PEGASUS DESCENDING

A Dave Robicheaux Novel

JAMES LEE BURKE

SIMON & SCHUSTER
New York   London   Toronto   Sydney

SIMON & SCHUSTER
Rockefeller Center
1230 Avenue of the Americas
New York, NY 10020

Title page photograph © Corbis

First Simon & Schuster trade paperback export edition 2006

SIMON & SCHUSTER and colophon are registered trademarks
of Simon & Schuster, Inc.

For information about special discounts for bulk purchases,
please contact Simon & Schuster Special Sales:
1-800-456-6798 or business@simonandschuster.com.

Book design by Ellen R. Sasahara

Manufactured in the United States of America

1   3   5   7   9   10   8   6   4   2

Library of Congress Cataloging-in-Publication Data
Burke, James Lee.
Pegasus descending : a Dave Robicheaux novel / James Lee Burke.
p.   cm.
1. Robicheaux, Dave (Fictitious character)—Fiction.
2. Police—Louisiana—New Iberia—Fiction.
3. New Iberia (La.)—Fiction. I. Title.
PS3552.U723P44 2006
813'.54—dc22   2006040341

ISBN-13: 978-0-7432-7772-3
ISBN-10:   0-7432-7772-4
ISBN-13: 978-0-7432-9812-4 (Pbk)
ISBN-10:   0-7432-9812-8 (Pbk)

For our grandchildren—
James Parker McDavid, Emma Marie Walsh,
Jack Owen Walsh, and James Lee Burke IV

I have yet many things to say unto you, but ye cannot bear them now.

—John 16:12

PEGASUS
DESCENDING

CHAPTER
1

IN THE EARLY 1980S, when I was still going steady with Jim
Beam straight-up and a beer back, I became part of an exchange program between NOPD and a training academy for police cadets in
Dade County, Florida. That meant I did a limited amount of work in
a Homicide unit at the Miami P.D. and taught a class in criminal justice at a community college way up on N.W. 27th Avenue, not far
from a place called Opa-Locka.

Opa-Locka was a gigantic pink stucco-and-plaster nightmare
designed to look like a complex of Arabian mosques. In the early
a.m., fog from either the ocean or the Glades, mixed with dust and
carbon monoxide, clung like strips of dirty cotton to the decrepit
minarets and cracked walls of the buildings. At night the streets were
lit by vapor lamps that glowed inside the fog with the dirty iridescence that you associate with security lighting in prison compounds.
The palms on the avenues were blighted by disease, the fronds clack-
ing dryly in the fouled air. The yards in the neighborhoods contained
more gray sand than grass. Homes that could contain little of value
were protected by bars on the windows and razor wire on the fences.
Lowrider gangbangers, the broken mufflers of their gas-guzzlers
throbbing against the asphalt, smashed liquor bottles on the sidewalks and no one said a word.

For me, it was a place where I didn't have to make comparisons
and where each dawn took on the watery hue of a tequila sunrise. If I
found myself at first light in Opa-Locka, my choices were usually

uncomplicated: I either continued drinking or entered an altered state known as delirium tremens.

Four or five nights a week I deconstructed myself in a bar where people had neither histories nor common geographic origins. Their friendships with one another began and ended at the front door. Most of them drank with a self-deprecating resignation and long ago had given up rationalizing the lives they led, I suspect allowing themselves a certain degree of peace. I never saw any indication they either knew or cared that I was a police officer. In fact, as I write these words today, I'm sure they recognized me as one of their own—a man who of his own volition had consigned himself to Dante's ninth circle, his hand clasped confidently around a mug of draft with a submerged jigger of whiskey coiling up from the bottom.

But there was one visitor to the bar whom I did call friend. His name was Dallas Klein, a kid who in late '71 had flown a slick through a blistering curtain of RPG and automatic weapons fire to pick up a bunch of stranded LURPs on the Cambodian border. He brought home two Purple Hearts, a Silver Star, and a nervous tic in his face that made you think a bee was buzzing around his left eye.

Like me, he loved Gulf Stream Race Track and the jai alai fronton up the road in Broward County. He also loved the craps table at a private club in Hollywood, a floating poker game in Little Havana, the dogs at Flagler, the trotters at Pompano, the Florida Derby at Hialeah, the rows of gleaming slot machines clanging with a downpour of coins on a cruise to Jamaica.

But he was a good kid, not a drunk, not mean-spirited or resentful yet about the addiction that had already cost him a fiancée and a twobedroom stucco house on a canal in Fort Lauderdale. He grinned at his losses, his eyes wrinkling at the corners, as though a humorous acknowledgment of his problem made it less than it was. On Saturdays he ate an early lunch of a hamburger and glass of milk at the bar while he studied the *Morning Telegraph,* his ink-black hair cut short, his face always good-natured. By one o'clock he and I would be out at the track together, convinced that we knew the future, the drone of the crowd mysteriously erasing any fears of mortality we may have possessed.

On a sunny weekday afternoon, when the jacaranda trees and bougainvillea were in bloom, Dallas strolled into the bar whistling a tune. He'd picked three NFL winners that week and today he'd hit a perfecta and a quinella at Hialeah. He bought a round of well drinks for the house and had dinners of T-bones and Irish potatoes brought in for him and me.

Then two men of a kind you never want to meet came through the front door, the taller one beckoning to the bartender, the shorter man scanning the tables, waiting for his eyes to adjust to the darkness of the bar's interior.

"Got to dee-dee, Dave. Call me," Dallas said, dropping his fork and steak knife in his plate, pulling his leather jacket off the back of his chair.

He was out the back door like a shot.

He made it as far as a lavender Cadillac where a man as big as the sky waited for him, his arms folded on his chest, his wraparound mirror shades swimming with distorted images of minarets and broken glass sprinkled along the top of a stucco wall.

The two men who had come in through the front of the bar followed Dallas outside. I hesitated, then wiped my mouth with my napkin and went outside, too.

The parking area had been created out of crushed building material that was spiked with weeds. The wind was blowing hard, and the royal palms out on the boulevard thrashed and twisted against a perfect blue sky. The three men whom I did not know had formed a circle around Dallas as though each of them had a fixed role he had played many times before.

The driver of the Caddy had the biggest neck I had ever seen on a human being. It was as wide as his jowls, his tie and collar pin like formal dress on a pig. He chewed gum and gazed at the palm trees whipping against the sky, as though he were disengaged from the conversation. The man who had spoken to the bartender was the talker. He wore polyester sports clothes and white loafers and looked like a consumptive, his hair as white as meringue, his shoulders stooped with bone loss, his face netted with the lines of a chain-smoker.

"Whitey is supposed to carry you for sixteen large?" he said.

"That ain't his money. He's paying a point and a half vig a week on that. No, Dallas, you don't talk, you listen. Everybody appreciates what you did for your country, but when you owe sixteen large, that war hero shit don't slide down the pipe."

But the man who caught my eye was the short one. He seemed wrapped too tight for his own body, the same way a meth addict seems to boil in his own juices. His mouth was like a horizontal keyhole, the corner of his upper lip exposing his teeth, as though he were starting to grin. He listened intently to every word in the conversation, waiting for the green light to flash, his eyes flickering with anticipation.

The consumptive man rested his palm on Dallas's shoulder. "*What?* You think we're being hard on you? You want Ernesto to drive us out in the Glades so we can talk there? Whitey likes you, kid. You got no idea how much he likes you, how kind you're being treated here."

"You gentlemen have a problem with my friend Dallas?" I asked.

In the quiet I could hear the palm fronds rattling above the stucco wall, a gust of wind tumbling a piece of newspaper past a spiked iron gate.

"No, *we* don't got a problem," the short man said, turning toward me, the sole of one shoe grinding on a piece of broken mortar. His hair was peroxided, feathered on the back of his neck. He wore platform shoes and a dark blue suit that was cut so the flaps stuck out from his waist, and a silver shirt dancing with light, and a silk kerchief tied around his throat. His eyes contained a cool green fire whose source a cautious man doesn't probe.

"Dallas has a phone call," I said.

"Take a message," the short man said.

"It's his mother. She really gets mad when Dallas doesn't come to the phone," I said.

"He's a cop," the driver of the Caddy said, removing his shades, pinching the glare out of his eyes.

The short man and the man in polyester sports clothes took my inventory. "You a cop?" the short man said, smiling for the first time.

"You never can tell," I replied.

"Nice place to hang out," he said.

"You bet. If you want a tab, I'll talk to the bartender," I said.

The short man laughed and accepted a stick of gum from the driver. Then he stepped close to Dallas and spoke to him in a whisper, one that caused the blood to drain out of Dallas's face.

After the three men had gotten back into their Caddy and driven away, I asked Dallas what the short man had said.

"Nothing. He's a jerk. Forget it," he said.

"Who's Whitey?"

"Whitey Bruxal. He runs a book out of a pizza joint in Hallendale."

"You're into him for sixteen grand?"

"I got a handle on it. It's not a problem."

Inside the bar, he pushed aside his food and ordered a Scotch with milk. After three more of the same, the color came back into his cheeks. He blew out his breath and rested his forehead on the heel of his hand.

"Wow," he said quietly, more to himself than to me.

"What did that dude say to you?" I asked.

"One-one-five Coconut Palm Drive."

"I don't follow," I said.

"I have a six-year-old daughter. She lives with her grandmother in the Grove. That's her address," he replied. He stared at me blankly, as though he could not assimilate his own words.

DALLAS INVITED ME to his apartment the next evening and cooked hamburgers for us on a hibachi out on a small balcony. Down below were blocks and blocks of one-story houses with gravel-and-tar roofs and yards in which the surfaces of plastic-sided swimming pools wrinkled in the wind. The sun looked broken and red on the horizon, without heat, veiled with smoke from a smoldering fire in the Glades. Dallas showed me pictures of his daughter taken in Orlando and in front of a Ferris wheel at Coney Island. One picture showed her in a snowsuit sewn with rabbit ears that flopped down from the hood. The little girl's hair was gold, her eyes blue, her smile magical.

"What happened to her mom?" I said.

"She took off with a guy who was running coke from the Islands in a cigarette boat. They hit a buoy at fifty knots south of Pine Key. Get this. The guy flew a Cobra in 'Nam. My wife always said she loved a pilot." He turned the burgers on the grill, his eyes concentrated on his task.

I knew what was coming next.

"Had a note under my door from Whitey this morning. I might have to take my little girl and blow Dodge," he said.

I cracked a beer and leaned on the railing. In the distance I could see car lights flowing down a wide bend in an expressway. I sipped from the beer and said nothing in reply to his statement.

"I made a salad. Why don't you dump it in a couple of bowls?" he said.

The silence hung between us. "I've got a couple of grand in a savings account. You want to borrow it?" I said, then raised the bottle to my mouth, waiting for the weary confirmation of the frailty and self-interest that exists in us all.

"No, thanks," he said.

I lowered the bottle and looked at him.

"It's just a matter of doing the smart thing," he said. "I got to think it through. Whitey's not a bad guy, he's just got his—"

"What?" I said.

"His own obligations. Miami is supposed to be an open city. No contract hits, no one guy gets a lock on the action. But nothing goes on here that doesn't get pieced off to the New York families. You see my drift?"

"Not really," I said, not wanting to know more about Dallas's involvement with Miami's underworld.

"What a life, huh?" he said.

"Yeah," I replied. "Make mine rare, will you?"

"Rare it is, Loot," he said, squeezing the grease out of a patty, wincing in the flare of smoke and flame.

I washed my hands before we ate. Dallas's work uniform hung inside a clear plastic dry cleaner's bag on a hook in the bathroom, the logo of an armored car company sewn above the coat pocket.

• • •

BUT DALLAS DID NOT BLOW DODGE. Instead, I saw him talking on a street corner in Opa-Locka with Ernesto, the leviathan driver of the lavender Cadillac. The two of them got in the Caddy and drove away, Dallas's face looking much older than he was. Twice I asked Dallas to go to the track with me, but he claimed he was not only broke but entering a twelve-step program for people with a gambling addiction. "I'll miss it, but everything comes to an end, right?" he said.

Spring came and I disengaged from Dallas and his problems. Besides, I had plenty of my own. I was trying to get through each morning with aspirin, vitamin B, and mouth spray, but my lend-lease colleagues at the Miami P.D. and the cadets in my class at the community college were onto me. My irritability, the tremble in my hands, my need for a vodka collins by noon became my persona. The pity and ennui I saw in the eyes of others followed me into my sleep.

I went three weeks without a drink. I jogged at dawn on Hollywood Beach, snorkeled at the tip of a coral jetty swarming with clown fish, pumped iron at Vic Tanney's, ate seafood and green salads at a surfside restaurant, and watched my body turn as hard and brown as a worn saddle.

Then on a beautiful Friday night, with no catalyst at work, with a song in my heart, I put on a new sports jacket, my shined loafers, and a pair of pressed slacks, and joined the crew up in Opa-Locka and pretended once again I could drop lighted matches in a gas tank without consequence.

That's when I got my second look at the short man who worked as a collector for Whitey Bruxal. He stood in the open doorway, scanning the interior, forcing others to walk around him. Then he went to the bar and spoke to the bartender, and I heard him use Dallas's name. The bartender shook his head and occupied himself with washing beer mugs in a tin sink. But the collector was not easily discouraged. He ordered a 7Up on ice and began peeling a hard-boiled egg on top of a paper napkin, wiping the tiny pieces of shell off his fingernails onto the paper, his eyes on the door.

Stay out of it, I heard a voice say inside my head.

I went to the men's room and came back to my table and sat down. The collector was salting his egg, chewing on the top of it reflectively while he stared out the front door into the street, his shoes hooked into the aluminum rails of the barstool. He wore stonewashed jeans and a yellow see-through shirt and a porkpie hat tipped forward on his brow. His back was triangular, like a martial arts fighter's, his facial skin as bright and hard-looking as ceramic.

I stood next to him at the bar and waited for him to turn toward me. "Live in the neighborhood?" I asked.

"*Right,*" he said.

"I never did catch your name."

"It's Elmer Fudd. What's yours?"

"I like those platform shoes. A lot of Superfly types are wearing those these days. Ever see that movie *Superfly*? It's about black dope pushers and pimps and white street punks who think they're made guys," I said.

He brushed off his fingers on his napkin and pulled at an earlobe, then motioned to the bartender. "Fix Smiley here whatever he's drinking," he said.

"You see, when you give names to other people, it's not just disrespectful, it's a form of presumption."

"'Presumption'?" he replied, nodding profoundly.

"Yeah, you're indicating you have the right to say whatever you wish to other people. It's not a good habit."

He nodded again. "Right now I'm waiting on somebody and I need a little solitude. Do me a favor and don't piss in my cage, okay?"

"Wouldn't dream of it," I said. "Were you in 'Nam? Dallas was. He's a good kid."

The collector got off the barstool and combed his hair, his eyes roving over the crooked smile on my face, the booze stains on my shirt, the table-wet on the sleeves of my new jacket, the fact that I had to keep one arm on the bar to steady myself. "I stacked time in a place you couldn't imagine in your worst dreams," he said.

"Yeah, I've heard the bitch suite up at Raiford is a hard ride," I said.

He put away his comb and looked at his reflection in the bar mirror. His cheeks were pooled with tiny pits, like the incisions of a knifepoint. He placed a roll of breath mints by my hand. "No, go ahead and take them. Gratis from Elmer Fudd. Enjoy."

MY TENURE WITH the exchange program was running out in June, and I wanted to carry good memories of South Florida back to New Orleans. I boat-fished out of Key West in the most beautiful water I had ever seen. It was green, as clear as glass, with pools of indigo blue in it that floated like broken clouds of ink. I visited the old federal prison at Fort Jefferson on a blistering-hot day and swore I could smell the land breeze blowing from Cuba. I slept in a pup tent on a coral shelf above water that was threaded with the smoky green phosphorescence of organisms that had no names. I saw the ocean turn wine-dark under a sky bursting with constellations and knew that the truth of Homer's line would never be diminished by time.

But wherever I went, a frozen daiquiri winked at me from an outdoor bar roofed by palm fronds; beaded cans of Budweiser protruded from the ice in a fisherman's cooler; a bottle of Cold Duck clamped between a woman's thighs burst alive with the pop of a cork and a geyser of foam.

Delirium tremens or not, I knew I was in for the whole ride.

During my last week in Miami, I drove up to Opa-Locka to pay my bar tab and buy a round for whoever was trying to escape the noonday heat. The bar was dark and cool inside, the street out beyond the colonnade baking under a white sun. I knocked back a brandy and soda, counted my change, and prepared to go. Through the front window I could see dust blowing along the pavement, heat waves bouncing off a parked car, a bare-chested black man drilling a jackhammer into the asphalt, his skin pouring sweat. I ordered another brandy and soda and looked at the order-out menu on the bar. Then I tossed the menu aside, dropped a half dollar into the jukebox, and kicked it on up into overdrive with four inches of Beam and a beer back.

By three-thirty I was seriously in the bag. Across the street, I saw an armored car pull up in front of the bank. It was a shimmering boxlike vehicle with a red-and-white paint job that pulsed in the heat like a fresh dental extraction. Three armed guards piled out, opened up the back, and began to lift big canvas satchels with padlocks on the tops onto the pavement. One of the guards was Dallas Klein.

I crossed the street, my drink in one hand, shading my eyes from the glare with the other.

"Where you been, fellow? I've had to knock 'em back for both of us," I said.

Dallas was standing in the shade of the bank, the armpits of his gray shirt dark with moisture. "I'm on the job, here, Dave. Catch you later," he said.

"What time you get off?"

"I said beat it."

"Say again?"

"This is a security area. You're not supposed to be here."

"You've got things mixed up, podna. I'm a police officer."

"What you are is shit-faced. Now stop making an ass out of your-self and go back in the bar."

I turned around and walked toward the colonnade, the sun like a wet flame on my skin. I looked back over my shoulder at Dallas, who was now busy with his work, hefting bags of money and carrying them into the bank. My face felt small and tight, the skin dead, freeze-dried in the heat.

"Something wrong, Dave?" the bartender asked.

"Yeah, my glass is empty. Double Beam, beer back," I said.

While he poured into a shot glass from a bourbon bottle with a chrome nipple on it, I blotted the humidity out of my eyes with a paper napkin, my ears still ringing from the insult Dallas had deliv-ered me. I looked back out the window at the armored car. But the scene had suddenly become surreal, divorced from any of my expec-tations about that day in my life. A white van came out of nowhere and braked behind the armored car. Four men with cut-down shot-guns jumped out on the sidewalk, leaving the driver behind the wheel. They were all dressed in work clothes, their hair and facial fea-tures a beige-colored blur under nylon stockings.

"Call nine-one-one, say, 'Armed robbery in progress,' and give this address," I said to the bartender.

I unsnapped the .25 automatic that was strapped to my right ankle. When I got off the barstool, one side of the room seemed to collapse under my foot.

"I wouldn't go out there," the bartender said.

"I'm a cop," I said.

I thought my grandiose words could somehow change the condition I was in. But in the bartender's eyes I saw a sad knowledge that no amount of rhetoric would ever influence. I walked unsteadily to the front door and jerked it open. The outside world ballooned through the door in a rush of superheated air and carbon monoxide. The street I looked out upon was no longer a part of South Florida. It was a wind-sculpted place in the desert, bleached the color of a biscuit by the sun, home to carrion birds and jackals and blowflies. It was the place that awaits us all, one we don't allow ourselves to see in our dreams. The .25 auto felt as small and light as plastic in my hand.

I positioned myself behind one of the Arabic columns under the colonnade and steadied my automatic against the stone. "Police officer! Put down your weapons and get on your faces!" I shouted.

But the men robbing the armored car did little more than glance in my direction, as they would at a minor annoyance. It was obvious their timing on the takedown of the car had gone amiss. The van had arrived seconds later than it should have, allowing the guards time to start carrying the canvas money satchels inside the bank. The car guards and the elderly bank guard were down on their knees, against the wall of the bank, their fingers laced behind their heads. The robbers simply needed to pick up the satchels that were within easy reach, head out of Opa-Locka, and dump the van, which was undoubtedly stolen. A few minutes later, they could have disappeared back into the anonymity of the city. But one of them had gotten greedy. One of them had gone into the bank to retrieve the satchels there, racking a round into the chamber of his shotgun.

A teller was already pushing the vault door shut. The robber shot him at point-blank range.

When the shooter emerged from the bank, he was dragging two satchels that were whipsawed with blood, his pump propped against his hip.

"I said on your faces, you motherfuckers!" I shouted.

The first shotgun blast from the robbers on the sidewalk patterned all over the column and the metal door of the bar. A second one caved the window. Then the robbers were shooting at me in unison, blowing dust and powdered stone in the air, peppering the metal door with indentations that looked like shiny nickels.

I crouched at the bottom of the column, unable to move or return fire without being chewed up. Then I heard someone shouting, "Go, go, go, go!" and the sounds of the van doors slamming shut.

It should have been over. But it wasn't. As the van pulled away from the curb, I was sure I heard the robber in the passenger seat speak to Dallas. "You're a joke, man," he said. Then he extended his shotgun straight out from the vehicle and blew most of Dallas Klein's head off.

CHAPTER 2

THE ROBBERY OF the armored car and the double homicide were never solved. I gave the FBI and the Dade County authorities as much information as I could about Dallas Klein's relationship to the bookie Whitey Bruxal and the three collectors who were trying to dun Dallas for his sixteen-thousand-dollar tab. But I was firing in the well. The three collectors all had alibis, were lawyered-up and deaf, dumb, and don't know from the jump. Whitey Bruxal returned from New Jersey of his own volition and allowed himself to be interviewed three times without benefit of counsel. I came to believe that the account I had given the authorities of Dallas's connection to the gamblers was being looked upon with the same degree of credibility cops usually give the words of all drunks and junkies: You can always tell when they're lying—their lips are moving.

I hung up my brief tenure with law enforcement in the tropics, attended my first A.A. meeting, a sunrise group that met in a grove of coconut palms on Fort Lauderdale Beach, and caught a flight the same day back to New Orleans.

That was over two decades ago. I believed Dallas made a deal with the devil and lost. I tried to stop the robbery and failed, but at least I tried, and I did not hold myself responsible for his death. At least, that was what I told myself. Later, I was fired from NOPD. Perhaps my dismissal was my fault, perhaps not. Frankly, I didn't care. I went back sober to my birthplace, New Iberia, Louisiana, a small city on

Bayou Teche, down by the Gulf of Mexico, and started my life over. It's always the first inning, I said. And this time I was right about something.

TODAY I'M A DETECTIVE with the Iberia Parish Sheriff's Department. I make a modest salary and live on Bayou Teche with my wife, Molly, who is a former nun, in a shotgun house shaded by oak trees that are at least two hundred years old. With a few exceptions, the cases I work are not spectacular ones. But in the spring of last year, on a lazy afternoon, just about the time the azaleas burst into bloom, I caught an unusual case that at first seemed inconsequential, the kind that gets buried in a file drawer or hopefully absorbed by a federal agency. Later, I would remember the pro forma beginnings of the investigation like the tremolo you might experience through the structure of an airplane just before oil from an engine streaks across your window.

A call came in from the operator of a truck stop on the parish line. A woman who was waiting on a tire repair had gone into the casino and removed a one-hundred-dollar bill from her purse, then had changed her mind and taken out a fifty and given it to the clerk.

"Sorry, I didn't realize I had a smaller denomination," she said.

"The hundred is no problem," the clerk said, waiting.

"No, that's okay," she replied.

He noticed she had two one-hundred bills tucked in her wallet, both of them stained along the edges with a red dye.

I parked the cruiser in front of the truck stop and entered through the side door, into the casino section, and saw a blond woman seated at a stool in front of a video poker machine, feeding a five-dollar bill into the slot. She was dressed in jeans and a yellow cowboy shirt. She sipped at her coffee, her face reflective as she studied the row of electronic playing cards on the screen.

"I'm Detective Dave Robicheaux, with the Iberia Sheriff's Department," I said.

"Hi," she said, turning her eyes on me. They were blue and full of light, without any sense of apprehension that I could see.

"You have some currency in your wallet that perhaps we need to take a look at," I said.

"Pardon me?"

"You were going to give the clerk a hundred-dollar bill. Could I see it?"

She smiled. "Sure," she said, and took her wallet from her purse. "Actually I have two of them. Are you looking for counterfeit money or something?"

"We let the Feds worry about stuff like that," I said, taking the bills from her hand. "Where'd you get these?"

"At a casino in Biloxi," she replied.

"You mind if I write down the serial numbers?" I said. "While we're at this, can you give me some identification?"

She handed me a Florida driver's license. "I'm living in Lafayette now. I'm not in trouble, am I?" she said. Her face was tilted up into mine, her eyes radiantly blue, sincere, not blinking.

"Can you show me something with your Lafayette address on it? I'd also like a phone number in case we have to reach you."

"I don't know what's going on," she said.

"Sometimes a low-yield explosive device containing marker dye is placed among bundles of currency that are stolen from banks or armored cars. When the device goes off, the currency is stained so the robbers can't use it."

"So maybe my hundreds are stolen?" she said, handing me a receipt for a twenty-three-hundred deposit on an apartment in Lafayette.

"Probably not. Dye ends up on money all the time. Your name is Trish Klein?"

"Yes, I just moved here from Miami."

"Ever hear of a guy named Dallas Klein?"

Her eyes held on mine, her thoughts, whatever they were, impossible to read. "Why do you ask?" she said.

"I knew a guy by that name who flew a chopper in Vietnam. He was from Miami."

"That was my father," she said.

I finished copying her address and phone number off her deposit receipt and handed it back to her. "It's nice to meet you, Ms. Klein. Your dad was a stand-up guy," I said.

"You knew him in Vietnam?"

"I knew him," I said. I glanced past her shoulder at the video screen. "You've got four kings. Welcome to Louisiana."

ON THE WAY BACK to the office, I asked myself why I hadn't told her I had been friends with her father in Miami. But maybe the memory was just too unpleasant to revisit, I thought. Maybe she had never learned that her father had been enticed into aiding and abetting the robbery of the armored car, if indeed that's what happened. Why let the past injure the innocent? I told myself.

No, that was not it. She had paused before she acknowledged her father. As any investigative law officer will tell you, when witnesses or suspects or even ordinary citizens hesitate before answering a question, it's because they are deciding whether they should either conceal information or outright lie about it.

It was almost 5 p.m. when I got back to the department. Wally, our dispatcher, told me there had been a homicide by gunshot wound on the bayou, amid a cluster of houses upstream from the sugar mill. I gave the serial numbers on the bills to a detective in our robbery unit and asked him to run them through our Internet connection to the U.S. Treasury Department. Then I tried to forget the image of Dallas Klein kneeling on a sidewalk, his fingers laced behind his head.

The sheriff of Iberia Parish was Helen Soileau. She had begun her career in law enforcement as a meter maid with NOPD, then had patrolled the Desire district and Gird Town and worked Narcotics in the French Quarter. She wore jeans or slacks, carried herself like a male athlete, and possessed a strange kind of androgynous beauty. Her face could be sensuous and warm, almost seductive, but it could change while you were talking to her, as though not only two genders but two different people lived inside her. People who saw her in one photograph often did not recognize her in another.

I not only admired Helen, I loved her. She was honest and loyal and never afraid. Anyone who showed disrespect regarding her sexuality did so only once.

A couple of years back, a New Iberia lowlife by the name of Jimmy Dean Styles, who ran a dump called the Boom Boom Room and who would eventually rape and murder a sixteen-year-old girl with a shotgun, was drinking from a bottle of chocolate milk behind his bar while he casually told Helen that even though he had overheard her male fellow officers ridiculing her at the McDonald's on East Main, he personally considered her "a dyke who's straight-up and don't take shit from nobody."

Then he upended his bottle of chocolate milk, his eyes smiling at the barb he had inserted under her skin.

Helen slipped her baton so quickly from the ring on her belt, he didn't even have time to flinch before glass and chocolate milk and blood exploded all over his face. Then Helen dropped her business card on the bar and said, "Have a nice day. Call me again if I can be of any more assistance." That was Helen Soileau.

I tapped on her office door, then opened it. "Wally says we have a homicide by the mill?" I said.

"The nine-one-one came in about fifteen minutes ago. The coroner should be there now. Where were you?"

"A couple of bills with dye on them showed up at the new truck stop. Who's the victim?"

She glanced down at a notepad. "Yvonne Darbonne. She waited tables at Victor's. You know her?"

"Yeah, I think I do. Her daddy used to cane-farm and run a bar up the bayou?"

"Bring the cruiser around and let's find out," she replied.

We drove through downtown and crossed the drawbridge over Bayou Teche at Burke Street, then crossed the bayou again and headed up a broken two-lane road that led past an enormous sugar mill that almost blocked out the sky. At night, during the grinding season, the fires and electric lights and the giant white clouds of steam that rose from the stacks could be seen from miles away, not unlike a medieval painting depicting Dante's vision of the next world.

Hunkered between the mill and bayou was a community of dull

green company-constructed houses left over from an earlier time. In the winter, the stench from the mill and the threadlike pieces of carbon floating off the smokestacks blew with a northern breeze directly onto the houses down below. The yards were dirt, packed as hard as brick, strung with wash lines, the broken windows repaired with tape and plastic bags. Several uniformed cops, two forensic chemists from the lab, the coroner, three cruisers, and an ambulance were already at the scene.

"Who called it in?" I asked Helen as we crossed a rain ditch and pulled into a dirt driveway.

"A neighbor heard the shot. She thought it was a firecracker, then she looked out the window and saw the girl on the ground."

"She didn't see anyone else?"

"She thought she heard a car drive away, but she saw no one."

The girl's father, whose name was Cesaire Darbonne, had just arrived. Even though he was almost seventy, he was a trim, comely man, with neatly parted steel-colored hair and pale turquoise eyes. His skin was brown, as smooth as tallow, marked on one arm by a chain of white scars that looked like small misshapen hearts. He was also coming apart at the seams.

Two cops had to restrain him from rushing to where his daughter lay in the backyard. They walked him back to a cruiser in the driveway and sat him down in the passenger seat, then stood in front of the open door so he couldn't get out. "That's my li'l girl back there. Her birt'day was tomorrow. Who done somet'ing like this to that li'l girl? She ain't but eighteen years old," he said.

But the answer was probably not one he wanted to hear. His daughter lay in the Johnson grass by a doorless wood garage, her body in the shape of a question mark. She was wearing a beige skirt and tennis shoes without socks and a T-shirt with a winged horse emblazoned on the front. A blue-black .22 revolver with walnut grips lay by her hand. The entry wound was in the center of her forehead. Her hair, which was dark red, had fallen down in a skein across her face.

I squatted down next to her and picked up the revolver by inserting a pencil through the trigger guard. The cylinder looked like one that had been drilled to hold Magnums, and all the chambers other than the one under hammer were loaded and appeared unfired. A cell phone lay in the grass, less than three feet away. Helen handed me a Ziploc evidence bag. "Powder burns?" she said.

"Enough to put out an eye," I replied.

Helen squatted down next to me, her forearms resting on her knees, her face lowered. "You ever see a woman shoot herself in the face?" she asked.

"Nope, but suicides do weird things," I replied.

Helen stood up, chewing on a weed stem. The sun went behind a cloud, then the wind came up and we could smell the heaviness of the bayou. "Bag the cell phone and get it to the lab. Find out who she was talking to before she caught the bus. Has the old man got other kids?"

"To my knowledge, Yvonne was the only one," I replied.

"Ready to do it?" she said.

"Not really," I said, rising to my feet, my knees popping like those of a man who was far too old for the task that had been given him.

Helen and I approached Mr. Darbonne, who was still sitting in the back of the cruiser. His khakis were starched and clean, his denim shirt freshly ironed. He looked up at us as though we were the bearers of information that somehow could change the events that had just crashed upon his life like an asteroid. I told him we were sorry about his loss, but my words didn't seem to register.

"Who was your daughter with today, Mr. Darbonne?" I asked.

"She gone over to the university for orientation. She was starting classes this summer," he replied. Then he realized he hadn't answered my question. "I ain't sure who she gone wit'."

"Was she dating anyone?" I asked.

"Maybe. She always met him in town. She didn't want to tell me who he was."

"Has she been depressed or angry or upset about anything?" Helen said.

"She was happy. She was a good girl. She didn't smoke or drink. She never been in no trouble. I was looking for work today in Jeanerette. If I'd stayed home, me—" His eyes started to water.

"Did she own a pistol?" I asked.

"What she gonna do wit' a gun? She read books. She wanted to study journalism and history. She wrote in her diary. She was always going to the movies."

Helen and I looked at each other. "Can you show us her room, sir?" I said.

The wood floors inside the house were scrubbed, the furniture dusted, the kitchen neat, the dishes washed, the beds made. An ancient purple couch was positioned in front of a small television set. Imitation lace doilies had been spread on the arms and headrest of the couch. In the hallway a black-and-white photo yellowed at the corners showed the father at a hunting camp, surrounded by friends in canvas coats and caps and rubber boots and a giant semicircle of dead ducks at their feet. Yvonne's dresser and shelves were covered with stuffed animals, worn paperback novels, and books on loan from the city library. Among the titles were *The Moon and Sixpence* and *The Scarlet Letter*.

"We'd like to take her diary with us, sir. I promise it will be returned to you," I said.

He hesitated. Then his eyes left mine and looked out the window. Two paramedics were placing a gurney in the back of the ambulance. The body bag that contained the earthly remains of Yvonne Darbonne had been zipped over her face, within seconds erasing the identity she had woken with that morning. The straps and vinyl that held her form against the gurney seemed to have shrunken her size and substance to insignificance. Cesaire Darbonne began to run toward the back door.

"Don't do that, sir. I give you my word your daughter's person will be treated with respect," Helen said, stepping in his way, holding up her palms against the air.

He turned from us and began to weep, his back shaking. "She met this boy in town 'cause she was 'shamed of her house. One night she walked all the way home from the bowling alley, wit' cars going by her at sixty miles an hour. I couldn't find work, me. I farmed t'irty acres of cane for forty years, but now I cain't find no work."

Before we left, we spoke to the neighbor who had made the

"shots fired" call. She was in her late-middle years and was a member of that ill-defined racial group sometimes called "Creoles" or sometimes "people of color." The term "Creole" originally meant a second-generation colonial whose parentage was either French or Spanish or both. Today, the term indicates someone whose bloodline is probably French, Indian, and Afro-American. This lady's name was Narcisse Ladrine and she insisted she had not witnessed the shooting or a car or person leaving the scene.

"But you heard a vehicle driving away?" I said.

"I ain't sure," she said. She wore a print dress that fit her like a potato sack and was so wash-faded you could see the outline of her undergarments through the fabric.

"Try to remember," I said. "Was it a sound like a truck? Did it make a lot of noise? Maybe the muffler was rusted out?"

"When you hear a gunshot, you ain't listening for other t'ings."

She had a point. "Did you see anyone else on the street?" I asked.

"There was a black man on a bicycle picking up bottles and cans out of the ditch." Then she thought about what she had just said. "Except that was a lot earlier. No, I ain't seen nobody else out there."

We went back up the road and checked with the security office at the sugar mill. No one there had seen any unusual activity near the mill or in the community of frame houses by the bayou. In fact, no one at the security office even knew a homicide had occurred there.

As we drove back toward the department, a rainstorm swept across the wetlands and pounded the cruiser and scattered hailstones like pieces of smoking dry ice on the road. Back at the office, I began the paperwork on the death of Yvonne Darbonne. I had completely forgotten the matter of the dye-marked one-hundred bills in the possession of Trish Klein, the daughter of my murdered gambling friend in Miami. Just before quitting time, Helen opened my door. "We got a hit on those serial numbers," she said. "The bills came from the robbery of a savings and loan company in Mobile."

Helen's announcement wasn't what I wanted to hear. "I'll get ahold of the woman tomorrow," I said.

"It gets better. The bills from the robbery have been showing up in casinos and at racetracks all along the Gulf Coast," she said.

"The Klein woman says she got hers at a casino in Biloxi."

"Here's an interesting footnote. The Treasury guys think the savings and loan company may be a laundry for the Mob. The wiseguys got ripped off by some bank thieves who didn't get the word. What's the background on this Klein woman?"

I told her about the shotgun slaying of Dallas Klein in Opa-Locka, Florida, years ago. Through my second-story window I could see rain hitting on the tops of the crypts in St. Peter's Cemetery.

"You were there when he died?" she said.

"Yeah," I said, my voice catching slightly.

"Wrap up our end on this and give it to the Feds. You copy on that?"

"Absolutely," I replied.

I DROVE HOME at 5 p.m. and parked my pickup truck under the porte cochere attached to the shotgun house where Molly and I live in what is called the historical district of New Iberia. Our home is a modest one compared to the Victorian and antebellum structures that define most of East Main, but nonetheless it is a beautiful old place, built of cypress and oak, long and square in shape, like a boxcar, with high ceilings and windows, a small gallery and peaked tin roof, and ventilated green shutters that you can latch over the glass during hurricane season.

The flower beds are planted with azaleas, lilies, hibiscus, philodendron, and rosebushes in the sun and caladiums and hydrangeas in the shade. The yard is over an acre in size and covered with pecan trees, slash pine, and live oaks. The back of the property slopes down to the Teche, and late at night barges and tugboats with green and red running lights drone heavily through the drawbridge at Burke Street on their way to Morgan City. At early dawn there is often ground fog in the trees and on the bayou, and inside it you can sometimes hear a gator flopping or ducks wimpling in the shallows.

Our elderly three-legged pet coon, named Tripod, lives in a hutch in the backyard. His sidekick is an unneutered male cat by the name of Snuggs. Snuggs has a neck like a fireplug and a body that ripples with muscle when he walks. He wears his chewed ears and the pink scars inside his short white hair like badges of honor. The only dogs he allows in the yard are those who have received Tripod's stamp of approval.

Our next-door neighbor is Miss Ellen Deschamps, an eighty-three-year-old graduate of Millsaps College who feeds every stray cat in New Iberia. She despises people who litter and once hit a man in the head with a bag of carrots for dumping his automobile's ashtray in the Winn-Dixie parking lot. She also considers Snuggs a profligate interloper but feeds him just the same. Early in the morning I can see Miss Ellen through the bamboo border on our property, feeding her cats or at work in her garden, the big pockets of her apron stuffed with tools and packets of seed. The image of Miss Ellen bending to her tasks on a daily basis, indifferent to the role of eccentric imposed on her by others, always makes me feel better about the world.

Our little spot on East Main is a fine place to live, and the woman I share it with is a person who lays no claim on courage or devotion or resilience but possesses all those virtues in exceptional fashion without ever being conscious of them. Before our marriage, her name was Sister Molly Boyle. In her religious life she had worked in a Maryknoll mission in Guatemala where the Indians were massacred by the army as an object lesson to leftist rebels. Later, she organized cane workers in St. Mary Parish, here in southwest Louisiana, and built homes for the poor. Then she left the religious order to which she belonged and married an alcoholic homicide detective with a long history of violence, and took up residence here, on Bayou Teche, along with Tripod and Snuggs and my adopted daughter, Alafair, who was studying psychology and English at Reed College in Portland.

"What's happenin', trooper?" she said when I walked into the kitchen.

She was washing and breaking up lettuce under the faucet, tearing it into chunks with her fingers. Her hair was dark red and cut short, and there was a spray of sun freckles on her arms, neck, and shoulders. Her father had been a retired United States Army line sergeant and later a police officer in Port Arthur, Texas. She spoke of him often and fondly, and I suspected some of her populist, blue-collar attitudes and her ability to do many things with her hands came from him.

I touched her neck and the tips of her hair, then squeezed her shoulders. Molly's hair was the same shade of red as the dead girl's by the mill, and I tried to push the image of the wound in the girl's forehead out of my mind. Molly turned around and looked at me. Her eyes were wide-set and bold and always hard to stare down. "Something happen today?" she said.

"There was a homicide up by the mill. A girl by the name of Yvonne Darbonne. She was about to start UL," I said.

"You knew her?"

"I know her dad. He lost his farm a few years back."

"She was murdered?"

"It looks like a suicide, but—"

"What?"

"Nothing. Let me help with supper," I said, and began taking dishes down from the cabinet.

By sunset the rain had stopped and I walked by myself down to the bayou's edge. In the west, the sky was the soft pink of a flamingo's wing, the air heavy and damp and clean-smelling. Water dripped from the trees onto the bayou's surface, creating a chain of rings that floated away in the current. But the mildness of the evening and the dripping sound of rainwater onto the bayou could not free me from the image of Yvonne Darbonne curled in the dirt, the red hair that had fallen over her wound tousled by the wind.

Suicides fall into categories. Some victims probably manufacture an internal psychodrama as a way of asking for help, then drift too far across the line. The clinically depressed do it in closed garages or with pills and booze while they listen to *Boléro* or "Clair de lune." Jumpers find audiences and sail out among the stars. Some fantasize a script in which they transcend their own deaths. In their imagination they watch from above while others find their bodies in horror and are trapped inside a legacy of guilt and grief for the rest of their lives.

But the ones who do it with high-powered firearms in the mouth or razors high up on the forearms, not on the wrists, are often filled with unrelieved rage at themselves. Female suicides are seldom if ever found in the last category.

Was Cesaire Darbonne's information correct about his daughter? Did she not drink or smoke? Had she always been happy? What could cause someone that young and beautiful and full of promise to fire a bullet into the center of her forehead? Or had someone else been at the scene also?

THE NEXT DAY our coroner, Koko Hebert, lumbered into my office. Koko was one of the saddest-looking human beings I had ever known. His body was shaped like a soft-sided pyramid. His breath wheezed in his chest. He stank of nicotine and beer sweat, and sometimes trailed an odor that was worse, one that made me think of a mortuary in Vietnam after the power had failed.

Koko's cynicism and anger were palpable. But his son had been killed in Iraq, and I had come to believe that his daily assault on the sensibilities of others was his own strange way of asking for help.

The grass was green and the sun was shining outside my window, but when Koko spread his buttocks on a chair in front of my desk, the sun might just as well have gone into eclipse. He took a huge drag off his cigarette, his brow furrowing as though his inhalation of cancer-causing chemicals were a moment of metaphysical importance.

"Would you not smoke in here?" I said.

He took a coffee cup off my desk and ground out his cigarette in it. "You want the post on the Darbonne girl or you want to tell me you don't have bad habits?" he asked.

"I'm happy you came by."

"Right. The lab call you yet?"

"Nope."

"We swabbed both her hands. She was the shooter. It's down as a suicide."

"You're sure?"

"You don't have confidence in the atomic absorption test?"

"Let's get something straight on this one, Koko. I appreciate the work you do. But I want the abrasive rhetoric out of my face."

I could hear the hum of the air conditioner in the silence. "There is no false positive here. She had powder residue on both hands. She inverted the pistol and fired it straight into her forehead. It's a suicide, plain and simple."

"Her father said she didn't drink or use. She was planning to start college. Why does a kid like that want to blow herself away? How did she end up in her own yard with a revolver her father never saw before?"

"Maybe I was looking at the wrong tox screen. The one that had Yvonne Darbonne's name on it showed she was loaded on alcohol, weed, and Ecstasy. When I opened her up, I thought I'd put my hand in a punch bowl, burgundy and fruit, to be exact. She had also engaged in recent sexual intercourse, with multiple partners. In my opinion, there was not forced penetration, either. There was one bruise on the thigh, but considering the number of partners she had, that's not unusual. I suspect she got stoned and loaded and was pumping it in four-four time."

"What do you get out of it, Koko?"

"Out of what?"

"Offending people, testing them."

He scratched the inside of his thigh, as though a mosquito bite were itching him beyond any level of tolerance. "If I go to meetings, can I learn how to use psychobabble like that?" he said.

I let out my breath and rubbed my temples. "What's the rest?" I asked.

"There is no 'rest.' She was drunk and stoned and she balled a bunch of guys who didn't bother to use rubbers," he said. "You're wondering why a kid like that would kill herself?"

RIGHT AFTER KOKO left the office, our forensic chemist, Mack Bertrand, called from the Acadiana Crime Lab. Mack was a decent, cheerful, pipe-smoking family man and one of the best crime scene investigators I had ever known. "We ran the weapon in the Darbonne shooting," he said. "It was reported stolen out of a fraternity house at Ole Miss in 1999."

"Any other prints besides the DOA's?"

"It was oiled and cleaned recently. There were a couple of smears, but not enough to run through AFIS. Where you going with this, Dave?"

"Probably nowhere."

"It's a suicide, podna. Her thumb pulled the trigger. Her finger-prints were on the back of the frame. I think she turned the pistol around and squeezed off one right into her face."

"What'd you get out of her cell phone?"

"Mostly numbers of kids at New Iberia High. Nothing unusual. Except . . ."

"Go ahead, Mack."

"She made two calls during the week to the home of Bello Lujan."

In my mind's eye I saw a sun-browned man wearing white jodh-purs, with swirls of black hair on his arms. At least that was Bello's image today, although I had known him in an earlier and much dif-ferent incarnation. "Why would she be calling a guy like that?" I said.

"He's got a kid at UL. Maybe Bello's kid and the vic knew each other." Then Mack paused. "Dave?"

"Yeah?"

"The girl took her life. Nothing will undo that. Bello wasn't born. He was poured out of a colostomy bag. Leave him alone."

"That's strong for you, Mack."

"Not when it comes to Bello Lujan," he replied.

HAVE YOU EVER SEEN SOMEONE cause a disastrous accident by driving so slowly that others are forced to pass him on a hill or curve? Or perhaps a driver running a yellow light, trapping a turning vehicle in the intersection so that it is exposed to high-speed traffic on its flank? The person responsible for the accident rarely looks in his rearview mirror and is seldom brought to justice. I wondered if that would prove to be the case with Yvonne Darbonne.

I looked at my watch. It was 11:05 and I still hadn't pursued the matter of the dye-marked bills in the possession of Dallas Klein's

daughter. I also had a hit-and-run homicide case on my desk, three
cold cases involving disappearances from ten years back, and a gangbanger shooting that had left two dope dealers on Ann Street peppered with rounds from a .25 auto.

Welcome to small-town America in the spring of 2005.

Yvonne Darbonne's diary lay on my desk. It had a sky-blue vinyl
cover with a sprinkle of sunflowers emblazoned on one corner. The
first entry was dated three months earlier. It read:

> Went with him to City Park and threw bread to the ducks
> and fox squirrels. He put his windbreaker on my shoulders
> when it got cold. His cheeks were red as apples.

She had written on perhaps thirty pages of the book. She had used
few names of people and no family names. The last entries seemed
filled with happiness and romance and did not indicate any sense of
emotional conflict that I could see. In fact, her handwriting and sentence structure and her general grasp of the world appeared to be
those of a sensible and mature person. I looked at my watch and all
the case files stacked on my desk and all the work sitting in my intake
basket. Yvonne Darbonne's death was going down as a suicide. My
function was over, I told myself. I placed the diary in a desk drawer,
closed the drawer, and drove to Lafayette to interview Trish Klein.

CHAPTER
3

SHE HAD TAKEN AN APARTMENT in an oak-shaded neighborhood not far from Girard Park. Her apartment complex was constructed of soft white brick, with a tile roof and Spanish ironwork along the balconies. Bougainvillea in full bloom dripped from the brick wall that surrounded the pool area. The swimming pool was heated, and even though the sun was high in the sky, steam rose from the water inside the shadows the live oaks made on the surface. Less than a quarter of a mile away, the Lafayette Oil Center might have been abuzz with concerns of profit and loss and images of black clouds rising into a desert sky from a burning pipeline in Iraq, but inside the enclosure of this particular residential complex, the year was 1955, and the moss in the trees and the gentleness of the day seemed to indicate that a less complicated era, at least temporarily, was still available to us.

Trish's apartment was on the first floor. I raised the brass knocker and heard chimes ring inside.

I had deliberately not called in advance in order to catch her unprepared. When she opened the door, I saw three young men and a woman in the living room with her. "Oh, Mr. Robicheaux," she said, stepping outside, pulling the door shut behind her. "If you'd called, I would have driven to New Iberia."

"I had to come to Lafayette anyway. Have any FBI agents talked to you yet?"

"FBI? No," she said. "This is about the hundred-dollar bills again?"

"It seems they were boosted from a savings and loan company in Mobile."

I watched for any change in her expression. But her eyes remained fixed on mine—pensive, blue, blinking perhaps once or twice. "Does that mean my money will be confiscated?"

"You'd better talk with the Feds about that."

She screwed her mouth into a button. "Well, if this is a federal case, why are you here?"

"We have jurisdiction in the passing of stolen money as well as the Feds. Also, I was a friend of your old man."

"I see. You're here in part because of my father?"

"Who are your guests?" I asked, ignoring her question, nodding at her door.

"Some people who want to help me start up a breeding farm."

"Can we go inside? I'd like to meet them."

"You think I stole those bills?"

"No, of course not. You're Dallas's daughter," I said.

I saw her jaw set and an irritable moment swim through her eyes. She looked searchingly into my face, her hand resting on the door-knob. "Yes, why don't you come in? Then maybe we can put an end to this business."

Her friends proved to be a strange collection. They were in their twenties or early thirties, and each seemed to claim a role for himself that appeared more an aspiration than a reality. They introduced themselves the way regulars in bars often do, as though last names are not important and an air of open familiarity is proof enough of one's goodwill. But unlike most people in bars, or at least people like me, there was almost a comic innocence about the friends of Trish Klein.

A diminutive man named Tommy, with bowed legs, a tubular-shaped nose, and a tiny mouth, said he was a horse jockey, although he was wider at the hips than most jockeys are and probably carried a prohibitive extra ten pounds on his stomach.

A deeply tanned man named Miguel in an immaculate white strap undershirt, with a tattoo of the Virgin Mary wrapped around his right shoulder, said he was a boxer. One eye was disfigured with scar tissue, the lid hanging at half-mast. His upper arms had the thick dimensions of someone who has put in long hours on the speed bag, but his wrists were thin, his hands too small for a professional fighter.

The third man introduced himself as Tyler and was all grins and energy and loquaciousness. He wore black jeans and gold chains and a pullover Hawaiian print shirt that ballooned on his skinny frame. His hair looked like it had been clipped with garden shears and blow-dried with an airplane propeller. He claimed to be a student of film and script writing, with screenplays under submission to Clint Eastwood and Martin Scorsese. When I asked if he had received any degree of response, he replied, "My agent is supposed to call. But I might do some networking on my own out there. I hear a deal sometimes just needs the right kind of nudge from the screenwriter."

The woman was named Lewinda. She stood up eye level with me to shake hands. She was plump and soft all over, peroxided, perfumed, and dressed in tight-fitting tan western slacks, ostrich-skin boots, and a purple shirt stitched with green and red flowers. She said she was a "country vocalist." Her smile was one of the sweetest I had ever seen on a human face, her accent a song in itself. But when she said she had sung "onstage" in both Wheeling, West Virginia, and Branson, Missouri, I had the feeling an anonymous moment "onstage" was about as good as it had gotten for Lewinda With No Last Name.

I drank coffee with Trish Klein's friends for a half hour and wondered if I was in a room filled with mental patients or the most interesting collection of scam artists I'd ever come across. I said good-bye at the door and started down the walkway toward the parking lot. I heard Trish Klein coming hard behind me. "That's it?" she said. "You drive twenty miles, then drink coffee and go back to your office?"

"Some days are like that. The Feds are going to pick this one up, anyway."

"Then why are you here? Don't give me any bullshit, either."

"I was there when your father died. I tried to stop it, but I was deep in the bag."

She stared at me, her mouth slightly parted. I could hear the wind in the trees as I let myself out the iron gate.

• • •

Back at the office, I went to work on a hit-and-run homicide that had probably occurred nine months to one year ago. The body had been discovered three weeks ago under a tangle of dead brush at the bottom of a coulee on a rural road where trash and garbage of every kind was regularly thrown from speeding automobiles and pickup trucks. Years ago, this particular road had experienced its own infamous fifteen minutes of importance through the book and film titled *Dead Man Walking*. On their graduation night, two high school kids had parked in the trees to neck. A pair of brothers from St. Martinville raped the girl and murdered both her and her boyfriend. Today, if you drive down this road, you will see amid the mounds of garbage a Styrofoam cross wrapped with a string of plastic flowers.

The skeletal remains at the bottom of the coulee, which in South Louisiana is what we call a naturally formed drainage ditch, came to be known as "Crustacean Man," because his bones and webbed vestiges of skin were dripping with crawfish when they were lifted out of the mud. Crustacean Man had no identification, had worn no jewelry, and did not have a belt on his trousers or even shoes on his feet. In all probability, he had been a derelict who had wandered north of the old Southern Pacific Railroad tracks. His hip was broken, his skull crushed. The coroner put his death down as hit-and-run vehicular homicide, a not uncommon event in a state that has one of the highest highway fatality rates ij the nation.

We had contacted numerous auto body repair shops in Acadiana, and used the media as much as possible for leads, but had gotten nowhere. Crustacean Man was probably destined for an anonymous burial and a posterity of a few sheets of paper inside a case file that would eventually be flung into a parish incinerator.

But there was one piece in the coroner's postmortem that didn't fit. I picked up the phone and punched in his number. "What's the haps, Koko?" I said, then continued before he had a chance to reply. "Crustacean Man's left hip was broken, but the fatal injury was to the right side of his head. How do you reconcile that?"

"'Reconcile,'" he said thoughtfully. "Let me write that down and look up the various definitions. 'Reconcile.' I like that word."

Koko, you are the most obnoxious human being I've ever had the misfortune to work with, I said to myself.

"What did you say?" he asked.

"Nothing," I said.

"Crustacean Man probably got hit broadside and slammed to the road, then he raised up as the vehicle went over him."

"Wouldn't he have been busted up all over?"

"Not necessarily."

"Was there any indication he was dragged?"

"I'm supposed to know this about a guy wild animals and the crawfish ate down to the bone?"

"I just don't understand how a guy could receive two massive injuries to two separate areas of the body but none anywhere else."

"Maybe the guy's head was smashed against the asphalt after he was broadsided. Or maybe against a post or telephone pole."

"There's no post or telephone pole near where he was found."

"Maybe a second vehicle ran over him."

"Two hit-and-run drivers on the same isolated road on the same night?"

He didn't reply. I could hear him breathing against the receiver. "Koko?" I said.

He hung up. I punched in his number again. "Your attitude sucks," I said.

"Maybe I've got some questions about this one, too," he said. "But you and I both know the guy is going into eternity as John Doe, killed by a person or persons unknown. Nobody cared about him when he was alive. Nobody gives a shit about him now. Now, stop jerking off at other people's expense."

Five minutes later, Wally, our hypertensive dispatcher and self-appointed departmental comic, buzzed my extension. "I got an FBI gal out here in shades and a suit and wit' top-heavy knockers. What you want me to do wit' her?" he said.

"Wally, what in God's name—" I began.

"She's in the can. She cain't hear me."

"That's not the point. This is supposed to be a professional—"

"She backed her car into a cruiser in the parking lot. Helen's outside looking at it now. I'll send her up to your office."

I walked to the window and looked down on Helen Soileau and a group of uniformed deputies staring at the crushed front end of a cruiser. A stream of green radiator fluid was draining into a pool on the asphalt. Behind me, someone tapped on my door. I looked through the glass at a tall woman in a powder-blue suit with hair the bright color of straw. She had propped one hand against the wall and was pulling off her shoe. When I opened the door, she looked up at me awkwardly, her left shoe gripped in her hand, the sole splayed with a flattened piece of pink bubble gum. "Yuck, I hate it when that happens," she said.

"Can I help you?" I said.

"I'm Special Agent Betsy Mossbacher. Phew, what a day," she replied, straightening up, then walking past me to the window, one shoe on, one shoe off. She looked down at the parking lot. "Oh, jeez."

"You're here about the bills from the Mobile savings and loan job?"

"Yeah, I'm getting off to kind of a bad start here. I just interviewed the Klein woman. You knew her father was killed in an armored car robbery? Can I sit down?"

"Yes," I said, uncertain as to which question I had just answered.

She sat in a chair by the side of my desk and began prying gum off her shoe with a pencil and wiping it onto a piece of paper over my wastebasket. "The Klein woman talked with you about her father?"

"She didn't have to. He was a friend of mine. I saw him killed."

Her face became thoughtful, her eyes looking into space, even though she kept digging gum off her shoe with her pencil. "You were the off-duty cop in front of the bar, right?"

I felt myself swallow. "You obviously ran my sheet, so why do you ask?"

"You were pinned down while these guys were shooting at you?"

"I was drunk."

She dropped her pencil in the wastebasket and fitted on her shoe. "I have to wash my hands," she said.

I was having a hard time assimilating Special Agent Betsy Moss-bacher. She seemed to combine ineptitude with abrasiveness and a way of speaking that required a cryptologist to understand what she was saying. Maybe Homeland Security had drained the FBI of its first team, I told myself. Or perhaps a case coordinator was sending her into the hinterland as a training exercise. Or maybe the investigation into two dye-marked bills was not only a waste of time but a way of getting Betsy Mossbacher out of somebody's hair. When she returned from the restroom, she blew out her breath, as though she had just completed a herculean task. "Quite a coincidence this gal ends up in your backyard, huh?" she said.

"The rim of the Gulf Coast is all one culture."

She seemed to chew the inside of her cheek. "Did you know Trish Klein roams around half of this country as well as Latin America?"

"No."

"She inherited a boxcar load of money from her grandmother. She owns beautiful horses. She's educated and has taste. But she says she got the hot bills at a low-rent hotel-and-casino in Mississippi, the kind of dump a roofers' union uses for its conventions. Does that make sense to you?"

"Check out her friends. They're like people who met at a bus depot and decided to live together," I said.

"You knew the savings and loan was a laundry for the Mob?"

I could feel my irritability growing. "So what?" I said.

"Maybe somebody squeezed Trish Klein's father and made him give up the armored car schedule."

"Dallas owed a lot of money to some bad dudes. I told this to the Feds many years ago."

"Was one of them a bookie by the name of Whitey Bruxal?"

"Since you came in here you've been asking me questions you already know the answer to. You saying maybe I don't tell the truth?"

She walked to the window again and gazed down on the cruiser she had struck. "You ever mess with cows?" she said.

"Excuse me?"

"In calving season you spend about six weeks learning about natural and unnatural law."

"You lost me," I said.

"The cows have got sunburned bags and you've got shit, piss, and blood up to your right armpit. You hardly sleep, you're cold most of the time, and you hear animals bawling day and night. When the mommies reject their calves, you graft the orphans to another mommy. You throw everybody a lot of cottonseed cake and pull it off and feel you've done a real good deed. Then one day you ship the whole bunch to the slaughterhouse. Some irony, huh?"

"I've always been poor at allegory," I said.

"The point is our best efforts are seldom good enough. You told Miami-Dade P.D. your buddy Dallas Klein was probably working with the men who boosted his armored car. Consciously or unconsciously, I think you blamed yourself for his death. Are you still carrying guilt, Detective Robicheaux? Is that why you seem to have a remarkable lack of curiosity about his daughter's behavior?"

She put a bright piece of red candy in her mouth and sucked on it. I looked her evenly in the eyes but did not answer her question, a bubble of anger rising in my chest like an old friend.

"Well," she said finally, then turned to go, somehow saddened, even aged, by our exchange.

"Where are you from?" I said.

"Chugwater, Wyoming."

"They must be frank as hell in Chugwater, Wyoming."

"That's what happens when you mess with cows," she replied.

I didn't need this.

CHAPTER
4

THAT EVENING I TOOK Yvonne Darbonne's diary home with me, and after supper walked down to the bayou with a folding chair and began to reread the thirty pages of entries that offered a small glimpse into the soul of an eighteen-year-old Cajun girl who had fallen in love with the world.

The last four pages contained the following entries:

We ate ice cream on the square in St. Martinville and walked out on the dock behind the old church. The moon was high above the oaks, and the moss looked like silver thread against the moon. He kissed me and wrapped me inside his coat. I could feel him against me, down there. . . .

Today we took a boat out to his father's camp in the swamp. I know he wants to do it, but he's afraid to ask. He touched my breast, then said he was sorry. I told him it's not wrong if people love each other. His eyes are dark brown, the way water is when starlight is trapped inside it. He hasn't asked me if I'm a virgin. I wonder if he'll think less of me. His goodness is in everything he does. . . .

Last night he introduced me to his friends. They're nice boys, I think, except for one. He has a hawk's eyes and a mouth that always looks hungry. I saw him watching me in the mirror when he thought no one was looking.

But Yvonne Darbonne's concern with an imperfection in her new-found world was brief. Her last entry returned to the boyfriend:

I told him I wanted him to do it and for him not to be afraid. When we were finished, he kissed my nipples and the tops of my fingers. It was hot in the cabin and his hair was wet and fell in curls on his forehead. I know now I love him in a way that's different from anyone else I've loved. I can't believe we'll be going to college together this summer. He wants to meet my father. He told me never to be ashamed of the place I lived.

Molly walked down the slope and placed her hand on my shoulder. "What are you reading?" she asked.

"The diary of the Darbonne girl. How does a kid like this end up shooting herself?"

I handed the diary to her, with my thumb inserted between the last two pages of entries. Molly turned the pages into the light and read for a moment, then closed the covers and looked into space.

"Who's the boy?" she asked.

"I'm not sure. Her cell phone contained the number of Bello Lujan. Evidently he's got a son at UL. Maybe he and Yvonne Darbonne were an item."

"The *Daily Iberian* said her death has been ruled a suicide."

"That doesn't mean someone else isn't responsible. Where did she get the revolver she shot herself with? Who's the bastard who left her drunk and stoned in the yard with a handgun?"

"Maybe she already had it."

"Her father says otherwise," I replied.

"Family members feel guilty. They often lie."

I took the diary from Molly's hand. "The weapon was stolen from a fraternity house at Ole Miss. How would Mr. Darbonne come to have possession of it?"

I could see a quiet sense of exasperation working its way into her face. "I don't know, Dave. I say don't grieve on what you can't change," she said.

I felt a sharp reply start to rise in my throat. But I kept my own counsel and looked across the bayou at the lights coming on in City Park. Then I followed Molly inside the house and helped her wash the dishes and put away the leftovers from supper.

I AWOKE AT FOUR in the morning and sat at the kitchen table in the darkness and listened to the sound of the wind in the trees. A few minutes later, Molly turned on the light and came into the kitchen in her robe and slippers. She sat down across the table from me. "The Darbonne girl?" she said.

"It's the language in her diary. There's no self-pity or anger in it," I replied.

Molly waited, then said, "Go ahead."

"People like Yvonne Darbonne don't kill themselves. It's that simple. Someone else did it."

Molly propped her elbows on the table, knitted her fingers together, and rested her chin on her fingers. She gazed wanly into my face, trying to hide her fatigue, her eyes filled with the foreboding sense that the dead were about to lay claim upon the quick.

SATURDAY MORNING I drove out to the home of Bello Lujan. His first name was actually Bellerophon, a name that on the surface seems absurd and grandiose in a working-class culture. But South Louisiana is filled with the names of ancient gods and heroes given to our French ancestors during the Reign of Terror when Robespierre and his friends attempted to purge Christian influence from French culture. The irony is that today Cajun pipefitters and waitresses sometimes bear names that Homer would recognize but not most contemporary Americans.

I can't say I ever liked Bello Lujan. He was aggressive, visceral in his language, naked in his attitudes about wealth and status. When you shook hands with him, he gave you a two-second squeeze that left no doubt about his physical potential. At a professional wrestling match in New Orleans, he got into an exchange of insults with one of the wrestlers and climbed into the ring with a wood stool and beat the wrestler bloody with it. Bello claimed that being a good loser required only one essential element—practice.

But even if I didn't like him, I tried to understand him or at least the background that had produced him. His father had been a pinball machine repairman who worked for a crime family that operated out of the old Underpass area in Lafayette. When his father was shot to death, Bello's family moved back and forth between the Iberville Project in New Orleans, the old brothel district in New Iberia, and a dirt-road rural slum in north Lafayette. He shined shoes in saloons and carhopped at a root beer drive-in owned by a mean-spirited man who never allowed him to eat his lunch or supper inside the building. Sometimes I would see Bello on a wintry day at the Southern Pacific station, his wood shine box hung by a leather strap on his shoulders, his face pinched in the cold as he waited to catch a customer stepping down from a Pullman car. Even though my own young life had been marked by privation, I knew Bello had paid more dues than I had. I also knew that he kept a longer memory than I and was not to be crossed.

Supposedly he made his early money in cockfighting and later in the oil and gas business. Others said he pimped for Lafayette's old crime family when they used to operate a pickup bar and brothel above the Underpass. If asked what he did for a living, he would grin good-naturedly and say, "Anything that makes money, podna."

But if there was a single characteristic always associated with Bello Lujan's reputation, it was the fact he could be an almost feral adversary when it came to protection of his interests and his family.

He lived with his wife and son in a big white house on rolling woodland along Bayou Teche, just outside Loreauville. His wife had been crippled in an automobile accident many years ago and seldom appeared in public. The details of the accident had softened around the edges with time, but a child had died in the other vehicle and some said Mrs. Lujan would have been charged had she not been so severely injured herself. Regardless, her lot had not been an easy one. Sometimes people saw her in her wheelchair, peering from behind the curtains in an upstairs window, her face as small and pointed as a bird's.

Across the road from the trellised entrance to Bello's driveway were thirty acres of the best pasture in the parish, where he raised thoroughbreds and gaited horses, all of it surrounded by white-painted plank fence. Bello was not simply a gentleman rancher, either. His horse trainers came from Kentucky; his thoroughbreds raced in both the Louisiana and Florida derbies. Winter and spring, Bello got to pose with the roses.

But there were rumors about the origins of his success at the track—stories about stolen seed, a manipulated high-end claim race in California, and doping the odds-on favorite with downers at a track in New Mexico.

I had called in advance. He greeted me in the driveway, dressed in white shorts and a golf shirt, his skin dark with tan, his arms swatched with whorls of shiny black hair. He crouched slightly, his fists raised like a boxer's. "Dave, you son of a gun, *comment la vie, neg*? I heard you sold off your boat dock. Too bad. I liked that place," he said. His accent was a singular one, a strange blend of hard-core coonass and the Italian-Irish inflections of blue-collar New Orleans.

"How's it hangin', Bello?" I said,

"How's *yours* hangin'?" he replied, still grinning, still full of play.

Then I told him why I was there.

"You want to talk to my son about that girl who killed herself?" he said. "Sorry to hear about something like that, but what's it got to do with Tony?" He turned his head toward the tennis court, where his son was whocking back balls fired at him by an automatic machine.

"Was he seeing Yvonne Darbonne?" I asked.

Bello rubbed at his nose with the heel of his hand. His brow was knitted, his wide-set, dark eyes busy with thought. "A young guy that good-looking has got a lot of girls around. How should I know? They come and go. I don't remember anybody by that name around here," he said.

I started across the lawn toward the tennis court. I could tell his son, Tony, saw me out of the corner of his eye, but he kept on stroking the ball, his cheeks like apples, his curly brown hair tied off his forehead with a bandanna, his hips thin, almost girlish. I heard Bello on my heels. "Hey, Dave, take it out of overdrive, here. That's my son, there. You're saying he's mixed up in somebody's death? I don't like that."

I turned around slowly, trying to fix a smile on my face before I spoke. "This is a homicide investigation, Bello. If you want this interview conducted down at the department, that's fine. In the meantime, I'm requesting that you stay out of it," I said.

He opened up his palms, as though bewildered. "It's Saturday morning. It's spring. The birds are singing. You hit my front lawn like a thunderstorm. I'm the problem?" he said.

I opened the door to the court and walked out on the dampened, rolled surface of the clay. Tony Lujan was deferential and polite in every way, repeatedly addressing me as "sir." But in South Louisiana, protocol is often a given and not substantive, particularly among young people of Tony's financial background.

"You knew Yvonne?" I said.

"Yes, sir."

"You knew her well?" I said, my eyes locked on his.

"She worked at Victor's Cafeteria. I'd see her there and maybe around town some."

"When's the last time you saw her?"

"The day before she died. We had some ice cream in the park."

"You have any idea why she'd want to kill herself?"

"No, sir."

"None?"

"No, sir."

"I think you knew her better than you're letting on," I said.

His eyes were starting to film.

"Hey, you answer his questions!" Bello said.

"We went out. We slept together," Tony said.

"Why'd you try to lie to me?" I asked.

The nylon windscreens on the court puffed in the breeze and creaked against their tethers. The color in the boy's cheeks had the broken shape of flame.

"You knock that off, Dave. He's cooperating, here," Bello said.

"You need to leave us alone, Bello," I said.

"Fuck you. This is my home. You don't come in here pushing people around," Bello replied.

There was nothing for it. Bello was obviously a suffocating, controlling presence in his son's life, and I knew that without a warrant I would get no more information out of either one of them. "If you think of anything that might be helpful, give me a call, will you?" I said to Tony, handing him my business card.

"Yes, sir, I will," he said.

I walked back to my truck, with Bello at my side, his eyes stripping the skin off my face. "You trying to make trouble here, Dave? You got an old beef with me about something?" he said.

"No," I said, opening the door to my truck.

"Then *what*?"

I didn't answer and started to get behind the wheel. Bello's hand sank into my arm. "You don't demean my family and blow me off," he said.

"A young woman is dead. Your son tried to conceal information about his relationship with her. Now, you take your hand off me."

"He's just a kid."

"Not anymore," I replied.

He stared at me, his face twitching, his lips seeming to form words that had no sound.

CLETE PURCEL, my old partner from NOPD Homicide, was not in a good mood that night. In fact, he had not been in a good mood all week, ever since a pipehead check writer and bail skip by the name of Frogman Andrepont had thrown a television set through his brother-in-law's picture-glass window onto the front lawn, then escaped across the roof while Clete ran from the backyard to the front of the house.

Clete had opened up his own P.I. and bail bond office on Main in New Iberia, but he still chased down bail skips for his former employers Wee Willie Bimstine and Nig Rosewater in New Orleans. So after Frogman missed his court appearance, Clete flushed him out of his brother-in-law's house, only to lose him in Henderson Swamp, where Clete blew out a tire highballing down the top of the levee and was almost eaten alive by mosquitoes.

But as a man on the run, Frogman had two disadvantages: His face looked exactly like a frog's, including the eye bags, distended throat, and even the reptilian skin; secondly, he was a degenerate gambler as well as a crack addict. In Frogman's case, this meant Louisiana's newest twenty-four-hour casino and all-purpose neon-lit hog trough was as close to paradise as the earth gets.

It was located in a parish to the north of us and was part of a larger complex that featured a clubhouse and horse track. But the horse races and the upscale dining areas were ultimately cosmetic. The real draw was the casino. The other bars in the parish were forced by law to close at 2 a.m. Not so with the casino. Regardless of the uproar raised by local saloon owners and law enforcement agencies and Mothers Against Drunk Driving, the booze at the casino flowed from moonrise to dawn. How could anyone doubt this was a great country? They only had to ask Frogman.

Seated at the bar, a martini in his hand, dressed western in case an unsophisticated country girl or two was floating around, Frogman had a sense of security and well-being that tempted him to forgive the state of Louisiana for all the time it had dropped on his head over the years. Actually he could afford to be generous. He'd just hit a three-hundred-dollar jackpot on the slot and had treated himself to a steak dinner and a split of champagne. He'd outsmarted that fat cracker Purcel, too, even if he'd had to remodel his brother-in-law's living room a little bit. Frogman tried to imagine his brother-in-law's face when he pulled into his driveway and saw his broken television set and picture-glass window lying in the flower bed. Maybe he should drop a postcard and explain. Why not? It was the right thing to do. He'd take care of it first thing tomorrow.

But Frogman's brother)in-law was not in a forgiving mood and had already dimed Frogman and his probable whereabouts to Clete Purcel. Saturday night Clete cruised the interior of the casino, not knowing that Frogman was taking a break from the machines and getting his ashes hauled by a Mexican prostitute in an Air Stream trailer out by the stables. So Clete set up shop at a blackjack table and quickly lost four hundred and seventy-three dollars.

"You lost how much?" I asked.

"The dealer had a pair of ta-tas that would make your eyes cross. She kept hanging them in my face every time I had to decide whether I wanted a hit. How can you think in a situation like that?" he said.

It was Sunday morning, and he was telling me all this in my backyard, in his own convoluted, exhaustive fashion, which usually indicated he had precipitated a disaster of some kind and was using every circuitous means possible to avoid taking responsibility for it.

Years ago Clete had fried his legitimate career in law enforcement with weed and pills and booze. He had also managed to kill a federally protected witness and had even done security in Vegas and Reno for a sadistic gangster by the name of Sally Dio, whose plane crashed into a mountain in western Montana. After Sally and several of his gumballs were combed out of the trees with garden rakes, investigators discovered Sally's engines were clogged with sand that someone had poured into the fuel tanks. Clete Purcel blew Big Fork, Montana, like the town was burning down.

He was hated and feared by both the Mob and many of his old colleagues at NOPD. His detractors tried to dismiss him as a drunk and an addict and a whoremonger, but in truth Clete Purcel was one of the most intelligent and decent men I ever knew, complex in ways that few could guess at.

He had been raised in the old Irish Channel and talked like it—an accent more akin to Southie or Flatbush than the Deep South. His hands were as big as hams, the knuckles half-mooned with scars. With regularity his massive shoulders and broad back ripped the seams of his tropical shirts. He had a small Irish mouth, the corners downturned, and sandy hair and green eyes that crinkled when he smiled. A black witness to one of his escapades described him as "an albino ape crawling across my rooftop in skivvies," and Clete wasn't offended.

He talked openly about his visceral appetites, his addictions, his romances with junkies and strippers, his alcoholic blackouts that turned into scorched-earth episodes that caused people to climb out of barroom windows. But inside his violence and his reckless disregard for his own welfare was another man, one who carried images and thought processes in his head that he seldom shared: a father who used to make a little boy kneel for hours at a time on grains of rice; a wife who dumped him because she couldn't sleep with a man who believed the ghost of a mamasan lived on his fire escape; the grinding sound of steel tracks through a Third World village, an arch of liquid flame, the smell of straw and animals burning, and the screams of tiny men in black pajamas trapped inside a spider hole.

These were the memories his booze and pills couldn't even make a dent in.

"What happened to Frogman?" I said.

"That's what I was trying to tell you," he said. "I got cleaned out at blackjack, so I was watching this great-looking broad shooting craps. You should have seen her ass when she bent over. Remember that song by Jimmy Clanton, 'Venus in Blue Jeans'? I was getting a boner just watching from the bar."

The kitchen window was open and I could see the curtains blowing inside the screen and hear Molly loading the dishwasher. "Clete, would you just—"

"Then I noticed this gal was probably part of a crew, maybe even running the crew. I think two of them had been counting cards at my blackjack table earlier. The gal crapped out twice, then the dice came back to her again. Soon as she picked them up from the stick man, a guy collides into the drink waitress and splashes cups of beer all over the place. That's when she switched the dice. It was smooth, too. The boxman didn't have a clue. She made seven passes in a row. Then she switched them back out, to one of the guys who'd been counting cards at my table."

"What's the point?" I said, my impatience growing.

We were sitting on the back steps. He squinted with one eye at the bayou, as though organizing his thoughts. "A half hour later she was back at the same table and switched them out again. Except this time she got greedy. She was doubling up her bets, until she had about

eight or nine grand on the felt. Everyone around the table was starting to go apeshit and stacking chips on the pass line. The boxman
called up a couple of security guys and I figured she was dead meat.
That's when Frogman showed up."

"He was in her crew?"

"Dig this. The boxman and security guys were just about to bust
the broad, then Frogman came stumbling into the crowd and went
down on the floor like he'd stepped on a high-voltage wire. At first I
thought it was part of the switch-off. I had to shove my way through
the crowd to look at him close-up. He was curled in a ball, shivering
all over, spit coming out of both sides of his mouth, then somebody
started yelling, 'The guy's having an epileptic fit!'

"Except I knew Frogman didn't have epilepsy. His hands were
shriveled up like claws against his chest and his eyes were popping
out of his head. I told the boxman to get a resuscitation cup out of
their first-aid kit, but he just stared at me like I was talking Sanskrit.
So I shouted at him, 'Nobody does mouth-to-mouth in a time of
AIDS. Get the cup out of your fucking first-aid kit.'

"You know what kind of medical aid they have in a dump like
that? French ticklers and aphrodisiacs you buy from the rubber
machine in the can. I couldn't believe what I had to do next. I don't
think Frogman Andrepont has gone near a toothbrush since he got
out of Angola five years ago. I grabbed his nose and opened up his
mouth and was just about to do the unthinkable, when the broad
with the bod that looks like Venus in blue jeans pushed me aside and
said, 'Move it over, bub.'

"She closed off Frogman's nostrils and blew air down his throat
and pounded on his chest until he finally made this terrible sucking
sound and started breathing again. The security guys still weren't sure
if they were watching a scam or not. They were checking the dice on
the table, but they couldn't find the ones she'd switched into the
game. Then the paramedics got there and Venus in blue jeans beat it
out the back door.

"I showed some deputies my papers on Frogman and cuffed him
to the gurney and was going to ride to the hospital in the ambulance
with him, when I saw Venus hauling that beautiful ass of hers across

the parking lot. I caught up with her and said, 'You just ripped off the casino and saved a guy's life at the same time. Grifters don't do that.'

"She was walking real fast and says, 'Grifter up your nose. Who do you think you are?'

"I go, 'I'm a private investigator. I was chasing a bail skip, the guy you saved. I got my clock cleaned at the blackjack table.'

"She says, 'You ought to stay out of casinos.'

"I say, 'What's your name?'

"She says, 'Trouble.'

"I go, 'How about a drink? Or something to eat?'

"She looks over my shoulder and sees the security guys coming for us. Then she looks all around for her friends, but she'd already lost them in the crowd. She goes, 'I'm up Shit's Creek, handsome. Can you get us out of here?' My big-boy started flipping around in my slacks, like it had gone on autopilot and was trying to break out of jail."

Molly shut the kitchen window.

"Sorry," Clete said.

"What happened?" I asked.

"She said her name is Trish Klein. She says you and her old man were buds. She says you were there when some guys took his head off with a shotgun."

I stared through the trees at the bayou, trying to assimilate Clete's story and connect it with the other information I had on Dallas Klein's daughter. But Clete wasn't finished. "This morning an FBI broad knocked on my door. Her name is Betsy Mossbacher and she's got a king-size broom up her ass. The Feds had a tail on Trish Klein last night, and now they've connected me with her and you with me. What's this bullshit about, Dave?"

"You're getting it on with grifters now?"

"Don't change the subject."

"I knew Trish Klein's father in Miami. He was a guard on an armored truck. He owed money to some wiseguys and I think they made him give up the truck's schedule. They cleaned the slate when they boosted the truck. I think Trish Klein is here on a vendetta. The

Feds think she was mixed up in taking down a savings and loan in Mobile that was a laundry operation for the Mob."

His big arms were propped on his knees, his face pointed straight ahead. But I could tell he was thinking about the girl now and not about her father.

"You were in the sack with her?" I asked.

"I wish. Do I look old, Dave? Tell me the truth," he said, fixing his eyes on mine.

CHAPTER
5

I F YOU EVER BECOME a low-bottom boozer, you will learn that the safest places to drink, provided you know the rules, are blue-collar saloons, pool halls, hillbilly juke joints, and blind pigs where two thirds of the clientele have rap sheets.

Upscale hotel bars and Dagwood-and-Blondie lounges in the suburbs have a low tolerance for drunks and shut you down or call security before you can get seriously in the bag. When you drink in a rat hole, you can get shit-faced out of your mind and not be molested as long as you understand that the critical issue is respect for people's privacy. Marginalized people don't want confrontation. Violence for them means life-threatening injuries, bail bond fees, fines paid at guilty court, and loss of work. It could also mean a trip back to a work camp or a mainline joint. They couldn't care less about your opinion of them. They just ask that you not violate their boundaries or pretend you understand the dues they have paid.

In New Iberia, most of the dope is sold on inner-city street corners by gangbangers. At dusk they assemble in dirt yards or in front of boarded-up shacks, their caps on backward, sometimes wearing gang colors, and wait for passing cars to slow by the curb. They're territorial, armed, street-smart, and dangerous if pushed into a corner. Most of them do not know who their fathers are and have sentimental attachments to their grandmothers. Oddly, few of them expect to do mainline time. None of them will deliberately challenge authority. Most important of all, none of them has any desire to become involved with respectable society, except on a business level.

But Tony Lujan and a friend knew none of these things about marginal people or chose to ignore them on Monday afternoon, when they decided to stop at the McDonald's on East Main, far from the black neighborhood where a dealer by the name of Monarch Little sold crystal meth and rock and sometimes brown skag to all comers, curb service free.

Monarch had a thick pink tongue that caused him to lisp, a gnarled forehead, and skin whose shiny pigmentation made me think of a walrus. He wore two-hundred-dollar tennis shoes with gas cushions in the soles, the stylized baggy pants of a professional weight lifter, and a huge ball cap turned sideways on his head, which, along with a washtub stomach and the shower of brown moles on his face, gave him the harmless appearance of a cartoon character.

But in a street beef, with nines, shanks, or Molotovs, Monarch did not take prisoners. As a teenager he had been in juvie three times, once for setting fire to the house of a city cop who had felt up his sister in the backseat of a cruiser. He marked his eighteenth birthday by shoving a pimp in the face and watching him tumble down a staircase. The pimp's brother, a human mastodon who had once torn a parking meter out of concrete and thrown it through a saloon window, put out the word he was going to cook Monarch in a pot. The pimp's brother caught four nine-millimeter rounds in the chest from a drive-by while he was watering his grass on Easter morning.

Monday afternoon the lawns of the Victorian and antebellum homes along East Main were sprinkled with azalea bloom. Great bluish-purple clumps of wisteria hung from the trellised entrances to terraced gardens that sloped down to Bayou Teche. The wind ruffled the canopy of oaks that arched over the street; the air was balmy and smelled of salt and warm flowers and the promise of rain. Monarch, with two of his cohorts, pulled into McDonald's and parked his Firebird next to an SUV, in the shade of a live oak tree. He went inside and ordered a bag of hamburgers and cartons of fries while his two friends listened to the stereo, the speakers pounding so loudly the window glass in other vehicles vibrated.

Tony Lujan sat in the passenger seat of the SUV, spooning frozen yogurt into his mouth. His friend, the driver, was darkly handsome, his cheeks sunken, his lips thick and sensuous, his hair growing in locks on his neck. He was dressed in black leather pants, a black vest, and a long-sleeved striped shirt, like a nineteenth-century gunfighter might wear.

"How about it on the Tupac?" he shouted at the black kids in the Firebird, at the same time flinging his half-eaten hamburger over the top of the SUV at a garbage can.

"Easy, Slim," Tony said, his eyes raising from his frozen yogurt.

The hamburger's trajectory was short. Half of a bun glazed across the Firebird's hood, stippling it with mustard.

Monarch had just walked out the front door of the McDonald's. He paused on the walkway, his bag of food in one hand, and fingered the skin under his neck chains. He walked to the driver's window of the SUV. "You just t'rew baby shit on my ride," he said.

"It was an accident," Tony said, leaning forward in the passenger seat so Monarch could see his face. He dipped his fingers into his shirt pocket and removed a five and a one. He extended the money toward Monarch. "It's six bucks at the car wash up on Lewis Street."

But the driver took Tony's extended wrist in his hand and moved it and the money back from the window. "You said 'baby *thit*'?" the driver asked Monarch, unable to suppress a laugh.

Monarch picked a leaf off his arm and watched it blow away in the wind. He pinched the saliva from the corners of his mouth and looked at the wetness on his fingers, then glanced at the university sticker on the back window. "You going to colletch?"

"*Colletch?* Yeah, man, that's us," the driver said. "Look, I'd really like to talk to you, but unless you dial down Snoopy Dog Dump or whatever, we're going to have to boogie, because right now I feel like somebody poured cement in my ears. How do you listen to that crap, anyway?"

"The mustard on my 'Bird need somebody to clean it off, not at no car wash, either," Monarch said.

"Look, this is from the heart, okay?" Tony Lujan's friend said. "That lisp you got probably isn't a speech defect. It's because you've got damaged hearing. You pronounce words the way you hear them, and you hear them incorrectly because you've blown out your eardrums listening to guys whose biggest talent is grabbing their dicks in front of an MTV camera."

Monarch tilted up his chin and massaged his throat. The moles on his face looked as hard and shiny as almonds. His stomach rose and fell under his shirt; his eyes seemed to grow sleepy. He reached down into his bag of hamburgers and fries and removed a wadded-up handful of paper napkins. Then he proceeded to wipe the mustard off his car hood, his expression flat, even yawning while he cleaned the last yellow smear off the paint.

He opened his door to get back in the Firebird, the edge of the door touching the side of the SUV.

"That damn nigger," Tony's friend said.

"Say what?" Monarch said.

"Cool it, Slim. The guy's not worth it," Tony said to his friend.

Monarch reached inside his Firebird, gathered an object in his hand, and dropped it in his pocket. Then he turned around and opened the passenger door of the SUV. "Both of y'all out on the pave," he said.

"You don't want to do this, man," Tony said.

"If a nigger scratch your 'sheen, we gotta check it out, call the insurance man, make sure everyt'ing get done right," Monarch said.

Tony's friend was already coming around the front of the SUV. "Hey, man, I told you we don't understand jungle drums. Can you translate ''sheen' for me?" He started laughing. "I'm sorry, man, you ever see those Tweety Bird cartoons? You sound just like him. I ain't dissing you. It's cool. You could turn it into a nightclub act. It's like Tweety Bird married Meat Loaf and they had a kid."

"That mean your 'machine,' see, and the reason I knowed you was going to colletch was I seen this 'sheen before, down on Ann Street, when you and a UL girl was scoring some Ex. See, we knowed who the UL girl was 'cause she was balling down the line long before she was balling you. Except none of us would ball her anymore 'cause of her gonorrhea. One guy still lets her give him head, but he say it ain't very good."

The street was quiet except for the rustle of the wind, a plastic cup rattling in the parking lot.

"Slim can hurt you, man," Tony said.

Monarch's right thumb was hooked on the edge of his pants pocket, his knuckles like pale quarters under his skin. His eyes shifted sideways, out toward the street. His hand worked its way into his pocket and Tony Lujan involuntarily stepped back. Monarch smiled and lifted his car keys jingling from his pocket. "Is that where I hit it, that li'l line in the dust?" he said, examining the SUV's door.

He rubbed away the dirt and then dug a bronze-colored key into the paint, peeling it back in a long curlicue, cutting through the primer, exposing a shiny strip of metal. His face clouded with concern. "No, that ain't where I hit it. It was just a smudge in the dirt. Or maybe I ain't hit it at all. What y'all t'ink?"

He raked a long silver line across the first one, forming an X, then straightened up and blew his nose softly into a Kleenex. No one had moved. While Monarch had vandalized the SUV, one of his cohorts had squirmed bare-chested through a window on the passenger side of the Firebird and had positioned himself on the window jamb, his underwear bunched on his stomach, a black bandanna tied down tightly on his scalp. In his right hand was a semiautomatic that he held flatly against the roof, the muzzle pointed at Tony Lujan and his friend Slim.

Monarch removed a roll of currency from his pocket and peeled off several bills. He crumpled the bills inside his soiled Kleenex and tossed the balled Kleenex on the seat of the SUV.

"Them dead presidents gonna take care of the scratch. Y'all want some more Ex, come see me. Get tired of white schoolgirl stuff, I can hep you there, too. In the meantime, check out Snoop and P. Diddy and improve your musical taste," he said. "You want to call us niggers, just don't do it where we can hear you."

A thick green vein that looked like knotted twine pulsed in Slim's forehead. He inhaled deeply, as though he were deciding whether or not to leap out the door of an airplane at a high altitude. Then he said, "Fuck you," and hit Monarch with a blow that slung a rope of spittle and blood across the Firebird's rolled white leather seat.

Monarch clutched his mouth with one hand, breathing hard through his nose, as though he could not allow himself to realize how badly he had been hurt. He stared at his palm, his lips as red and shiny as a clown's. He stepped toward Slim, his hands balling into fists.

"Don't touch me," Slim said.

Monarch swung at the air, off balance, tripping on his shoelaces, his body caroming off Slim's shoulder.

Slim pushed him away, whirled, and delivered a tae kwon do kick that exploded on Monarch's eye and snapped his head sideways, knocking him against the Firebird. Then Slim's foot shot out again, spearing Monarch in the center of his face.

"Clear my line of fire, Monarch! That motherfucker dead!" the shirtless kid in the black head scarf shouted.

But Monarch behaved like a king. With a siren pealing in the distance, his mouth and nose streaming blood, a piece of broken tooth glistening on his chin, he lifted one hand as though he were giving a benediction, his body positioned between his armed friend and the boy whose nickname was Slim. "Lose the—" he began. He pressed his palm against his mouth, swallowed, and tried again. "Lose the nine. I tripped on the curb. We was just getting burgers. Don't know nothing about these motherfuckers here. Don't got nothing against them," he said.

Then he sat down heavily on the white leather seat of his Firebird and vomited on his shoes.

LAST YEAR, for economic reasons, our city police force was subsumed by the sheriff's office, creating one jurisdiction out of both the city and parish, which meant that all 911 police emergency calls went automatically into the sheriff's department, regardless if the police emergency had taken place inside or outside the city limits.

I had just left a mayoral meeting downtown when Helen Soileau called me on my handheld radio. "Where are you?" she said.

"In the parking lot, behind City Hall," I replied.

"There's a racial beef of some kind going down at McDonald's.

Monarch Little and Bello Lujan's kid may be involved in it. I've got two cars on the way. Can you get down there?"

"I'm on my way."

"One of the black kids may have a gun. Watch your ass, Streak. But get a fire extinguisher on this. Nobody gets hurt out there."

I dropped the handheld on the seat of the cruiser I was using and turned into the one-way traffic on East Main, the gray-green arch of live oaks sliding by overhead, then swung around on St. Peter and headed back in the opposite direction, toward the McDonald's.

New Iberia is not New Orleans and we do not share its violent history, one that in the past has included a homicide rate equaled only by that of Washington, D.C. Here, whites and people of color work and live side by side. But nonetheless a peculiar kind of racial ill ease still exists in our small city on Bayou Teche. Maybe it's indicative of the shadow that the pre–civil rights era still casts upon all the states of the old Confederacy. Perhaps we fear our own memories. I think as white people we know deep down inside ourselves the exact nature of the deeds we or our predecessors committed against people of color. I think we know that if our roles were reversed, if we had suffered the same degree of injury that was imposed upon the Negro race, we would not be particularly magnanimous when payback time rolled around. I think we know that in all probability we would cut the throats of the people who had made our lives miserable.

So we are excessively conscious of manners and protocol in dealing with one another. Unfortunately, we have no control over a rogue cop with a sexual agenda or a closet racist at the post office or a newly elected black official wetting his lips his first night on the city council or a white college kid who thinks he can splatter a gangbanger's grits on a sidewalk without all of us paying his tab.

Two uniformed deputies were already on the scene when I reached the McDonald's, but they obviously had their hands full. A crowd had gathered, and two carloads of Monarch's friends had pulled to the curb and were forming a phalanx on the sidewalk. A witness evidently had told the deputies that one of the black kids in the Firebird had dumped a semiautomatic in the trash barrel, and the deputies were now trying to search all five kids from the fray for concealed weapons while at the same time keeping an eye on the crowd and Monarch's newly arrived compatriots.

But most of the real trouble was coming from only one person— Tony Lujan's friend. He had been told to lean against the side of the SUV and to spread his feet, but he kept turning around and talking without stop, feeding his own anger, one cheek flecked with blood from Monarch's mouth.

I shoved him against the SUV, hard, and kicked his feet wider apart. "We make the rules, podna. Time for you to take Trappist vows," I said.

"Take what?" he said.

"That means shut your face," I said.

I motioned the deputy away and began to shake down Tony Lujan's friend. When I ran my hands down under his arms I could feel his body humming with energy, the way you can feel an electrical current coursing through a heavily insulated power line.

"Put your wrists behind you," I said.

"You're arresting me? These guys pulled a gun on us. They vandalized my vehicle."

But he put his hands behind him just the same. On one hand he wore a high school graduation ring, on the other a gold ring inset with a ruby and the insignia of his fraternity. I snipped the cuffs on each of his wrists and began walking him toward the backseat of my cruiser. Already his manner had changed and I realized he was exactly like all the middle-class kids we run in for possession or DWI. Many of them are the children of physicians and attorneys and prominent businesspeople. When they deal with someone dressed in a suit, or in sports clothes, as I was, someone who represents a form of authority they associate with their parents, their vocabulary becomes sanitized and their manners miraculously reappear. In fact, their degree of humility and cooperation is so impressive, they usually skate on the charges or at worst receive probationary sentences.

"Watch your head," I said as I put him in the backseat of the cruiser.

"Sir, we told you the truth about what happened out there," he said. "The fat black guy keyed my father's new paint job. If I had it to do over, I'd just drive away and eat the loss. But that kid with the rag on his head aimed a nine-millimeter at us. Over nothing."

"What's your name?" I asked.

"Sam Bruxal. But everybody calls me Slim."

"You took down Monarch Little, Slim. At gunpoint. That's impressive. But I'd watch my ass for a while. What's your last name again?"

"Bruxal," he said.

"Ever hear of a guy by the name of Whitey Bruxal?"

"That's my father," he said, his eyes lifting into mine.

"From Florida?"

"That's right. We moved to Lafayette from Miami five years ago."

"Really?" I said, looking at him now with much more interest.

"Yeah, what's going on?"

"I'd like to have a chance to meet your dad."

"Oh, you'll meet him, all right," Slim replied, then realized he had allowed his manufactured persona to slip. "I mean—"

"Yeah, I know exactly what you mean, kid," I said, and rejoined the deputies, one of whom had hooked up Monarch Little and was about to take him to emergency receiving at Iberia General.

The deputy was a stout, red-haired man with a brush mustache who had been one of the city cops absorbed into the sheriff's department when the two agencies merged last year. He was a retired NCO and was called "Top" by his colleagues, although he had been a cook in the Marine Corps and never a first sergeant. Top's admonition about surviving in a bureaucracy was simple: "Make friends with all the clerks and don't get in the way of a supervisor who wants to be on the links by two p.m."

"Let me talk to Monarch a minute, will you, Top?" I said.

"Take him home to dinner with you," he replied.

Monarch was seated in the back of the cruiser, his wrists cuffed in front of him so he could hold a blood-spotted towel to his mouth and nose.

"You going to make it, Monarch?" I said.

"I done tole y'all, I tripped on the curb and busted my face. Ain't filing no charges. Don't even remember what happened," he replied.

Through the back window I saw Helen pull into the parking lot, the reflected image of a giant live oak sliding off her windshield. "You got a history with Slim Bruxal?" I said.

"Who?"

"The guy who remodeled your face."

"A white guy picked me up after I fell. That the one you talking about?"

"Cute," I said.

But Monarch was no longer looking at me. His eyes were on Helen, who had walked over to the trash barrel where a deputy had just recovered the nine-millimeter dumped by Monarch's friend. "I'm ready to go to the hospital. I swallowed blood. I t'ink I'm gonna t'row up again," he said, pressing the towel to his face.

"Sheriff Soileau might want to talk with you first."

"I ain't got nothing to say."

I straightened up from the passenger window and looked across the top of the cruiser. "He's all yours, Top," I said.

Helen came up to me after the cruiser had disappeared down the street. "Looks like you got the cap on it," she said.

"I wouldn't say that at all," I replied.

"Oh?"

"That tall white kid is the son of a Miami bookie by the name of Whitey Bruxal. I think Whitey Bruxal is the guy who got a friend of mine killed in an armored car robbery twenty years ago. It's no accident my dead friend's daughter, Trish Klein, is in this area."

I saw the connections start to come together in Helen's eyes. "Whatever the Klein woman's issues are, they're federal. Unless she manages to kill somebody in our jurisdiction, I don't want to hear that name again," she said.

"One other thing. I got the impression Monarch wanted to get a lot of gone between you and him."

"His mother was a washerwoman who worked for my father. She also turned tricks at the Boom Boom Room. I used to take him for sno-balls in City Park," she said. "Funny how it shakes out some-times, huh, bwana?"

I'D HAD A SLIP from my A.A. program the previous year. The causes aren't important now, but the consequence was the worst bender I ever went on—a two-day blackout that left me on the edges of delir-ium tremens and with the very real conviction I had committed a homicide. The damage I did to myself was of the kind that alcoholics sometimes do not recover from—the kind when you burn the cables on your elevator and punch a hole in the basement and keep right on going.

But I went back to meetings and pumped iron and ran in the park, and relearned one of the basic tenets of A.A.—that there is no posses-sion more valuable than a sober sunrise, and any drunk who demands more out of life than that will probably not have it.

Unfortunately the nocturnal hours were never good to me. In my dreams I would be drunk again, loathsome even unto myself, a public spectacle whom people treated with either pity or contempt. I would wake from the dream, my throat parched, and walk off balance into the kitchen for a glass of water, unable to extract myself from memo-ries about people and places that I had thought no longer belonged to my life. But the feelings released from my unconscious by the dream would not leave me. It's like blood splatter on the soul. You don't rinse it off easily. My hand would tremble on the faucet.

The dawn always came as a form of release. The gargoyles and the polka-dotted giraffes disappeared in the light of day, and my night-mares burned into a soft and harmless glow, like a pistol flare dying inside a mist.

But as William Faulkner said, and as I was about to learn, the past is not only still with us, the past is not even the past.

The warning call from Wally, our dispatcher, came in the next day on my cell while I was having midmorning coffee at Victor's Cafeteria. "Some guy named Whitey Bruxal and a geek wit' him was just in here to see Helen. I told them Helen was in Baton Rouge. You know these guys?" he said.

"Bruxal is the father of the white kid we busted in the beef at McDonald's yesterday," I replied.

"He was seriously out of joint. When I tole him Helen wasn't here, he wanted to talk to you."

"What did you tell him?"

"That you wasn't here, that he needed to lower his voice, that this ain't New Orleans."

"Why New Orleans?"

"He talks like he comes from there."

I suspected Wally had confused Bruxal's accent, which was probably eastern seaboard, with the Irish-Italian inflections that are characteristic of blue-collar people born in New Orleans. "Why'd you call me, Wally?" I said.

"He's on his way to Victor's."

"You told him I was here?"

"The janitor did. Want me to chew him out? He was seventy-t'ree last week."

I paid my check and was about to go out the door when I saw a waxed black Humvee, wrapped with chrome, pull up to the curb. A muscular man in a powder-blue suit, with peroxided blond hair and cords in his neck and tiny pits in his cheeks, cut the engine and got out on the sidewalk. He saw me about to push open the glass door. "He's here," he said to a man in the passenger seat.

I did not recognize the passenger in the Humvee, but the driver had the familiarity of someone you have met in a dream, or perhaps at a time in your life when you saw the world through a glass darkly and went about making a religion out of your own dismemberment, inviting as many people as possible to bring saws and tongs to the task. The blond man pulled open the door and came inside, bringing the hot smell of the street with him.

"I told Whitey it was you. Same name, same guy, just a little older," he said. "Remember me?"

"I'm not sure," I lied.

"Elmer Fudd, from that bar in Opa-Locka, the one looked like a French Foreign Legion fort in the Sahara. Last time we saw each other, I gave you some breath mints."

"If you want to talk to me, you need to come into my office at the Iberia Parish Sheriff's Department," I said.

"I don't want to talk to you. But *he* does," the blond man said, glancing toward his friend.

Whitey Bruxal wasn't what I expected. Miami has always been an open city for the Mafia, which means that no one is allowed a lock on the action and no one gets clipped while he's there on R & R. Consequently, during the winter season the city is filled with the lower echelons of the New York crime families. The ones I used to see on the beach had the anatomical proportions of upended tadpoles, with barrel chests, no hips, and legs that looked like tendrils, their phalluses as pronounced as bananas inside their Speedos.

But Bruxal was not a run-of-the-mill South Florida bookie. His physique reminded me of a gymnast or a man who plays tennis singles with a mean eye, under a white sun, never thinking of it as just a game. "You the guy who busted my kid?" he said, smiling at the corner of his mouth.

"I'm the detective who hooked him up and took him in. The charges are up to the prosecutor's office," I replied.

"I'll fill you in. The D.A. is talking about felony assault."

"I doubt that," I said, and walked past him, out onto the sidewalk.

He followed me. His hair was white and thick, clipped G.I., as stiff as a brush, his skin tanned, his shirt tight on his chest and shoulders. "Doubt it why?" he said.

"Monarch Little is a dealer and general lowlife, but he usually takes his own bounce. I doubt he'll press charges."

"I got a problem here. Those black kids pointed a gun at my son," he said, still smiling at the corner of his mouth.

"Yeah?"

"I haven't heard anything about charges against the blacks. Way I see it, my son and his friend Tony Lujan are the wronged parties. I'm supposed to feel good the head gangbanger isn't trying to send my boy to prison?"

"They may take a hit on a firearms charge. Why not wait and see?"

"That's what you do when a concrete truck is coming down the center stripe at you?"

He was not an unpleasant man, and his beef with the prosecutor's office not without foundation. But I could not get rid of the image of my friend Dallas Klein, kneeling in the shade of an Opa-Locka bank, just before a shotgun was fired directly into his face.

"I've got a problem of my own, Mr. Bruxal," I said.

The blond man, who had been listening quietly, couldn't suppress a laugh.

"That's funny?" I said to him.

His eyes were bright green, his mouth spread open on one side out of his teeth. "You got boons pulling guns on people and you're telling the victim's father *you* got a problem?" he replied.

"What's your name?"

"Lefty Raguza." When he spoke his name, his face was charged with energy, his eyes dancing, his chin lifted.

"Thanks," I said, writing his name in a notebook.

"What's that for?" he asked.

"We like to research who's in town, who's not. You know how it is. Got to keep the down-home folks happy," I replied, winking at him.

"You need to finish your statement to me, Mr. Robicheaux," Bruxal said, a tanker truck loaded with gasoline passing behind him.

Don't say it, I thought. "I think if a kid by the name of Dallas Klein had never met you and your friend here, he'd still be alive," I said.

Bruxal looked at the blond man named Lefty Raguza. The blond man shrugged his shoulders, indicating he did not understand the reference either. "Who's this Dallas Whatever?" Bruxal asked.

"Your man here already acknowledged he remembers me. He remembers me because we met in Opa-Locka, Florida, when he was trying to collect sixteen grand Dallas owed your sports book. Just to make sure everything is clear here, I want you to know I'm the dude who dimed you with Miami P.D. and the FBI on the armored car boost."

Bruxal had a square chin and big bones in his cheeks. His expression remained good-natured, his brow unlined, but it was obvious he was thinking, his mind processing information, considering and rejecting various forms of response. "Tell you what, I'd like to talk with you more, but I'm going to do like my lawyer says and butt out. I'll ask you a favor, though. You mind?"

"Be my guest," I replied.

"If you got to hook up my son again, call me first? Slim's dick is too big for his brains, but he's a good kid. I didn't have any judgment at that age. How about you? Your sizzle stick get in the way of your brains sometimes, Mr. Robicheaux?"

A moment later I watched him drive away in his Humvee with ...e man who had once ridiculed me when I was stone-drunk. Bruxal was slick. He had not challenged me on a personal level and he had not made any statement that was demonstrably a lie, the handle that every cop looks for in a guilty man. Instead, he had made a personal entreaty on behalf of his son and put the moral onus on me.

I had a feeling I was going to see a lot more of Whitey Bruxal.

BACK AT THE OFFICE I ran his name through the National Crime Information Center. It was not helpful. Bruxal had been interviewed several times by the FBI and Miami P.D. in the aftermath of the armored car heist and the murder of Dallas Klein and the bank teller, but he had never been directly connected to either the robbery or the homicide. Of course, this was information I already had. He had been arrested in Flatbush for driving with an expired operator's license and fined once in the Crown Heights section of Brooklyn as a co-conspirator in the distribution of Irish Sweepstakes tickets. His third arrest was in West Palm Beach, check this out, for littering. He had been sentenced to six consecutive Saturdays on a sanitation truck.

If Bugsy Siegel had set the standard, Bruxal had fallen far short of the mark.

But the hit I got on Lefty Thomas Leo Raguza was another matter. He had done time both in Georgia and inside the Flat Top at Raiford Pen for assault with a deadly weapon and had spent a year in the Broward County Stockade for criminal possession of a firearm, a charge that had been knocked down from attempted murder. It took me less than a half hour to find his old parole officer in Fort Lauderdale.

"Tommy Lee Raguza? You bet I remember him," he said.

"He goes by Lefty now."

"That's right, he boxed in Raiford. You've got a real bucket of shit on your hands, pal."

"Can you break that down?"

"When it comes to Tommy Lee Raguza, I'm not up to the task. I'll fax you a psychiatric evaluation from his file. Get this, that psych report came in *before* we had to cut him loose. It'll make you feel warm and fuzzy inside."

The two-page evaluation that came through the department's fax machine was a study in failure, not simply societal and institutional failure but the kind that reaches all the way back through the evolution of the species. After a long typed description of Lefty or Tommy Lee Raguza's psychological and behavioral problems, all couched in Freudian terms, the psychiatrist made this handwritten addendum at the bottom:

> Medical science does not provide an adequate vocabulary to describe a man like this. He is probably the cruelest human being I have ever had the misfortune to meet. There is no element in his background, environmental or genetic, that would explain the dispassionate level of iniquity in this man and the level of pleasure he takes in injuring both people and animals. Frankly, I think this man is evil and should be separated from human society for the rest of his life. Unfortunately that will probably not happen.

This was the man now living in Acadiana, where parishioners still make the sign of the cross when they pass a Catholic church and cannot believe that an American president would lie to them.

I went back to work on Bruxal and ran his name through Google. I found information there that told me far more about him and his present intentions than his criminal jacket did. His name had appeared in several articles published in the Lafayette *Daily Advertiser,* the Baton Rouge *Advocate,* and the *Times-Picayune* in New Orleans. Whitey Bruxal had become a major player in Louisiana's blossoming casino industry.

Gambling, like prostitution and every other imaginable vice, has a long history in the state. In the nineteenth century the gambling halls along Canal were perhaps the most notorious in the country, not only for their lucrativeness but also for the number of knifings and shootings that took place inside them. The Confederate general P.G.T. Beauregard, who fired the first shot on Fort Sumter, made a fortune after the war as the head of the state lottery. Governor Huey P. Long literally gave Louisiana to Frank Costello, who in turn empowered a crime family in New Orleans to set up and control all organized vice throughout the southern half of the state. The gambling machines were made by a Mob-owned company in Chicago, but the credit line that purchased them came from right here in New Iberia.

During the mid-1950s, the most despised man in the state was an attorney general who tried to shut down the brothels and deep-six the slots out in the Gulf. The gambling joints and cathouses in St. Landry Parish were run by the sheriff. Every pool hall and blue-collar bar from Lake Charles to the Mississippi line contained football cards, punchboards, and payoff pinball machines. Cops in uniform worked as card dealers and bartenders in nightclubs that deliberately served minors. I could go on, but what difference does it make? The illegal gambling industry of the past is nothing in comparison to its legalized descendant.

A few years back our governor, who supposedly was in debt millions of dollars to the Vegas syndicate, proved himself a great friend to casino gambling in Louisiana. Today, he and his son are serving time in a federal penitentiary, along with our last three state insurance commissioners. No matter. From Shreveport on the northwestern tip of the state to Lake Charles in the south, the casinos and racetracks soak up all the Texas trade they can get their hands on. New Orleans takes the trade from everywhere, including old people the casinos bus into town from retirement homes in Mississippi. The Indians on the rez are happier than pigs rolling in slop. In fact, everyone is delighted with the new era of gaming in Louisiana, except, of course, the uneducated and the compulsive who lose their life's savings and the owners of bars and restaurants who have to shut down their businesses because they can't compete with the giveaway prices at the casinos.

I went into Helen's office and told her about my encounter with Whitey Bruxal and his friend Lefty Raguza at Victor's Cafeteria.

"Bruxal doesn't like the way we're handling things?" she said.

"He thinks his son and Tony Lujan are getting dumped on. I told him the black kids might go down on the firearms charge."

"The lab says there are a half-dozen different prints on the nine-millimeter we found in the trash can. So far nobody from McDonald's has been willing to identify which black kid was holding it. I don't think the D.A. is going to carry the ball very far on this one."

"It looks like Bruxal is mixed up with some floating casinos and a couple of tracks here. I think a lot of big players from Florida have found a new home in Louisiana. Bruxal's hunting on the game reserve."

She nodded slowly, as though respectfully absorbing my words. But I knew I was bringing problems and complexities into her day that she didn't need. She had heard it all before, and nothing I said would ever change the historical problems of our state. I only wish I had listened more often to my own counsel.

"Trish Klein is here to take Bruxal down, Helen. She was switching out dice at the new casino," I continued.

"Good. We'll let Calamity Jane take care of it."

"Who?"

"That FBI field agent, Betsy Mossbacher. She was just in here." Helen glanced at her watch. "She's due back here in six minutes. Talk with her, then get her out the door."

"Something happen?"

"You might say that," she replied.

CHAPTER

6

EXACTLY SIX MINUTES LATER Betsy Mossbacher was at my office door. She wore Levi's and boots and a black western shirt with pearl-colored snap buttons. Her face had the taut intensity of someone who has just been slapped.

"Would you like to sit down?" I asked.

"This won't take long—"

I cut her off. "If something is going on between you and my boss, I don't want to get caught in the middle of it," I said.

"She called the FBI 'Fart, Barf, and Itch.'"

"That's an old NOPD heirloom."

"I don't care what it is. I told her we expect a degree of professionalism from her and her department, unless I walked into the tongue-and-groove club by mistake."

"You said that to Helen Soileau?"

She widened her eyes and took a deep breath. "You don't seem to get what this investigation is about. This Klein woman is trouble—for us and herself. But she seems to have special status with you because of your relationship with her dead father."

"We already covered that, Agent Mossbacher."

"Your friend Clete Purcel helped her elude a surveillance in a casino where she was switching out the dice. But you didn't relay that information to us."

"I don't think that's my job."

I could see the heat intensify in her face. "Listen, we have a couple

68

of large issues on the burner—Whitey Bruxal and the robbery of a savings and loan. I don't know how much you know of Bruxal, but he's an extremely intelligent man and not to be underestimated. You know who Meyer Lansky was?"

"The financial brains of the Mob."

"Bruxal used to hang in a Miami coffee shop called Wolfie's. Lansky would challenge anyone in the place to stump him with a mathematical problem. The only person who ever did it was Whitey Bruxal. Lansky was so impressed, he used to take Bruxal fishing with him on a charter. God, I need a drink of water. Why do I have days like this?"

It was like listening to two people talking out of one face. The words "rolling chaos" went through my mind, and I hoped fervently she had no idea what I was thinking. "I'll get you a cup from the cooler," I said.

"Forget it. You busted Bruxal's son in that racial beef in front of McDonald's. This is the first handle we've had on him. We want to use it."

"You had me under surveillance?"

"No, I was passing by McDonald's and saw it go down."

"I see. And you want to go after Whitey Bruxal by prosecuting his boy?"

Her eyes shifted off mine, and I knew the idea was not hers, that it had come down from someone over her. "Monarch Little needs to file charges against Bruxal's kid," she said.

"Tell it to Monarch. See what kind of reaction you get."

"That's where you can help us."

"Not me," I replied.

She paused. "Bruxal got your friend in Miami killed. Maybe he gave the order for it."

It was quiet in the room. I could hear raindrops ticking on the window glass. "You know that for a fact?"

"The people above me seem to."

"Then you tell those sonsofbitches they'd better prosecute him."

She paused again and I saw a strange glint come in her eye. "Want me to quote you?"

"Absolutely."

For the first time that day, she smiled. "They said you were a bit unusual."

"Who's 'they'?"

"I'm just one of the field grunts. What do I know? Tell your boss I'm sorry I tracked horseshit on her carpet," she said.

"That's a metaphor?"

"No, I had it on my boots. Give Monarch Little a tumble. Whitey Bruxal is a bad guy. Back in Chugwater, he'd be split open, salted, and tacked on a fence post."

"I've got to visit this place someday," I replied.

Two days passed and I heard no more from Betsy Mossbacher. On Friday I went back to my file on Crustacean Man, the victim of a hit-and-run whose earthly remains had been left as food for crawfish at the bottom of a coulee. I still did not buy Koko Hebert's explanation of Crustacean Man's death. I had investigated many hit-and-run homicides over the years, both in Iberia Parish and New Orleans, and I had never seen one instance in which the victim had received two massive traumas on opposite sides of his body and no obvious ancillary damage that linked the two.

If they were bounced off the grille into the air and they caromed off the windshield, you knew it. If they were dragged under the vehicle, the damage was usually horrendous and pervasive. I looked at the photos taken of the remains at the crime scene. The body looked like one that could have fallen out of a boxcar at Bergen-Belsen. The skin was as tight as a lamp shade against the bone, the round mouth and eyes like the soundless scream in the famous painting by Edvard Munch.

Who are you, partner? What did somebody do to you?

Then a strange conjunction of thoughts came together in my head. Betsy Mossbacher had tried to pressure me into persuading Monarch Little to press charges against Whitey Bruxal's son. Although it was a cynical legal maneuver, it was a good one. I suspected that Slim Bruxal, in spite of his good manners, was a vicious fraternity punk who had taken immense pleasure in tearing up Monarch Little's face, and consequently deserved any fate the court dropped on his head. By the same token, Monarch had been cruising for a serious fall a long time. If his denouement happened to come from Whitey Bruxal, those were the breaks.

In the meantime, Monarch was of special interest to me for another reason. Before he had started dealing narcotics, he had worked for two or three shade-tree mechanics and backyard body-and-fender men. In fact, Monarch was something of an artist at his craft and could have made a career out of customizing and restoring vintage collectibles. But Monarch had discovered it was easier and more profitable to steal automobiles than it was to repair them.

I FOUND HIM under a shade tree, with five of his men, in the city's old red-light district. The wind rustled the leaves in the tree, and a rusted weight set rested inside the dirt apron that extended from the trunk out to the tree's drip line. Monarch and his friends were listening to music from the radio in Monarch's Firebird, and drinking Coca-Cola and crushed ice from paper cups that they threw on the ground or in the street when they finished.

It could have been a midafternoon scene in any inner-city neighborhood, but it wasn't. The old brothels are gone or boarded up with plywood and are nests for rats now, but at one time they serviced Confederate soldiers from Camp Pratt, out by Spanish Lake, in the early months of the Civil War; then the same women in them serviced any number of the twenty thousand Yankee soldiers who marched through New Iberia in pursuit of General Alfred Mouton and his boys in sun-faded butternut. Decades later, the five-dollar white cribs on Railroad Avenue and the three-dollar black ones on Hopkins continued to flourish, right up until the sexual revolution of the 1960s. But the industry did not disappear. It morphed into a much more pernicious and complex enterprise.

The whores are window dressing today. The issue is dope. The whores work for it, men like Monarch sell it, cops go on a pad for it, pimps use it as their control mechanism, attorneys make careers defending its purveyors, the government subsidizes the cottage industries that screen for it. Its influence is systemic and I doubt if there is one kid in our parish who doesn't know where he can buy it if he wants it. College kids get laid on Ex; black kids carrying nine-millimeters melt their heads with crack; and whores do crystal because it burns off their fast-food fat and keeps them competitive in the trade.

The short version? It's an ugly business and it dehumanizes everyone involved with it. Anyone who thinks otherwise should do an up-close observation of one day in the life of a crack baby.

"What's the haps, Monarch?" I said.

He was sitting in the passenger seat of his Firebird, his feet stretched out on the dirt beyond the curb. His mouth was pursed from the thickness of the stitches inside his gums. He drank out of his soda cup, tilting it gently to his mouth, letting the mixture of Coke and melting ice slide over his tongue. "No haps, Mr. Dee," he said.

"Just call me Dave."

"Call you Mr. Dee."

"I need to talk with you in a confidential fashion, know what I mean?" I said.

He seemed to think about my proposal, his gaze wandering to a small grocery on the corner, kids riding their bikes along a trash-strewn ditch, a tattered wisp of rope, which used to support a tire swing, swaying from an oak limb overhead. He nodded at one of his friends, and without saying a word all five of them walked to the grocery store and went inside. Monarch got up from the car seat and positioned himself in front of the weight set under the tree. "This about them UL boys?" he said.

"You going to file on the Bruxal kid?" I said.

"Who?" he replied.

He bent over, hooking his palms under the weight bar, his stomach distended like an overflowing tub of bread dough. Then he lifted what I counted to be at least a hundred and forty pounds of steel plate. He curled the bar into his chest ten times, his back straight, his knees locked, his upper arms tightening into croquet balls. He set the bar down on the ground and stepped back from it, breathing slowly through his nose.

"Don't try to square your problem with the Bruxal kid on your own. His old man is a gangster, the real article, a Brooklyn wiseguy who uses a hired psychopath to take care of his personal problems."

"What you saying is he was a hump for them dagos in Miami."

"That's one way to put it."

He bent over to pick up the weights again. I put my hand on his shoulder. It felt like concrete under his shirt. "Forget the Mr. Universe routine for a minute. You want to take this kid down, I'll help you. In the meantime, you watch your back."

"Since when y'all started going out of your way to jam up rich white boys?"

"Slim Bruxal is a special case."

"Yeah, he special, all right. That's why the FBI been trying to plug my dick into a wall socket. They after his old man, ain't they?"

"Maybe. What've they got on you?"

"Some agents come by my house. They say they might be looking at me for t'ree-strikes-and-you-out."

"How many adult convictions do you have?"

"Two. But right now I'm a li'l warm on a deal wasn't my fault. My cousin hid his works at my house so his P.O. wouldn't catch him wit' them. I didn't know they was there. A DEA narc busted my cousin and my cousin give me up. His syringe and spoon and a half ounce of tar was under my lavatory. So they say I either flip or I go down for the whole ride. That's life wit'out no parole, Mr. Dee."

He hefted up the weight bar and curled it toward his sternum, releasing it slowly so that the tension built unmercifully in his forearms, his face impassive to the pain burning in his tendons.

He put on a good show, but he was caught and he knew it. The Feds would probably squeeze him until blood was coming out of his fingernails. I wondered how stand-up Monarch really was. Enough to do mainline time? If the FBI flipped him, they wouldn't use him just on the Bruxal case, either. He would become a permanent rat, at the beck and call of the Bureau whenever they wanted him.

Monarch had made his own choices and I couldn't feel sorry for him. He wasn't an addict; he was a dealer. He robbed his customers of their souls and profited off the misery of his own people. But he was not without certain qualities, and he didn't ask for the kind of world he had been born into.

He did ten curls and dropped the weights in the dirt. I tapped his upper arm with my fist. "You take steroids?" I asked.

"You ever see steroid freaks take a shower at the health club?"

"Come to think of it, no," I replied.

"That's 'cause they don't take showers at the health club. That's 'cause their package usually looks like smoked oysters."

"Nine months to a year ago, somebody did a hit-and-run on a guy out in the parish. I wondered if you heard of anyone needing body or fender work about that time, somebody who didn't want to go to a regular shop?"

"I could ax around. That gonna buy me some juice wit' the t'ree-strikes-and-you-out sit'ation?"

"Probably not."

"Then don't hold your breat'."

I looked at him for a long time. "You're an intelligent man. You could be anything you want to be," I said.

"So?"

"Why don't you wise up and stop taking it on your knees from white people?" I said.

"Say that again?"

"The people you work for live in mansions in Miami and the Islands. While you pimp and deal product on street corners for chump change, they're depositing millions in offshore accounts. You take the weight and stack the time for white guys who wouldn't wipe their ass with you."

"Ain't nobody talks to me like that. *Nobody*, Mr. Dee."

"Somebody better, because you're about to become a professional snitch or a bar of shower soap in Marion Pen. We're talking about jailing with the Aryan Brotherhood, Monarch. In Marion, they eat gangbangers for bedtime snacks."

Even in the deep shade of the oak tree, I thought I saw his pulse beating in his throat.

• • •

THAT NIGHT I DREAMED of horses galloping in a large dusty pen, without sound, their muscles rippling like oily rope. In the distance were meadows and softly rounded green hills and a fast-running stream that was bordered by cottonwood trees. In the herd were buckskins, palominos, piebalds, Appaloosas, Arabian creams, duns, bays, sorrels, and strawberry roans, their mouths strung with saliva, their collective breath like the pounding of Indian war drums. The sky was forked with lightning, the air pungent with the promise of rain. But there was no water inside the pen, only heat and clouds of dust and powdered manure. Then a red mare lifted out of the herd on extended wings, her rear hooves kicking open the pen gate as she rose into the sky. Suddenly, in the dream, I heard the sound of the other horses thundering toward the stream and the shade of the cottonwoods.

In the morning I could not get the dream out of my head. It was Saturday, and Molly, Clete, and I had planned to go fishing at Henderson Swamp that afternoon. But I told Molly I had to run an errand first, and I went to the office and pulled out my file on Yvonne Darbonne. One of the crime scene photos had been taken at an angle to her body, so even though she lay on her side in the position of a question mark, the lens was pointed directly at her face and chest.

A red winged horse was emblazoned on the front of her T-shirt, and through a magnifying glass I could make out the name of a racetrack inside the folds of the fabric under her breasts. It was the name of the new track and casino north of Lafayette where Trish Klein had been switching out dice at the craps table.

I looked at my watch. It wasn't quite noon. Clete was supposed to meet Molly and me at the house at two. There was still time for a visit to the home of Bello Lujan and his son, Tony.

FIFTEEN MINUTES LATER I was standing on the front porch of the Lujan house, just outside Loreauville, the sun winking at me through a mimosa tree, the wind puffing a fringed pale green canopy by the bayou's edge, where a buffet table was covered with half-eaten food and empty Cold Duck bottles. Tony answered the door—barefoot, shirtless, a towel hung around his neck, his hair still wet from a shower. Behind him, I saw a college-age girl thumbing through a magazine on a couch. She looked at me uncertainly, then picked up her drink glass and went into the kitchen. Tony still had not spoken.

"You're not going to ask me in?" I said.

"Yes, sir, sure," he said.

"Y'all have a party last night?" I said, stepping inside. Mounted on the staircase wall was a mechanical apparatus that would allow a seated infirm person to ride up and down the stairs.

"My parents did. They hosted my fraternity and our little sisters," he replied.

"Your little sisters?"

"It's a sorority we call our little sisters."

"Where are your parents?"

"My father went to New Orleans for the rest of the weekend. My mother is upstairs. You want to talk to her?"

"No, my question is to you, Tony. Say, who's your friend back there in the kitchen?"

"A girl I go to UL with."

"Was she a friend of Yvonne Darbonne, too?"

A flush of color spread across his cheeks. But I had come to believe that Tony Lujan was less shy and awkward than he was fearful and ridden with guilt.

"I'm not sure what you're saying," he said.

I didn't pursue it. "Actually, I came out here because of a photo taken of Yvonne before she was put into a body bag. She was wearing a T-shirt with a winged horse on it. Know the one I mean?"

"I gave it to her," he replied. "It's a promo shirt from the new casino and track. My dad's an investor in it. He's partners with Mr. Bruxal. That's how I got to know Slim. My dad was going to give Yvonne a job in the restaurant."

"That's funny. Your father told me he didn't know her."

His face drained. "I thought maybe you were here about those black guys. My dad thinks they might try to file a civil suit and milk us for whatever they can get. That's why I thought you wanted to talk to my parents."

Tony Lujan's attitude toward law enforcement was one that no amount of experience has ever allowed me to deal with in an adequate way. Every police officer who reads this knows what I'm talking about, too. Certain groups of people in our society genuinely believe police agencies have only one purpose for existing, and that is to protect and serve the interests of a chosen few. Guess which income bracket they belong to.

I had gotten what I wanted and probably should have left at that point. But I didn't. "See, we don't get involved in civil suits, Tony. In fact, it's the prosecutor's office that determines which criminal charges we pursue in a given case. Personally, I don't think you need to worry about a guy like Monarch Little fooling around with civil suits. The truth is, Monarch Little is one badass motherfucker who swallows his blood in a fight and comes at you right between the lights. He's not above doing serious collateral damage, either."

I heard a glass break in the kitchen.

I WAS HOOKING UP my boat trailer to my truck when Clete's Caddy bounced into the driveway, his spinning rod propped up in the backseat, a Rapala flopping on the tip. "Ready to rock?" he said.

"Almost," I said.

He got out and watched me load our rods, tackle boxes, and the cooler into the boat. He was wearing shined loafers, cream-colored golf slacks, and a Hawaiian shirt I hadn't seen before.

"Dressed kind of sharp, aren't you?" I said.

"Not really," he replied, ripping the tab on a beer, looking off casually at the thick green arch of oak limbs over East Main. "Where's Molly?"

"Right there," I said, nodding toward the porte cochere, where Molly was coming out the side door with an armload of food. "What are you up to, Cletus?"

"Maybe I like to wear some decent threads once in a while. Will you give it a rest?"

Because my pickup truck was not big enough for the three of us, he followed us in the Caddy to Henderson Swamp. In the rearview mirror, I could see he was sneaking sips from a beer can on the floorboards. I thought about stopping and possibly preventing legal trouble on the road, but reason and caution and even common sense held little sway in the life of Clete Purcel. I was even more convinced of that fact when I saw him upend the can, crush it in his fist, and drop it over his shoulder into the backseat, where any cop who stopped him would be able to see it.

"What are you looking at?" Molly said.

"Clete."

"What about him?"

"That's like asking about the flight plan of an asteroid."

She looked at me quizzically, but I didn't try to explain further.

I backed the trailer down the concrete ramp at Henderson and we slid the boat into the water. It was a perfect afternoon for fishing. The day was hot, the wind down, the water dead-still in the coves. Out on the vast expanse of bays and channels and islands of willow and gum trees that comprised the swamp, I could see other fishermen anchored hard by the pilings of the interstate highway and the desiccated wood platforms of oil rigs that had long ago been torn down and hauled away. The air contained the bright, clean smell of rain in the south, which meant the barometer was dropping and the bass and bream would begin feeding as soon as one raindrop dented the surface of the water.

Molly and I sat in the boat's stern and Clete sat up on the bass seat by the bow, flicking his Rapala in the lee of the willows that grew along the entrance to a wide bay. He had spread a paper towel over the seat cushion and I noticed that whenever he took a hit off a can of Budweiser or ate one of the po'boy sandwiches Molly had made, he leaned forward to avoid staining his clothes. At six o'clock he looked at his watch, removed his aviator shades and his porkpie hat, and combed his hair. His face was red from beer and sunburn, the area around his eyes still pale. He grinned happily. "Look at that sky," he said.

Then a bass that must have weighed eight pounds rolled the surface by a nest of lily pads and took Clete's Rapala with such force it blew water up into the willows. "Jesus Christ," Clete said, dropping his beer can in his lap.

I got the net from under the seat and Molly swung the electric trolling motor about to keep Clete's line at eleven o'clock from the bow so the bass would not tangle it with ours. Clete cranked the handle on his reel and jerked the tip of his rod up at the same time, bowing his rod into a severe arch.

"Ease up," I said. "I'll get the net under him."

The bass broke the surface in a flash of gold and green and a roll of its white belly, then it stripped the monofilament off Clete's drag and dove for the bottom, sawing the line against the boat.

"Pull your line around the bow and let him run," I said.

Too late. The line snapped and the tip of Clete's rod sprang back toward his face. "Wow," he said, wiping at the beer on his slacks with a paper towel.

"Tie on a Mepps. We'll try the next island up the channel," I said.

"No, that's it for me," he replied.

"You want to quit?" I said, incredulously.

"It's been a great day. I don't always have to catch fish."

"Right," I said.

Molly looked at me. "I could go for a red snapper dinner up at the restaurant," she said.

We had at least an hour of good fishing left and I wanted to stay out, but Molly had obviously chosen to act charitably toward Clete's mercurial behavior and I didn't have it in me to go against her wishes. "You bet," I said.

Molly cranked the engine, and we headed across a long bay toward the landing. The surface of the water was the color of tarnished bronze against the sunset, and the new bloom on the cypress trees lifted like green feathers in the wind. Cars with their lights on streamed across the elevated causeway behind us, and ahead I could see the boat ramp and the levee and a lighted restaurant on pilings, with a walkway that extended out over the water.

We winched the boat back up the trailer, then I saw Clete's face soften as he glanced up at the railing on the restaurant walkway. "I better head on out. Thanks for the afternoon," he said.

A solitary woman stood on the walkway, her face turned into the sunset, her hair moving in the wind.

"Who's your lady friend?" I asked, afraid of the answer I would get.

"I love you, Streak, but at some point in your life, can you give me some space?" he said.

Then I saw the woman's profile against the sky.

"Just keep it in your pants," I said.

He lifted his tackle box out of the boat and said good-bye to Molly but not to me. He walked toward the restaurant, his big hand gripped tightly on the disconnected sections of his rod, the back of his neck thick and glowing with heat.

"I can't believe you said that," Molly said.

"He's used to it," I replied.

A few minutes later, as Molly and I walked up to the restaurant for a meal, Clete and the woman drove past us on the rocks to the levee, the moon rising above his pink convertible. The woman's face was young and radiant and lovely in the glow from the dashboard. She lifted a highball glass to her mouth, never looking in my direction. May the angels fly with you, Cletus, I said to myself.

"Who was that?" Molly said.

"A grifter by the name of Trish Klein. The kind of gal who knows how to break Clete's heart."

CHAPTER
7

I HAD THOUGHT MONARCH might be stand-up, might let the FBI do its worse, even if that meant he had to go down on what recidivists used to call "the bitch," short for "habitual offender," which was the old-time term for the Clinton-era equivalent known as the three-strikes-and-you're-out law.

But on Monday morning Monarch came to the prosecutor's office with his attorney and filed felony assault charges against Slim Bruxal. It was obvious the previous night had not been an easy one for him. He was raccoon-eyed, morose, and stank of beer sweat and weed. When he tripped on a carpet and knocked his head against a door, two teenage girls snickered.

I suspected Monarch's life was about to unravel. How badly was up for debate. But there are no secrets in our small city on the Teche. In a short time the word would be on the street that Monarch Little had become a hump for the Feds to avoid taking his own bounce. It wouldn't be improbable for his peers to conclude that he was not to be trusted and that he might start dimeing the same gangbangers who now hovered around him like candle moths.

In the meantime, he had empowered the Iberia Parish district attorney to go forward with assault charges against Slim Bruxal, by extension giving the FBI enormous leverage they could use against Slim's father, Whitey Bruxal, in what I guessed was a RICO investigation.

I saw Monarch in the parking lot, on the way to his Firebird.

"You hep set this up, Mr. Dee?" he asked.

"I never jammed you, Monarch. Show a little respect," I replied.

"Before I come down to the courthouse, I tried to join the army."

"Really?" I said, my face deliberately empty.

"Guy said I might have a weight problem."

It was hot and bright in the parking lot, and the crypts in St. Peter's Cemetery looked white and hard-edged in the light, the weeds wilted and stained yellow by herbicide. Several deputies in uniform walked past us, talking among themselves, their cigarette smoke hanging in the dead air. "I need to talk to you," I said to Monarch.

"I ain't feeling so good right now. I'm going home and sleep."

"Suit yourself," I said.

"Hey, you the man called me a pimp. I sell dope, but I ain't no pimp. Maybe you the one need a little humbleness."

THE PROSECUTOR'S OFFICE lost no time serving the arrest warrant on Slim Bruxal. By lunchtime the same day, two Lafayette city police officers and an Iberia Parish detective were at Slim's fraternity house, a few blocks from the university campus. Evidently he was not in a cooperative mood. The arrest report stated that after he was hooked up, he fought with officers and fell down a flight of stairs. I recognized the name of one of the arresting officers. His name had a way of appearing in news stories involving the apprehension of suspects who always seemed to resist arrest. The newspaper prose describing this type of event is usually written in the passive voice, which means the journalist copied it from the arrest report and used no other source. The telltale line to look for in this kind of print story is "The suspect was subdued." Slim Bruxal got subdued and probably had it coming. I also suspected that if Slim stayed in custody, his cookie bag would get stepped on extra hard again.

But I wasn't a player in Slim Bruxal's fate and I tried to concentrate on the ebb and flow of petty concerns that constituted most of my ordinary business day. These included a terrorist bomb scare involving a suitcase someone abandoned in front of Victor's Cafeteria; a sexual battery charge filed by a man who claimed his three-hundred-pound wife was forcing him to have sex with her four times a week; the disappearance from a picnic bench of a roasted pig, which turned out to have been eaten by a nine-foot alligator we found floating contentedly in the family swimming pool; the flight of a homemade airplane down the bayou, three feet off the water, that ended with the crash landing of the plane on a cockfighting farm and the shredding by propeller of at least a dozen roosters; the theft of bones from crypts in St. Peter's Cemetery by a bunch of kids with rings in their lips and nostrils and pentagrams tattooed on their shaved heads. How the bones could add to what the kids had already done to their faces and heads remained a mystery.

A house creep cut a hole through an attic roof to avoid setting off the alarm system and electrocuted himself when he tapped into a breaker box. A biker blitzed on weed and downers roared through a church picnic in City Park, punched a hole in a hedge, and almost decapitated himself on a wash line. But my favorite caper of the week was a 911 call we received from a meth addict who was outraged that his dealer had shown up at the door without the drugs the caller had paid for, committing fraud, according to the caller, and adding insult to injury by robbing him at gunpoint of seventy-eight dollars and his stash.

It was 3:16 p.m. when I looked at my watch. I couldn't concentrate any longer on the Pool, my term for that army of merry pranksters and miscreants who wend their way endlessly through the turnstiles of the system. I dropped all the paperwork on my desk into a drawer and headed for Monarch Little's house, where he lived in a rural black slum paradoxically located on a pastoral stretch of oak-shaded land along Bayou Teche, not far from the sugar mill community where Yvonne Darbonne had died.

I knocked on the screen door. Monarch's house was made of clapboard, with a peaked tin roof, and was set amid a cluster of water oaks and pecan trees and slash pines down by the water's edge. An old Coca-Cola machine beaded with moisture throbbed under an improvised porte cochere where his Firebird was parked. He was wearing boxer shorts and a strap undershirt when he opened the door. "What you want now?" he asked.

"Can I come in?"

"Don't matter to me."

If Monarch was getting rich in the dope trade, the interior of his house didn't show it. The furniture was worn, the wallpaper spotted with rainwater, the linoleum in the kitchen split and wedged upward in a dirty fissure. A floor fan vibrated in front of a stuffed couch where he had probably been napping when I knocked.

"I think Slim Bruxal's old man was mixed up in the murder of a friend of mine," I said. "That means I want to see Whitey Bruxal brought up on homicide charges. That doesn't mean I want to see you turned into fish chum."

"I ain't buying this, Mr. Dee."

"You calling me a liar?"

"No, you just got your own reasons for doing what you doing. It don't have nothing to do wit' me."

"I saw my friend shot point-blank in the face with a twelve-gauge. I tried to convince both the Feds and Miami-Dade P.D. that Bruxal or his friends were behind it. But I was a drunk back then and didn't have much credibility. Now I have a chance to nail him. But I'm not going to do it by feeding a guy to the sharks. It's not a complicated idea."

"That's all fine, but right now I ain't got a lot of selections, starting wit' how I make a living."

I handed him my business card with a name and telephone number I had already penciled on the back. "This is the name of the United States Attorney in Baton Rouge. He's a friend of mine. You tell him you're cooperating with the FBI, but you need some protection. You have that right. Because you have a sheet doesn't mean you don't have constitutional guarantees."

"Yeah, we all be having constitutional guarantees, but that ain't my way."

"You know what 'bruising the freight' means?"

"Yeah."

"Well, that's what happened to Slim Bruxal when he got busted today. He also got dumped in a cell with a couple of black guys who haven't had a fresh bar of white soap in a while. Who do you think the Bruxal family is going to blame for all this?"

He sat down on the couch and looked at his feet. "They took my nine," he said.

"Who?"

"Them FBI agents. They say ain't nobody gonna bot'er me."

I sat down on a wood chair across from him. I removed my business card from between his fingers and wrote two more telephone numbers on it, then handed it back to him. "If I'm not at the department, you can call me at my house or on my cell," I said.

Outside, the willows along the bayou were bending in the breeze, an old man and a child were cane-fishing in the shade, a pretty countrywoman in a sunbonnet was hoeing out a vegetable garden, a strand of black hair curled on her cheek. I had a feeling these ordinary moments in the ordinary day of ordinary people were possessions that Monarch would soon pay a great deal to own.

"Them FBI agents want Bruxal to put up a kite on me, don't they? Miss Helen sent you out here to warn me?"

I didn't want to tell him that Helen had nothing to do with my visit. "You loaded their gun, podna. They're just doing their job. They win, you lose. The question is how badly do you lose. Just don't take things into your own hands. That's why I gave you those phone numbers."

I got up to go.

"You still interested in somebody who might have done a hit-and-run last year sometime?" he asked.

"What about it?"

"Friend of mine up the bayou got a li'l shop in his backyard. Last summer a man brung a big Buick in there wit' the headlight knocked in and the right fender scratched up. Said he hit a deer. Said he heard my friend done real fine work and he didn't feel like paying the Buick dealer a lot of money when my friend could do the job just as good."

"Who was the guy?"

Monarch looked up at me and let his eyes hold on mine. "You gonna t'ink I set it up."

"Who was it, Monarch?"

"Better go out to my friend's place and ax him yourself."

• • •

THE FRIEND'S AUTO REPAIR BUSINESS was conducted in a pole shed behind an ancient, rust-leaking trailer that sagged on cinder blocks, just outside St. Martinville. The sun was down in the sky now, red and dust-veiled above a line of live oaks on the opposite side of Bayou Teche. The air was breathless, the clouds crackling with electricity in the south. Monarch's friend was one of the most unusual-looking human beings I had ever seen. He was an albino, with negroid features and gold hair and pink-tinted eyes, his entire body encased in long-sleeved coveralls zipped to the throat. He had been working next to a gas-fired forge. I couldn't imagine what the temperature was like inside his clothes, but he grinned constantly just the same, as though a grin were the only expression he knew. He seemed delighted at my visit. I had the feeling he was one of those rare individuals who genuinely loves life and has no issue with the world or grievance against his fellow man, regardless of what they may have done or not done to him.

"Your name is Prospect Desmoreau?" I said.

"That's me," he said. But like every other mismatched element in his makeup, his accent didn't fit. It was genuine peckerwood, a yeoman dialect that runs through the pine forests and plains from West Virginia into West Texas, one that probably goes back to the early days of the Republic. "Hep you with something?"

"Monarch Little said a man brought you a Buick last summer that had been damaged from a collision with a deer."

"He sure did. I fixed it good as new, too."

"Did this man act hinky to you?"

"No, suh."

"What was this fellow's name?"

Prospect Desmoreau looked at the wind ruffling the bayou, an amber blaze of late sunlight on its surface. But no matter where his eye traveled, he never stopped grinning. "Mr. Bello brought it in," he said.

"Bellerophon Lujan?"

"Yes, suh. He give me a twenty-dollar tip."

"Where was the damage?"

"Passenger-side fender, passenger-side headlight."

"Did you see any material on the car body that indicated Mr. Bello hit a deer? Hair, a piece of antler embedded in the headlight?"

"Looked to me like somebody had already hosed it down and wiped it off. People do that sometimes when they plow into livestock and such. You looking for somebody done a hit-and-run on a pedestrian?"

"That pretty well sums it up, Prospect."

"There was blood inside the headlight glass. I didn't see no deer hair, though. Least none I remember. Don't mean wasn't none there."

"There's no way you saved the headlight glass, huh?" I said, putting my notebook back in my shirt pocket.

"You want to look at it?"

"Sir?"

"I got a pileful of trash and junk on the other side of the barn. 'Bout every two years I haul it to the dump. I know right where that glass is at, 'cause I seen it just the other day when I was hunting around in the pile for a radio speaker I pulled out of a 'fifty-five Chevy."

"Broken glass with blood on it?"

"Yes, suh. It's been under an old piece of tarp. I seen it."

I stared at him stupidly. "Prospect, I think you're a remarkable man," I said.

"Women tell me that all the time."

He dragged a large tangle of canvas off the pile, spilling a shower of wet pine needles and pooled water onto the ground. He lifted a jagged half-moon piece of broken glass from a circle of chrome molding. "Right there on the edge, you can still see the blood."

I took a Ziploc bag from my back pocket and spread it open. "Just drop it right in there, partner. I need that molding, too. Is there anything else in here from Mr. Bello's Buick?"

"No, suh, I don't think so."

"On another subject, how well do you know Monarch Little?"

"I taught him body-and-fender work. Taught him when he was knee-high to a tree frog."

"Too bad he doesn't make use of it."

"Folks don't always get to choose what they do," he replied.

"You seem like a smarter man than that," I said.

"His mama is at M.D. Anderson in Houston. She's had every kind of cancer there is. Monarch ain't tole you that?" he said, his pink-tinted eyes squinting in the sunlight.

I DROVE DIRECTLY to the Acadiana Crime Lab and logged in the evidence with Mack Bertrand. It was late and I could tell Mack was anxious to get home to supper and his wife and family. "What are you looking for on this?" he asked.

"A DNA match or an exclusion on Crustacean Man."

"How soon you need it?"

"The owner of the vehicle is probably Bello Lujan. I doubt he's a big flight risk."

Mack raised his eyebrows. "Use the process as a buffer between you and him, Dave. No matter what he does, don't react, don't let it get personal."

"What's the big deal about Bello?"

"I think he's a driven man. He came to our church for a while, but we had to encourage him to attend one that's probably more suited to his needs."

"Can you translate the hieroglyphics for me?"

"He's got sex on the brain, he's full of guilt, he shouts in the middle of the service. He may be dangerous, at least to himself. We sent him to some Holy Rollers who speak in tongues. But I'm not sure even they can deal with him. Does that give you a better perspective?"

I couldn't help but laugh.

"What a sense of humor. I'll have the DNA report for you in three days," he said.

THAT EVENING I tried to disconnect my thoughts from Bello Lujan, in the same way that as a child I tried not to believe that a school-yard bully had become an inextricable part of my life. But I also remembered how, for some unexplainable reason, my path and the bully's crossed regularly, as though by design, and regardless of what I did to avoid encountering him, my actions always led me back to a choice between public humiliation or the end of a fist.

Saturday morning I had visited Bello's home and questioned his son, Tony, about the T-shirt emblazoned with the image of Pegasus that Yvonne Darbonne had been wearing the day she died. Inadvertently, Tony Lujan had told me his father was an investor in the track and casino advertised on the shirt and that he had planned to give her a job in the casino restaurant. This was after Bello had denied knowing anyone by the name of Yvonne Darbonne.

I had managed to expose the school bully as a liar. I should have known he would come calling as soon as he returned from his weekend visit to New Orleans.

"There's a man standing in the front yard," Molly said.

I looked out the window. Bello's Buick was parked in the driveway, his son in the passenger seat, but Bello was staring at the street, as though he couldn't make up his mind what he should do next. I walked out on the gallery. A sun-shower had just stopped, and water was ticking out of the trees.

I remembered Mack Bertrand's cautionary words about using procedure as a buffer between me and Bello Lujan. "I suspect this is a business call. If that's the case, I'd rather talk about it at the office, Bello," I said.

"You questioned my boy while I was in New Orleans. About the T-shirt that dead girl was wearing," he said.

The sunlight was tea-colored through the oak branches overhead, the air cool from the rain, the sky throbbing with the sound of tree frogs. It was too fine an evening for an angry encounter with a primitive, tormented, and violent man. I stepped off the gallery into the yard so I would not be perceived as speaking down to him. But I did not offer him my hand. "Come see me tomorrow, partner."

"My boy told you I was going to give the dead girl a job waitressing at the track clubhouse. I told you I didn't remember her name. That's 'cause I give jobs to lots of kids, particularly ones wanting to go to college. You making me out a hypocrite in front of my family?"

"That's a term of your own choosing."

"You cracking wise now?"

"What I'm doing is telling you to get out of here."

"You told my son this colored kid, what's his name, Monarch Little, is a badass motherfucker who might put out his lights?"

"I don't think I phrased it exactly that way."

"Come over here, Tony!" Bello said.

His son stepped out of the car. His face was bloodless in the shade, his jaws slowly chewing a piece of gum.

"What did Mr. Robicheaux here say to you?" Bello asked.

"It's like you say, Daddy."

"He said that colored boy was gonna cool you out?"

"Not in those words," Tony said.

"He said this kid was a badass motherfucker and was gonna hurt you?"

"Yes, sir."

"My son is lying, here?" Bello said to me.

You don't argue with drunks and you don't engage with stupid or irrational people. But when they insist that you are the source of all the unhappiness in their lives and denigrate you without letup, when they stand so close to you that you can smell their enmity in their sweat, at some point you have to take it to them, if for no other reason than self-respect. At least that's what I told myself.

"You've got a lot more to worry about than just me," I said.

"No, my life is fine. It's *you* that's the problem. I didn't finish high school or go to college. But I did pretty good. Maybe that don't always sit too well with some people. Think that might be the trouble here, Dave?"

I rested one hand on the hood of the Buick. I rubbed the finish and the passenger-side headlight molding and brushed away a leaf that was stuck to the glass. "Fine car you have here. Ever have any work done on it? Looks like somebody might have had a sander on your fender."

He tried to keep his face empty, but I saw my words take hold in his eyes. Tony gazed down the driveway at the bayou as though he had never seen it before.

"I always treated you good," Bello said. "We both go back to the old days, when people talked French and kids like us didn't have ten cents to go to a picture show. How come you can't show respect for our mutual experience? How come you treat me like some kind of bum?"

"Because you lied to me."

The skin on his face flexed, just as though I had spit on it. I started back toward the gallery, wondering if he was not about to attack me. Just as I reached the steps, I felt his fingers touch me through my shirt.

"That's my only son, there," he said. "He's gonna be a doctor. He never done anything to deliberately hurt anybody, particularly not to some poor girl who shot herself. Why you trying to mess him up? You got colored kids shooting each other in the streets. Why you got to go after my boy?"

But the hand had already been dealt, for both Bello and me and his son as well. None of us, at that moment, could have guessed at the outcome. I heard a flapping of wings above our heads, like a giant leathery bird rising from the oak tree's crown into the sky.

CHAPTER
8

THURSDAY MORNING, Mack Bertrand called from the crime lab. "The blood on the Buick headlight fragment came from Crustacean Man," he said.

"No gray area, no contamination, no dilution of the specimen, none of that stuff?"

"This one is dead-bang. It even gets better. You actually brought me two specimens."

"Say again?"

"A microscopic piece of bone was on the inside of the molding. My guess is it came from the collision of the fender against Crustacean Man's hip."

"You don't think it came from the blow to his head?"

"Maybe. But the body-and-fender guy told you the glass and molding came from the passenger side of the vehicle, right?"

"Correct."

"Crustacean Man's left hip was crushed. My guess is he either walked in front of the vehicle or he was walking on the side of the road, in the same direction as the Buick, when he was hit."

"Here's the problem with that scenario, Mack. The cause of death was massive trauma to the right-hand side of the cranium. Death was probably instantaneous. He ended up in the coulee, which means he wasn't slammed to the asphalt. He wasn't knocked into a post or telephone pole, either."

"You're saying the fatal injury wasn't caused by the Buick? Maybe a second vehicle killed him?" Mack said.

"There's another possibility."

"What?"

"The second blow didn't come from a vehicle," I said.

"Maybe he got hit by a chunk of meteorite. Ease up on the batter, Dave," he said.

A few minutes later I went into Helen's office and told her of Mack Bertrand's findings. She was hunched over her desk, her short sleeves folded in tight cuffs on her arms. She thought for a moment before she spoke. "Okay, so we've got a dirty vehicle, but we can't put Bello Lujan behind the wheel," she said.

"We can make a case for destroying evidence and aiding and abetting."

"Provided we can prove he had knowledge a crime was actually committed. What if his kid was the driver? What if one of the kid's fraternity brothers borrowed the car? How about the wife?"

"She's an invalid. She doesn't drive. These wouldn't be issues if the victim wasn't a wino," I said.

"If there were no gravity, monkey shit wouldn't fall out of trees, either."

"I don't think this is a simple hit-and-run, Helen. Something else is involved."

"Like what?" she asked.

"I don't know."

"Dave, there are times I want to kill you, I mean actually pound your head with my fists."

I gazed out the window, choosing reticence as the better part of valor.

"Go back to that business about it not being a simple hit-and-run," she said.

"Mack believes the Buick either struck Crustacean Man in the hip while he was walking down the right-hand side of the road, or Crustacean Man walked out in front of the car. But neither Mack nor Koko can explain the origin of the fatal injury, which was to the head."

"I think we're starting to drown in more information than we need here. Look, somebody hit this guy with the Buick. He was left to die on the side of the road. The DNA evidence on that is absolute. Somebody is going down for what we can prove happened. Whoever it is, Bello or somebody else, will probably not receive the punishment he deserves. But we're going to do our jobs as best we can and leave the rest of it to God. Am I putting this in words you can understand?"

"Bello's son is the key."

"Why?"

"Because his face is full of secrets."

"Be honest with me. Are you trying to tie all this to the suicide of Yvonne Darbonne?"

"I have the feeling it's connected. But I can't tell you how."

She rubbed the back of her neck, her starched shirt tightening across her chest. Then she laughed to herself.

"Want to let me in on it?" I asked.

"No, I want to keep you as a friend. Get a warrant on Bello and bring his kid in as a potential material witness."

Time to deep-six the role as receptacle for Helen's invective at my expense, I thought. "Tony Lujan's name is now involved in three separate investigations—the assault on Monarch Little, the shooting death of Yvonne Darbonne, and a vehicular homicide. You think I'm obsessive or being unfair to him? How often does the average premed student get in this much trouble?"

Helen rolled her eyes and brushed a strand of hair off her forehead, but this time she had nothing to say.

After lunch, she and I met with our district attorney, Lonnie Marceaux. When I first met Lonnie a few years ago, I had thought he was one of those people whose attention span is limited either by an inability to absorb detailed information or a lack of interest in subject matter that isn't directly related to their well-being. I was wrong. At least partially. Lonnie was usually three or four jumps ahead in the conversation. He had been Phi Beta Kappa at Tulane and had published in the *Stanford Law Review*. But the real content of his thoughts on any particular issue remained a matter of conjecture.

Lonnie was blade-faced, six and one half feet tall, and had a body like whipcord from the marathons he ran in New Orleans, Dallas, and Boston. His scalp glistened through his crew cut; his energies were augmented rather than diminished by the two hours a day he spent on a StairMaster. When he turned down a position as United States Attorney in Baton Rouge, his peers were amazed at his sudden diffidence. But it didn't take us long to see the true nature of Lonnie's ambitious design. In spite of his own upscale background, he charmed blue-collar juries. The press always referred to Lonnie as "charismatic" and "clean-cut." No high-profile case in Iberia Parish ever went to an ADA, and God help the man or woman Lonnie got in his bomb sights. He was on his way up in the sweet sewer of Louisiana politics and I believe long ago had decided it was better to be first in Gaul rather than second in Rome.

Lonnie kept nodding his head as Helen and I explained the chain of evidence on Bello Lujan's involvement with Crustacean Man's death. Then he crossed his legs and began playing with a rubber band, stretching and twisting it into rhomboids and triangles on his fingers, while he spoke with his gaze focused above our heads. "So the kid is the weak sister, we squeeze him, scare the piss out of him, and force him to come clean on who clobbered the homeless guy with the Buick?"

But before we could answer, he resumed talking. "Okay, let's do that. But a couple of things we have to remember. Monarch Little gave you the lead on the bloody headlight. Bello's defense attorney is going to point out to a jury that Monarch has a vested interest in screwing the Lujan family."

"How could Monarch plant DNA on the Lujans' Buick?" I said.

"'Nobody ever lost money underestimating the intelligence of the American public.' Know who said that?"

"No, but please tell us," Helen said.

Lonnie gave her a look. "That great American sociologist P. T. Barnum."

"You said there were a couple of items we need to remember," I said.

"When it comes to Bello Lujan, we're not the first in line. The FBI already has this guy under investigation. You've met Special Agent Betsy Mossbacher?" Lonnie said.

"How could I forget? How many federal agents track horseshit on your carpet?" Helen said.

Lonnie gave her another look, then began playing with his rubber band again. I had the feeling Helen was one of the few people who could stick thumbtacks deep into Lonnie's scalp. "They're after Bello and Whitey Bruxal," he said. "However, my guess is they have some conflicts among themselves about the real goal of their investigation. The Mossbacher woman seems more intent on bringing down this televangelist Colin Alridge. You ever meet him?"

I had. Colin Alridge was a homegrown product who had returned to New Orleans a national celebrity. He was not simply telegenic, either. In person, he seemed to exude goodness and rectitude. Outside of Mickey Rooney in his role as Andy Hardy, I could not think of a public figure who was more representative of Norman Rockwell's America. But I didn't respond to Lonnie's question, in part because I wanted to know Lonnie's attitude toward Alridge. More candidly, I didn't trust Lonnie. His prosecutorial eye seemed to be selective, and he chose his enemies with discretion.

"Alridge has probably been fronting points for the Indian casinos in the central portion of the state at the expense of those on the Texas state line," he said. "A lot of people around here have no objection to a guy like Alridge helping the local economy. A lot of these same people get their paychecks from Bello Lujan and by extension Whitey Bruxal. Which means a lot of people around here might not like the idea of Crustacean Man messing up the cash flow. You with me?"

"You want to back off on the warrant for right now?" Helen said.

"Helen, why not listen a little more attentively to what's being said? My point is the Feds are already investigating crimes committed in our backyard. So how does that make us look? Like bumbling hicks. So the question presents itself: How do we take the initiative away from the FBI and act like the elected servants we're supposed to be? The answer is we drop the hammer on our own miscreants and, while we're at it, see if we can't show this televangelical asshole that just because you were born in Louisiana, you don't get to wipe your feet on Iberia Parish. Is this starting to gel for you, Helen?"

It was so quiet I could hear the air-conditioning in the vents. "We'll have Bello and his son in custody by close of business," I said.

"Good," Lonnie said, rocking back in his chair, raising one finger in the air. "One other thing—I want daily updates on every aspect of this investigation. Any memoranda are eyes-only. All conversations regarding the investigation stay within our immediate circle. Any sharing of information with federal authorities will be performed by this office and this office only. Are we all on the same page here?"

"I'll notify you as soon as we bring Bello and Tony Lujan in," I said.

I had slipped his punch, but he didn't seem to take note of it. "Helen?" he said.

Her face was thoughtful, even placid, before she spoke. "No, I can't think of a thing to say, Lonnie. Nothing at all. But if I do, I'll give you a buzz."

THE NEXT MORNING, Friday, Bello Lujan was placed under arrest for destruction of evidence in a vehicular homicide. He was not told that simultaneously his son was being removed from a classroom at UL by me, a uniformed Iberia Parish sheriff's deputy, and a Lafayette City Police detective. When Tony Lujan protested, we cuffed his wrists behind him and led him across the quadrangle, just as a bell rang and his peers poured out of the surrounding buildings and filled the colonnaded walkway that surrounded the main campus. Tony's face was as red as raw hamburger.

We left him cuffed behind the wire screen in the cruiser and headed for New Iberia, with me in the passenger seat and Top, our retired Marine Corps NCO, behind the wheel.

"You treated me like I'm a rapist or a drug dealer in front of all those people. You can't do that unless you charge me with something," Tony said.

"We don't have to charge you, because you're not under arrest," I said.

"Then why am I in handcuffs?"

"You gave us a bad time," I replied.

"If I'm not under arrest, take the cuffs off."

"When we stop," I said.

I saw Top look into the rearview mirror. His red hair was turning gray and two pale furrows ran through it on each side of his pate. His mustache looked as stiff as a toothbrush. "I'm not as forgiving as Dave, here," he said.

"What I'd do?"

"You stepped on my spit shine. You scratched the leather on my brand-new shoes. Those are forty-dollar shoes."

"I'm sorry," Tony said.

"How would you like it if somebody stepped on your new shoes?" Top said.

"This is crazy. I want to call my father."

"Your father is under arrest. I don't think he's going to be of much help to you," I said.

"Arrest for what?"

I turned around in the seat so he could look directly into my face. "Either you or he or your mother killed a homeless man with your automobile. Y'all thought you could get away with something like that, Tony? How old are you, anyway?"

"Twenty." The handcuffs were on tight and he had to lean forward on the car seat to keep from pinching them into his wrists.

"You're studying to be a doctor?" I said.

"I'm in my second year of premed."

"And you're starting out your career with blood splatter all over you?" I said.

"I didn't kill anybody."

"How did the dead guy's blood get on your headlight?" Top said.

"I'm not saying anything else. I want to talk to my father. I want to talk to a lawyer."

"Glad to hear that, kid, because I'm very upset over what you did to my shoes," Top said. "You just graduated from 'friend of the court' to 'punch of the day' in the stockade shower. I hear if you close your eyes and pretend you're a girl, it's not so bad after a couple of months."

Then both Top and I turned to stone and watched the billboards and fields of young sugarcane slide past the windows. After we had crossed into Iberia Parish, I gestured toward a turnoff. We left the four-lane and drove through a community of shacks and rain ditches that were strewn with litter and vinyl bags of raw garbage that had been flung from passing vehicles. Thunderclouds moved across the sun and the countryside dropped into shadow. The wind smelled like rain and chemical fertilizer and dead animals that had been left on the roadside. Beyond a line of trees I could see the ugly gray outline of the parish prison and the silvery coils of razor wire along the fences.

"Stop here," I told Top.

"He wants to lawyer-up. He's a fraternity punk who deserves to fall in his own shit. Don't end up with a bad jacket, here," Top said.

"I'm going to do it my way. Now stop the car."

I got out of the cruiser and opened the back door. Tony looked at me cautiously. "Outside," I said.

"What are we doing?"

I reached inside and pulled him out on the road, then marched him toward a clump of cedar trees. He twisted his head back toward the road, his face stretched tight with fear. "People at UL know we left together. You can't do this," he said.

"Shut up," I said. I pushed him into the shade of the trees. He began to struggle, and I shoved him against a tree trunk and held him there. "I'm going to uncuff you now. The conversation we have out here is between you and me. You're being treated like an intelligent man. Try to act like one."

I unlocked the cuffs, pulled them free of his wrists, and turned him around. His face was gray, his breath rife with funk.

"Your old man didn't kill the homeless man, did he?"

"No, sir."

"Did your mother?"

"She has bad night vision. She doesn't even have a license. You can check."

"So that leaves you."

He was shaking his head even before I finished the sentence. "If I'd killed a homeless guy, it would have been an accident. Why would I want to hide it?"

"But it's obvious you know when and how it happened."

"I didn't kill anybody."

"You said your mother has bad night vision. How do you know the homeless guy was struck at night?"

He closed then opened his eyes, like a man who has just stepped on the trapdoor of a hangman's scaffold. "You got to let me see a lawyer. It's in the Constitution, isn't it? I'm guaranteed at least a phone call, right?"

"Listen to me. A man with no name was killed by an automobile your family owns and drives. The dead man was probably a wino, a guy with few if any friends, no family, and no known origins. He was the kind of guy who gets bagged and tagged and dropped in a hole in ground, case closed. Except that's not going to happen here. That guy had a right to live, just like you and I do. Whoever ran over him is going to be indicted and sent to trial. I give you my absolute word on that, Tony. You believe me when I say that?"

"Yes, sir."

"You're a young man and young people make mistakes. Usually the cause is a lack of judgment. People get scared, they can't think straight, they make bad decisions. They want to run from the deed they've committed because it's almost as though it didn't happen, it's not *them,* it's like someone else did it. If they could only go home, this terrible moment in their lives would be erased. That's what happened, didn't it, Tony? You just didn't think straight. It's only human in a situation like that. Tell us your version of events before somebody else does. Don't take a fall you don't deserve. That's not stand-up, it's dumb. Just tell the truth and trust the people trying to help you."

He watched me carefully while I spoke, his face turned slightly aside, as though he didn't want the full measure of my words to undo his defenses. But I had not convinced him. I took another run at ip.

"You ever read Stephen Crane?" I said.

"The writer?"

"Yeah, the writer."

"No," he said.

"Crane said few of us are nouns. Most of us are adverbs. No tragedy is orchestrated by one individual. An event we blame ourselves for may have been years in the making and may have much more to do with others than ourselves. Without recognition of that fact, we never acquire any wisdom about anything. Our case name for the homeless guy is Crustacean Man. Help us give back this guy his name. You can start correcting things, turning them around, right now, as we speak. It's that easy."

His eyes were locked on mine, his eyelids stitched to his brows. His bottom lip was white on the corner where he was biting down on it, to the point I thought the skin would break. I could almost hear words forming in his throat. Then his gaze broke and the moment was lost. "I want to talk to my father. What have you done with him?" he said.

"Your old man can take care of himself," I replied.

"He might actually go to prison?"

"It's a good possibility."

He started to cry. It was the first time I had seen Tony Lujan show any concern for anyone but himself. I took out a clean, folded handkerchief and handed it to him. "We're done here. I'm not going to question you any more. Other people will talk to you later," I said.

He cleared his throat and spit. He looked at the clouds scudding across the sky and the gray outline of the parish stockade. "I need to confess something," he said.

I waited for him to speak, but he didn't. "What is it?" I said.

"I'm holding."

"You're dealing?"

"No," he said. He unbuttoned his shirt pocket and removed a small plastic bag rolled around three joints. "I smoke one or two a day, that's all. I know if I'm arrested at the jail, I'll be searched and then charged for holding."

I took the bag from him, shook the joints out, and ground them under my heel. "So you're not holding now," I said, and stuffed the bag back in his pocket.

I started walking toward the cruiser, with Tony perhaps ten feet behind me. I heard him quicken his step to catch up with me.

"That was a pretty decent thing to do, Mr. Robicheaux," he said.

"Don't deceive yourself, kid. What I told you back there in the trees wasn't a ruse. You had your chance and you blew it. The people I work with are going to twist your head off and spit in it," I replied.

I HAD NOT SEEN Clete Purcel since Saturday evening, when he had driven away from the boat landing at Henderson Swamp with Trish Klein, his face and hers glowing like those of youthful lovers in the sunset. I left three messages on his cell phone, and also went by his office, only to find it closed. Friday I went by his office again, and this time his part-time secretary, Hulga Volkmann, was behind the desk. She was a big, rosy-complected, cheerful, and scatterbrained woman who wore flower-print dresses and perfume that would numb the olfactory senses of an elephant.

"He went to New Orleans for a day or so, then called from Cancún. He'll be back tonight," she said.

"Clete's in Mexico?" I said.

"Or was it Bimini?" she said.

Clete Purcel's romantic problems did not occur as a result of his having love affairs with biker girls and neurotic artists and strippers. Instead, they usually began when he got involved with any woman who was halfway normal, in other words, the type of person he didn't believe he deserved. Any attempt to convince him that he was attractive to women other than pipeheads and narcissistic meltdowns was futile. In Clete's mind, he was still the son of a milkman in the Irish Channel, with skinned knuckles from fights on the school ground and welts across his butt from his father's razor strop. Nice girls didn't hang with a guy who had a scar like a pink inner-tube patch through one eyebrow, put there by a black warlord from the Gird Town Deuces. Nice girls didn't hang with a former jarhead who still heard the downdraft of helicopter blades in his sleep.

"Is Clete with a lady by the name of Trish Klein?" I asked the secretary.

"He was with someone. I heard a lot of noise in the background. I think he was in a casino," Hulga said.

Clete lived down the bayou in a Depression-era motor court, one that still did not have telephones in the cottages and was covered by the shade of oaks hundreds of years old. At ten Saturday morning, I knocked on his door. He answered it in his skivvies and an undershirt, smiling sleepily. "How you doin', big mon?" he said. A square bandage was taped high up on his left shoulder.

"Why don't you tell your friends where you are once in a while?"

"Oh, Trish and I drove over to the Big Sleazy for the day, then one thing led to another. You know how it goes. You want coffee?"

"I don't want to hear Darwin's history of the planet. Did you let her hustle you?"

"Lighten up on the terminology," he replied, filling a metal coffeepot at the sink.

"What happened to your shoulder?"

"Nothing. A scratch. I had to get a tetanus shot."

"I think Trish Klein is playing you, Cletus," I said, instantly regretting my words.

"Hell, yes. Why would a great-looking broad be interested in an over-the-hill P.I. who's got a worse jacket than most perps?"

"I didn't say that. Your weakness is your good heart. People take advantage of it."

"Good try. Get the milk out of the icebox, will you? God!"

"God *what*?"

"I woke up feeling great. I haven't had any booze in two days. Trish and I are going to a street dance in Lafayette tonight. Then you come in here and walk around on my libido with golf shoes. Plus you insult Trish."

"I worry about you. You were gone four days without telling me where you were."

He tossed a loaf of bread into my hands. "Make some toast."

"What happened in New Orleans?"

"Ever hear of a guy named Lefty Raguza?"

"He's a psychopath who works for a bookie and general shithead by the name of Whitey Bruxal."

"I had to straighten him out. It wasn't a major event. You don't figure him for a listener, huh?"

"What have you done, Clete?"

Then he told me of the beginnings of his romantic involvement with the girl whose nickname he had taken from a song by Jimmy Clanton.

CHAPTER
9

LAST SUNDAY MORNING he and Trish Klein had headed down the four-lane toward New Orleans, the top down, the cane blowing in the fields on each side of them, then they skirted a sun-shower at Morgan City and turned into a convenience store to put up the top. It was still early and there were few vehicles on the highway. A Ford Explorer that had been a quarter mile behind Clete went past the convenience store, a blond man at the wheel, then the road was empty again, the wind balmy and flecked with rain.

"I love it here. You can almost smell the Gulf. That's the only thing I miss about Miami—the smell of the ocean in the morning," Trish said.

"You lived by the water?" Clete said.

She had taken a bandanna off her head and was shaking out her hair. Clete couldn't keep his eyes off her. Nor could he read her or her intentions, or judge whether or not he had any chance with her. All he knew was she had the most beautiful blue eyes and heart-shaped face he had ever seen. "We had a house in Coconut Grove. My grandmother kept a sailboat. We used to sail down into the Keys when the kingfish were running," she said.

"That must have been great," he said, his gaze wandering over her eyes and mouth, her words not really registering.

"You want to go now?" she asked.

"Pardon?"

"It's starting to rain."

"Right," he said.

They drove back onto the four-lane and crossed the bridge over the wide sweep of the Atchafalaya River. From the bridge's apex, Morgan City looked like a Caribbean port, with its palm-dotted streets, red-tiled roofs, biscuit-colored stucco buildings, and shotgun houses fronted by ceiling-high windows and ventilated green shutters. As Clete descended the bridge, he glanced into the rearview mirror and saw the Ford Explorer again. The blond man was hunched over the wheel, wearing shades, cutting in and out of the passing lane. Then he dropped behind a semi and disappeared from view.

Clete and Trish crossed another bridge at Des Allemands and ate deep-fried soft-shell crabs in a restaurant by a waterway where the banks were still thickly wooded and undeveloped and houseboats were moored under the overhang of the trees. When they got back on the highway, Clete saw the Explorer swing behind him. Clete took the exit to Luling and approached the huge steel bridge spanning the Mississippi. The Explorer dropped back four cars but stayed with him.

At one point the blond man threw some trash out the window, perhaps a fast-food container, something that splattered and bounced across the pavement.

"Know anybody who drives a dark green Explorer?" Clete said.

"Nobody I can think of." Trish leaned forward so she could see into the side mirror. "I don't see one. Where is it?"

"He's about three cars back now. A blond guy with shades on, throwing garbage on the road."

"No, that doesn't sound like anybody I know. He's following us?"

"He's probably just a jerk. Sometimes I think we should make littering a capital offense, you know, have a few roadside executions. It would really solve a lot of environmental problems here."

He could feel her looking at the side of his face. When he glanced at her, she was smiling, her eyes lit with a tenderness that made his loins go weak.

"What'd I say?" he asked.

"Nothing. You're just a sweet guy." She touched his shoulder with her fingertips. Clete forgot about the man in the Explorer and wondered if he wasn't being played.

They drove down I-10 to New Orleans and parked in a multilevel garage in the French Quarter. A storm was blowing off Lake Pontchartrain and the air smelled like salt and warm concrete when the first drops of rain hit it. They walked to the casino, at the bottom of Canal, and Clete could hear the horn blowing on the paddle-wheel excursion boat out on the river. He paused at the steps leading into the casino, under a row of transplanted palms that lifted and straightened in the breeze.

"Sure you want to go in here? Wouldn't you like to take a boat ride instead?" he said.

"Come on, I'm just going to play a couple of slots. Then I've got a surprise for you."

"What kind of surprise?"

"You'll see." She winked at him.

He told himself he was pulling the rip cord if she went near the craps table or if she started playing blackjack and a member of her crew was in place at the table or watching the game from the crowd. Clete had never been a gambler, but he had learned most of the casino hustles when he had run security for Sally Dio in Vegas and Reno. One of the best scams going involved card counting. Actually, it wasn't even a scam. It was a matter of having more brains than the house. A good card counter could determine at which point a blackjack deck contained a preponderance of cards in the high numbers, usually 10 through king. The high numbers in the shoe raised the odds that the dealer, who was required to take a hit on 16 or less, would go bust. The player just had to stand pat and let the dealer beat himself.

There was a hitch, however. The casino cameras and pit managers could tell when a card counter's betting pattern had changed. So a crew made use of a player who always bet the same high amount of money but did not take a seat at the table and commence betting until he received a signal from a colleague in the crowd. The player would stay at the table as long as the odds remained in his favor, then linger briefly after the shuffle, losing a few bets if necessary. Finally he would glance at his watch, pick up his winnings, and stroll over to a craps or roulette table, where he would be absorbed into the crowd.

Clete ordered a vodka collins at the bar and watched while Trish wandered between the rows of slot machines. Was she casing the joint? Did she and her crew plan to take it down? He couldn't tell. But she was no garden-variety grifter. Nor was she a degenerate gambler. So what were they doing here?

The recycled air was like cigarette smoke that had been trapped for days in a refrigerator full of spoiled cheese. Half the people on the floor had B.O. and reminded Clete of outpatients at the methadone clinic. The rest were peckerwoods in shiny suits and vinyl shoes, with haircuts that resembled plastic wigs that didn't fit their heads. What a dump, he thought. The people who ran it would probably comp Hermann Göring.

Then he saw the blond driver of the Explorer watching him from behind a column by the entrance. The blond man wore a silk neckerchief and a magenta-colored silk shirt that was molded against his lats and shoulders and tapered waist. His facial skin was bright and hard-looking, like polished ceramic, his eyes a mystery behind his shades. He pulled a cigarette out of his pack with his mouth and cupped the flame from a gold lighter to it.

Clete thought about bracing him, then decided to let the hired help handle it. He introduced himself to a security man by the craps table, out of sight of the blond man, opening his P.I. badge holder in his palm. "I have an office on St. Ann in the Quarter and one in New Iberia," he said. "I think a dude hanging by the entrance is bird-dogging me and my lady friend. Blond hair, shades, reddish-purple shirt, kerchief around the neck. He's been following me since Morgan City. But I've got no idea who he is."

The security man listened attentively. He was trim and well dressed, his whitewalled hair freshly barbered. "You said your name was Purcel?"

"Right."

"You used to be with NOPD?"

"What about it?"

"I heard your name mentioned at Second District headquarters, that's all."

Clete waited for him to go on, but he didn't. The security man stepped away from the craps table and glanced casually toward the front of the casino. "Wait here."

"Maybe the guy doesn't know I made him. I'd appreciate being left out of it."

But the security man walked off without acknowledging Clete's last statement, and Clete concluded the reference to his past history at the Second District wasn't a positive indicator of his situation. The security man began talking to the blond man, the silhouette of a potted palm between them and Clete. But he quickly became a listener rather than a talker. He listened and then he listened some more. The blond man slipped what looked like a photo from his pocket and the two men examined it together, the blond man tapping on it for emphasis. Then the blond man gave the photo to the security man, obviously to keep.

When the security man returned to the craps area, he had the photo cupped in his palm. It showed Trish Klein at a blackjack table, laughing, a drink in her hand, one of her crew on the stool next to her. She had five cards turned up on the green felt in front of her, the total sum of which was under 21.

"Is this your girlfriend?" the security man asked.

"That's the lady I'm with."

"She's in the Griffin Book."

"That looks like a photo of somebody who just hit a five-card Johnny. That gets you blackballed here?"

"You and your friend are welcome to play the slots, Mr. Purcel. Just stay away from the tables. If you get near them, you'll be escorted from the building."

"Really?" Clete said, stepping closer to him. "How about my initial question? Who's this geek with the shades following me around?"

"He does the same kind of work I do, at least in my off-duty capacity. You and Miss Klein enjoy yourselves. At the slot machines."

Clete's face was burning. "We need to get something straight here."

"No, we don't. Thank you for visiting the casino," the security man said, and walked off.

Suddenly Clete's shirt felt too tight for his chest. Inside the steady din of coins rattling into metal trays and the excited yelling around the craps table, he could hear the hoarseness of his own breathing and a sound like wind roaring in his ears. It took him five minutes to find Trish, who was watching a blackjack game, one knuckle poised on her chin, a thoughtful expression on her face. Thirty feet away, two security men were talking to each other, glancing in her direction.

"Time to boogie," Clete said.

"What for?"

"I want to show you the battleground at Chalmette."

She seemed to consider the idea.

Please, God, Clete thought.

"All right," she said. "But don't forget I have a surprise."

He put one arm over her shoulders, and the two of them began walking toward the entrance. Through the glass doors he could see the dark green of the palm fronds in the rain and the lighted storefronts along Canal. We're almost there, he thought.

"I have to stop by the restroom," she said.

"Now?" he said.

"Yes," she said, giving him a look. "I might be a minute or two."

"Sure," he said, his eyes sweeping the casino. "I'll wait at the bar. Take your time."

Just cool it, he told himself. You can't always dee-dee out of Indian country when you want. Sometimes you just have to brass it out.

He took a seat at the bar and ordered a soda and lime slice. It was a mistake. He heard a stool squeak on its swivel and felt a presence near his left arm, almost like an energy field that had the potential of a beehive.

Clete took the soda and lime from the bartender's hand, then turned and looked into the sunglasses of the blond man in the reddish-purple shirt.

"Your gash go to the can?" the man asked.

"What did you say?"

"I said did the lady, your gash, stop by the john?"

Clete took a sip from his glass, then put the lime slice in his mouth and chewed it. "What's your name, buddy?"

"Lefty Raguza," the man said, and offered his hand. When Clete didn't take it, he removed his shades and grinned. His eyes made Clete think of a cool green fire, an intense combination of color and light that didn't indicate thought patterns or moods so much as incipient cruelty that had no specific target.

Clete drank the rest of his soda and crunched ice between his molars. He looked into the bar mirror when he spoke. "Here are the ground rules for you, Lefty. You don't bird-dog us, you keep your mouth off certain people, and if I see you passing around photos of my lady again, I'm going to rip your wiring out."

"She looks like a sweet piece of ass is all I was saying. That's meant as a compliment. Prime cut is prime cut. So far, what I'm doing here isn't personal. If I were you, I'd let things remain like that."

Clete gazed into the moral vacuity of Lefty Raguza's eyes. Then he got off the stool, left a five-dollar bill on the bar, and waited for Trish by the door of the women's restroom.

"You okay?" she said.

"Sure, I'm solid," he replied.

"You're red as a boiled crab."

"I could go for some of those right now. I know a joint over on Iberville. Then we'll go out to Chalmette. I'm extremely copacetic today."

But Clete was neither solid nor copacetic. They walked into the Quarter, in the rain, staying under the colonnades, the music from the clubs drifting out on the sidewalk, but he couldn't get the words of the man named Lefty Raguza out of his head. He stopped in front of a café that was brightly lit and cheerful inside and patted his pants pocket. "I think I left my keys at the bar. Have a coffee in the café and I'll be right back," he said.

"Don't you want to call the casino first?"

"No, I'm sure I left them at the bar. It's not a problem," he said.

He didn't wait for her to reply. When he got back to the casino, his loafers were sopping with rainwater. He dried his face with a paper napkin from the bar and scanned the casino but didn't see Lefty Raguza. "There was a guy sitting next to me, a friend of mine, a guy with a neckerchief and shades, you see where he went?" he said to the bartender.

"To the men's room," the bartender replied.

The crowd had grown, and Clete had to thread his way through the people at the machines and tables. His eyes were watering in the cigarette smoke, his ears ringing, his heart pounding in his chest. He passed a neatly folded and stacked fire hose inside a glass door that had been inset in the wall, then entered the restroom. Lefty Raguza was positioned in front of a urinal, his feet slightly spread, one hand propped against the wall, his face turned toward the far wall.

"Put your flopper in your pants and turn around," Clete said.

Two other men had been washing their hands. They glanced simultaneously in Clete's direction, then left the room without looking back. Lefty Raguza shook himself off and flexed his knees, tucking his phallus back inside his slacks. Then he turned, grinning from behind his shades, and kicked Clete between the thighs as casually as he would punt a football.

Clete felt a wave of nausea and pain surge through his lower body that was like broken glass being forced up his penis and out his rectum. He fell backward through a stall door, crashing into a toilet bowl, his fingernails raking down the sides of the walls. He could feel the wet rim of the bowl against his back and piss on the seat of his slacks.

Lefty Raguza was staring down at him, a small, triangular-shaped leather case in his hand. "You attacked me in the can and got your ass kicked. Don't screw with Whitey, don't screw with me. Show your gash what happened here. Tell her she can have the same. Ready for it, big man?"

Ready for what? Clete thought. He tried to raise himself, but the pain inside his groin made his eyes brim with water.

Lefty Raguza unsnapped the leather case in his hand and removed a metal tool that was like a machinist's punch with a short crosspiece at the top designed to fit the palm and a hilt one inch from the point. "You're getting off easy, Blimpo. So act like a man and take your medicine," he said.

Then he leaned down and jabbed the tool into Clete's shoulder, thudding it hard with the heel of his hand, feeling for bone, twisting it sideways before removing it. He cleaned the point on a piece of toilet paper. "Now beat feet. I got to finish my piss," he said.

Clete stumbled toward the door, his hand pressed to the wound under his shoulder bone. The door swung open in his face. Two black men and a white man about to enter the room stepped aside, avoiding eye contact with him, then walked off as though the last five seconds in their lives had not happened.

Clete worked his way along the wall in the concourse to the glass enclosure that housed the emergency fire hose. He fitted his palm inside the handle and ripped the door loose, expecting an alarm to go off. But none did.

The hose was a masterpiece of engineering. It was full-throated at the valve, perhaps four inches across, probably directly connected into a main that could blow paint off a battleship. The nozzle was brass, with a lever to adjust the outflow, the hose itself made of a canvaslike material that unfolded neatly from the stack and slapped on the carpet. Clete pushed the lever on the main valve and watched the hose straighten and harden like an enormous, thick-bodied snake.

Lefty Raguza was combing his hair in the mirror when Clete kicked open the restroom door and dragged the hose inside with him. "Here's a postcard from New Iberia, motherfucker," he said. Then he pulled back the lever on the nozzle.

The jet of water blew the shades off Raguza's face, then blew Raguza into the tile wall. Clete tugged the hose deeper into the room, keeping it trained on Raguza, knocking him down when he tried to get up, skittering him into the urinals, remolding his mouth and cheeks, flattening the flesh against bone and teeth so that his face looked like he was caught in a wind tunnel.

Raguza almost got to his feet when Clete blew him into a stall, trapping him between the toilet and stall wall. Raguza was gasping for breath, his feet fighting for purchase, one arm sunk deep inside the bowl, his head thudding against the wall like a rubber ball tethered to a paddle.

Clete shut down the nozzle and dropped the hose on the floor. The restroom was flooded, the doorway packed with onlookers, security guards in uniform trying to fight their way through.

"This guy was starting a fire. He said something about hiding a bomb. Somebody better get the cops," Clete said.

Suddenly the crowd headed in all directions, the words "fire" and "bomb" rippling like flame across the casino floor. "Hey, you, come back here!" a security man yelled.

But Clete was now ensconced in the middle of the throng pouring onto Canal. The mist was gray and swirling, as thick and damp as wet cotton, the palm fronds fraying overhead, and he could smell beignets cooking somewhere and the heavy green odor of the Gulf. His shoulder throbbed, his genitals were swollen, his shirt was streaked with blood and his slacks with urine and bathroom disinfectant, but somehow he knew it was going to be a grand day after all. He crossed into the Quarter, splashing through pools of rainwater, wondering if Trish would still be at the café, wondering, for just a moment, why she had not come looking for him.

He felt his spirits begin to sink. Maybe Dave had been right; maybe he had been a special kind of fool this time out. He was not only over the hill and addicted to most of the major vices, he was still the violent, chaotic, immature man intelligent women might find exciting and even interesting for the short haul but whom they eventually got rid of, as they would an untrained house pet.

Then he saw Trish coming down the street, without umbrella or raincoat, almost being hit by a car at the intersection, her lovely, heart-shaped face filled with concern and pity when she realized the condition he was in. "Oh, Clete, what did they do to you?" she said, her fingers touching his eyes, his hair, his mouth. "What did they do to you, honey?"

"Just a little discussion with a guy. What was that surprise you were talking about?"

She hooked her arm through his and began to pull him across the street toward the parking garage. "I'm taking you to the hospital," she said, ignoring his question. "It was that guy following us, wasn't it? I shouldn't have let you go back there. I hate myself for this."

A passing car blew a wall of water across both Clete and Trish.

She used a handkerchief to wipe it out of his eyes, her face turned up to his like a flower opening into light. He wrapped both his arms around her and lifted her up on his chest and carried her in that fashion all the way to the car.

HE SPENT THE NIGHT in a hospital up St. Charles Avenue. In the morning she picked him up in his Caddy and they drove to a marina on Lake Pontchartrain. A gleaming white seaplane waited for them at the end of a dock, rocking in the chop, the wide slate-green expanse of the lake in the background. "Wow, where we going?" Clete said.

"How about dinner in Mexico?" she said.

"Why you doing this, Trish?"

"Because you saved me from getting busted. Because you take chances for other people. Because I like you, big stuff." She pressed her knuckles playfully into his stomach.

When they were both inside, the pilot fired the engines and the plane gathered speed across the water, a white froth whipping from the backdraft. Then the plane lurched suddenly into the sky, climbing higher and higher, until Clete could see the alluvial fan of the Mississippi and the immense, soft gray-green outline of the Louisiana wetlands.

"Where to in Mexico?" he said.

"Cancún," she said, then paused for a beat. "More or less."

More or less? But there was still a pink mist inside his head from the Demerol drip at the hospital, and he didn't pursue it. He lay back in the seat and shut his eyes and let the steady vibration of the engines put him to sleep. He dreamed of a jungle in southeastern Asia, one that always flickered whitely under trip flares or bloomed with red-black geysers of fire and dirt from booby-trapped 105 duds. But now the jungle contained no sign of threat and breathed with the sounds of wind and the patter of rain ticking on the canopy overhead.

When he awoke, the seaplane was descending through thunderheads, the windows streaked with rain. Then they were below the squall, flying low over water that had the translucence of green Jell-O. The coral reefs were strung with gossamer fans and shadowed by floating pools of hot blue that looked like they had been poured from a bottle of ink.

But Trish and Clete's destination was not the postcard picture he had witnessed from the plane. They landed in a bay full of fish-kill and rode across the interior in a misfiring taxi to a village that buzzed with flies and smelled of chickenshit and herbicide. The villagers were all Indians, who waved at Trish when they saw her through the taxi's back windows. The houses were constructed of unpainted cinder blocks, the cookstove often a sheet of corrugated tin set on rocks under a lean-to. The community water wells were dug within a few feet of hog and goat pens. The only telephone lines Clete could see went into a cantina and a police station.

Trish had said little since they had gotten off the plane, and in fact had become reflective and somber. The taxi turned up a rutted road that led to a yellow building with a peaked tar-paper roof.

"I got involved with the guerrillas in El Sal in the eighties," he said. "I don't think any of this will change in our lifetimes."

"So we shouldn't try?"

He looked at the yellow building. "What is this place?"

"A home for handicapped kids. Either their parents don't want them or are not equipped to raise them. Without the home, most of them would spend their lives on the street."

Some of the children at the home had been born blind or without hands or feet, or with misshapen faces and twisted spines and spastic nervous systems. Some drooled and made unintelligible sounds. Others were harelipped, clubfooted, or had dwarf or bowed legs. Some had never walked.

When Clete was introduced to them, his smile felt like a surgical wound. He told Trish he had to use the restroom.

"Out back, the cinder-block building under the cistern. It has plumbing," she said.

When he got outside, his eyes were brimming with tears. He washed his face in an aluminum basin and blew his nose on his handkerchief, then returned to the yellow building, a grin on his face.

The personnel at the home were Mennonites and Catholic lay missionaries, and seemed to glow with a level of humanity that Clete

thought had little to do with political or perhaps even religious conviction. In fact, they seemed to be uncomplicated people who had little or no interest in the larger world and did not view themselves as
exceptional and would probably not understand why anyone would
treat them as such.

When Clete got back on the plane, he felt ten years older and for
some reason could not even remember the details of what he had
done the previous day, even the hosing down of Lefty Raguza at the
casino. "You just visit here sometimes?" he asked Trish.

"No, I work here several months a year."

"Who finances this place?"

"A bunch of assholes who don't know they finance it," she replied.

"Ever boost a savings and loan in Mobile?"

Her response was a deep-throated laugh.

CHAPTER
10

THE FACT THAT NO Jewish, Hispanic, Asian, Mideastern, or black person had ever been admitted to Tony Lujan's fraternity did not seem significant to him. Clubs were meant to be private in nature. Like families. There was no law that said you had to let people of different religions and races marry into your family, was there? He had heard about a Jewish pledge who had been blackballed—a kid who later dropped out of college and got blinded in Iraq, but that was before Tony had joined the fraternity. Whenever he heard mention of the Jewish kid getting sandbagged by his fraternity brothers, he walked away from the conversation. Tony didn't like problems, particularly when they were caused by wrongheaded people. If the kid was Jewish, why didn't he just go to Tulane? It wasn't Tony's freight to carry.

Tomorrow morning, Tuesday, he and his attorney were scheduled to meet with the Iberia Parish district attorney. The D.A. had already presented the available choices for Tony in the most draconian terms. He would either accept a grant of immunity for his cooperation in the investigation of his father or be considered a suspect himself. Either way, he or his father was going to prison. Or maybe both of them would. "You've got the key to the jailhouse door," the district attorney had said. "We'll try to protect you up at Angola, but you wouldn't be the first white college boy to get spread-eagled on the bars. Let me know what you decide."

The image made Tony's skin crawl, his buttocks constrict.

All this because of a wino on a road. All this because Monarch Little, in order to save his own black ass, had told the cops where his old man had gotten the Buick repaired. What had he ever done to Monarch Little? He hadn't even known Monarch Little existed until the run-in at McDonald's.

Tony could not get tomorrow's meeting with the D.A. out of his mind. There had to be a way out. He had told his lawyer he had no knowledge about the wino's death, but it was obvious the lawyer didn't believe him.

"Your father or you ran over the guy, Tony," the lawyer had said. "Unless you lent the car to somebody. You think that might have happened?"

"It could have," Tony replied, watching the lawyer's face.

"Forget I mentioned that," the lawyer said.

Would his courage fail him? Could he take the weight and actually risk time on Angola Farm, where he would hoe soybeans under mounted guards who carried quirts and shotguns? Was he actually as small and frightened and weak as he felt? The D.A. obviously thought so. For the first time in his life, he understood why people killed themselves.

When he did not think his morning could get any worse, the professor in his political science class started in on institutionalized class and ethnic prejudice, asking Tony, in front of a hundred other students, if he believed campus fraternities and sororities had the right to discriminate in their admission policies.

"Isn't 'discrimination' just another word for judgment?" Tony said. "People discriminate in the kind of food they eat or what part of town they live in. That's how standards are established. People have a right to choose, don't they, sir?"

"Let's put it another way. Is the issue one of inclusion or exclusion?" the professor asked from behind his lectern, which was mounted on a stage, high above the class. "Doesn't a fraternity pride itself on who it keeps out rather than who it lets in? What's the value of money if it doesn't buy privilege? 'Melting pot' sounds good on paper, but the mix may not always be good for everyone. Is that the case, Tony?"

Tony couldn't keep track of the professor's logic, but he knew it was a trap of some kind, an effort to make him look like a pampered rich kid who didn't care about the rights of others. He could feel words forming in his mouth that he knew he shouldn't speak.

"I don't think fraternities and sororities are the problem. I think the problem is people who—"

"Who what?" the professor said. His face was effeminate and narrow and stippled with gin roses, his teeth small and sharp inside a neatly trimmed gray-and-brown beard that reminded Tony of mouse fur.

"People who are professional victims," Tony said. Then he thought of a joke he had heard at the fraternity, one whose implication he didn't actually share. But the professor had tried to tar him. All right, let's see how far the professor wanted to run with it. "Like the NAACP—the National Association of Always Complaining People. I mean, should people feel guilty because they work hard and make a lot of money?"

The lecture hall became absolutely quiet. The black students in the room put their pens down and either looked into space or twisted in their seats to get a better view of Tony Lujan.

"You raise an interesting point," the professor said. "Maybe the vote of one group in our society should count more than another group. But which group fights the wars? Rich people or poor people? It seems that blue-collar young men and women go to war in greater numbers than rich ones. So using your own logic, shouldn't their vote count for more than yours or mine?"

Tony's head was pounding, his forehead breaking with sweat. This was about something else. The professor had been Tony's freshman adviser and had relatives in New Iberia. Did the professor know about Yvonne Darbonne? Was this about Yvonne? Was he calling Tony an elitist hypocrite? Tony felt the room spinning around him. "I didn't mean to offend anyone, sir. I apologize for my remark."

Then he realized his apology was actually sincere, and for just a moment he felt good about himself. Out of the corner of his eye he saw several black students pick up their pens again.

"I appreciate your candor, Tony. This is a political science class. If you have a thorn in your head, this is the place to pull it out." The professor looked at the clock on the back wall. "See you all on Wednesday."

Candor? What was candor?

After the lecture hall had emptied, Tony still sat in his desk, his eyes fastened on the professor, who was putting his notes and books in a briefcase. The professor glanced up and smoothed his beard. "Something you want to ask me?" he said.

"What did you mean by that, Dr. Edwards?"

"By what?"

"This being the place to pull a thorn out. Were you saying something about me? Just tell the truth."

"Supposedly that's why I get paid."

"Sir?"

"I get paid to tell the truth." The professor gave it up. "I was saying that the idea of class superiority has one basic function—it allows people to justify their exploitation of their fellow human beings. The exploitation happens on many levels, Tony, the most common of which is financial or sexual. It's taught in fraternities, it's taught in churches. People screw down and marry up."

Tony got up from his seat and approached the lectern, his stomach churning, a sound like an electrical short buzzing in his head. "Are you accusing me of sexually using a girl from a poor family?"

"Excuse me?"

"I didn't have anything to do with her death," he said. "We had something special. It just didn't last. It just went to hell, all at once. I don't even know why."

"I'm afraid I don't—"

"You were talking about Yvonne. You were doing it in front of the whole class."

The professor stared at him. "You have a few minutes, Tony? Why don't you and I go for a cup of coffee?"

Tony looked at the confusion in the professor's face and realized the terrible mistake he had made. "I'm sorry, I misunderstood. I'm not feeling too good, Dr. Edwards. I didn't mean to bother you."

"You're a fine boy. One day you'll discover who you are and

none of this will matter." The professor seemed to smile with a level of compassion Tony did not think him capable of. But was it compassion, or perhaps something else? "Come talk to me when you have a chance. We'll have a drink in my backyard. I can make a grand martini."

But Tony was already walking rapidly up the aisle toward the exit, his footsteps echoing in the empty room, his face red with shame.

THE FRATERNITY HOUSE had been created out of a large white three-story Victorian home, one whose gables and cornices were visible through the crepe myrtle and azaleas and live oaks like the hard edges of a medieval fortress. The pledges mowed the lawn, raked the leaves, and trimmed the hedges, and kids whose families couldn't afford the fraternity's costs worked off their room and board by cooking and serving meals and cleaning the house.

Tony shared a room on the third floor with Slim Bruxal, one with a small balcony that provided a magnificent view of the trees and rooftops in the neighborhood. The room was the most desirable in the house, and when Slim requested it, none of his fraternity brothers objected, although others had more seniority than Slim and wanted it.

Tony's insides were like water when he returned to the house from his poli-sci class. He tried to tell Slim about what had happened, how he had made a fool out of himself, how Dr. Edwards had looked at him as though he were an object of pity.

While Tony sat on the side of his unmade bed and went through every detail of his public embarrassment in class, Slim stood barechested at a full-length mirror, combing his hair, examining his facial skin for imperfections, checking to see if the barber had etched his sideburns sufficiently. "I got news for you. Dr. Edwards is an alcoholic fudge-packer. He pushes that pinko douche rinse whenever he gets the chance. Be proud you stood up to him."

"I'm scared, Slim."

"Of what?"

"My lawyer and I meet with the D.A. tomorrow."

"Tell him to stuff it, just like I did. The Feds are using Monarch Little and the Iberia D.A. to get at my old man. They don't got jack on either one of us. Winos get run over all the time. You're an innocent man. Keep remembering that. They're targeting you because of who your father is."

"They'll send him to prison."

"No, they won't. My old man eats guys like that D.A. for lunch. Back in Miami, these local schmucks wouldn't have been allowed to clean his toilet."

"I feel real bad. I keep seeing that guy on the road. I keep thinking about Yvonne. Why did she go nuts like that?"

"How do I know? She had mental problems. Yvonne doesn't have anything to do with this. You keep the two issues separate. I don't want to see you like this."

"I can't help it. I'm coming apart."

Slim studied Tony in the mirror and slipped his comb in his back pocket. He sat down next to him and put his arm over Tony's shoulders. Tony could smell the clean odor of Slim's skin, the tinge of testosterone from his armpit. Slim squeezed him fraternally to get him out of his funk. "In no time you'll be the house's top cocksman again. Trust me, nobody cares about a winehead who walked in front of a car."

"That's not what happened, Slim."

"Yeah, it is."

"I can't hurt my folks like this."

Slim's eyes were filled with the kind of thoughts he never shared. He massaged the back of Tony's neck a long time, then glanced through the partially opened door and saw two junior classmen studying at a table in the room across the hall. He got up from the bed and quietly shut the door.

An hour later Tony drove his silver Lexus to St. John's Cathedral, a nineteenth-century brick church with twin bell towers a few blocks from Lafayette's old downtown area. If asked, he probably would not have been able to tell anyone what he was doing there. Before her accident, his mother had dutifully attended the local Episcopalian church, served graciously on all its social committees, and had believed in absolutely none of it. Ironically, Tony became convinced of the spiritual world's authenticity by his father. Bellerophon Lujan feared no man, but he would quit plowing or avoid proximity to any livestock at the first creak of electricity in the clouds. He was terrified of the prospect of hell and the consequences of his own libidinous nature, and believed it was the devil's hand that constantly subverted his attempts to achieve social respectability, which in Bellerophon's mind was the same as morality. For Bello, God was an abstraction, but the devil was real and reminded Bello of his presence each morning when Bello awoke throbbing and hard, chained to unrequited dreams that followed him into the day.

Tony walked across the church lawn to the St. John Oak and sat down on a stone bench. The oak was supposedly over four hundred years old. The limbs were so thick and so heavy, they not only touched the ground but had formed huge elbows that allowed the limbs to continue growing into the sunlight. The breeze was cool under the tree and smelled of flowers in the garden planted by the rectory. A young priest was watering the flowers with a hose, amusing himself by placing his thumb over the end of the hose and firing a jet into a nest of mud daubers. He caught Tony looking at him and grinned self-consciously.

Tony did not know how long he sat on the stone bench. He could have stayed there forever. The limbs of the live oak were hung with Spanish moss and encrusted with lichen, the stone under him cool to his touch. How did he get mixed up in so much trouble? Why did Yvonne have to go and kill herself? In his mind he created a fantasy in which he walked through the front door of the church and out the back, free of all the misery that had come into his life since he had started hanging out with Slim Bruxal.

But in truth he couldn't put it on Slim. He had sought out Slim; it wasn't the other way around. There were rumors about Slim's expulsion for cheating at LSU and a fight with a Texas Aggie in the restroom at Tiger Stadium, one that left the Aggie ruptured and bleeding inside from a broken rib. But Slim had another side to him. He listened to Tony and always sensed what Tony needed to hear. Slim took no guff from anyone. He understood what it was like to have a father he admired, even loved, but who was looked down upon by others. In fact, sometimes Tony looked at Slim soaping himself in the shower and experienced feelings he didn't like to dwell upon.

Then Tony realized the priest had turned off the garden hose and was walking toward him. He started to get up and leave. In fact, he didn't even know why he was there. Should he just tell this stranger about Yvonne and the dead homeless man and the fact that tomorrow he might betray his own family? The man in black pants and a smudged T-shirt was probably not much older than he was, except he was slight of build, almost frail. A baseball glove hung from his belt and another one was folded in his hand, a grass-stained ball buried in the pocket.

"Feel like a little pitch-and-catch?" he said.

"I pulled my arm in a fraternity game. I probably won't be that good at it."

"Neither am I. See that piece of cardboard where there used to be a stained-glass pane? My forkball got out of control."

Tony fitted the spare glove on his hand, and he and the priest began flinging the ball back and forth under the oak's drip line, the sunlight breaking like slivers of glass behind the cathedral's silhouette. Then the priest skipped one across the grass to him. Tony fielded it backhand, then fired it straight into the priest's glove, straight and hard, with no trajectory, with an accuracy that surprised even himself.

The priest sent another grounder at him. Tony bobbled it at first, the ball caroming off the heel of his hand. But he pulled it out of midair with his right hand and side-armed it, *whap,* back into the priest's waiting glove.

"You're pretty good," the priest said.

"Not really," he said, doing a poor job of hiding his pride.

"Try me now," the priest said.

Tony threw a high-hopper that the priest caught easily and tossed back without interest. The next two were faster, at an angle, grounders-with-eyes. The priest was good, scooping them up with his body positioned in front of the ball, his return throw fired from behind the ear. The next one Tony threw was a hummer, whizzing across the lawn like a shot. The priest caught it on the run, spearing it after it took a bad hop on a tree root, whirling and side-arming it back in a half turn.

The ball flew by Tony's outstretched glove and hit a passing car on the street. "Oh, boy," he heard the priest say.

"I'll go after it, Father," Tony said.

"Are you kidding? This is the third time this has happened this week. Time to take cover," the priest said.

Moments later, the priest hid the two gloves in a flower bed, furtively looking around the corner of the building. His face was bright and sweaty in the shade, his eyes wide with apprehension.

"You're really a minister?" Tony said.

"Well, I'm sure not Derek Jeter."

"I think the ball hit the car window."

"I know. That's why I'm here and not on the street looking for it. Come on, I have a couple of cold sodas in my cooler."

He squatted down on the grass and popped off the top of a small ice chest. He lifted out a can of Pepsi, ripped the tab, and handed it up to Tony. "Were you worried about something out there?" he said.

"Me? No, not really."

"You a Catholic?"

"No."

"If you want to tell me about something, it won't go any farther than this garden."

Had all this been a ruse? Tony wondered. Another do-gooder with an agenda? The priest lifted up his T-shirt and wiped his face with it, staring out at the traffic on the street.

"My girlfriend killed herself. She was stoned out of her head and maybe went to bed with several men before she did it. I might be arrested tomorrow for the death of a homeless man. I think maybe I'm a coward. I may commit a terrible act of betrayal and send one of my parents to prison."

The priest's mouth parted silently. His face was still flushed from play, the hair on his arms speckled with dirt from his work in the garden. His eyes glistened. "I'm sorry," he said.

Sorry about what? Yvonne's death? Sorry he had nothing to offer? What was he saying?

But the priest's gaze had drifted toward the street, where Slim Bruxal's SUV had just pulled behind Tony's Lexus. The SUV was loaded with kids from the fraternity house. At least two of them were wearing T-shirts imprinted with the faces of Robert E. Lee and Stonewall Jackson, which had been one of several ways the fraternity signaled its feelings on the question of race.

"I have to go," Tony said.

"Who are those guys?" the priest said.

"My friends."

The priest looked again at the kids getting out of Slim's vehicle. "You didn't tell me your name."

"I don't know who I am, Father. I don't know anything anymore."

"Stay," the priest said.

But Tony had already fitted a crooked smile on his face and directed his steps toward his friends, who waited for him by the curb. The speckled shade under the St. John Oak seemed to slip off his skin like water sliding off stone.

IT WAS HOT AND DRY that evening, and heat lightning flickered against a black sky in the south. Molly and I ate a late dinner of cold cuts and potato salad and iced tea on the picnic table in the backyard with Snuggs and Tripod. The air was thick with birds, the bayou coated with a pall of smoke from meat fires in the park.

"I think it's going to storm," Molly said. "You can feel the barometer dropping."

Just as she spoke, the wind touched the leaves over our heads and I felt a breath of cool air against my cheek, smelled a hint of distant rain. The phone rang in the kitchen. Molly got up to answer it.

"Let the machine take it," I said.

She sat back down. Then she tapped herself on the forehead with the heel of her hand. "I forgot."

"Forgot what?"

"A kid called just before you got home. He wouldn't leave a number. He said he'd call back later."

"What's his name?"

"Tony?"

"Tony Lujan?"

"He just said 'Tony.' He sounded like he'd been drinking."

"He probably was. That's Bello Lujan's kid. The D.A. and the Feds are about to chain-drag him down East Main."

The phone rang again. This time I went inside and answered it. It was Wally, our dispatcher, working the late shift and, I suspected, trying to pass on his discontent about it.

"We got Monarch Little in a holding cell. He t'rew his food t'rew the bars. What do you t'ink we ought to do?"

"Tell him to clean it up. Why you calling me with this, Wally?"

"'Cause he wants to talk to Helen, but she ain't here."

"What's he in for?"

"Illegal firearms possession. Maybe littering, too, 'cause he left his burned car on the street."

"I'm not in the mood for it, partner."

"His car caught fire, down at the corner where he sells dope. Soon as the fire truck gets there, shotgun shells start blowing up inside the car. There was a sawed-off double-barrel on the floor. The firemen found what was left of a truck flare on the backseat. Want to come down?"

"No."

There was a pause. "Dave?"

"What?"

"One of the uniforms called Monarch a bucket of black gorilla shit. Monarch axed him if it was true the uniform's mother still does it dog-style in Master P's backyard. The same uniform tole me he was recommending suicide watch for Monarch. I go off shift in t'ree hours. I don't want no accidents happening here after I'm gone."

I took the receiver from my ear and pinched the fatigue out of my eyes. "I'll be down in a few minutes."

"T'anks. I knew you wouldn't mind."

I asked Molly to save my dinner and went down to the jail, where Monarch sat in a holding cell, barefoot, beltless, his gold neck chains locked up in a personal possessions envelope. One eye had a deep red blood clot in the corner, the eyebrow ridged, split in the middle.

"Who popped you?" I asked.

"Slipped down getting into the cruiser. Check the arrest report if you t'ink I'm lying. I cain't get ahold of that FBI woman. I'm suppose to be in Witness Protection, not in no holding cell."

"This may come as a shock, but Witness Protection doesn't empower a person to go on committing crimes."

"That cut-down shotgun ain't mine. I ain't never seen it before."

"Why were you on the corner?"

"I wasn't on the corner. I was in the back room of the li'l store there, drinking a soda wit' my friends. I go there every afternoon to have a soda. Then my 'Bird explodes. Next t'ing I know, I got a racial problem wit' a cracker don't have no bidness in a black neighborhood." He brushed at his eye with the back of his wrist.

"Did you mouth off to the arresting officer?"

"I tole him what I tole you—that ain't my gun. He t'ought my 'Bird burning up was funny. He said too bad I wasn't taking a nap in it."

"I'll see if I can get you kicked. But I want you in my office at oh-eight-hundred tomorrow morning."

His eyes wandered around the opposite wall and up on the ceiling. "That's military talk, ain't it? Kind of stuff John Wayne like to snap off."

"Sometimes you make me wish I was black, Monarch."

"Why?"

"So I could beat the crap out of you and not feel guilty about it," I said.

But Monarch was not destined to make the street that night. Before I could get in touch with Helen, Wally took a 911 call from a community of rusted trailers, shacks, weed-grown yards, and piled garbage that was so egregious in the social decay it represented that it seemed planned rather than accidental. The 911 caller said he had heard shots, four of them, that afternoon, down by the bayou. He had thought the shooter was target-practicing and consequently had paid little attention to it. At sunset he had let his dog out to run in the sugarcane. The dog had come back from the field with blood on its muzzle.

So far, the only deputy at the crime scene was our retired Marine

NCO, Top. He had driven his cruiser down a turnrow in the field, his flasher bar rippling with color, and was now standing with the driver's door open, gazing at the sun's last reflection on the bayou. A hundred yards up the bayou, the turn bridge's lights were on, and close to the four corners, a juke joint rimmed by a shell parking lot thundered with music. Behind us, inside the deep evening shade of clustered cedar and locust trees and slash pines, children rode bicycles among trailers and shacks where no one ever responded to a knock on a door without first checking to see who the visitor was.

"Where's the vic?" I said.

Top picked up a rock and threw it at a dog that was slinking through the Johnson grass toward the back of a tin-sided tractor shed. "Still need to ask?"

"What's that smell?"

"You don't want to know."

I took a flashlight from my glove box and walked to the rear of the shed. I have investigated many homicides over the years. They're all bad and none are easy to look at. Rarely does a fictionalized treatment do them justice. The physical details vary, but the most unforgettable image in any homicide is the stark sense of violation and theft and utter helplessness in the victim's face. I knew all these things before I rounded the corner of the shed. But I wasn't prepared for what I saw. I stepped backward, a handkerchief pressed to my mouth, the victim's remains glistening in the beam of my flashlight.

The murder weapon was undoubtedly a shotgun, discharged within inches of the face, the shells probably loaded with double-aught bucks. The victim's right jaw had been blown away, exposing his teeth and tongue. His skullcap had been splattered on the shed wall in a spray of white bone and brain matter. The shooter had put at least one round into the victim's stomach, virtually disemboweling him. Feral dogs had done the rest. A chrome-plated .25-caliber automatic lay amid a network of dandelions, just beyond the tips of the victim's right hand. In the distance, I saw the flashers of emergency vehicles coming hard down the road.

I went back to my truck and pulled on a pair of polyethylene gloves and stuck three Ziploc bags in my back pocket, although I would have to wait for the crime scene photographer to be done before I picked up any evidence.

"Got any idea who he is?" Top asked.

I didn't answer.

"Streak?" he said.

"I'm not sure, Top," I said.

But it was hard to ignore the victim's Ralph Lauren shirt, his girlish hips, and his curly brown hair, sun-bleached on the tips, probably by many hours on a tennis court. I squatted down next to him and eased his wallet out of his back pocket, swiping at a cloud of gnats in my face.

The wallet was fat with a sheaf of hundred-dollar bills. I slipped the driver's license out of a leather slot for plastic cards and shined my light on it. Then I realized I had almost stepped on two twelve-gauge shell casings that lay just behind me, perhaps five feet out from the shed wall. I rose from the ground and kept my face turned into the breeze, away from the odor that caused my nostrils to clench up each time I breathed it. Helen Soileau and Koko Hebert were walking toward me through the grass.

"You ID the vic?" Helen said.

"Yeah," I said, my voice thick.

Koko shined his light on the body. "We'll need a front-end loader to get the guy into a bag," he said.

Helen's eyes stayed fastened on my face.

I handed her Tony Lujan's driver's license. Blood from his wounds had seeped into his wallet and dried on his photograph. "I'll make the family notification, but I want backup when I do it," I said.

CHAPTER
11

Earlier that evening I had tried to get Monarch Little kicked loose on a weapons charge that in all probability would never have gone to trial, since the cut-down shotgun had been seized from his vehicle when he was not anywhere near it. My failure to get Monarch back on the street would probably remain the kindest deed I ever did for him.

People handle grief in different ways. I once looked into the eyes of a Vietnamese woman and realized that sorrow can sometimes possess a depth that goes deeper than the bottom of one's soul. I knew if I looked too long into this woman's eyes, I would drown in their luminosity and silence and lose the sunlight in my own life.

I believe Bello's sorrow was as great as that Vietnamese woman's, and I was almost thankful that as a primitive and ignorant man, he chose to channel it into rage and threats of violence against others, because then I didn't have to look into his eyes and see the depth of his loss.

He had met us at his front door, in a crimson robe and house slippers, a bowl of ice cream and blueberries in his hand. He looked at Helen and me and the two uniformed deputies with us and at the flasher lights pulsing on our vehicles, and I saw his jaw tighten and his nostrils swell with air. A college-age girl sat on the sofa behind him. She was the same person I had seen when I had first interviewed Tony Lujan at his house.

"What's happened to my boy?" Bello said.

"Can we come in?" I said.

"No, you tell me where my boy is," he replied.

"There's been a shooting out by the Boom Boom Room," I said. "We don't have a positive ID yet, but Tony's wallet and driver's license and credit cards were on the body. We're very sorry to tell you this, but we're pretty sure the victim is your son." Then I waited.

He set the bowl of ice cream on a stand by the door. "You get the fucking collard greens out of your mouth. What do you mean you found his wallet but you ain't sure about a positive ID?"

Bugs were swimming in the yellow glow of the porch light. The breeze had died and my clothes felt like damp burlap on my skin.

"The victim was killed with a shotgun. Positive ID will have to be made with fingerprints," I said.

I could see his face crinkling up, his bottom lip trembling. The girl rose from the sofa and placed her hand on his shoulder. She was slim and attractive, not more than twenty, with a narrow face, like a model's, and shiny chestnut hair that hung to her shoulders. "Maybe you ought to ask them to come in, Mr. Bello," she said.

Instead, he knotted my shirt in his fist. "It was that nigger, wasn't it? Tell me the troot, or I'll knock your fucking head into the driveway," he said.

"You'll release me or go to jail," I said.

But he twisted the fabric of my shirt tighter in his hand, at the same time pushing me out into the darkness. "That nigger killed my boy. You motherfuckers wouldn't do anything about him, and now he's killed my boy," he said.

Out of the corner of my eye, I saw Helen gesture at the two uniformed deputies. They were both big men who had been roughnecks on offshore oil rigs before they became police officers. But it took all of us, including Helen, to cuff Bello and get him in the backseat of a cruiser. When we closed the door on him, he broke out the window with his head and spit on me.

Helen took a section of paper towel from a roll on the seat of her cruiser and cleaned the spittle off my sleeve and wrist and back. She crumpled the towel and threw it in Bello's face. Then she stared down at him through the broken window, her hands on her hips, her fingers touching her slapjack. "We all grieve for your loss, Mr. Lujan, but everybody here is fed up with your abuse. You either act like a sensible human being or I'll pull the cuffs off you myself and beat the living shit out of you. Look into my face and tell me I won't do it."

He glared up at her, rheumy-eyed, his jaws unshaved, his face aged by ten years in the last ten minutes. "Y'all ain't understood me. The nigger called. He set my boy up."

"What?" Helen said.

"Ax Lydia up there on the porch. The nigger talked to her. He drove away to meet him."

"Who drove away?" I said.

"Tony. My son drove away to meet that nigger, Monarch Little."

Helen and I looked at each other. I walked back under the porch light. "You're Lydia?" I said to the girl standing there.

"Yes, sir," she replied.

"Let's go inside."

"I haven't done anything."

"I didn't say you had. Who else is here?"

"Mrs. Lujan. She's upstairs."

I left the door slightly ajar, so it wouldn't lock Helen out. Although I had been in the Lujan home briefly once before, I hadn't taken adequate note of its design and decor and the contradictions they suggested. The floors were maple that glowed with a honeylike radiance, the molding and window frames done with fine-grained recovered cypress that was probably two hundred years old. The rugs were an immaculate white, the couches made of soft leather that was the color of elephant hide. A lighted crystal chandelier hung over a mahogany table in the dining room, a silver bowl filled with water and floating camellias in the center. It was hard to believe that this was the home of Bello Lujan.

"A black guy called here earlier?" I said.

"Yes, sir, he said he was Monarch Little."

"You talked to him? You, yourself?"

"Yeah, I mean yes, sir. I was talking with him when Tony came home from UL. Tony was, like, a little drunk and maybe a little stoned, too. Then he drove off."

"Let's have a seat," I said, and took a notebook and pen from my shirt pocket. "What's your last name, Lydia?"

"Thibodaux. My father runs the restaurant at the new casino. I go to UL with Tony."

"Do you know Monarch Little personally? You know his voice when you hear it, Lydia?"

"I've seen him around." Her eyes became uncertain. She glanced at the closed front door, then up the stairs. "He sells dope. Like, if you want to score weed or Ex, everybody says he's the guy to see."

"What did Monarch say to you?"

"First, there's, like, all this rap music blaring in the background. I could hardly hear. I told him Tony wasn't home and he should call back later. He goes, 'Tell him I can prove the cops planted blood on his daddy's broken headlight. Tell him to call me back on this phone.' I go, 'Which phone?,' like, I'm supposed to know where he's calling from. Just then Tony comes in the door, blowing fumes all over the place."

"Tony talked to Monarch?"

"Yeah. No. He just listened. Then he took the phone away from his ear and looked at it, like Monarch had hung up on him or something."

"What did Tony say to you?"

"He went upstairs and got a bunch of cash out of his drawer. He said he'd be back in an hour. He said he was going to get Mr. Bello out of trouble. We were supposed to see *The Kingdom of Heaven*. If we had just gone to supper and the show, none of this would have happened. It's like bad things keep happening for no reason."

"Which bad things?"

"All the bad things that have happened to Tony and Mr. Bello." Her gaze was averted now, neutral in expression, as though she were distancing herself from her own statement.

I looked at my notes and the sequence of events she had described. I believed that Lydia Thibodaux was telling me elements of the truth about the events of that evening, but obviously not all of them. "Did you ever buy dope from Monarch, Lydia? Did you ever hear his voice up close?"

"I was with some people once who bought some from him on Ann Street, like where all those gangbangers hang out. Like maybe a year ago."

"You think Monarch is a dangerous dude?"

"That's what some people say."

"Then why would you and Mr. Bello not call the cops?"

"Sir?"

"You told Mr. Bello that Monarch had arranged to meet his son. You also knew Tony was stoned. Why would you and Mr. Bello let Tony walk into the lion's mouth with a wallet full of cash?"

She sucked in her cheeks and looked straight ahead, her hands folded demurely in her lap.

"Y'all were willing to let Tony suborn perjury?" I said.

"Do what?" she said, making a face.

"Bribe a man to lie."

She was disarmed and afraid now, confused about terminology and unsure about the implications of her own rhetoric. It was the kind of moment in an interview when you ask a question the subject is not expecting. "Did you date Tony?" I said.

"Sometimes we went out," she replied, momentarily relieved. Then her face clouded again. "I don't know what you mean by 'date.'"

"Yvonne Darbonne was about the same age as you. She had everything to live for. Can you tell me why she ended up shot to death, Lydia? Can you help us with that question? Why'd that young girl have to die?"

But Lydia Thibodaux's reply surprised me. "I don't know why. Tony didn't talk about her. He said they only went out a couple of times. I think it was more than that, though. I think Tony wasn't honest with me. I don't think I ever had a real chance with him. I loved Tony and—"

The events of the evening and her memories about Tony Lujan, whatever they were, seemed to take their toll all at once. I studied her face and the fatigue in it and the look of theft in her eyes and felt for the first time that night she was speaking the complete truth. I heard a board creak at the top of the stairs.

A woman in a wheelchair had pushed herself precariously close to the edge of the landing and was trying to see beyond the angle into the living room. Her skin was as white as milk, as though the blood had been drained from her veins or her skin denied exposure to sunlight. Her legs were wasted, her arms marked with the bruises of someone who has had long-term intravenous injections. She kept peering around the edge of the banister, like a person rarely allowed a glimpse of the larger world.

"Who's down there, please?" she said. "I saw the emergency lights outside. Has Tony been hurt?"

WE FOUND TONY LUJAN'S silver Lexus in the morning, parked inside a cluster of persimmon trees and water oaks a hundred yards from the crime scene. We also found impressions of multiple vehicles in the Johnson grass behind the tractor shed where Tony died. Early Tuesday morning Mack Bertrand went to work on the crime scene, the two discharged shotgun shells I had picked up by Tony's body, and the cut-down double-barrel the firemen had found inside Monarch's burned-out automobile.

Mack was one of the most thorough forensic chemists I had ever known. He didn't speculate, take shortcuts, or complain when he was obviously overloaded. In many instances, he worked holidays and canceled his own vacation time when we needed evidence to get a genuine bad guy off the streets in a hurry. But by the same token, he would not cooperate with a zealous and politically ambitious district attorney who wanted the evidence skewed in the prosecution's favor. The latter tendency sometimes got him in trouble.

At noon he came into my office, his white shirt crinkling, his hair wet and neatly combed, his ever present briar pipe nestled in a pouch he carried on his belt. "I'll treat you to lunch at Victor's," he said.

"You got it, Mack," I said.

We strolled toward Main Street together. The wind was up and white clouds were rolling overhead, marbling the crypts in St. Peter's Cemetery. "The cut-down double-barrel from Monarch Little's car is the weapon that fired the two twelve-gauge hulls y'all found at the crime scene," he said.

"You're that sure?" I said. Identification of shell casings doesn't come close to the precise science associated with identification of a bullet that has been fired through the spiral grooves inside the barrel of a pistol or a rifle.

"Reasonably sure on one round. Absolutely sure on the second one. The right-hand firing pin on the cut-down has a tiny steel burr on it. The pin is slightly damaged or offset as well. It leaves an almost imperceptible notch when it strikes the shell. I tested the right-hand firing pin five times, and the notch appeared in exactly the same place on the casing each time. Same notch, same position. There's no way those shells were fired by another shotgun."

"How about Monarch's prints?" I asked.

"Not his, not anybody's."

We were almost past the cemetery now. Mack kept his face straight ahead as we crossed the street, his necktie flapping in the wind.

"No one's?" I said.

"Yeah, that's what I said. There was some fire-retardant foam on the barrel but not on the stock. In my opinion, that gun was thoroughly wiped down. You might talk to the firemen."

"Firemen don't wipe down guns taken from burning vehicles," I said.

"That's my point."

I had said Mack didn't speculate. He didn't. But he was a man of conscience and he brought attention to situations that didn't add up.

"In other words, why would Monarch Little go to the trouble of wiping his prints off a weapon used in a homicide and then leave it in his automobile for anyone to find?" I said.

"What do I know?" he said.

"What else did you come up with from the crime scene?"

"No latents on the shells you recovered. The twenty-five auto was fully loaded and not fired recently. It's Italian junk and appears to be unregistered. The tire impressions on the Johnson grass came from a number of vehicles. I think a couple of hookers from the Boom Boom Room use that area to reduce their motel overhead. I must have found a dozen used condoms in the weeds."

"Is the post in yet?" I asked.

"No, why?"

"I was wondering what number shot the shooter used."

"I dug some lead out of the shed wall. Double-aught bucks," Mack said.

In my mind's eye I saw Dallas Klein kneeling on a sidewalk, just before somebody fired a load of the same numbered shot into his face. Mack caught my expression. "Heavy stuff," I said.

"That model shotgun hasn't been manufactured for two decades. There's no registration on the serial number," Mack continued. "The rust buildup where the barrels were cut off suggest somebody probably hacksawed them off years ago. There's little powder residue in the mechanisms and the wear on the firing pins is minimal. I'd say it's been fired only a few times."

"So it appears to have had only one function—to serve as an illegal firearm?"

"If that means anything," he replied.

"You don't make Monarch for this, do you?"

"A guy who sells crystal to his own people, including high school kids? I'd make Monarch Little for anything. I'm just giving you the arithmetic."

But I knew Mack better than that. While we waited for a light to change, he began scraping at the bowl of his pipe with a small penknife, blowing the crust off the blade, away from his person. It was warm and cool at the same time in the sunlight, the air smelling like rain and dust. "Lonnie Marceaux called me this morning," he said. "He's ready to rock with Monarch. I told him what I just told you."

"You told him the lack of latents on the murder weapon didn't add up with the fact it was left on the floor of Monarch's car for a fireman to find?"

"Not in so many words, but Lonnie got the drift. I don't think he liked what he heard. You ever go up against a left-handed pitcher who was always pulling at his belt or the bill of his cap?"

"Look for a Vaseline ball?"

"With Lonnie, more like a forkball between the lamps," he replied.

A downpour broke just as we reached Victor's. We went inside and joined the noontime crowd.

HIGH-PROFILE TRIALS are high-profile because they are usually emblematic of causes and issues far greater in cultural and social importance than the individuals whose immediate lives are involved. In western Kansas, amid an ocean of green wheat, two sociopaths invade a home looking for a money cache that doesn't exist and end up butchering a farm family whose members possessed all the virtues we admire. The story shocks and captivates the entire country because the farm family is us. A black ex–football player appears to be dead-bang guilty of slicing up two innocent people but skates because the jury hates the Los Angeles Police Department. A female culinary celebrity who profits from insider stock-trading information takes the bounce for Enron executives who ruined the lives of tens of thousands of retirees. That's the nature of theater. The same horrendous crimes, committed by nonrepresentative individuals, draw no attention whatsoever. Every attorney knows this, every cop, every police reporter. Sometimes justice is done, sometimes not.

But in the meantime major careers get made or destroyed. Lonnie Marceaux had called me at 8:05 that morning and had gotten as much raw information from me as possible about the murder of Tony Lujan.

After I returned from lunch at Victor's, Helen and I reported for a meeting with Lonnie in the prosecutor's office. The surprise was not the fact he had called a meeting immediately following the Lujan homicide. The surprise was the fact Betsy Mossbacher had been invited and that she showed up on such short notice. As a rule, FBI agents cannot be accused of having great amounts of humility when it comes to dealing with state and local law enforcement. But she arrived in the hallway one minute before the meeting was to commence, wearing jeans, boots, and an orange shirt tucked inside a wide leather belt. It was sprinkling outside, and there were drops of water in her hair. She brushed them onto the floor, then dried her hand on her jeans. "Phew, how many times does the weather change in one day here?" she said.

"South Louisiana is a giant sponge. That's why we keep in constant motion. If you stand still, you'll either sink or be eaten alive by giant insects," I said.

Betsy Mossbacher laughed, but Helen remained stone-faced and silent, obviously because of her resentment over Betsy Mossbacher's early reference to her as a member of what she called "the tongue-and-groove club."

"How are you, Sheriff Soileau?" Betsy said.

"Fine. How's life at the Bureau?" Helen replied.

"Oh, we chase the ragheads around. You know how it is."

"*What?*" Helen said.

"I just wanted to see if you were listening," Betsy said.

Great start for the afternoon, I thought.

But personality conflicts were not really on my mind. The fact that Lonnie Marceaux had called a meeting with Helen prematurely in the investigation of the Lujan homicide, even inviting an FBI agent to attend, meant the purpose was entirely political. More specifically, it meant the purpose was entirely about the career of Lonnie Marceaux.

After we were seated in his office on the second floor of the courthouse, he closed the door and sat down in his swivel chair, leaning backward, stretching out his long legs, as though he were entering a moment of profound thought, his scalp glistening through his crew cut. Behind him was a fine overview of the old part of town and the enormous live oaks that arched over small frame houses.

"Thanks for coming today. I've already gotten some feedback from our forensic chemist, Mack Bertrand, and our coroner, Koko Hebert," he said, his gaze lingering a moment on Betsy Mossbacher's casual dress. "I'm afraid this case is going to have some racial overtones we don't need. That means we need to move forward with as much dispatch as possible and keep things in perspective, which translates into keeping them simple." He glanced again at Betsy Mossbacher, probably to see if she was aware of the deference he had shown her by using people's titles so she could follow the discussion. "Has Koko talked to you yet, Dave?"

"No, he hasn't," I replied.

"Well, there's not a lot in the post we don't already know. Tony

Lujan was murdered with buckshot fired at him from almost point-blank range. Koko thinks he was hit four times, which means that whoever did it probably bore Tony a special hatred. Mack's report on the twelve-gauge found in Monarch Little's car is absolute in its conclusions. The cut-down twelve is the murder weapon."

"How about the lack of latents?" I said.

"What about it?"

"Monarch wiped off his gun, then left it lying on the floor of his car, just before somebody tossed a truck flare on the seat?"

Lonnie scratched the back of his head with one finger. "I don't believe the absence of latents is particularly unusual, especially with a career street mutt like Monarch. With these guys, wiping down a gun is probably an automatic reflex. Plus, I don't think Monarch is that bright. Also, he had no way of knowing the gun has a defective firing pin that leaves a singular mark on a shell casing. After he did the Lujan kid, he probably thought he was home free. What do you think, Helen?"

"I haven't talked with Mack or read his report. I don't have an opinion," she said.

"Can you get on that ASAP?" Lonnie said.

"Soon as I get out of this meeting," she replied.

Lonnie looked at her, searching for second meaning in her statement.

"I get the sense we're already narrowing down the investigation to one suspect," I said.

"Wrong. Right now we're talking about a 'person of interest,' and his name happens to be Monarch Little. He's in jail, too, and that's where he needs to stay," Lonnie said.

"I've just started to track the victim's movements and whereabouts preceding his death," I said. "I've talked on the phone to two of his fraternity brothers and I'm going to interview them in person at three o'clock. Evidently Tony Lujan went over to St. John's Cathedral in Lafayette yesterday and talked to a priest, or at least was playing pitch-and-catch with him. The fraternity brothers said Tony was agitated and depressed and maybe wanted to unload his conscience about something."

"Of course he was depressed. He was supposed to be in my office today and either take the fall for Crustacean Man or let his father go down for it."

"Let me finish here, if I can," I said, blinking to show I didn't intend offense, that the problem was my own inability to speak succinctly and not Lonnie's imperious attitude. "I also have the impression he was doing some weed and drinking. In other words, he was in an impaired state when he talked to the caller who identified himself as Monarch Little. The only semireliable witness we have in the moments leading up to Tony's death is a part-time girlfriend by the name of Lydia Thibodaux. She says she talked to Monarch when he called Tony's house to set up the meeting, but she gets pretty vague when it comes to actual voice identification. I have a sense—"

"Have you gotten the Lujans' telephone records?" Lonnie interrupted.

"There were three calls to the house yesterday afternoon. One from a solicitor, one to confirm a pizza order, and one from a pay phone. The pay phone was—"

"I don't think you're reading me correctly, Dave. We're going to examine every possible lead in this case, but it's going to be done in an expeditious way, without any foot-dragging. I'm not going to let this turn into a racial issue, and everybody in this room knows that's what's going to happen if Monarch Little has his way. I'm not letting the do-gooders and the ACLU use us for their agenda, either."

"Hear me out, Lonnie. Tony's roommate was Slim Bruxal. So far I haven't been able to find him. He was gone from the fraternity house yesterday and his father claims he hasn't seen him since last week. Slim and some other fraternity kids followed Tony to St. John's and found him playing pitch-and-catch with the priest. Before we start dropping the jailhouse on Monarch's head, we need to get Slim Bruxal in here and find out what he was doing when Tony was killed."

I could tell Lonnie didn't like my bringing up Slim Bruxal's name in front of Betsy Mossbacher, in all probability because he planned to launch his own investigation into Whitey Bruxal's ties with racketeering and exclude the FBI.

"So haul his ass in here. But what you're going to get from Slim Bruxal is shit and you know it," Lonnie said.

"You'll have to excuse me for being a bit dense, but can you explain to me why I've been invited here?" Betsy said.

"Professional courtesy, Agent Mossbacher," Lonnie replied. "You were in the process of moving Monarch into Witness Protection. In my opinion, that process has become a moot issue. We'll cooperate in every way we can with your investigation into racketeering inside the gaming industry, but right now we have a homicide to deal with. In case you're interested, at age eighteen Monarch was probably involved in the shooting death of a man who was watering his lawn on Easter morning. He also set fire to the house of a city policeman."

"That's interesting. I wonder why he's been on the street all this time," she replied.

Lonnie grinned and glanced out the window, as though he were checking the weather. "You forced Monarch to file charges against the Bruxal boy in order to get at his father. That makes perfect sense. But now it looks like your confidential informant or whatever you want to call him has committed a homicide in an extortion attempt gone bad. So you're going to have to go after Whitey Bruxal on your own, or at least without strings on Monarch Little. He's our problem now and we're going to handle him and *it* from now on out."

He turned away from her and looked back at me and Helen. "I'd like to talk with both of you again by close of business today. Media are already all over this, and there's at least one alternative newspaper in Lafayette that loves to throw matches at gasoline. We're not going to let this turn into a gangbanger and race issue. This is not Los Angeles or New Orleans. Our tourism is booming and I plan to see that it stays that way. This is a good city. Our streets aren't going to be turned into free-fire zones because of one black asshole and a spoiled white kid who probably ran over a homeless man and left him to die on the road."

It was obvious he was proselytizing about local concerns in order to exclude Betsy Mossbacher from the conversation and encourage her to leave the meeting. But it didn't work.

"No disrespect meant, Mr. Marceaux, but do you believe either

the Bureau or the DOJ is going to change its policies because of anything said at this meeting?"

"I'm trying to be candid about our priorities, Agent Mossbacher.
You and your people can do whatever you want. That's how you usually operate anyway, isn't it?"

Betsy Mossbacher got up from her chair, then reached down for
her purse. Her bright, straw-colored hair was still damp on the tips
and stuck to the back of her neck. "You don't have your brand on
that black kid's backside. He's still a confidential informant cooperating with a federal investigation, and he'd better be regarded as such
by your office. In my opinion, you're pushing your own investigators
to come to conclusions they're not ready to make. I'm going to take
official note of all this, so don't be surprised if you invite a civil rights
beef you didn't have before you called this meeting."

Lonnie pinched his eyes and pretended to suppress a yawn. "I hear
you. Glad you dropped by. Let me get the door for you," he said, rising from his chair.

Then I witnessed one of those rare moments, in a male-dominated
environment, when a woman can wrap herself in her own integrity
and create an impregnable shield around herself. Lonnie had pulled
open the door and was waiting for Betsy Mossbacher to leave, but
she didn't. Instead, she stood silently, five feet from the door's thresh-
old, waiting for his pantomime to end, her eyes focused into the hallway. He tried to wait her out, then realized he had been trapped into
making a fool of himself.

He eased the door closed. "I beg your pardon, Agent Mossbacher," he said, and returned to his desk.

"No problem," she said. Then she opened the door for herself and
closed it behind her.

I saw a tug at the corner of Helen Soileau's mouth.

Lonnie cleared his throat and fiddled with a ballpoint pen on his
desk. "I want to say something for the record. I believe Monarch did
Bello Lujan's boy. But I'm going to leave that determination up to
y'all. That said, there's obviously a much larger story at work here.
Those federal agents wouldn't take the time to spit on us if we were
burning to death. They want Whitey Bruxal in a cage and maybe

Bello Lujan, too. I suspect the Mossbacher woman is a closet liberal who wants to bring down this televangelical lobbyist Colin Alridge. It's my position we don't need the goddamn federal government to do any of the aforementioned. Bruxal has tried to bribe two or three people to get his video poker machines into Iberia Parish. That puts him in our jurisdiction. Y'all with me on this?"

"I haven't thought it all through, Lonnie," I said.

"Glad to see such a positive attitude. How about you, Helen?"

"To tell the truth, I think I should have been reading Mack's report and the post on Tony Lujan rather than attending this meeting," she said. "I'll get back to you ASAP."

It wasn't the best of days for Lonnie Marceaux.

A few minutes later, as I was checking out a cruiser to go to Lafayette, I saw Helen make a point of speaking to Betsy Mossbacher at the entrance to the courthouse. Helen saw me watching her, just before she headed back to her office.

"Don't say a word," she said.

"My mind was totally blank," I said.

Then a laugh coughed out of her throat. "That Calamity Jane is something else, isn't she?"

LATER, I INTERVIEWED the Catholic priest at St. John's who threw baseballs through church windows. I also interviewed a collection of fraternity kids who until the previous day had believed inclusion in a whites-only non-Jewish social organization could protect them from death. I still couldn't find Slim Bruxal. The only light moment in the afternoon came when I was leaving the interview with the priest. He asked me if I would like to catch a few grounders with him. And I said why not.

CHAPTER
12

I WOKE AT FIVE-THIRTY the next morning to the sound of mock-ingbirds in the trees and a boat with a deep draft working its way downstream from the drawbridge at Burke Street. Our home was a wonderful place to wake on an early summer morning. Sometimes ground fog hung on the bayou, and inside it I would hear a gator slap its tail in the lily pads or a nutria or a muskrat roll off a cypress knee into the water. Sometimes I imagined I saw Confederate longboats, sharpshooters humped low inside, the oars muffled, floating silently with the current toward the Yankees' skirmish line at Nelson's Canal.

It didn't matter what the weather was like. Morning with Molly and Snuggs and Tripod was always a grand time, and the arrival of the day had little to do with clocks. Just before first light I would hear the milkman crossing the lawn, fat bottles of cream clinking in his wire basket, then a solid thump on the ceiling when Snuggs dropped from an oak limb onto the roof, right above our bedroom. Molly would stir in her sleep, her hip rounded by the sheet, her hot rump brushing against me. I would put my fingers in her hair, trace them down her shoulders and back, and along the deep curve in her waist. I'd kiss her baby fat and the two red sun moles below her navel. I'd kiss her breasts and stomach and mouth and eyes, then slip her close against me, burying my face in the thick smell of her hair.

When she made love, she did it without stint or reservation or buried resentment because of a cross word or imagined slight. Molly's charity and smile followed her into bed, and in the morning her skin

gave off a warm fragrance just like flowers in a garden. In the blue-
ness of the dawn I would hear the steady rhythm of her breath in my
ear while Miss Ellen Deschamps called to her cats from her back
porch, and I would start the day with the absolute knowledge that no
evil could hold sway in our lives.

When I got to the office, the investigation into the murder of Tony
Lujan awaited me in a way I didn't expect. Wally had written a name
and a cell number on a pink message slip and had put it in my mailbox. At the bottom of the slip he had penciled the notation: "Call him
between 9:15 and 10."

"Who's J. J. Castille?" I said.

"Some colletch kid."

"Which college kid?"

"He says you was at his fraternity house yesterday."

"Wally, I'd really appreciate it if you didn't present information in
teaspoons."

His shirt pocket was fat with cellophane-wrapped cigars, which he
rolled around in his mouth but never lighted because of his high blood
pressure. "The kid, J. J. Castille, says he's in class till nine-fifteen. He
says you saw him at his fraternity house yesterday but you didn't talk
to him. He says he wants to talk wit' you now. That's how come he
called the office."

"Thank you."

"He also said not to call him at the fraternity house. He said use
the cell. That's why I wrote down the cell number on the note.
Anyt'ing else I can interpret for you?"

"No, that's just fine."

"You sure?"

In the army or prison, you learn not to make enemies with anyone
in records or the kitchen. In law enforcement, you don't admonish
your dispatcher.

As I walked to my office, I couldn't put a face with the name on
the message slip. But I did remember a thin-chested kid at Tony's fraternity house who had hung in the background, his expression full of
conflict. At 9:20 a.m. I punched J. J. Castille's cell number into my
desk phone.

"Hello?" a voice said. In the background I could hear music and many voices talking and the clatter of dishes.

"This is Detective Dave Robicheaux with the Iberia Parish Sheriff's Department. I'm returning a call made by J. J. Castille. Are you Mr. Castille?"

"Yes, sir. I need to talk with you."

"Is this about Tony Lujan?"

"Yeah, I guess."

"You guess?"

"It's about him and Slim Bruxal. It's about something they were saying at the house. Maybe it's not important." The pitch of his voice dropped when he mentioned Bruxal's name.

"It's important," I said.

"I can't talk here."

"Do you have a car?"

"No, sir."

"I'll come over there. Where do you want to meet?"

He didn't reply immediately. "I just thought I should pass it on."

"I understand that. You're doing the right thing, partner. Just tell me where you want to meet."

"You know the UL campus?"

"I went to school there."

"I'll be between Cypress Lake and the music building."

I checked out an unmarked car, clamped a magnetized flasher on the roof, and was at the campus in under thirty minutes. I pulled into a driveway between a cypress-dotted lake and the old brick music building known as Burke Hall. I saw a kid squatted down on the bank, tossing crumbs from a hot dog bun to a school of perch that popped and roiled the surface when they took the bread. His brown hair grew on his neck and hung in his eyes, and he wore a T-shirt that was washed so thin it looked like cheesecloth hanging on his shoulders.

He rose to greet me but didn't shake hands. Instead, he looked over his shoulder at the elevated walkway that led into the Student Union.

"You going to summer school, J.J.?" I said.

"Yeah, but I work in the cafeteria, too. A lot of guys take off for the summer, but I want to get through premed early so's I can go on to Tulane. I got a scholarship through the Naval ROTC program there."

He had clean features and brown eyes that were too large for his face and a pronounced Cajun accent. He looked back over his shoulder again. Through the cypress trees I could see kids walking in and out of the building.

"No one is paying any attention to us, J.J. Want to tell me what this is about? My boss doesn't want me gone from the office too long." I tried to smile.

"I was studying across the hallway from Slim and Tony's room the day Tony got murdered. Our doors were open and I could hear them talking about the guy who was run over on the road. Slim kept calling him 'the wino.' He said the wino died 'cause he walked out in front of a car."

"Tony's car?"

J.J. thought about it. "No, he said 'a car.' Slim said winos walked out in front of cars all the time and got killed and nobody cared. Then Tony said, 'That's not what happened, Slim.'"

He blew out his breath.

"What else did they say?"

"Nothing. Slim closed the door. Slim's a rough guy. He's not supposed to have the top room, but nobody says anything about it."

I gave him my business card. "If you remember anything else, call me again, will you? But right now it's important to remember you did the right thing. You don't have any reason to feel guilty or ashamed or afraid. Do you know where Slim Bruxal is now?"

"He was back at the house this morning. He said he'd been in New Orleans with a girl."

"Slim's at the house now?"

"Far as I know. Am I going to have to testify in court?"

"I'm not sure. Would you be willing to do that?"

He cleared his throat and didn't answer.

"Did you know Yvonne Darbonne?" I asked.

"She came to the house with Tony once or twice. At least I think it was with Tony. I really didn't know her." He looked at me briefly, then his eyes left mine. The wind was cool blowing through the cypress trees on the lake, but his skin was flushed, his forehead shiny with perspiration.

"What are you not telling me?" I said.

"They say she pulled a train."

"She did a gang bang?"

"They call it 'pulling a train.' They say she was wiped out of her head and took on a bunch of guys upstairs in the house. It was after a kegger or something. There was a lot of Ecstasy and acid floating around. The way these guys talked, Tony didn't know about it. I heard she was messed up in the head and committed suicide."

"Yeah, she did. But she wasn't messed up before she met Tony Lujan. Did she pull the train the day she died?"

"I don't know. I wasn't there. I work and study all the time. I don't know who the guys were, either. There's stuff goes on at the house I don't get mixed up in."

The lake was dark in the shade, wrinkled by the wind, the hyacinths blooming with yellow flowers out in the sunlight. "You seem like a good guy, J.J. Why do you hang around with a collection of shits like this bunch?"

"They're not all bad."

"Maybe not. But enough of them are. Come see me in New Iberia if you want to go fishing sometime. In the meantime, hang on to my business card, okay?" I said.

I DROVE DIRECTLY to the fraternity house. Two kids were raking leaves in the front yard when I walked up to the porch. "Is Slim here?" I said.

"Out back," one of them replied, hardly looking up from his work.

"Did he just get back from New Orleans?" I said, checking J. J. Castille's story.

"Search me," the same kid said.

I walked around the side of the house into the backyard. The St.

Augustine grass was uncut, the yard enclosed by thick hedges, the sunshine filtered by pecan and oak trees. Slim Bruxal stood below a speed bag that was mounted on the crossbar of two iron stanchions. He wore a workout shirt that had been scissored into strips and gym shoes and a pair of string-tie gym shorts low on his hips. His fists looked as hard and tight as apples inside his red gloves as he turned the speed bag into a blur, *tada-tada-tada-tada,* the exposed skin on his back crisscrossed with sweat.

"You're a hard man to find," I said.

He turned and looked at me, his eyes hot, his brow knitted, like someone pulling himself out of an angry thought. He removed his right glove by clamping it under his left arm, then extended his hand. "How you doing, Mr. Robicheaux?"

I turned away from him, as though I were distracted by the blowing of a car horn on the street, my hand at my side. "You were with your girl the last couple of days?"

"Girl? I was seeing my therapist in New Orleans. She's also a grief counselor," he replied, lowering his hand.

"Can I have her name and number?"

"What for?"

"We're trying to exclude everyone we can in our investigation into Tony's death. That's so we can concentrate on nailing the right guy."

He gave me a woman's name and a phone number in the Garden District, up St. Charles Avenue.

"You want the right guy?" he said. "He looks like a pile of soggy meat loaf with warts on it. I hear he's sitting on his fat black ass in your jail."

"When was the last time you saw Tony?"

"I think you already know that."

"Pretend I don't."

"We took him for a couple of beers Monday afternoon. We tried to cheer him up. Then he left the bar and drove back to New Iberia."

"Was anyone with him?"

"No, sir." He blotted his face with a towel and tossed the towel on the grass. The sun was directly in his eyes, making it even harder for him to hide his irritability. "Look, Tony was my friend. I don't like being under the microscope for this. He was depressed and we were worried about him. One of the guys had seen him playing baseball with a priest at St. John's. So we went over there and tried to cheer him up. Then he ends up being killed by this animal Monarch Little."

"Yeah, I can see how you're frustrated by all this. But something doesn't flush here."

"Flush?"

"Yeah, there's one element in your story that bothers me."

"Bothers *you*. My best friend is dead and *you're* bothered?" he replied, his mask slipping, his face hot and glistening in the sun's glare.

"You said you were worried about Tony's being depressed. So you tracked him down at a church where he was playing baseball with a minister and took him to a bar. You removed him from an environment where he might have gotten some genuine help. Does that sound reasonable to you?"

"I'm not knocking anybody's church."

"Nobody said you were. But between you and me, I think you're trying to put the slide on me. You wouldn't do that, would you?"

He tried to shine me on, his face suffusing with feigned goodwill and humility.

"What happened to Yvonne Darbonne? Were you one of the dudes who gangbanged her?" I said.

"I don't have to take this," he said.

"You're right, you don't. Keep up the work on the speed bag. You look good. I know the boxing coach up at Angola. His best middleweight got shanked in the shower. He'd love to have you on the team."

"Don't patronize me, Mr. Robicheaux. I'm not Tony Lujan." He tilted his chin up when he spoke.

AS SOON AS I GOT BACK to the office, I received a call from Mack Bertrand at the lab. "Monarch Little's prints were on the pay phone that was used to call the Lujan house Monday evening," he said.

"How many other prints were on it?"

"Six sets that were identifiable, all belonging to people with criminal records."

"The phone is on the corner where he hangs out?"

"Right," he said.

"It's another nail in Monarch's coffin, but it's still circumstantial."

"How'd you make out in your meeting with Lonnie Marceaux?"

"I think Lonnie found a horse he can ride all the way to Washington."

"Have you talked to Helen since you got back from Lafayette?"

"Not yet," I said.

"She got a call from *The New York Times* this morning. Somebody leaked a story about a possible local investigation into this televangelical character who's mixed up with Whitey Bruxal."

But I really wasn't interested in Lonnie's attempts to manipulate the media. "Do you still have DNA swabs from the autopsy on Yvonne Darbonne?" I asked.

"Yeah, why?"

"I believe her death was a homicide."

"I respect what you say, Dave, but this time I'm on Koko Hebert's side. Yvonne Darbonne shot herself."

"Maybe she pulled the trigger. But others helped her do it."

"Want to drive yourself crazy? You've found the perfect way to do it," he said.

A few minutes later I went down to Helen's office and told her about my interviews with J. J. Castille and Slim Bruxal. She listened silently, occasionally making a note on a legal pad, waiting until I finished before she spoke. "You think maybe in this instance things aren't that complicated after all?" she asked, her eyes on the top of her pencil as she drew a little doodle on the pad.

"What do you mean?"

"That Monarch did it. He was resentful, needed money, and miserable in his role as a federal snitch. So he figured he'd score a few bucks off a rich white boy and get even at the same time. Except the rich white boy took a gun to the meeting spot and Monarch blew him apart."

"It's not that simple. According to J. J. Castille, Slim Bruxal and

Tony had specific knowledge about the death of the hit-and-run on Crustacean Man. I think Bruxal is a player in this."

"Right now we're talking about Tony Lujan, not Crustacean Man. You don't like fraternity kids, Dave. I don't think you're entirely objective about this case."

"I'm not objective about this particular group of fraternity kids, so lay off it, Helen. In my view, the kids who gangbanged Yvonne Darbonne are one cut above sociopaths."

"All right, bwana."

"All right what?"

"You made your point."

I was sitting in a chair in front of her desk. I got up and went to the window behind her, an act a subordinate in a sheriff's office would not normally do. But Helen and I had been friends and investigative partners long before she became sheriff. "Lonnie leaked the story to *The New York Times*?" I said.

"Probably," she replied.

"What did you tell the reporter when he called?"

"That I loved their gardening and culinary articles."

"What did he say to that?"

"It was a she. She sounded cute, too." She looked up and winked. You didn't put the slide on Helen Soileau.

EVEN THOUGH MONARCH LITTLE might have turned federal informant, he was still considered a high flight risk by the parish court and his bail on the illegal weapons charge had been set at seventy-five thousand dollars. He had also been transferred to the parish prison, an institution that earned itself a degree of national notoriety in the early 1990s for a practice known as "detention chair confinement" and the gagging of bound prisoners.

Just before quitting time, I drove through the gates of the prison compound, the coils of razor wire atop the fences trembling with a silvery light. I hung my badge holder on my belt, checked my holstered .45 at the admissions counter, and asked that Monarch be brought out to an interview room.

When I began my career in law enforcement, walking a beat in the lower Magazine area with Clete Purcel, a career house creep who had pulled time twice in Arkansas, considered years ago to be the worst of the worst among American prison systems, told me he had learned character in jail. Because of my youth and inexperience, I thought his remark grandiose if not ridiculous. But like most cops, I came to respect the dues that a stand-up or "solid con" has to pay. For an individual to survive the system with his integrity and personal identity intact requires enormous amounts of physical courage, humility, wisdom about people, and the ability to eat pain without resenting oneself. The era of the redneck gunbull may have slipped into history, but the atavistic and sexual energies of people in captivity have not. Ask any fish what his first shower experience was like after he wised off to the wrong guy.

Lonnie Marceaux had said Monarch wasn't particularly bright. He was wrong. Monarch had a wolf's intelligence and could sniff weakness, fear, or strength in an adversary in the same way an animal does. And even though he acted the role of a smart-ass with me, in the can he showed respect to inmates and prison personnel alike. More important, he never violated a confidence and never ratted out another inmate, even if his silence cost him lockdown or isolation.

At least that had been his reputation before word reached the parish prison that Monarch was no longer an inner-city king but just another hump on a federal pad.

A turnkey walked him down a corridor to the interview room, Monarch outfitted in jailhouse orange. He was also draped in waist and leg chains.

"Why the traveling junkyard, Cap?" I said.

"District attorney's orders," the turnkey replied.

"I'd appreciate your unhooking him," I said.

"Can't do it, Streak. Holler on the gate when you're done."

After the turnkey was gone, Monarch sat down in a wood chair, his chains tinkling, his manacled hands locked against his torso. "This gonna take long? They serving supper in a few minutes," he said.

"You in lockup?"

"Gen pop. Ain't axed for lockup."

"Some bad dudes in general pop."

"Yeah, most of them use to work for me. Come on, Mr. Dee. You got better t'ings to do, ain't you?"

"They're about to put a homicide jacket on you, Monarch."

"Like you ain't part of it?"

"You have a violent history. Dusting a rich white boy wouldn't be inconsistent with some of your past behavior."

My statement was simplistic. In truth, I wanted him to contradict it.

"You talking about that drive-by on the dude who said he was gonna cook me in a pot?"

"He put up a kite on you, then got capped watering his grass."

"He got capped 'cause he stepped on some dago's dope so many times there wasn't nothing left of it but baby laxative."

"You burned down a police officer's house."

Monarch twisted a crick out of his neck, his chains clinking, his manacled hands rolling into balls at his sides. "There use to be a cop 'round here liked to run black girls in for soliciting, even when they wasn't soliciting. Except they didn't end up down at the jail. They ended up copping his stick in the back of his cruiser. So a fire broke out under his house one night. Too bad he wasn't home."

"Where'd you get the cut-down that was in your car?"

"You seen it?"

"Yeah, in an evidence locker."

"Then you know more about it than I do, 'cause I ain't never seen it and I ain't got no idea how it got in my car. You a smart cop. The FBI was already jamming me. Why would I leave a sawed-off shotgun in my car?"

"You called Tony's house and tried to extort money from him. Your prints were on the pay phone where the call was made. You set up a meet with Tony. Your voice has been identified."

"I ain't called nobody. I'm t'rew here. Tell the screw I'm ready to go eat. Y'all got a nigger in the box. Y'all ain't gonna look for nobody else."

"That's a lie."

"Where you been, man? I'm sitting here in chains. I ain't did nothing. Whoever smoked that white boy is laughing at y'all." He stood up from his chair. "On the gate!" he yelled, his love handles bunching over his waist chain.

IN THE MORNING I got lucky. Wally buzzed my phone and told me a kid by the name of J. J. Castille was in the waiting room and wanted to see me.

"Send him up," I said.

"He's got a package in his hand. He wouldn't tell me what it was."

"I know him. He's okay."

"He's on his way."

A moment later J.J. tapped on my glass and I motioned him inside. "You want to go fishing?" I asked.

"I got something here I thought you might want. I don't know if it's important or not. But I don't feel good about a lot of things that have happened at the house. Anyway, here it is." He set a rectangular object on my desk. It was wrapped in brown paper and taped down at the edges.

I told him to have a chair, then began unwrapping the paper.

"I work for room and board at the house, and I'm supposed to clean up all the junk and loose trash people leave behind at the end of each semester," he said. "So I found a boxful of junk down in the basement, and that videocassette was in there. I started to throw it out, then I thought maybe somebody tossed it in there by mistake. So I stuck it in the VCR and watched a little bit of it. I'm probably wasting your time."

"Let's take a look," I said.

We went downstairs to a small room that contained a computer, a fax and Xerox machine, and a television set that we used to view surveillance videos. I shoved J.J.'s cassette into the VCR. A collage of meaningless scenes appeared on the screen—a crowd of revelers at a sports bar, Mardi Gras floats, a kid mooning from an upstairs window, a wedding party emerging from a church, the bride in white, her face glowing with happiness.

I pushed the fast-forward button.

"Stop! Right there, back it up," J.J. said.

I eased back to footage of a touch football game, then eased forward and froze the frame on a lawn party in progress. The St. Augustine grass was in full sun, live oaks and towering slash pines and a blue sky backdropping the dancers. From the lack of shadows, I guessed the video was shot close to noon.

"That's her, isn't it? Right in the middle," J.J. said.

I pressed the play button and Yvonne Darbonne came to life on the screen. She was barefoot and dressed in a sleeveless blue tank top that exposed her bra straps, and a beige skirt that stretched tight high up on her rump as she raised herself on the balls of her feet and lifted her hands into the air. John Lee Hooker's "Boom Boom" was playing in the background.

The lens swept across the crowd but quickly returned to Yvonne Darbonne. She looked absolutely beautiful—sensuous, innocent, filled with joy, in love with the world.

Then the music stopped, the camera swung across the tops of the trees, and for just a moment I heard a popping sound and the ringing of metal against metal, like a flag and chain blowing on an aluminum pole.

I reran the scene three times and wondered if the footage was of any value at all. She was not wearing the clothes she had died in. There was no time or date indicator attached to the footage, and to J.J.'s knowledge none of the guests he could identify was linked personally to Yvonne.

"I was right, huh, waste of time?" he said.

I stared at the image of Yvonne that I had frozen on the screen. Her eyes were closed, her pug nose lifted into the sunlight, her exposed shoulders red with fresh sunburn.

"It's hard to tell, J.J. Can I keep this?"

"Sure, it was being thrown out."

"Stay in touch. We'll entertain the bass one of these days."

But he didn't get up from his chair. He picked at his nails, his brow furrowed. "There's one other thing I didn't tell you. I'm in premed, just like Tony was."

"Yeah?"

"Tony had the tests for a bunch of my science classes, including the finals for chemistry. I think he got them from Slim. Tony offered to let me use his copy of an anatomy test. He said it wasn't cheating. He said the test was just a study guide. But another guy told me Slim paid him to break into a file drawer in a professor's office."

"Were Slim and Tony selling the tests?"

"I didn't ask."

"Okay, partner. Thanks for coming in." But before he went out the door, I had one more question for him. "Did you use the help on the anatomy exam?"

"No, sir. I made a D on it," he said, grinning self-effacingly.

I gave him the thumbs-up sign.

A few minutes later I called Koko Hebert at his office. "Was the Darbonne girl sunburned?" I asked.

"Why you want to know?"

"Because that's my job."

"No, your job is being a full-time compulsive-obsessive neurotic pain in the ass."

"If you don't like the way I do things, take it up with the sheriff or the D.A. I sympathize with your loss of a family member, Koko, but I'm not going to be the target of your anger anymore."

The receiver was quiet for a long time. "Koko?" I said.

"I heard you. I'm pulling up her file. Yeah, there was a certain degree of erythema on her shoulders and the back of her neck. It probably occurred a few hours before her death."

"But she was wearing a T-shirt at the time of her death, wasn't she?"

"Right," he said.

"Would the burn be more consistent with someone wearing a sleeveless tank top?"

"Probably."

"I didn't mean to be rough around the edges a minute ago," I said.

"Anything else?" he asked.

"No, that's it. I just—"

He hung up.

CHAPTER
13

CLETE PURCEL WAS NOT sleeping well these days. His shoulder ached where Lefty Raguza had driven a steel tool almost to the bone, and, worse, he could not think straight about Trish Klein, nor was he any longer sure about his own motivations in getting involved with her. Was he just an aging fool trying to regain his lost youth? Was she playing him? Were the sounds she made in bed manufactured?

Why would a woman with her looks, money, and education mess around with a disgraced ex-policeman who skated on the edges of alcoholism and criminality? The question implied an answer he hated to even think about. Was that exactly the kind of man she was looking for, or rather needed, to perpetrate a vendetta on Whitey Bruxal for her father's murder?

Her retinue was made up of pretenders. The horse jockey ate hamburgers like potato chips. The prizefighter had sticks for wrists. The country songstress carried a tune like a piano falling down a stairwell. The Hollywood screenwriter admitted his only experience in the industry had consisted of running a film projector at a neighborhood theater in Skokie, Illinois. As grifters scamming casinos, they weren't bad. But did they actually boost banks? The answer was probably yes. And that's what disturbed Clete most.

He had known their kind back in the late 1960s. They came from traditional blue-collar and middle-income homes, and became imbued with a political or social cause that allowed them to justify criminal acts normally associated with Willie Sutton or Alvin Karpis.

The irony lay in their level of success. Most criminals get nailed in the aftermath of their crimes, largely because of their lifestyles and their associations. But the sixties bunch was not composed of junkies, degenerate gamblers, whoremongers, or porn addicts, nor did they hang out with recidivists or network with professional fences and money launderers. Instead, they lived in the suburbs, felt no guilt whatsoever about their crimes, jogged five miles before breakfast, and considered themselves patriotic and decent. In custody, they didn't attempt to defend their actions any more than they would have attempted to explain the nature of light to a blind man.

Clete sat on the side of his bed, his electric coffeepot bubbling on the counter in his small kitchen, the early sun glowing through the closed slats of his blinds. He knew Trish liked him, but that didn't mean she loved him, nor did it mean she wouldn't use him. He had learned in Vietnam there were three groups of people who got you killed—pencil pushers, amateurs, and idealists. Trish didn't fit into the first category but she qualified for the other two. So far, his involvement with her had cost him a visit from the FBI, a stab wound in the shoulder, and possibly a warrant for the fire hose caper and bomb scare at the casino on Canal. How big a bounce was he willing to take in order to feel he was thirty again?

He ate four scrambled eggs and a slab of ham in his skivvies, shaved and showered, then dressed in a new suit, fitted on his porkpie hat, and went outside to greet the day.

The previous night he had pulled a vinyl cover over his Caddy to protect it from bird droppings. But someone had unhooked the elastic loops from the bumpers and folded back the cover in a neat stack on the ground, then had tiger-striped the paint job with acid. There was also a silver indentation the width and flat shape of a screwdriver tip under the gas flap, and Clete guessed the flap had been prized in order to pour sugar or sand into the tank.

He used his cell phone to call Triple A for a wrecker, then called me at the office. "I think Lefty Raguza paid me a visit last night," he said, and described the condition of his car.

"You should have pressed assault charges against him when you had the chance, Clete," I replied.

"You know how much business that fire hose situation probably cost the casino? I'll be lucky if I don't have to blow the state."

It was pointless to argue with Clete. Besides, he was right. His history of mayhem and environmental destruction both inside and outside the New Orleans Police Department preempted any chance of his being presumed innocent in a conflict between Clete and a business enterprise that brought millions of tourist dollars into Orleans Parish. "You'll need an investigative report for your insurance. I'll send somebody out," I said.

"Thanks. Raguza didn't do this on his own. Whitey Bruxal had to give his approval."

"You don't know that."

"Wake up, Streak. These guys have used the state of Florida for toilet paper since the 1920s. You're spending your time on people at the bottom of the food chain. Fraternity pissants and black street pukes aren't the problem. The word is Whitey Bruxal has bought juice with a televangelical lobbyist who closes down Bruxal's competition. Like Trish says, you hurt the big guys in their pocketbook."

"Stay away from that woman," I said.

But he had already closed his cell phone.

I HAD ALWAYS BELIEVED Colin Alridge was far too complex a man to be dismissed as a tawdry charlatan. His father had been an insurance executive who mixed pleasure with business in both Fort Lauderdale and New Orleans, his mother a survivor of internment by the Japanese in the occupied Philippines. After the father drank up the family money and shot himself, Colin attended a poor-boy Bible college in South Carolina, wandered around the Upper South as an encyclopedia salesman, then became a regular on a Sunday-morning religious program that was broadcast out of Roanoke, Virginia. Colin quickly learned that his good looks, corn-bread accent, and family-oriented Christian message were a combination that could ring like coins bouncing on gold plate. More important, he discovered that beyond the television camera there was a huge political constituency hungry for conversion and affirmation, provided that it was conveyed by someone they could trust.

It's inadequate to describe him as handsome. It was the totality of his appearance that charmed his audiences and made him an iconic figure sought out by political and religious groups all over the country. He was clean-cut, immaculately groomed, straightforward, his face marked with an ever present serenity that was obviously born of inner conviction. Working-class women who touched his hand called him "godly." When he whispered his message of love and redemption into a microphone, their faces crumpled and their eyes swam with tears.

He returned to his birthplace and bought a modest home on Camp Street, in the Garden District, and often appeared at shelters for battered women and the homeless. But there were stories about a second home outside Bay St. Louis, one with a breathtaking view of the Gulf. The deed was in the name of the incorporated ministry that others administered for him, but the rich and the powerful were often seen dining on the deck with Colin at sunset, the blood-streaked skies and rustle of palms a triumphal backdrop to those who had successfully managed to give unto both God and Caesar.

Colin Alridge had remained free of the type of scandals that had brought down many of his predecessors. If there was a repressed libertine inside him, no one ever saw it. He was devoted to his work and I suspect sincere when he often mentioned his mother as the source of his political and spiritual convictions. Even I sometimes wondered if the rumors about his ties to casino gambling were manufactured by his political enemies. Why would anyone who had achieved so much risk it all by involving himself with a Miami lowlife like Whitey Bruxal?

Clete Purcel had his Caddy towed into the shop, then drove in a rental to Whitey Bruxal's business office on an oak-shaded stretch of Pinhook Road near the Lafayette Oil Center. But Whitey Bruxal was not there and his receptionist said she had no idea where he was.

Clete looked around at the deep carpet and heavy, ornate furniture in the reception area. The office was located next to a motel built of soft South Carolina brick, and through the windows he could see the shadows of the live oaks out on Pinhook Road and the sun winking on the motel swimming pool. "You got a nice location here," he said. When she didn't respond, he added, "Whitey just blows in and out but doesn't tell his employees where he is?"

"Would you like to leave your name and phone number?" the receptionist said. Her hair was platinum, her tan probably chemically induced. She picked a piece of lint off her skin and dropped it in a wastebasket.

"Is Lefty Raguza around?" Clete asked.

"I think Mr. Raguza is at the track."

"Too bad. Tell Whitey Clete Purcel was by. He doesn't need to call. I'll drop by another time. Or maybe catch him at his house. He goes to his house sometimes, doesn't he, when he's not blowing in and out of the office?"

Her eyes drifted up into his, her expression as bored as she could possibly make it.

"That's what I thought. Thanks for your time. Give Lefty my best. Tell him I'll be getting together with him soon," he said. "Could I have one of those business cards?"

She nodded her head toward a container on her desk, her attention concentrated on her computer screen.

Clete wrote on the back of the business card and handed it to her. "Give this to Whitey, will you?" he said.

She took the card with two fingers and set it beside her keyboard without looking at it. Then she glanced down at the message written in a tight blue calligraphy across the card. It read:

The guy your people capped in Opa-Locka had the Silver Star and two Purple Hearts. Why don't you give me a call, shitbag? I'd like to chat you up on that.

The receptionist's face sagged slightly, then she picked up her purse and walked into the restroom, her eyes focused far out in front of her.

Outside, Clete stood in the shade of an oak, wondering what he had just accomplished. The answer was easy: Nothing. In fact, his behavior had been foolish, he told himself. Contrary to his own admonition, he was once again engaging the lowlifes on their own turf, issuing challenges that brought him into conflict with disposable douche bags like Lefty Raguza.

What was it that guys like Whitey Bruxal wanted? Again, the answer was easy: Respectability. The legalization of gambling throughout most of the United States was a wet dream come true for the vestiges of the old Syndicate. The money they used to make from the numbers racket, money that they always had trouble laundering, was nothing compared to the income from the casinos, tracks, and lotteries they now operated with the blessing of federal and state licensing agencies. In fact, not only had the government presented them with a gift that was beyond the Mob's wildest imaginings, they had been able to attach educational funding to gambling bills all over the country, which turned schoolteachers into their most loyal supporters. Was this a great country or not?

Maybe it was time to piss in the punch bowl, Clete thought. He looked at his watch, then headed for New Orleans.

En route he called his part-time secretary at the office he still operated on St. Ann Street in the Quarter. She was a former nun by the name of Alice Werenhaus, a stolid pile of a woman whose veneer of Christianity belied a personality that even the previous bishop had feared. In fact, I think Nig Rosewater and Wee Willie Bimstine's bail skips were more afraid of facing Miss Alice than they were Clete. But she and Clete had hit it off famously, in part, I suspected, because the pagan in each of them recognized the other.

She called Clete back by the time he crossed the Atchafalaya and gave him the probable schedule for the rest of Colin Alridge's day.

"High tea at the Pontchartrain Hotel?" Clete said.

"He entertains elderly ladies there. Actually, he doesn't seem like a bad man," she said.

"Don't let this dude snow you, Miss Alice."

"Have you gotten yourself into something, Mr. Purcel?"

"Everything is copacetic. No problems. Believe me."

"The police department keeps calling about this episode at the casino. They say a lot of water damage was done to the carpets."

"Don't listen to them. It was just a misunderstanding. Thanks for your help. Got to go now." He closed the cell phone before she could ask any more questions.

But she called back thirty seconds later. "You take care of yourself, Mr. Purcel!" she said.

He could do worse than have Miss Alice on his side, he thought.

Just before 3 p.m. he drove down St. Charles and parked across from the Pontchartrain. Sure enough, inside the cool, pastel-colored reaches of the hotel, he found Colin Alridge seated at a long, linen-covered table, speaking to a group of ladies who must have been in their eighties. A tea service was set at each end of the table, and Colin sat in the center, turning his head back and forth, his eyes lingering on each face, his sincerity and goodwill like a candle in the midst of an otherwise empty dining room.

It was not the scene Clete had anticipated when he left Lafayette. He had envisioned catching Alridge in a crowded restaurant, perhaps among the monied interests that seemed to find their way into Alridge's inner circle. Maybe even some of the Giacano minions would be there, he had told himself. But what if they *had* been there? What would he have done: pull a fire hose out of the wall and create another disaster for himself like the one at the casino? He stopped at the bar and ordered a double Jack with a beer back. "How long does Billy Graham Junior work the crowd?" he asked the bartender.

"Sir?" the bartender said.

"When does Boy Bone Smoker get finished with the ladies?"

The bartender, who wore a white jacket and black pants, leaned forward on his elbow. He had a pencil mustache and black hair that was cut short and parted neatly, like a 1930s leading man. "I happen to be gay myself. You don't like it, drink somewhere else."

The afternoon was not working out as Clete had planned. He finished his Jack, ordered another, and left three one-dollar bills as a tip for the bartender. The bartender picked them up and stuffed them in a cup on the bottle counter, not speaking, his face without expression. Clete had not eaten, and by three forty-five he was half in the bag. "Sorry about that crack. It's been one of those days," he said.

The bartender poured him a shot and waved off the five Clete put on the bar.

"You know who Whitey Bruxal is?" Clete asked.

"He's a gambler."

"Ever see him in here?"

"Yeah, he stays here sometimes."

"Ever see him with the guy over there at the table?"

"Are you kidding?"

At four o'clock, the group of elderly ladies began filing out of the dining room. Clete picked up his drink and walked over to Alridge, who was just saying good-bye to a lady on a walker. He clapped Alridge hard on the shoulder. "Need to talk to you," he said.

"Pardon me?" Alridge said, turning slowly.

"We've got a big mess over in New Iberia. Your name keeps coming up in it. You know Whitey Bruxal and Bellerophon Lujan, right? Lujan's boy got blown away with a twelve-gauge and it looks like a gangbanger might ride the needle for it. The gang-banger is a bucket of black whale sperm by the name of Monarch Little. Too bad the Lujan kid got mixed up with him. You need a drink?"

But Clete realized his grandiose manner was manufactured, that he was not in control. His face felt hot and swollen, as though it had been stung by bees; his own words sounded foreign and discon-nected, outside himself. He propped one hand on a chair to steady himself. Colin Alridge stared at him in amazement.

"I couldn't process all that. What was that about the Lujan boy?" Alridge said.

"You know him?"

"I know Mrs. Lujan. Sit down. What is your name?"

Clete had not been prepared for Alridge's response. "Tony Lujan's old man is part owner of the casinos you front points for," he said. "You're in bed with some nasty guys, Mr. Alridge, so I thought you'd like to get an update on their everyday lives."

"Who are you?"

"Clete Purcel. I'm a private investigator. I've got a hole in my shoulder a guy named Lefty Raguza put there. He also poured acid all over my car early this morning. He works for Whitey Bruxal. You and Whitey pretty tight?"

But Alridge seemed to take no notice of the implication in Clete's question. He pushed a chair out for Clete, then took one for himself. "You have to start over, sir. Tony Lujan was *murdered*?"

"You don't watch the news?"

"No, most of the time I don't. Who did you say killed him?"

"The Lujan kid had a beef with some gangbangers. But what happened later is a matter of debate. Maybe the larger case involves Whitey Bruxal and the Feds. I thought you might have some feedback on that."

Alridge rested his forehead on his hand, obviously bereaved, his composure lost. Then his eyes climbed up into Clete's face. "And you think Tony Lujan's death has something to do with me?"

"You tell me."

"You can't begin to comprehend how offensive you are."

Now it was Clete who felt undone. The pain and the level of insult in Alridge's face were real. Clete tried to hold his eyes on Alridge's but felt himself blink. "Whitey Bruxal gave the orders to blow the head off an armored truck guard. The word is you're backing his play here in Louisiana, so—"

"I don't have any idea what you're talking about. You deal with your own demons, Mr. Purcel. I have to call Mrs. Lujan," Alridge said.

He rose from his chair, seeming to tower over Clete. Then he hesitated, his face fraught with concern. "Are you all right to drive?" he said.

"Am I all—"

Alridge gestured to the bartender. "Call a cab for this gentleman, will you, Harold?"

"Yes, sir, Mr. Alridge," the bartender replied.

"You hold on, bub," Clete said, getting to his feet.

Alridge touched him gently on the shoulder. "You did what you thought you had to do, Mr. Purcel. Rest here a little bit and have a cup of coffee. I'm happy to have met you."

Clete searched for a dignified response but could think of none. He watched Colin Alridge walk out of the room. His hands felt thick and stiff and useless on top of the linen-covered table. His face was dilated like a balloon, his ears ringing in the quiet, his mouth bitter with the aftertaste of midafternoon whiskey. He wondered if the role of public fool came in incremental fashion with age, or if you simply crossed a line one day and found yourself in a room full of echoes that sounded almost like laughter.

THAT EVENING he sat next to me in a canvas chair on the bayou, at the back of my property, flipping a cork and baited hook from a cane pole out on the edge of the current. The evening sky was green, the wind cool in the trees, and the lights had just come on in the park across the water. A dragonfly lit on the Clete's cork and floated with it past the flowers blooming among the hyacinths.

"I felt like two cents. Did I read this guy all wrong?" he said.

"Who cares? You're a good guy, Cletus. You've always been on the right side of things. You don't have to prove anything," I said.

He had eaten and showered after returning from New Orleans, but his face still had an empty look, like that of a man who has just awakened from sleep and isn't sure where he is. Clete had been on the full-tilt boogie for more than three decades now, and I wondered if the bill was starting to come due.

"The crazy thing is, I don't even know why I went after this guy," he said.

"Because you don't like frauds and guys who use religion to sell wars."

He rubbed one eye with his fist. "The guy seemed on the square."

"He's not, Clete. He's a con man, and the guy he's probably conned the most is himself. But let's get off the dime here. Alridge knows Bello Lujan's wife?"

"Yeah, he was upset about the kid getting blown away. I think it really put a nail in his head."

"Like maybe he feels guilt about it?"

"Something like that. Or maybe he knows why Lujan was killed."

"So I'm glad you went after him."

"Really?" he said, looking me at me directly for the first time since his return from New Orleans.

"Really," I said.

ONE TIME WHILE SWACKED on Cambodian red and a quart of stolen Scotch, a sergeant in my platoon who had served in World War II, Korea, and Vietnam told me he was the wisest man he had ever known.

"Why's that?" I asked.

"Because I've spent a lifetime seeing people in duress," he replied.

"So?" I said.

"That's when the best and worst in people comes out. When they're in duress. Most of the time the best comes out. Sometimes it don't."

"What happens when the worst comes out?" I asked.

"You got to remember who you are so you don't become like the people around you. Each night you tell yourself over and over you got a special place inside you where you live. It's like a private cathedral nobody can touch. That's the secret to sanity, Loot. But you can't tell anybody about your special place."

"Why not?" I asked.

"Because once they know you got that private place in your head, they'll strap you down and kill your brain cells with electroshock."

I was about to have the opportunity to test the wisdom of the sergeant's words.

CHAPTER
14

MONARCH LITTLE'S BAIL was reduced Monday morning on the firearms violation to twenty-five thousand dollars. Through a friendly bondsman who allowed his clients to pay off his ten percent fee on the installment plan, Monarch was back on the street in time for lunch at the same McDonald's where he'd gotten into it with Slim Bruxal and Tony Lujan.

But the problem with Monarch's release from jail didn't lie with Monarch, at least not directly. Helen called me into her office at 1 p.m.

"How much tolerance do you have for Bello Lujan?" she asked.

"Considering the fact he broke out a window in a cruiser with his head in order to spit on me, not very much," I replied.

"You're probably the only person in the department he'll listen to," she said.

I knew where she was headed. "No, Bello is not my responsibility. If you want a nursemaid for this guy, find somebody else," I said.

"He respects you."

"Bello is an animal. He doesn't respect anybody or anything."

Helen drummed her fingers softly on her desk pad, her eyes lowered. "We've come a long way since the civil rights era, Dave. I don't want to see that progress undone."

"Then figure out a way to put Bello in a cage. Just leave me out of it. I don't like getting spit on. I don't like getting used, either."

She snuffed now in her nose. "I can't blame you for your feelings. Don't worry about it. I'll work out something else," she said. She swiveled around in her chair and gazed out the window.

"That's it?" I said.

"That's it," she said.

When your slider isn't working and your fastball couldn't find the strike zone if it had eyes on it, what's the only pitch to throw? The answer is always the same: the humble change-up. You hold the ball deep in your palm, then let the batter's overwrought watch spring destroy his timing. Helen had just floated a beaut down the pipe. I went back to my office and tried to bury myself in paperwork, but I couldn't get Bellerophon Lujan and the primitive, violent mind-set he represented out of my thoughts.

He was a creature out of the past, but one that every southerner of my generation recognizes and instinctively avoids if possible. It's facile to call his kind racist. In fact, race is almost a cosmetic issue when it comes to understanding the Bello Lujans of the world. They're often fond of black people individually but they resent if not despise them as a group. Their anger lives like a benign form of clap in their blood. Instead of destroying them, it energizes them, defines who they are, and allows them to use social outrage to intimidate other whites.

Their ignorance is a given. In fact, they take pride in it and use it as a weapon. The threat of violence is implicit in all their rhetoric and in the bold stare of their eyes. Their greatest fear as well as their greatest enemy is knowledge of themselves. Like Plato's prisoners in "The Allegory of the Cave," they will perpetrate any hateful act, including murder, on the individual who tries to set them free from their chains.

South Louisiana's cultural mores have always been French Catholic in origin, and hence the Klan has never had a strong foothold here, at least not since Reconstruction and the short-lived influence of the White League. But that doesn't mean that violence and cruelty and the sexual exploitation of Negroes did not occur here. When I was in high school, white kids went nigger-knocking along rural roads, shooting people of color with BB guns or throwing M-80s on their galleries or hurling "torpedoes," tightly compacted balls that exploded upon impact, against the paint jobs of their cars and pickup trucks. I remembered seeing Bello leaning out of a speeding junker, his face split with a grin, just before he splattered a black man dressed for church with a half-eaten mayonnaise and tomato sandwich.

But there was a much darker story that had circulated about Bello, one that gradually died but one that was never quite laid to rest, either. Years ago, in a parish to the north of us, a middle-aged white woman who operated a grocery store on a dirt road had just closed the store for the night when a man of mixed blood, one she later described as a "red-bone," tapped on the glass and said he needed milk for his baby. The store owner peered through the glass and thought she saw the humped silhouette of a woman in the front seat of his automobile. She was certain she heard the muffled cries of an infant.

She unlocked the door and let the man in. He walked past her to the cooler in back, an odor like fermented fruit and stale sweat sliding off her face. She turned her back and continued counting the day's receipts. She heard him slip a heavy glass container of milk from the cooler and place it on the counter. She turned around to take his money, just as his fist exploded on her nose and mouth. Then he came through the swinging gate on the corner, pinned her to the floor, and beat her bloody with both fists. After he sodomized her, he raked the cash off the counter into a paper bag with his forearm, picked up the bottle of milk, and started to leave. But a two-dollar bill thumbtacked on the wall caught his eye. He pulled the bill loose from the tacks and left the store, the bell over the door tinkling behind him.

A light-skinned Negro who lived in his car and made his living sharpening knives was stopped and questioned at a roadblock on the parish line two hours later. He could not account for his whereabouts that night, except to say he had pulled off the road at sunset to take a nap under a tree. He stank of sweat and Hawaiian Punch that he had laced with sloe gin. A crumpled paper bag of the kind used by the grocery store owner lay on the backseat, along with an empty baby bottle. Both of his hands were swollen, his knuckles skinned.

His court-appointed attorney introduced evidence to show that the paper bag found in the defendant's car was manufactured by a company that sold the same type of paper bags all over the state. The lawyer also found a witness who testified that the defendant had been involved in a fistfight two days before his arrest. The black man took the stand and told the jury a hitchhiker had left the baby bottle in the car. But on cross-examination he contradicted himself about where he had picked up the hitchhiker and where he had dropped her off. He also could not explain the fact that at the time of his arrest he had a two-dollar bill in his possession.

The knife sharpener was sentenced to death by electrocution. But in the ensuing weeks, several of the jurors developed problems of conscience. They mentioned the fact that the two-dollar bill found on the Negro man had no thumbtack holes or apparent indentations on the corners. More important, they remembered that originally the victim had identified her attacker as a "red-bone," a person of mixed Indian, Negro, and white blood. The man arrested at the roadblock was clearly a mulatto, with no distinguishing Indian features whatsoever.

Then one night during an electrical storm, three men wearing masks broke the condemned man out of the parish prison, but not to set him free. They beat him senseless with a sap, gagged and handcuffed him, and took him deep into the Atchafalaya Basin in a powerboat. On the edge of the river, while lightning lit the endless gray miles of flooded gum and cypress trees, they dragged him up on a sandspit and pulled his trousers down over his buttocks. One of them produced a cane knife from the boat, then the three began to argue in French over who had the most right to deliver the first cut. But they had made the mistake of cuffing the condemned man's wrists in front of him. He got to his feet, his trousers tangling around his ankles as he staggered to the edge of the sandspit and plunged into the river.

By all odds he should have drowned. Instead, he clung to a pile of river trash and uprooted cypress trees, the rain stinging his face, and floated downriver until sunrise, when a man on a houseboat fished him out of the water with a boat hook.

Three weeks later, Louisiana's traveling executioner arrived in town with the flatbed truck that carried the boomed-down generators and rubber-encased cables that powered the instrument of his trade. The mulatto who had escaped a lynching in the Atchafalaya Basin was buckled down in an oak chair and jolted three times against the straps while the victim and her husband sat in folding chairs and watched.

Two months after that, a man and his wife were arrested outside

Oklahoma City for the robbery and sadistic murder of a family who operated a roadside fruit stand. They were caught only because they were turned in by a relative upon whom they had dumped their infant child. They denied ever having been in the state of Louisiana, but a receipt from an Opelousas motel, dated the night before the attack on the female grocery store owner, was found under the front seat of their automobile. The man was half Choctaw Indian. In his wallet was a worn two-dollar bill, each corner pierced by what appeared to be a thumbtack.

Bellerophon Lujan's name surfaced again and again whenever the story of the attempted lynching was told. His father had been a close friend of the rape victim's family. His uncle had gone to Angola for killing a Negro farmworker with a hoe. Bello was notorious for bragging on his sexual conquests of black women, and it was obvious to any reasonable person that his anger toward the Negro race seemed to exist in direct proportion to his libidinal fascination with them. Whenever the subject of race came up in a barroom conversation, Bello's eyes became lustrous with secret thoughts and memories he did not share.

Shortly after 2 p.m. I checked out a cruiser and drove to Bello's horse farm up the Teche. After I rang the chimes, I waited in the shade of his porch, watching the shadows of clouds sliding across his pastureland. In the side yard I heard a flapping sound, like fabric lifting in the wind, and a clinking of metal upon metal. Then I remembered where I had heard those sounds before. I started to walk around the side of the house, when a big black woman in a nurse's uniform, her white hair held in place by chemical spray, opened the front door. "Yes, suh?" she said.

"I'm Detective Dave Robicheaux, here to see Mr. Lujan," I said, opening my badge holder.

"He's not here, suh."

"Where is he, please?"

"He didn't say where he was going." She had been looking me straight in the eye, but her gaze broke. "He took the dog wit' him. So maybe they went to the park. Or maybe downtown somewheres." Her eyes came back on mine.

"Is that Mr. Robicheaux, Regina?" a voice said from the sunporch.

But I kept my attention on the black woman. "Come out on the front porch with me," I said.

"Suh?"

I stepped backward, taking her hand in mine. She followed me outside, glancing back once.

"What's Mr. Bello up to, Miss Regina?" I asked.

"I'm making ten dollars an hour here. I cain't lose this job."

"Tell me where he went."

"He took the rottweiler. That dog mean t'rew and t'rew. You don't walk a dog like that in the park, no."

"Go back inside and tell Mrs. Lujan I'll be right there," I said.

"Suh?"

I said it again. This time I placed my hand reassuringly on her upper arm. "I give you my word no one will know what you just told me," I said.

She went back inside the house uncertainly, leaving the door ajar. With my back to the house, I opened my cell phone and punched in the number to Helen's office.

"Sheriff Soileau," she said.

"I'm at Bello's house now. Mrs. Lujan's nurse says he left here with a rottweiler. Better get somebody over to Monarch's place."

"You got it, bwana," she said.

I stepped inside the living room and saw Mrs. Lujan out on the sunporch, staring at me from her wheelchair. She was dressed in a flowery blouse and beige skirt, but the seasonal cheeriness of the colors only accentuated the pallor of her skin and the obvious deterioration of her bone structure. Through the windows I could see freshly mowed St. Augustine grass and a bank of shade trees in the background and a pale green canopy set up on aluminum poles. The canopy was swelling with wind, a loose chain on one corner rattling against a pole.

"Are you here about Tony?" she asked.

"Monarch Little has been released from jail on bond. We're concerned your husband might want to take the law into his own hands," I replied.

She watched me in the same way a bird watches a potential predator from atop its nest. She was originally from the Carrollton district
of New Orleans and had come to Lafayette to study drama at the university when she was only a girl. Her parents, who had been successful antique dealers, were killed in a commercial airline accident her
freshman year. Mrs. Lujan, whose first name was Valerie, left school
and went to work for a man who made breakfast-room furniture out
of compressed sawdust and sold it to the owners of double-wides and
prefab homes during the domestic oil boom of the 1970s. Then she
met Bellerophon Lujan and perhaps decided that the dreams of a
young drama major were just that—dreams that a mature woman
tries to put aside with only a brief pang of the heart.

"You're here because you're worried about the man who killed my
son? Who disfigured him so badly he's virtually unrecognizable?" she
said.

"I'm sorry for your loss, Mrs. Lujan," I said. But it was obvious
she was not interested in my sympathies. "Monarch Little hasn't been
charged in the murder of your son. He was in jail on a firearms violation. His bond was reduced and now he's back on the street. And
that's why I'm here."

Her face was almost skeletal, her hair like corn silk, her eyes filled
with both sorrow and the analytical glint of someone who has probably been systematically deceived. She reminded me of a figure in a
Modigliani painting, attenuated, her bones like rubber, her body
robbed of both beauty and hope by an unkind hand. "You're saying
there's doubt about this man's guilt?" she said.

"In my mind, yes."

"Why?"

"The investigation is ongoing."

"Please answer my question."

"I don't think Monarch Little is a killer."

She stared out the window at the lawn and the wind puffing the
canopy that had been used at garden parties in a happier time. "You
were one of the policemen who found Tony?"

"Yes, I was."

"Do you think my son suffered?"

"No, I don't think he did." I let my eyes go flat so they did not focus on her face.

"But the truth is you don't know?" she said.

"In this kind of instance—"

"Don't patronize me, Mr. Robicheaux."

My words were of no value. I suspected her grief had now become her only possession and in all probability she would nurse it unto the grave. I looked out the window at the green canopy rippling in the wind and the chain tinkling on the aluminum pole.

"I have a videotape of Yvonne Darbonne dancing at a lawn party. In the background there's a sound like canvas popping and a chain rattling against metal. I think that video was shot in your yard, Mrs. Lujan."

She lifted her chin. Her eyes were small and green, recessed unequally in her face. "And what if it was?"

"You knew Yvonne Darbonne?"

"I'm not sure that I did. Would you answer my question, please?"

I felt a surge of anger in my chest, less because of her imperious attitude than her callousness toward someone else's loss. "She died of a gunshot wound in the center of her forehead. She was eighteen years old. I think she was at your house the day of her death. She had red hair and was wearing a short skirt and sleeveless blue tank top at the party. She was dancing to a recording of John Lee Hooker's 'Boom Boom.' Does any of that sound familiar to you?"

"I don't like the way you're addressing me."

"Mr. Darbonne lost his child to a violent act, just like you lost yours. Why should you take offense because I ask whether or not the girl was at your house? Why is that a problem for you, Mrs. Lujan?"

"Get out."

I placed my business card on a glass tabletop next to her wheelchair. There was a small pitcher of orange juice and crushed ice, with sprigs of mint in it, sitting on the table. The refraction of sunlight from the pitcher looked like shards of glass on her skin.

"Either your son or your husband ran over and killed a homeless man. Moral outrage won't change that fact," I said.

"Your cruelty seems to have no bounds," she replied.

• • •

BELLO HAD GONE FIRST to Monarch Little's home, located in a blue-collar neighborhood that was gradually becoming all black. A woman had been hanging wash in her backyard when she saw Bello come up the dirt driveway, the rottweiler straining at the leash he had double-wrapped around his fist. "You know where Mr. Little is?" he asked, smiling at her.

"No, suh," she replied.

"You been out in the yard long? Or maybe at your kitchen window? Or maybe out on your gallery, pounding out your broom?" He was grinning at nothing now, his eyes roving about aimlessly, the dog stringing saliva into the dirt.

"He come in a while ago, then left again," the woman replied. She was overweight, her dress blowing on her body like a tent, her arms wrapped with a skin infection that leached them of their color.

"Wasn't driving that Firebird, though, was he? 'Cause it got burnt up," Bello said.

She wasn't going to reply, then she looked again at his face and felt the words break involuntarily from her throat. "He was wit' his cousin, in a beat-up truck. It's got boards stuck up on the sides to haul yard trash wit'."

"Where they gone to?" Bello was still grinning, his eyes never quite lighting on her. He lifted up on the dog's choke chain, tightening it until the dog stiffened and sat down in the dirt. "Tell me where he's at. I owe him some money."

"That corner where they always standing around under the tree. I heard them say they was going to the li'l sto' there," she said.

"The corner they sell dope at?"

"I don't know nothing about that."

"But that's the corner you're talking about, isn't it?"

"Yes, suh."

"If I don't find him, you don't need to tell him I was here, do you?"

"No, suh," she replied, shaking her head quickly.

"T'ank you," he said. He turned the dog in a circle and walked it back to his Buick, making a snicking sound behind his teeth.

• • •

I HAD JUST LEFT Bello's house when I got the dispatcher's call. I hit the siren and the flasher and headed down Loreauville Road, cane fields and horse farms and clumps of live oaks racing past me.

THE AIR-CONDITIONING UNIT in Bello's Buick was turned up full blast as he approached the corner that had always served as a secondary home for Monarch and his friends. Bello's dog sat on the front seat, its yellow eyes looking dully out the window, its choke chain dripping like ice from its neck. The frigid interior of the Buick, with its deep leather seats and clean smell, digital instrument panels, and silent power train, seemed a galaxy away from the dusty, superheated, and litter-strewn environment on the corner. A black kid drinking from a quart bottle of ale eyeballed Bello's car, waiting to see if the driver would roll down the window, indicating he wanted to make a buy.

Bello slowed the Buick against the curb, the white orb of sun suddenly disappearing behind the massive canopy of the shade tree. He turned off the ignition, cracked the windows, and waited for his eyes to adjust to the change in light before he got out of the car. Bello had never had a cautionary sense about people of color, and had never thought of them, at least individually, as a viable challenge to his authority as a white man. In the past, they had always done what he told them. That's the way it was. If they believed otherwise, a phone call to an employer or a manager of rental properties could bring about a level of religious conversion that even a beating could not.

But something had changed at the corner. The gangbangers were there, as always, playing cards, drinking soda pop or beer, or taking turns at the weight set, their hair matted down with black silk scarfs, even in the heat; but they seemed disconnected from Monarch, in the same way that candle moths lose their flight pattern when their light source is removed. Monarch and his cousin, a yardman who looked like he was made from coat-hanger wire, were eating spearmint sno-balls with tiny wood spoons at a plank table under the tree. The yardman's paint-skinned truck, garden tools bungee-corded to the sides, was parked in the background. Monarch was wearing jeans and old tennis shoes and a colorless denim shirt, the sleeves scissored off at the armpits. He looked at the spangled sunlight bouncing off the windshield of Bello's Buick but gave no indication he recognized the man behind the wheel.

A bare-chested black kid, not over seventeen, his shirt wadded up and hanging from his back pocket, tapped on Bello's window. His arms were without muscular tone, soft, his chin grown with fuzz that looked like black thread. Bello smiled when he rolled down the window. "Yeah?" Bello said.

"Want some weed?" the kid asked.

"That's not what I had in mind," Bello replied.

"You name it, I got it, man," the kid said, his arm propped on the roof, exposing his armpit. He gazed nonchalantly down the street.

"You gonna hook me up wit' some cooze?" Bello said.

"There's a lady or two I can introduce you to."

"I got a special one in mind," Bello said, squinting up at him.

"Yeah?"

"Your mama. She still working rough trade?"

The black kid kept his gaze averted and did not look back at him. "Why you want to do that, man?" he said.

"'Cause you put your fucking hand on my car," Bello said. Then he opened the door and stepped out into the heat. "Want to meet my dog?"

"No, suh," the boy said, stepping back, lifting his hands in front of him. "T'ought you was someone else, suh."

Bello snapped his fingers softly and the rottweiler dropped to the asphalt behind him. Bello closed the car door and picked up the animal's leash. Everyone on the corner was staring at him now, everyone except Monarch Little, who continued eating his sno-ball with his tiny wood spoon, digging out the last grains of spearmint-flavored ice from the bottom of the cone.

Bello stepped up on the curb. The wind puffed the oak tree overhead, and tiny yellow leaves drifted down into the shade. Monarch's cousin rose from the table and walked to a trash barrel by his truck and dropped his empty sno-ball cone inside. The cousin's strap over-alls looked made from rags, the weave almost washed out of the fab-ric. His facial expression was bladed, filled with cautionary lights.

"Been t'inking about me?" Bello said to Monarch.

"Don't know who you are. Ain't interested, either," Monarch replied.

"You fixing to find out. You should have stayed in jail, yeah."

Monarch seemed to think a long time before he spoke. "I ain't did it. That dog ain't gonna make me say I did, either. The people on this corner ain't gonna hurt you, so you ain't got to be afraid. But don't come down here no more t'reatening people wit' dogs, no."

"My son was gonna be a doctor. You took that from me," Bello said.

Monarch waved an index finger back and forth. "I ain't took nothing from you. Do what you gonna do. But you better look around you. This ain't your pond. Now, I'm walking away from here. I don't want no trouble."

Monarch got up from the table, a net of sunlight and shadow slid-ing over his skin.

That's when Bello unsnapped the leash from the rottweiler's choke chain and said, "*Sic le neg!*"

The dog took only two bounds before it was airborne and aimed right at Monarch's chest. Monarch twisted away and wrapped his arms across his face, waiting for the dog's teeth to sink into his flesh. Instead, he felt a suck of air past his head and heard metal *whang* on bone. Then the dog's great weight bounced off him, and when he opened his eyes, the dog lay in the dust, its body quivering, its fur split across the crown of its skull.

Monarch's cousin lowered the shovel he had used on the dog, pointing its tip into the dirt, letting his callused palm slip down the shaft. One of his eyes constantly watered, and he pressed a handker-chief into the socket, all the time watching Bello with his other eye, so that in an odd way he looked like two people, one managing himself while the other studied an adversary. "A mistake got made here 'cause folks was in hot blood. Don't mean it got to continue, suh," he said.

"You tear my dog's head off and lecture me?" Bello said.

The corner was completely silent except for the wind coursing through the leaves overhead. A locomotive engine blew in the distance, the sound climbing into the hot sky.

"My cousin ain't done you nothing. You come here blaming us for your grief. Now you got more of it, not less. But it ain't on us," Monarch said.

No one could say later what thoughts or perhaps memories went through Bello's mind at that moment. Did he remember a kid with a shoe-shine box waiting in the cold at the Southern Pacific station? Or the one who worked for tips at the root beer drive-in, where the owner did not allow him to eat his lunch or supper inside the building? Or did he realize, at that particular moment, that no matter what he accomplished in life, he would never separate himself from that class of white men who were considered by other whites to be no better on the social ladder than Negroes and, worse yet, considered even less in stature by people of color themselves?

He ripped into Monarch with both fists. But once again Bello had misjudged both his situation and his adversary. Monarch slipped the first punch, ate the second one, then got Bello in a bear hug, pinning his hands at his sides, crushing the air from his lungs. Bello struggled helplessly against Monarch's huge arms, his body pressed hard against Monarch's girth, his shoes leaving the ground.

"Tear him up, Monarch!" somebody yelled.

But instead Monarch wrestled Bello against the Buick, trapping him there, holding him tight against the hot metal while sheriff's deputies spilled out of three cruisers, Monarch's sweat mixing with Bello's inside a cone of heat and dust and the smell of engine oil and rubber tires. The expression of despair and loss and a lifetime of impotent rage on Bello's face was one I will never forget. No greater injury could have been imposed upon him. A black man had not only bested him in public but had treated him with mercy and pity while others watched, a deed that Bello was incapable of forgiving.

CHAPTER
15

THE NEXT MORNING, Lonnie Marceaux buzzed my extension and said he wanted to see me in his office. When I got there, a barber was wiping shaving cream from Lonnie's sideburns and snipping hair out of his nose. The barber held up a mirror for Lonnie to examine his work. Lonnie touched at a spot by his hairline. "Just a tad more on top," he said.

The barber used his comb and clippers briefly, then held up the mirror again.

"No challenge is too much for your talents, Robert. Thanks for coming over," Lonnie said. He handed the barber three ten-dollar bills held crisply between two fingers.

The barber thanked him and folded the apron carefully so that no hair dropped on the floor, then nodded at me and left the room.

"I have a crowded schedule some days," Lonnie said, looking at a steel pocket mirror he kept in his desk drawer.

"It's that time of year," I said.

He didn't make the connection. In fact, I didn't care whether or not there was one to make.

"Bellerophon Lujan is in jail?" he said.

I looked at my watch. "He's probably out by now."

He made a tent out of his hands and patted the pads of his fingers against one another, a thought buried like an insect between his eyes. "We're getting reports on this friend of yours, Clete Purcel. Evidently

185

he caused some massive property damage at the casino in New Orleans."

"Then that's between him and them."

"Not if he's inserting himself into one of our investigations."

"You'll have to take that up with Clete."

"I don't need to. I have you. You're the other half of the coin."

"You brought me over here about Clete Purcel?"

"You're not hearing me. I got a call from a couple of guys in New Orleans, fraternity brothers who have interests in common with Colin Alridge and want to know why Purcel was hassling their boy in the tearoom at the Pontchartrain Hotel."

"What's their problem? From what I understand, Alridge handled himself in a pretty dignified manner," I said.

"I honest-to-God believe you have trouble with the English language, Dave. My words have no effect on you. If anybody brings down Alridge, it's going to be us. NOPD might let Purcel wipe his shit all over their parish, but that's not going to happen in New Iberia. If Purcel was bird-dogging Alridge, you knew about it. I've already told you every element of this investigation will be coordinated out of this office. But I've got a feeling you're using a surrogate to pursue your own agenda."

"You're mistaken."

"I'd like to believe that."

"Believe it."

He rocked back in his swivel chair and let his gaze drift out the window. The sky was full of yellow dust and leaves that were gusting out of the trees. "So what did your pal find out?"

"Colin Alridge seems to be a friend of Mrs. Lujan. Maybe a spiritual adviser or something like that."

"Spiritual adviser, my ass."

"Clete said Alridge seemed upset about Tony Lujan's death, like maybe he felt guilty over it."

Lonnie made a snuffing sound in his nose and brushed a piece of clipped hair out of one nostril. "Did you pass this information on to Helen?"

"It's not information. It's speculation on the part of a private investigator."

"There are a lot of bad traits I can accept in people, Dave, but disingenuousness isn't one of them." He held his eyes on mine. "No, I'm not going to be euphemistic here. I won't put up with lying."

I felt a flame spread across my back, the way it can wrap around you when you have shingles. I watched the dust blowing across the tops of the trees out in the street, newspaper swirling off the asphalt. "I hope it rains. It's been awfully hot," I said. "Give me a call if I can provide you with any more help."

"We're not finished here," he said.

"That's what you think."

BUT INDIRECTLY Lonnie Marceaux had made a point. Clete's speculation about Colin Alridge's involvement with the Lujan family wasn't to be ignored. I called Mrs. Lujan and asked if I could visit her at her home again.

"No, you may not," she said.

"I'll come with a warrant if I have to." I could hear her breathing against the receiver. "Is your husband there, Mrs. Lujan?"

"My husband is in jail. You should know that."

"No, he's not."

She was silent again. Then she said, "What time did he get out?"

"I'm not sure."

"Find out and call me back," she said, and hung up.

I rang the jail, then redialed Mrs. Lujan's number.

"He was out at nine-seventeen a.m." It was now a quarter to noon.

"Have you seen him since his release?"

"No, ma'am."

"If you wanted to find him, would you know where to look?"

"I'm not sure."

"I could give you two or three addresses. Guess which part of town they're in. Guess who lives at those addresses."

"I wouldn't know, Mrs. Lujan."

"You wouldn't know? Do you smoke cigarettes?"

"I don't."

"Do you know where to buy some?"

This time I didn't answer.

"My husband is an inflexible man and doesn't allow smoking in our home. Please buy me a package of Camels and bring them to the house. Can you do that for me, Mr. Robicheaux?"

"My pleasure," I said.

"Mr. Robicheaux?"

"Yes?"

"Also bring the video. The one you said shows the Darbonne girl at our garden party. Bring that with the cigarettes."

Thirty minutes later, the maid let me in the front door. Outside, the sun was white in the sky, the windows running with humidity, but the interior of the house was frigid. There was no sign of Bello or his car. Mrs. Lujan gestured at me from the sunporch, her fingers curling back toward her palm.

"Sit," she said. Then she waited, her eyes on my face.

"You want the cigarettes?" I said.

"Take one out and give it to me."

I removed the cellophane from the package and slipped a cigarette loose for her. She held it between two fingers and waited. I took a folder of matches from my shirt pocket and lit her cigarette and blew out the match. There was no ashtray on the glass tabletop that separated me from her wheelchair, and I set the match on the edge of a coffee saucer and placed the package of cigarettes next to it. She turned her face to one side when she exhaled the smoke, then looked at me quizzically. "You think I'm strange?" she said.

"It's not my job to make those kinds of judgments."

"Put the video in the machine," she said.

I shoved the cassette into the VCR and watched the first images come up on the screen. She continued to smoke as I fast-forwarded the tape, her eyes rheumy, sunken like green marbles into bread dough. She seemed to radiate sickness in the same way that an unchanged bandage or an infected wound does. I even wondered if the diminution of her bone structure had less to do with an automobile accident than a cancerous anger that lived inside her.

I stopped the tape on the garden party, backed it up, and recommenced it. Once again, Yvonne Darbonne was dancing to the signature composition of John Lee Hooker, her shoulders powdered with freckles, her pug nose turned up at the sky.

"That's the girl who shot herself?" Mrs. Lujan said.

"Do you remember her?"

"She was pretty. Tony brought her here. Then he left, and she was dancing by herself. She was wearing that tank top. She spilled sangria on it."

"Go on."

"I was watching the dancers from the upstairs window. She looked up at me and smiled and pointed at the stain on her top. It was wet and dark on the material. Her breasts were molded against the cloth and I remember thinking she didn't belong out there, at least not with the likes of Slim Bruxal. I waved at her to come inside. I wanted to give her a clean blouse to wear."

"Why didn't you?"

"I saw her talk to Slim, then to Bello. She walked under the orange tree, below my line of vision, then I couldn't see her anymore. I heard the door slam. The side door is right under my bedroom, and when it slams I can always feel the vibration through the floor. So I know she went into the house. Then I heard the door slam a second time."

Mrs. Lujan drew in on the cigarette and blew out the smoke and watched it flatten against the window. Her makeup was caked, her mouth stitched with wrinkles that were as thin as cat's whiskers, her eyes looking at an image, imagined or real, trapped inside her head.

"Who followed Yvonne Darbonne into the house?" I asked.

"There's a game room behind the den. Bello keeps the curtains drawn so the western sun doesn't get in. It's the place where he goes to be alone. I heard something thump against the wall down there. I kept waiting to hear another thump, the way you do when a sound wakes you up in the middle of the night. But I didn't. All I heard were voices."

"Voices?"

"I heard a girl's. I heard it come up through the pipe in the lavatory. It was loud, then it stopped, and I couldn't hear anything except the sound of water running. I think somebody turned on the shower down there. I can always tell when it's the shower in the game room. The stall is made of tin. The water makes a drumming sound on the sides. I wanted to think she was just taking a shower. But that's not why somebody turned on the water, is it?"

I waited before I spoke again. "What do you think happened down there, Mrs. Lujan?"

"I used the intercom to call Sidney, the colored man in the kitchen. It took over fifteen minutes to get him up here. I told him to go down to the game room and see who was in there. But he refused."

"Pardon?"

"He said he had left a tray of drinks on the landing and had to take them out on the lawn before somebody tripped on them. But I knew he was lying."

"I'm not with you."

"Sidney couldn't look at me. His eyeballs kept rolling around in his head. I told him to stop acting like Stepin Fetchit and get down there. Ten minutes later I called him on the intercom again. He still hadn't gone into the game room."

"Why wouldn't he do as you told him, Mrs. Lujan?"

She wore dentures, and they looked hard and stiff inside her mouth, her flesh by contrast soft and trembling against them. "Because he was afraid of what he would have to tell me. Because he was afraid of my goddamn husband," she said.

Her eyes were moist now, the flat of her fist pressed against her mouth.

"There's something else I have to ask you, Mrs. Lujan," I said.

When she looked up at me, the whites of her eyes were threaded with tiny red lines.

"I think Colin Alridge has knowledge about your son's death. I think he may know why Tony was murdered. I believe you gave Alridge information you won't give us," I said. "Monarch Little didn't kill your boy, did he?"

She stared into space, as though reviewing all the words she had said and listened to and all the images her own words had caused her to see inside her head and the confession of personal failure and inadequacy she had just made to a stranger. Her face grew still and composed and she looked up at me again, this time her eyes free of pain, her thoughts clear.

"I've been a fool, Mr. Robicheaux. You are what I've heard others say of you. You're a dishonorable and self-serving man, and I should not have confided in you. You'll leave a black animal on the street while the blood of his victim runs in the gutter. There is only one type of person who does that, sir, someone who feels an intolerable sense of guilt about himself. Take your videocassette with you when you leave. Don't return without a warrant, either."

THAT NIGHT I lay beside Molly in the dark and tried to sleep. I have never given much credence to the notion that the dead are held captive by the weight of tombstones placed on their chests. I believe they slip loose from their fastenings of rotted satin and mold board and tree roots and the clay itself and visit us in nocturnal moments that we are allowed to dismiss as dreams. They're in our midst, still hanging on for reasons of their own. Sometimes I think their visitation has less to do with their own motives than ours. I think sometimes it is we who need the dead rather than the other way around.

Once, I saw the specter of my drowned father standing in the surf, rain dancing on his hard hat while he gave me the thumbs-up sign. Annie, my murdered wife, spoke to me inside the static on a telephone line during an electric storm. Sometimes at dusk, when the wind swirled through the sugarcane in a field, denting and flattening it just like elephant grass under the downdraft of a helicopter, I was sure I saw men from my platoon, all KIA, waiting for the Jolly Green to descend from the sky.

A therapist told me these experiences were a psychotic reaction to events I couldn't control. The therapist was a decent and well-meaning man and I didn't argue with him. But I know what I saw and heard, and just like anyone who has stacked time in what Saint John of the Cross described as the dark night of the soul, I long ago gave up either defending myself or arguing with those who have never had their ticket punched.

It was hot and breathless outside, and the sound of dry thunder, like crackling cellophane, leaked from clouds that gave no rain. Through the back window I could see vapor lamps burning in City Park and a layer of dust floating on the bayou's surface. I could see the shadows of the oaks moving in my yard when the wind puffed through the canopy. I could see beads of humidity, as bright as quick-silver, slipping down the giant serrated leaves of the philodendron, and the humped shape of a gator lumbering crookedly across the mudbank, suddenly plunging into water and disappearing inside the lily pads. I saw all these things just as I heard helicopter blades roaring by overhead, and for just a second, for no reason that made any sense, I saw Dallas Klein getting to his knees on a hot street swirling with yellow dust in Opa-Locka, Florida, like a man preparing himself for his own decapitation.

I sat up in bed, unsure if I was awake or dreaming. I looked down the slope to the bayou, and all was as it had been a few moments earlier, except my heart was racing and I could smell my own odor rising from inside my T-shirt. I felt Molly's weight shift in the bed.

"Did you have a dream?" she said.

"A chopper flew over the house and woke me up. It was probably a guy on his way out to a rig."

"Did you dream about the war?"

"No, I don't dream about it much anymore. It was just the sudden sound of helicopter blades that woke me, that's all."

But you don't tell a lie to a Catholic nun and get away with it. Molly went into the kitchen and returned with a glass of lemonade for each of us. We sat there in the dark and drank the lemonade and watched the trees flare against the sky. She placed her hand on top of mine and squeezed it. "You never have to keep secrets from me," she said.

"I know."

"You know it but you don't believe it."

"I believe you're everything that's good, Molly Boyle."

She lay down next to me, the curve of her body close against me, her arm across my chest, the fragrance of her hair cool in my face. And that's the way I went to sleep, inside the fragrance and body heat of Molly Boyle, and I did not wake until dawn.

BUT IN THE MORNING I could not shake the vision I had seen of Dallas Klein kneeling on a sidewalk in Opa-Locka, Florida. Was the vision simply a matter of unresolved guilt about his death? Or was it a warning?

Because I carried a badge, I sometimes presumed. Sometimes in my vanity I saw myself as a light bearer, possessed of an invulnerability that ordinary men and women did not share. There were times when I actually believed my badge was indeed a shield. Soldiers experience the same false sense of confidence after surviving their first combat. Gamblers think they have magic painted on them when they pick a perfecta out of the air or draw successfully to an inside straight. The high of a boozer doesn't even come close to any of the aforementioned.

All of it is an illusion. Our appointment in Samarra is made for us without our consent, and Death finds us of its own accord and in its own time. Cops rarely die in firefights with bank robbers. They're shot to death during routine traffic stops or while responding to domestic disturbances. As a rule, their killers couldn't masturbate without a diagram.

I had taken too much for granted in my attitude about the killers of Dallas Klein. The people who had killed him were not only cold-blooded, they were cynical and cruel and I believe totally committed to a life of evil. They exploited Dallas's weakness as a compulsive gambler to rob him of his honesty, his valorous war record, his self-respect, and finally his life. His executioner had even ridiculed him before pulling the trigger on the shotgun, calling him "a joke," ensuring he would realize before he died how badly he had been used.

I had no doubt Whitey Bruxal was behind the armored car heist. But Lefty Raguza's role was another matter. Could he have been at the scene? He'd had an alibi, but an alibi for a guy like Raguza was never further than a phone call away. I had heard the shooter speak just before the van steered around the armored car, but the alcohol in my blood and the gunfire and glass caving out of the saloon window onto the concrete and the *whang* of buckshot into the metal door behind him had turned my ears into cauliflower. I had tried a thousand times to re-create the voice in my head, always with the same result. I had witnessed an execution, and my recall of it was absolutely worthless.

The killer had been someone for whom cruelty and sexual pleasure were interchangeable, a man who I suspected not only killed for enjoyment but who experienced the moment as a form of benediction bestowed upon him by his own id.

Did this describe Lefty Raguza?

And Clete had not only baited Whitey Bruxal and gotten into it with Raguza, he was in the sack with Trish Klein, an amateur grifter who thought she could use a collection of self-deluded blue-collar kids to bring down her father's killer.

In the meantime, Lonnie Marceaux was playing both ends against the middle and using both the district attorney's office and the sheriff's department to further his own political ambitions.

I believed Whitey Bruxal and Lefty Raguza had come to Louisiana with the same sense of excitement and expectation generated in hogs when they get a downwind sniff of a trough brimming with swill. We were amateurs and they knew it. They bought politicians and media people for chump change, and fleeced Social Security recipients and twenty-five-dollar-an-hour offshore oil drillers alike, while convincing them that casinos increased their quality of life.

Lonnie Marceaux thought he was going to take Bruxal off at the neck. Inside Lonnie's worldview, Helen Soileau and I were as important as his fingernail parings. Yesterday I had walked out on a meeting with him, as though somehow that changed the fact he was skewing an investigation to serve his own ends. Maybe it was time to set the record straight in a more definitive fashion. I picked up my phone and called his office. "I'd like to drop by for a minute," I said.

"What for?" he asked.

"To apologize."

"People go off half-cocked sometimes. Don't worry about it," he said.

"I appreciate your attitude. But I'd like to apologize in person."

"That's not necessary."

"Yeah, it is. I'll be right over."

When I entered his office he was standing by his desk, putting files in a briefcase. His long-sleeved white shirt had glittering strips in it, like tin ribbons, and it hung on his frame without a fold or crease in it, as though the sense of freshness and efficiency he brought to the job could not be diminished by the heat of the day. He glanced up from his briefcase and grinned. "You don't have a splinter in your butt about something, do you?" he asked.

"I haven't been adequately forthcoming with you, Lonnie. I don't think Monarch Little is our killer. If anybody had motivation to kill the Lujan kid, it was Slim Bruxal or his old man."

"What motivation is that?"

"Tony Lujan was the weak sister in the death of Crustacean Man. He was going to roll over on Slim."

"But you don't know that."

"I know that Monarch Little is too convenient a target for your office."

"Is he, now?"

"He's a gangbanger and dope dealer, and large crowds aren't going to be saying rosaries for him if he rides the needle. There won't be a civil rights issue about him, either. Most black civic leaders wouldn't take the time to piss on his grave."

"You're telling me, to my face, I'm framing an innocent man?"

"If you pop Monarch, you win three ways. You clear the homicide, you take a dealer off the street permanently, and you've still got Slim Bruxal on an assault beef. You can freeze out the Feds and use Slim to squeeze his old man and by extension Colin Alridge."

"You know, if it weren't for your age and the fact we're both civilized men, I think I'd break your nose."

"Your magnanimity is humbling, Lonnie, but anytime you'd like to walk into the restroom and bolt the door, I'd be glad to accommodate you."

"I want you off the case."

"Talk to Helen."

"That's perfect."

"Run that by me again?"

"If it wasn't for Helen Soileau, you couldn't get a job picking up litter in City Park. She's covered your sorry ass for so long, people think she's either stopped being a queer or you're her portable muff diver. But I'm not going to let either her or you—"

That's as far as he got. I hit him so hard the blow peppered blood across the window glass. He went straight down on his buttocks like a man whose legs had caved into broken ceramic.

CHAPTER
16

THAT DAY I HAD PLANNED to meet Molly at home for lunch. She worked at a Catholic foundation down the bayou that built homes for poor people, and twice a week she prepared an extraordinary lunch before she left for work, then returned home before noon and laid it on the kitchen table so it would be ready when I walked through the door.

Today she had heated up a pot of white rice and a fricassee chicken that had already cooked down into a soft stew of onions, pimientos, floating pieces of meat, chopped-up peppers, and brown gravy. She had set flowery place mats on the table, and heaped a tight ball of steaming rice in each of our gumbo bowls, and placed jelly glasses and a pitcher of iced tea filled with lemon slices and sprigs of mint in the center. It was a simple meal, but one that few men can come home to at noontime on a workday.

I sat down with her, and she said grace for both of us, one hand touching mine. Snuggs was stretched out on a throw rug in front of a floor fan, his short fur stiffening in the breeze. Through the back window I could see a spray of gold and red four-o'clocks opening in the shade of a live oak and blue jays flying in and out of the sunlight. I filled a spoon with rice and stewed chicken and put it in my mouth.

"What happened to your finger?" Molly asked.

"You mean that little cut?" I replied, removing my hand from the table and picking up the napkin in my lap.

"I don't call that a little cut. It looks like somebody bit you."

I laughed and tried to shine her on.

"*Dave?*"

"Huh?"

"Answer my question."

"I had a little run-in with Lonnie Marceaux."

"The district attorney? Clarify run-in."

"Yeah, that's the one," I replied, ignoring the second part of her statement, bending over the bowl, putting another spoonful in my mouth, my eyes flat now.

"You punched the Iberia Parish district attorney?"

"It was more or less a one-shot affair. Hey, Snuggs, you want a piece of chicken?"

Molly was staring across the table now, her mouth open. "You're playing a joke, aren't you?"

"He called Helen a queer. He accused me of—" I didn't continue.

"What? Say it."

I told her. Then I added, "So I dropped him. I wish I'd kicked his teeth in."

"I don't care what he said. You can't attack people with your fists whenever someone offends you."

"Louisiana law allows what it calls provocation. It goes back to the dueling code. Lonnie is a fraternity pissant and should have had his head shoved in a commode a long time ago."

"What does his fraternity history have to do with anything?"

"It—"

But she wasn't interested in my response. She rested her forehead on her fingers, her other hand clenched on her napkin, her eyes wet. I felt miserable. "Don't be like that, Molly," I said.

"Your enemies know your weakness. You take the bait every time."

"I don't see it that way."

"Oh, Dave," she said, and went into the bathroom and closed the door. I could hear the water running, then I heard the faucet squeak and the pipe shut down. But she didn't come out.

"Molly?" I said through the door.

She didn't answer. Behind me, I heard Snuggs go out the swinging flap I had cut for him in the kitchen door. I drove back to the office in the heat, my lunch unfinished, the sky bitten with dust, my face burning with shame.

AT THE DEPARTMENT a number of felt-tip notes were taped to my office door. The following excerpts indicated the general sentiments of my colleagues toward Lonnie Marceaux:

WAY TO GO, ROBICHEAUX!
STOMP ASS AND TAKE NAMES, BIG DAVE!
HEY, STREAK, LIKE WAYLON SAYS, IT AINT THE YEAR
THAT COUNTS BUT WHAT'S UNDER THE HOOD.

Helen was not so congratulatory. "He's at Iberia General now with a concussion. He also has a tooth broken off at the gum," she said.

She was walking back and forth in front of her office window, her navy blue pants and denim shirt and masculine physique backlit by a sulfurous glare in the sky.

"I'm not sorry I did it. He had it coming. I say fuck him, Helen."

"*What?*"

"He treats us like douche bags. He's been consistently disrespectful to you and the department. You don't negotiate with a guy like that. You reach down into his wiring and rip it out."

"Since when is it your job to defend me or this department?"

"It's not my job. That's the point."

She hooked her thumbs in her gunbelt, the question hanging in her eyes. I looked away from her.

"You popped him because of something he said about me?" she said.

"He called you a queer. He accused me of performing cunnilingus on you." I cleared my throat and shifted in the chair, unconsciously touching my knuckles.

She took her thumbs out of her belt and gazed out the window, her lips pursed. She fooled with one ear, her jaw flexing on a piece of chewing gum. There were ridges of muscle, like rolls of dimes, in the backs of her arms. "He hasn't filed charges yet," she said.

"He's not going to, either."

"How do you know that?"

"Because he doesn't have a leg to stand on. Because he's a gutless fraud."

"Pops, you have one character defect I've never been able to deal with."

"Really?"

"I can never guess what your feelings are on a given subject. God, you're a case. Dropping the district attorney in his own office. That's a beaut." She smiled at me, her face infused with genuine warmth. In fact, it was radiant and filled with the kind of humanity that I suspect is purchased by living in two genders, and lovely in ways I cannot adequately describe.

GOVERNOR HUEY LONG, known as the Kingfish, became the prototype for all the southern demagogues who would follow him. According to legend, Huey kept a little black book he called his "sonofabitch file." Whenever he met a man he disliked, he wrote his name in it. If someone wondered why Huey had entered the individual's name in the book, the answer was simple: When the opportunity presented itself, Huey would destroy that man's life.

What I had not said to Helen was that men like Lonnie Marceaux and Huey Long had ice water in their veins and kept long memories. I still believed Lonnie would not come after me immediately because a public airing of our confrontation would cause him political embarrassment. But for three years he would have the option of filing charges against me, and that option would hang over me during the entirety of our investigation into the murder of Tony Lujan. My guess was Lonnie would eventually have his revenge, but like all cowards, he would use a three-cushion shot to get it.

In the meantime, I had to keep an investigative clarity of line in the death of Tony Lujan, regardless of my feelings about Lonnie

Marceaux. I didn't buy Monarch Little for the murder. He was just too easy a target. Black dirtbags make wonderful dartboards for prosecutors in need of defendants with cartoonlike dimensions. Unfortunately for Monarch, he had the social grace of a hog on ice and was the kind of defendant juries love to boil into grease and pour down a sewer grate. But nevertheless, Monarch was not stupid. Even if he had shot the Lujan boy, he would not have left the murder weapon on the floor of his Firebird. Also, Monarch was a pragmatist. The person who had murdered Tony Lujan had deliberately disfigured the body postmortem and I suspected had been driven by the kind of insatiable rage we associate with sexually motivated psychopaths.

Just when I had convinced myself that Monarch was being set up, that the old southern incubus of racial scapegoating was once again rearing its head in our midst, I received a telephone call that was like a brick toppling down a stone well.

"Mr. Robicheaux?"

The voice was young, female, threaded with trepidation.

"Yes, this is Dave Robicheaux. What can I do for you?"

"It's Lydia Thibodaux, Tony's friend."

"How are you?" I said, straightening up in my chair.

"You questioned me the night Tony died. I told you things—" She stopped and started over. "Dr. Edwards is my academic adviser at UL. He was kind of like a friend to Tony. Slim was in one of his classes, too. I told him the truth about what happened. He said I needed to talk with you and straighten everything out. A lot of people say Dr. Edwards is gay, but I don't care. What does it matter if he's gay?"

I couldn't follow her. "Straighten out what?"

"I told you I wasn't sure it was Monarch who called up and asked Tony to meet him. That wasn't true. I know Monarch's voice. I bought some weed from him. More than once."

"Can you come to my office?"

For a moment I thought the line had gone dead. Don't lose her, I told myself. "It's all right. We'll talk on the phone. I appreciate your cooperating with us. You're sure it was Monarch Little?" I said.

"As sure as you can be just by listening to somebody over the phone. How many people lisp like that? He sounds like he has wires all over his teeth."

"What else did you want to straighten out, Lydia?"

"Sir?"

"You said there were 'things' you told me that were not correct. You used the plural."

"Maybe Slim was with Tony."

"Say that again."

"Before Tony left to meet Monarch, I told him it was crazy to go meet a drug dealer when he was already in so much trouble. Tony said he'd be all right because Slim would go with him. He said, 'Slim can handle the action. Monarch already learned he'd—' "

"Say it, Lydia."

"He said, 'Monarch already learned he'd better not fuck with Slim.' Tony always looked up to Slim. It never made sense to me. Slim is no good."

"What do you base that on?"

"He's mean. His fraternity brothers act like he's their friend, but the truth is they're afraid of him. I told Dr. Edwards that. I mean, I told him Slim scared me."

I was writing on a yellow legal pad while she talked. "What did Dr. Edwards have to say about that?"

"He said Tony and Slim both wore masks. He said not to be afraid of someone who can't live with the person who's inside his skin. He said it was too bad Tony couldn't have learned that lesson. I don't know what he meant. What do you think he meant?"

"I'm not sure. Was Tony maybe unusual or different in some way?" I asked, wondering if I was now pushing the envelope.

"Sir?"

"Let me meet you someplace."

"I have to go to work now. I'm helping my father at the restaurant."

"Your father runs the restaurant at the new casino?"

"What does that have to do with anything?"

"Nothing," I said.

"I was just trying to undo a lie I told you. Now you're trying to make me say bad things about Tony. Monarch Little killed him, didn't he? Why are you protecting a piece of scum like that? I wish I hadn't called you, Mr. Robicheaux. You're on the side of black people. It's always like this. They do whatever they want."

I started to reply, but she broke the connection.

Had I been completely wrong? Did Monarch do it after all? Was my enmity toward Lonnie Marceaux so extreme that I would take up the cause of a dope dealer who had set up and murdered a hapless college kid whose father had already psychologically damaged him beyond repair? Was I one of those who always saw a person of color as a victim of social injustice?

I didn't like to think about the answer.

THE TEMPERATURE HIT ninety-nine that afternoon. The trees along East Main were almost indistinguishable from one another inside the haze of heat and humidity and dust that covered the town. The tide was out and Bayou Teche had sunken inside its banks, and in the harshness of the sunlight, alligator gars roiled the water next to clumps of lily pads that had burned yellow on the edges. As I drove home, the wind was hot and smelled of tar and carbon monoxide, and even though I had left my air-conditioned offices only five minutes ago, I could feel sweat running down my sides like trails of ants.

Molly was not an angry or resentful woman, nor was she one who judged or sought to punish. But her disappointment in others could lie buried in her face as deep as a stone bruise. Perhaps she thought violence could be exorcised from an individual in the same way demons were cast out by medieval clerics. No, that was my own resentful thinking at work. Molly believed too much in others. At least, she probably believed too much in me.

We said little at supper and even less as we washed the dishes and put them away. As the light went out of the sky and the trees filled with thousands of birds, we found ways to occupy ourselves with chores that did not involve the other. Just before ten o'clock, when I usually watched the news, I heard her moving about in the kitchen, opening the icebox, setting down a plate on the table.

"Dave?" she said.

I got up from my soft chair in the living room and went to the kitchen door. She had on her nightgown and I could see the spray of freckles on her shoulders. "What's up?" I said.

"I fixed you a piece of pie and some milk."

"Are you having any?"

"I'm pretty tired. I think I'm just going to bed."

"I see," I said.

"The heat seems to affect me more than it used to."

"It's been a hot one."

"Good night," she said.

"Yeah, good night," I replied.

I lay on the couch and watched the local news until ten-thirty, then I stared at CNN for the amount of time it took me to fall asleep, in my clothes, a floor fan blowing in my face, my wife on the other side of the bedroom wall.

SOME PEOPLE IN A.A. say coincidence is your Higher Power acting anonymously. I'm not sure about that, but on Thursday morning, after I had already left for work, Tripod began to tremble and to cough and rasp deep in his throat, as though he had swallowed a hairball. Molly took him to a veterinary clinic, one that also boarded and groomed animals. While she was waiting for the veterinarian, a blade-faced, well-dressed man with an athletic build, six and a half feet tall, entered the room with a French poodle on a leash. The poodle's fur was dyed pink. Molly had put Tripod in a cardboard box lined with newspaper and a vinyl garbage bag, and had fold-tucked the flaps on the top over Tripod's head and placed the box by her foot. But Tripod had wedged his head between the flaps and had just started a survey of the room when the poodle's scent struck his nostrils.

Lonnie Marceaux was filling out a form on a clipboard at the intake window, the poodle's leash lying on the floor. The poodle turned toward Tripod's box and made a soft growling sound, like the purr of a distant motorboat. Tripod jerked his head down through the flaps and skittered around in the box, coughing violently, his weight flopping sideways on the stump of his missing hind foot.

"Sir! Sir! Would you take control of your animal? He's frightening my coon," Molly said.

"Sasha is harmless, believe me," Lonnie said.

"The coon doesn't know that. I'm not sure I do, either," she replied.

He nodded as though he understood the urgency of her request but kept writing. In the meantime, Tripod's paws skittered and scratched inside the cardboard and his incontinence kicked into major download.

"Sir, you're causing problems you can't guess at. There's a tether post for your pet in the other room," Molly said.

"Sorry, I don't quite understand."

"This is a very old and sick raccoon. Your dog is terrifying him. Now, try to act with a little decency."

"Please accept my apologies," Lonnie said, bending over to pick up the poodle's leash. Then he sat down three chairs away from Molly and Tripod and began reading a magazine, impervious to Molly's stare.

Molly gathered Tripod's box in her arms and rose from her chair just as the receptionist slid back the glass on the intake window. "Mr. Marceaux, did you want your poodle shampooed *and* clipped?" she asked.

"Give her the works. She's going to a show this weekend," he said, looking at the receptionist over the top of his magazine.

"You're Lonnie Marceaux, the district attorney?" Molly said.

"I am," he replied pleasantly.

"I must be the dumbest woman on the planet," she said, and started toward the other waiting room.

"Are we back to my poodle again?"

Just then, the bottom broke out of the box and Tripod plummeted to the floor, landing on his back with a sickening thump.

Molly squatted down and picked him up, his bladder emptying down her forearms. "Poor Tripod," she said.

"Madam, I'm not responsible for your diffi—" Lonnie began.

"Shut up," she said. "I took my husband to task for punching you in the mouth. Now I wish he'd knocked your teeth down your throat. I've known some self-important idiots in public office, but you're pathetic."

"You're Mrs. Robicheaux?"

"Duh."

MOLLY CALLED MY OFFICE as soon as she returned home with Tripod.

"He was poisoned?" I said.

"The vet's not sure, but that's what he thinks," she replied. "Tripod probably vomited most of it back up. The vet wants to see him again in two days, but most of the poison is probably out of his system."

"What's Tripod doing right now?"

"Sleeping on a blanket in front of the floor fan."

"Run that stuff about Lonnie Marceaux by me again."

"Who cares about a jerk like that? Come home for lunch," she said.

"What did you say to him?"

"It's not important. Why waste time talking about it? I'll see you at lunch. Keep your powder dry."

"What's that mean?"

"Guess."

MOLLY DIDN'T GO ABOUT THINGS HALFWAY. What some might refer to as a conjugal expression of amends was, in the case of Molly Boyle, like being subsumed by an Elizabethan sonnet devoted to celebration of Eros and the ethereal interludes he offered from all the dross of everyday life. Her skin, which was fine-grained and smooth and taut from years of farmwork in Central America, took on a flush that was like the cool burn of the sun out on the Gulf in late autumn. The pillow was imprinted with the smell of her hair, the sheets damp from the sweat on her thighs and back. When I closed my eyes, I thought of breakers sliding across a beach into clumps of bougainvillea and a coral cove where schooled-up kingfish flitted next to a patch of floating hot blue, and I thought of a great hard-bodied fish curling out of a wave and plunging into a rain ring. She came under me, her womb actually scalding, then got on top of me and did it again, her breath drawing slowly in and out as though a piece of ice were evaporating on her tongue.

We took a shower together and dressed, and I checked on Tripod again and smoothed his fur with a brush that was used for no other purpose. "Who did this to you, old partner?" I said.

I went into the backyard and checked Tripod's bowls. There was clean water in one bowl and a half-eaten strip of a sardine in the other. Most of the time, if he was not in the house, he stayed on his chain and wasn't allowed to roam because of his age and his propensity for getting into trouble. There seemed little chance that he had eaten either tainted or poisoned food by accident.

Through the bamboo border on the side yard, I saw Miss Ellen Deschamps sprinkling her rose garden in the shade. Miss Ellen was our one-woman, or rather one-lady, neighborhood crime watch program. Parish sheriffs, zoning boards, and city mayors could come and go, but Miss Ellen's standards did not change with the political season. She served high tea on her upstairs balcony at exactly 3 p.m. every weekday and had her black yardman deliver handwritten invitations to her guests. Any resident on East Main who did not properly attend to the upkeep of his home and lawn and flower beds would receive a polite note from Miss Ellen. If that failed, she put on formal dress, including white gloves, and marched to the home of the offending party and invited him out on his own porch, in full view of the street, to have an extended conversation about the importance of setting a good example for the less fortunate.

"Miss Ellen, did you see anyone prowling around our house in the last day or so?" I asked.

She twisted the water faucet shut and walked toward me. She wore a wide straw hat and a blue sundress and an apron with big pockets for her garden tools. Miss Ellen had a way of never speaking to others from a distance, as though honesty and candor always required her to look directly into a person's eyes when she spoke. "He said he was a friend of yours. He said he was staying with you."

"Who?" I asked.

"A blond man who tied a canoe at the foot of your property. It was at dawn. He opened a can of sardines and fed the raccoon."

"This wasn't a friend. Tripod was poisoned."

I saw something shrink inside her. "I thought he might have been vacationing here. He was very relaxed and polite. He came out of the fog and made a point of saying hello. He said he didn't want to startle me."

"Was he a tall or short man?"

"No, he wasn't tall."

"How about an accent or tattoos?"

She seemed to look into her memory, then she shook her head. "He had tiny pits in his cheeks, like needle holes."

"This afternoon somebody from the department will bring you a few mug shots. Maybe you can pick this fellow out for us."

But she wasn't hearing me. Her face made me think of paper that had been held too close to a heat source. It seemed to have wrinkled from within, as though someone had pinched off a piece of her soul. "Mr. Robicheaux, I'm very sorry I didn't notify you. Is your raccoon—"

"He's fine, Miss Ellen. Don't feel bad about this. You've been very helpful."

"No, I haven't," she said. "I should have called your house."

"I think you've already told me who this guy is. You've done a good deed here."

"Do you really mean that?"

"I do."

"Thank you, Mr. Robicheaux."

"Miss Ellen?"

"Yes?"

"If you see this man again, don't talk with him. Call me or the sheriff's department," I said.

"This man is genuinely wicked, isn't he?"

"Yes, he is."

I watched her go back to work in her garden, troweling a hole for a potted caladium, the damp black soil she had created out of coffee grinds and compost sprinkled on her forearms like grains of pepper. But I knew Miss Ellen had not returned to the normalcy that characterized an ordinary day in her life as caretaker of East Main. The lie told her by the man in the canoe had diminished her faith in her fellow man, and if wounds can remain green, this one I suspected was at the top of the list.

On the way back to the house, I saw a tube of roach paste lying inside the bamboo border of my property.

That afternoon, a uniformed deputy showed Miss Ellen a half-dozen booking-room photos. The deputy radioed in that she took all of two seconds to tap her finger on the face of Lefty Raguza.

Why would Raguza commit such a senseless act of cruelty? If you ask any of these guys why they do anything (and by "these guys" I mean those who long ago have stopped any pretense of self-justification), the answer is always the same: "I felt like it."

I called Joe Dupree, an old friend at the Lafayette P.D. who had transferred from Homicide to the Sex Crimes Unit to Vice. The last helicopter may have lifted off the roof of the American embassy in Saigon in 1975, but thirty years later Joe was still humping a pack on a night trail, an M-60 across his shoulders, his arms spread on the stock and barrel like a man on a cross. He was addicted to speed, booze, bad women, and the conviction that no force on earth could remove his fear of sleep. I had long ago given up trying to help Joe, but I still admired his courage, his integrity as a cop, and the fact that he stacked his own time and didn't complain about the burden he carried.

"This guy does scut work for Whitey Bruxal?" he said.

"More or less. Maybe he helped take down an armored car in Miami. Two people got killed in the heist. One of them was a friend of mine."

"Why would he want to poison your coon?"

"Maybe Whitey Bruxal is starting to feel the heat and wants to provoke me into self-destructing. Or maybe it has to do with Clete Purcel. He bounced Raguza around a little bit."

"I can't quite visualize 'bounced.'"

"Clete blew him all over a restroom with a fire hose."

I heard Joe laugh. "You want me to have a talk with Raguza?"

"That's like talking to a closetful of clothes moths. I need a serious handle on him, something that can jam him up and leave him with bad choices."

"I'll see what I can come up with. Look, on the subject of Whitey Bruxal, I took a strange call from his wife three days ago."

"You're not working Vice anymore?"

"We think Bruxal is laundering meth money. For a while I was in charge of a surveillance at his house. Anyway, his old lady seems to be a real nutcase. Check this out: He met her at what's called the Wild Hog Festival in Collier County, Florida. People who are half-human come out of the Glades and—"

"Joe, I've got a time squeeze going here."

"She tells me in this mushmouth cracker accent that the gas man stole twenty dollars out of her purse. So I told myself this was a good time to see the inside of Bruxal's house. When I get out there, she tells me she found the twenty-dollar bill on the floor and there was no problem, that the gas man had checked out a leak by the barbecue pit and had come inside to turn off and relight her pilots but she was mistaken about the missing twenty dollars."

"So I say, 'You had a gas leak out here?'"

"She said the meter reader smelled it by the barbecue pit out on the breezeway and a repairman came in to turn off all the pilots on the hot water heaters so they could see if gas was still going through the meter. She said the repairman asked her to sit on the glider in the yard in case there was any danger."

"I said, 'Your husband wasn't home?'"

"She goes, 'No, he was out of town. Why you ask that?'"

"Then she tells me these guys were in and out of her house for a half hour. I called the gas company when I got back to the department. They said no meter reader had been out to the Bruxal residence since last month."

"Feds?" I said.

"They're chasing terrorists."

"Thanks for your help, Joe."

"We're firing pop guns against the side of an aircraft carrier," he said.

"I don't see it that way."

"The gambling industry in this country pulls in hundreds of billions a year. Guys like us earn paychecks that have the purchase power of toilet paper. Who do you think is gonna walk out of the smoke?"

"So we'll piss in their shoes."

"That's why I always liked you, Dave. Innocent all the way to the boneyard."

I LOOKED AT the case files on my desk and couldn't begin to compute the amount of time I needed to pursue the investigation into the murder of Tony Lujan, the possible rape and subsequent suicide of Yvonne Darbonne, and the vehicular hit-and-run death of Crustacean Man. I was convinced all three cases were tied to one another, but I wasn't sure how. To complicate matters, Tony's part-time girlfriend had told me she was absolutely sure Monarch had called the Lujan home and arranged a meeting with Tony shortly before he was killed at close range with a twelve-gauge shotgun. My earlier belief that Monarch was not a killer now seemed more and more like the thinking of a politically correct fool.

My file folders on Tony Lujan, Yvonne Darbonne, and Crustacean Man were thick with handwritten notes, crime scene photos, summations of witness interviews, postmortem forms, cassette tapes of 911 calls, forensic reports, and national database printouts on firearms and ballistics. The clerical work I had done on all three cases was impressive to look at. The truth was, all three investigations had become circular and virtually worthless in terms of prosecutorial value. But in my opinion there was still one individual out there besides the killer who had knowledge about the causes behind Tony's death. If so, he had obviously not been willing to come forward, even though he was ostensibly a religious man. I had met him once before, at the home of the Chalons family, one that was notorious for its involvement with casinos on the Texas-Louisiana state line. Maybe it was time to test the legitimacy of Colin Alridge's claim on spirituality.

I called Alice Werenhaus, Clete's secretary at his New Orleans office, and in a half hour she called back and told me where I could find Alridge. I signed out of the department and told Helen I would be out of town until at least the next morning.

CHAPTER
17

THE TWO-STORY HOME that was deeded in the name of his ministry was built of lacquered logs on a bluff that overlooked the Mississippi Sound and a stretch of shell-streaked beach spiked with salt grass. To the west the alluvial flow of the Mississippi River formed an enormous brown cloud of silt and mud along the Louisiana coastline, but just east of the river's mouth, the Gulf was green, capped with waves all the way to the southern horizon, and pelicans glided above the water like fighter-bombers in formation.

It was almost dusk when I drove down a broken asphalt lane through pine trees to his front gate. I expected that he would have private security in place around his home, but there was none that I could see, only a railed fence around a yard planted with flowers and St. Augustine grass.

I knocked on the front door, but no one answered and I could hear no sound from inside the house. The borders of the deck were hung with baskets of impatiens and geraniums, and inside the railing were iron chairs that had been painted white and a glass-topped table shaded by a canvas umbrella. The sky was aflame with the sunset, the pine trees north of the dunes whipping in the evening wind. The fragrance of the flowers, the salt air, the resinous smell of the trees that reminded the viewer he was still in the state of Mississippi were like a perfect moment in time, an encapsulation of everything that was aesthetic in the Deep South.

But there were no people. No children playing on the beach, no woman reading on the deck, no gardener snipping flowers for a vase that would be placed with burning candles on a dining room table. For reasons that perhaps made no sense, I thought of the paintings of the young Adolf Hitler when he had supported himself as a sidewalk artist. Hitler's street scenes and buildings were geometrically precise, the lines like the edges of knives, but there were no people on the streets or inside the buildings, as though the human family had been vacuumed off the planet.

On the far side of Alridge's house were a dock and boat slip and a channel that was fed by the bay at high tide. No boat was moored at the dock, but a bright rainbowlike film of gasoline and oil floated next to one of the pilings. A cooler and an orange life jacket and a cheap spinning rod lay in a pile on the planks, as though the owner had started to take them with him in his boat, then had lost interest in his purpose.

I went back to my truck, pushed back the seat, and closed my eyes. As the sun sank behind the pines and the summer light turned green and dark across the sky, I heard the drone of an outboard in the distance. I took my field glasses out of the glove box and focused them on a twelve-foot aluminum boat bouncing through the whitecaps, farther out than I would have been willing to go in a boat that size.

As Colin Alridge came up the channel, canted sideways on the rear seat, his hand on the throttle, his expression showed mild curiosity at my presence but no sense of alarm. He cut the gas and let his boat slide into the dock on its wake.

"My name is Detective Dave Robicheaux, with the Iberia Parish Sheriff's Department," I said, opening my badge holder. "We met a year or so ago in Jeanerette."

"Yes, I remember you. How are you?" he said.

Without waiting for me to answer, he looped the painter of his boat around a post on the dock and stepped off the bow onto the planks. He was wearing beltless, wash-faded Levi's and a print shirt. His skin was slightly burned by the sun, adding an air of ruggedness to his boyish good looks.

"You left your fishing gear and cooler behind," I said.

"I'm not that keen on fishing, really. I just like to get out in the wind."

"I'm investigating the death of Tony Lujan. I thought you might be able to help me out."

"I don't see how," he said, gathering up his fishing rod, cooler, and life jacket, glancing sideways at me.

"I've interviewed Tony's mother at some length. Evidently you're a good friend of the family."

"I know Mrs. Lujan. She's a supporter of my ministry, if that's what you mean."

"Did she tell you Tony's life was in danger?"

He gave me a quizzical look. "Where did you get that?" he said. But again he didn't wait for me to answer. "Mrs. Lujan is a private person. She shares very little about the tragedies in her life."

Alridge had just made his first and second mistakes. Like all people with something to hide, he telegraphed his fear by trying to fill the environment around him with his own words. Also, he answered questions with questions or made oblique statements that were factually true but did not address the issue. I was convinced he was dirty from the jump, but it was going to be a long haul to prove it.

I pulled at my ear. "Can we sit down?" I asked.

"I'm expecting some people over."

"You're not wearing a watch," I said, and smiled.

"Pardon?"

"You have people coming over but you went out in your boat and didn't bother to wear a watch."

"You're an observant man," he said. He grinned and removed a pocketwatch from his jeans. "Let's go up on the deck for a few minutes. But then I have to take a shower and put something together for dinner."

He dropped his cooler and life jacket and spinning rod on the grass, then mounted the wood steps to the deck. "Watch that third step. It's a little rotted," he said, glancing back at me.

Colin Alridge was not only slick, he was likable. But I had known his kind before. They tested your charity by forcing you to believe in them. To reject their sincerity, their mix of patriotism and religion and love of family, was somehow to reject your own country. Ultimately, they used the suffering of others to justify their own actions. Colin Alridge's support for foreign wars was unequivocal, regardless of the issues involved. His rhetoric was lofty, his eyes clear, his principles as present in his manner as a flag popping in the breeze. Tony Lujan might be a thorn in his conscience, but not one so great that a Band-Aid or two couldn't heal it.

I sat down in one of the scrolled-iron chairs on the deck and stared at my shoes a moment. "I think Tony Lujan was involved in the death of a homeless man. I think his mother told you what her son had done. You didn't come forward with that information, Mr. Alridge. That's called aiding and abetting after the fact."

"Maybe what you say is true. Maybe it's not. But as an ordained minister I have certain protections under the law."

"We can settle some things here or we can do it in front of a grand jury. The word is Bello Lujan and Whitey Bruxal and a few other casino operators launder money through a Washington lobbyist, who in turn gives it to your ministry. Then you exercise your influence on your religious constituency to shut down their competitors. Frankly, I don't have any interest in your ties to the gambling industry. But I've got three open homicide cases on my hands, and I believe you've got the key to at least one of them."

The evening light had receded into a single strip of purple and red clouds on the western horizon, but even in the gloom I could see my words take hold in Alridge's face, as though he had been bitch-slapped in public.

"You need to speak to my attorney," he said.

"Fuck your attorney. If you want to shill for Whitey Bruxal and Bello Lujan, that's your business. But Tony Lujan and maybe Slim Bruxal, that's Whitey's kid, ran over a derelict and left him to die on the side of a road. We call the derelict Crustacean Man because we have no other name to put on him. But I guarantee you, Mr. Alridge, before this is over, that guy is going to have a name and somebody is going to take the bounce for his death. If you're aiding and abetting, your next evangelical crusade is going to be on closed-circuit TV in Angola Pen."

He rose from his chair, flipping open his cell phone, almost spiking himself in the eye on one of the umbrella's points. "I just hit the speed dial to the ministry's security service. They'll help you find your way to your vehicle."

I stood up and looked at the sunset. The air was filled with the heavy, damp, green smell of the Gulf, and I said or perhaps thought a prayer of thanks for the fact I didn't have to live inside Colin Alridge's skin. "One cautionary word before I go," I said. "I used to find ways to skirt on the edge of blowing out my own doors. That's how depression works. It's like being drunk, except you don't know you're drunk, and you find ways to set yourself up for the Big Exit because you can't deal with the guilt that's stitched like a black tumor across your brain. I'd give some thought to my problems, Mr. Alridge, before I stepped across a line and found myself irrevocably on the way to being dead for a very long time."

Then I walked back down the steps and followed a sandy path toward my truck, the wind cool and gusting off the bay through the pines. When I looked over my shoulder, Alridge was still on his deck, his hands propped on the railing, like a ship's captain peering out onto the ocean, every light in his house blazing against the darkness.

THAT NIGHT I SLEPT in a motel in Slidell, on the northeast side of Lake Pontchartrain, and early the next morning I returned to New Iberia. I felt better for having confronted Alridge, but I was no closer to resolving the contradictions at work in the Lujan homicide. With rare exception, homicides are committed for reasons of money, sex, or power, or any combination thereof. What was the motivation in Tony's death? If Monarch Little was the shooter, it was because he had tried to extort money from Tony and the extortion attempt had gone south. But Tony's occasional girlfriend, Lydia Thibodaux, had indicated Slim Bruxal had gone to the meeting with Tony. Where was Slim while Tony was being blown apart, or was Slim in fact the shooter?

It was possible. Slim was probably mixed up in the death of Crustacean Man and feared that Tony would flip for the D.A. By killing

Tony and putting it on Monarch, he would take out two problems at once. But in my mind's eye I could still see the point-blank wounds delivered to Tony's skullcap, jaw, and viscera. The person who killed Tony had borne him a special hatred and was not simply a cynical pragmatist getting a problem out of the way.

Who kills with that kind of insatiable rage?

Someone whose anger and desire for revenge comes straight out of the libido.

I looked at the clock. It was 1:21 p.m. on Friday. What better time to catch an academic about to flee a faculty meeting for the solace of a dry martini in his backyard? I called the political science department at UL in Lafayette and was told that Dr. Frank Edwards had already gone for the day.

"Could I have his home telephone number?" I asked.

"We're not allowed to give that out," the secretary said.

"I'm a police officer."

"So why don't you look in the phone directory?" she said.

I flipped open the Lafayette phone book and found the number at the top of the page. The address was in an oak-shaded neighborhood in an old part of town, one of those urban enclaves where people hold on to their accents and their eccentricities and take a peculiar pride in the genteel poverty that often marks their lives. The phone rang for a long time before a man picked up. I assumed he was not one who made use of answering machines. "Yes?" he said.

"May I speak to Dr. Edwards?"

"I'm Dr. Edwards."

"This is Detective Dave Robicheaux of the Iberia Parish Sheriff's Department. I'd like to talk with you about Tony Lujan and Slim Bruxal," I said.

For a moment I thought the line had gone dead. "Are you there, Professor?"

"Lydia Thibodaux contacted you?"

"She said you encouraged her to come forward with information about Slim and Tony. I appreciate your having done that."

Again the line went silent.

"I'd like to come over to Lafayette and talk with you in person," I said.

"Yes, I guess you would," he said, with a sense of resignation I didn't understand. "I'll be at home. How important will this turn out to be?"

"Excuse me?"

"Are we talking about a trial, public testimony, that sort of thing?"

"I'm not sure. Is there a problem, sir?"

"That depends on whether or not you think young brownshirts belong in our universities."

I took the four-lane into Lafayette, and in forty-five minutes was through the university district and driving down a quiet residential street where the sidewalks had been broken and pitched by the huge tree roots that grew under them. Inside the filtered light and the ambience of shade-blooming flowers, the palms and Spanish daggers that grew under a canopy of live oaks, the air vines and lichen-stained goldfish ponds and the late-Victorian frame houses whose rain gutters bled rust down the walls, you could have sworn you were looking at a misplaced piece of history ripped out of the year 1910.

The political science professor was reading on the gallery of his two-story house, one knee crossed, a wood-bladed fan turning overhead, a shot glass and a small pitcher by his foot. A plump, middle-aged white man in mismatched gardening clothes was watering the caladiums at the base of an oak tree with a sprinkling can. When he heard the piked gate squeak open, he smiled politely in my direction, then walked casually into the backyard with his sprinkling can, his soft buttocks tight against his pants.

"You're Dr. Edwards?" I said to the man on the gallery.

He glanced at my badge, which was clipped on my belt. "Would you like a glass of anisette? It's ice-cold," he said.

"No, thanks." I walked up on the gallery, the boards under my feet sinking with my weight. I sat on the edge of a wide, deep-set straw chair. "Could you explain that remark about young brownshirts?"

The professor was dressed in linen slacks and sandals and a tropical shirt that exposed the bones in his chest. His beard was clipped close to the skin, his teeth tiny and tea-colored inside his mouth. He closed his book on his knee.

"I think the purpose of your visit involves Slim Bruxal more than it does Tony Lujan. Slim conjures up a certain image. I think of arm-bands and people with heavy boots stomping down a street in Nuremberg. But ultimately I guess he's a victim, too."

"Not in my view. You told Lydia Thibodaux that Slim and Tony both wore masks. You told her not to be afraid of someone who couldn't live with the person inside his skin. You were talking about Slim?"

He filled his shot glass with anisette, then sipped from it, as though testing its coldness, before draining the entire glass. He wiped his lips with the tips of his fingers, his eyes focused on the columns of sun-light in his yard, the motes of dust and desiccated leaves swimming inside them.

"There's a nightclub here, where friends of a kindred spirit tend to gather," he said. "It features its own kind of entertainment. Are you with me, sir?"

"I think so."

"Most people who frequent this club have no problem with who they are. But others find excuses to be there."

"We need to get to it, Dr. Edwards."

"Slim and his friends would make themselves available at the bar. Of course, the men who picked them up would be robbed. They would also have their teeth kicked in. Not only teeth but ribs, scro-tums, or any other place Slim could get his foot."

"You know this for a fact?"

"Do you think I'd make up something like this? Do you know the risk I'm taking by telling you this?"

"With Bruxal?"

He looked away in annoyance, and frankly I couldn't blame him for it.

"Was Tony Lujan gay?" I asked.

"Maybe he hadn't decided on what he was."

"You think he came on to Slim?"

"Tony had a dependent personality. He was frightened. His girl-friend had committed suicide. I suspect he had undefined longings that . . ."

"Go on."

"For what purpose? Tony's dead. I'm going to ask one favor of you, Detective Robicheaux."

"Yes, sir?"

"If the content of this conversation is passed on to Slim Bruxal or his attorney, I want to be notified immediately."

"I'm not sure I can do that."

"It's so good to have met you," he replied, opening his book again, focusing his eyes disjointedly on the page.

THE TRAFFIC WAS HEAVY on the four-lane, and I took the old highway past Spanish Lake into New Iberia. The sun had gone behind the clouds in the west, and the air was dry and hot and dust was rising from the cane fields. I'm not qualified to speak on the question or causes of global warming, but anyone who believes Louisiana's climate is similar to the one in which I grew up has a serious thinking disorder. When I was a child, summer thunderstorms would sweep across the wetlands at almost exactly three o'clock every afternoon. Today, weeks will pass with no rain at all. The wind will turn into a blowtorch, the ground into flint, the sky into a huge cloud of cinnamon-colored dust. As I drove past Spanish Lake, I could see electricity forking inside a bank of distant thunderclouds and smell an odor on the wind like fish spawning, like first raindrops lighting on a scorching sidewalk.

I got back to the department just in time to return the cruiser and punch out for the day. Just as I was leaving the office, my phone rang. It was Joe Dupree, my friend at the Lafayette P.D. "You wanted a handle on this bozo Lefty Raguza. I didn't come up with a whole lot, but here it is. He does security work at a couple of casinos and the new track in Opelousas. He's got no arrests in Louisiana, not even traffic citations, but I suspect he's cruising on the edge of it."

"How do you mean?"

"He smokes a lot of China white because he doesn't like to use needles anymore. He also likes to bust up women with his fists, usually someone who's down to seeds and stems. He hangs in a dump in North Lafayette."

"A rough-trade joint?"

"No, it's a zebra hangout. From what I hear, the broads he picks up never see it coming. Then they're on the floor, spitting out their teeth. Dave?"

"Yeah?"

"If you have a tête-à-tête with this guy, not a lot of people around here are gonna be wringing their hands or calling up the ACLU."

He gave me the address of a club north of the Four Corners district in Lafayette.

I headed home in my truck and by the time I reached my driveway I could feel the barometer dropping and see birds descending out of the sky into the trees. Then, like a blessing from heaven, the clouds broke loose and hailstones as big as mothballs clattered down on our tin roof.

Molly and I opened all the windows and flooded the house with the cool smell of the storm, then fixed potato salad, ham-and-onion sandwiches, and iced tea, and ate supper in the kitchen. We brought Tripod and Snuggs inside and gave each of them a bowl of ice cream, which they ate in front of the floor fan, their fur lifting in the breeze. Steam rose off the bayou, then the sky went totally black with the storm and the lights came on in City Park and you could see torrents of leaves blowing out of the trees and falling on the water.

But in spite of the fine evening the rain had brought us, I couldn't stop thinking about the implications of my interview with Dr. Edwards. I believed him to be a man of conscience who had been willing to put his reputation and his academic career at risk in order to see justice done. Perhaps more significantly, he had also been willing to invite the violent potential of Slim Bruxal into his life. The legal importance of my interview with Dr. Edwards was doubtful. That fact, I'm sure, was not lost on him. The fact he had remained willing to go forward with it anyway said a lot about Dr. Edwards's character. It also said a lot about Slim Bruxal and the ferocious energies of homophobes who can't deal with the female hiding inside them.

But another piece of unfinished business was on my mind as well. As I watched Tripod eating from his ice cream bowl in front of the fan, I thought about the many years he had shared our house, and our lives, as an adopted member of the family. I thought about the war he had waged with Batist, the elderly black man who had run our bait shop, over custody of the candy bars and fried pies Batist kept on a display rack by the cash register. I remembered how Alafair, as a little girl, had snuck Tripod through her screen window and hid him under the covers after he had been expelled from the house for doing various kinds of mischief. I thought about how Tripod had always been a loyal and loving pet who never strayed more than fifty yards from his home because it had always been a safe place where he could trust the people who lived or visited there.

Then in my mind's eye I saw a blond man with tiny pits pooled in his cheeks squeezing a tube of roach paste into Tripod's bowl.

All these things, along with the fact that Monarch Little had lied to me, gave me no rest.

"Pax Christi is having a meeting at Grand Coteau tonight. I think I should go. I missed the last one. Do you mind?" Molly said.

"No, just be careful on the road," I said.

As soon as Molly had backed her car into East Main, I took my Remington twelve-gauge from the closet and sat down on the side of the bed with it and a box of pumpkin balls and double-aught bucks. Years ago I had sawed off the barrel at the pump handle, sanded the serrations smooth with emery paper, and removed the sportsman's plug from the magazine. I fed the shells into the tube, one after the other, until I felt the magazine spring come tight against my thumb. Then I called Clete Purcel at his motor court and told him I would pick him up in ten minutes.

"What's shakin', big mon?" he said.

"The Bobbsey Twins from Homicide ride again," I replied.

"Ah," he said, like a starving man dipping a spoonful of chocolate ripple into his mouth.

CHAPTER
18

THE SKY WAS STILL BLACK and charged with lightning, the cypress and oak trees along the Teche thrashing in the wind, when I parked my truck in front of Monarch Little's house. Through the front window I could see him working a crossword puzzle on his knee, his brow knitted, a small pencil clenched in his meaty hand. I kicked open the front door and entered the living room in a gust of wind and water. I threw my rain hat in his face.

"You really piss me off, Monarch. And it's not just because you're a dope dealer. It's because you're genuinely stupid," I said.

His mouth hung open.

"You know the definition of stupid?" I said. "Stupid is when you have your head stuffed so far up your fat ass you think you can help your cause by lying in a homicide investigation."

He looked past me at my truck. Clete was sitting in the passenger seat, drinking from a can of beer, the raindrops sliding down the window in the porch light.

"Who's that?" he asked.

"A friend of mine who gets even more pissed off than I do at stupid people. Pick up my hat."

"Mr. Dee, I—"

"If I have to pick it up, I'm going to slap you silly with it."

"Why you hurting me like this?" He reached down and handed me my hat. I started to hit him with it, then stopped.

"You lied to me. A lie is an act of theft. It steals people's faith and

224

makes them resent themselves. No, don't open your mouth. *Wrong* time to open your mouth, Monarch. If you try to lie to me again, I'm going out the door and let you drown in your own shit. Am I getting through here?"

"You kick open my—"

I slapped his head with my hat, twice, whipping it hard across his scalp. He took both blows full force and didn't raise his hands to protect himself. He even tried to stare me down, but his eyes were shiny now and his lower lip was trembling.

"Answer my question," I said.

"I didn't have no money. I got to bring my mother home from M.D. Anderson. She got to have nurses, special care, special diet, trips back and fort' to Houston. I t'ought I'd jack Tony Lujan for a couple of grand. So I called him up and said I'd meet him out by the Boom Boom Room. Then I started t'inking. What if he called Slim Bruxal? What if some of them colletch boys showed up wit' ball bats? What if Mr. Bello showed up and decided to pop me down by the bayou? So I ain't gone. Next t'ing I know, my car's on fire and shotgun shells are blowing up inside it."

I pressed out the folds in my rain hat and smoothed the brim. "You'll take a polygraph on that?"

"I'll ax Miss Betsy if I should."

"The FBI agent?"

"Yeah, who you t'ink? She been my friend."

"Do you know what the term 'uneducable' means?"

"No, I ain't that smart. But at least Miss Betsy ain't slapped me wit' her hat and she ain't talked to me like I'm a dumb nigger."

I had stepped into it again, taking on the role of a white man from an earlier generation talking to a black street kid who had grown up in a free-fire zone. I wanted to blame my ineptitude on Monarch, but in truth I had acted imperiously toward a man who was clinging to the sides of the planet with suction cups. Even worse, I had been deliberately cruel, an act that under any circumstances is inexcusable.

"You ever hear anything about Tony Lujan or Slim Bruxal being homosexual?" I asked.

He wiped at his nose with his wrist, then I saw several disconnected thoughts start to come together in his eyes. "You saying, like, was they lovers?"

"Not exactly."

"You saying, like, maybe they had a fight, and Slim took him out with the shotgun and put it on me?"

"Could be. Or maybe Tony came on to him and Slim couldn't deal with it. My point is, I think you're an innocent man."

He lowered his head and fiddled with his hands. When he looked up again, there were tears on his eyelashes. "I got allergies. Every time the wet'er changes, my nose starts running. I got to get me a prescription for it."

I sat down on a tattered footstool in front of him. A bolt of lightning struck on the far side of the bayou, and the entire rural slum in which Monarch lived—the pecan trees, the crepe myrtle, the slash pines, the junker cars slick with rain, the clapboard shacks and tarpaper roofs—was caught inside a cobalt glow that collapsed in on itself as quickly as it came.

"I apologize for hitting you. I didn't have the right to speak down to you, either," I said. "Believe it or not, I respect you. You treated Bello Lujan with mercy when you could have broken his neck and gotten away with it. You're a stand-up guy, Monarch. It's too bad you're on the wrong side of the fence."

"What's 'uneducable' or whatever mean?"

"It means Betsy Mossbacher is probably straight-up, but watch out for the DOJ. They'll use you, then spit you out like yesterday's chewing gum. You heard it first from the Iberia Parish Sheriff's Department."

"I ain't up to this no more."

THE CLUB WHERE Lefty Raguza hung out was located north of the Four Corners area in Lafayette, on a backstreet that for years had marked the border between a poor black neighborhood of dirt streets and rental shotgun cabins and a similar neighborhood of poor whites and what are sometimes called Creoles or people of color. Before the civil rights era, the bar had been one where dark-skinned people moved back and forth across the color line as the situation demanded. In back, inside a grove of pine and cedar trees, was a cluster of dilapidated cabins where many an interracial tryst was conducted.

Over the years the streets had become paved and the privies replaced by indoor plumbing, but the Caribbean nature of the neighborhood and the function of the bar, one that Joe Dupree had referred to as a zebra hangout, remained unchanged.

I turned off the asphalt into a gravel parking lot that was pooled with gray water and layered with flattened beer cans. The club was oblong, built of both cinder blocks and wood, all of it painted red and purple, the corrugated roof the color of an old nickel. Behind the building, a transformer on a pole was leaking sparks into the darkness, but a gasoline generator was roaring inside a wooden shed, powering the lights inside the bar. When I turned off the ignition, killing the windshield wipers, the rain cascaded down the glass.

"That's his Ford Explorer," Clete said.

"You're sure?" I said.

"He followed me all the way to New Orleans in it."

Clete's humped shape, his porkpie hat tilted down on his forehead, was silhouetted against a streetlight. My twelve-gauge pump rested between his thighs, the barrel leaning away from him, against the dash.

"I'm going through the front door. Watch the back," I said.

"How far you want to take this?"

"That's up to Raguza."

"I know you, Dave. You get us into rooms without doors or windows, then give yourself absolution for leaving hair on the walls."

"This from *you*?"

"If you want to smoke the guy, I got a throw-down on my ankle. But get him out of the bar before you do it."

"You're exaggerating the nature of the situation, Clete."

"Right," he said.

I unclipped my holster and my .45 from my belt and set them on the floor of the cab. Then I took my slapjack out of my raincoat pocket and set it on top of the holster. "Satisfied?"

"Where's your hideaway?" he asked.

"Which hideaway?" I said.

He tapped the edge of his loafer against my right ankle. "What's that, a steel brace?"

"Stay in the truck."

He pulled at his belt and made a face, but this time it wasn't about me. "You got any Tums? I ate some shrimp spaghetti for lunch that smelled like three-day-old fish bait."

I got out in the rain. The power wire on the pole fell into the darkness, then struck a pool of water and snapped like a coach whip. Clete got out on the other side of the truck, the shotgun stiff and hard-looking inside his raincoat. He walked heavily toward the rear of the club, his big shoulders bent forward, the back of his neck glistening with rainwater.

I pushed open the front door and stepped inside the smoky, air-conditioned coolness of the club. A long wood bar ran the length of one wall. The people drinking there glanced at the door and the inrush of rain, as though expecting an event, a messenger, a harbinger that would indicate a change in their lives. Then they returned to their drinks or watching their reflections in the bar mirror, hypnotized somehow by the stylized ways they smoked their own cigarettes.

In an alcove to the right of the bar was a cone of yellow light, under which Lefty Raguza stood by a pool table, chalking the tip of his cue. He wore a pleated short-sleeved lavender shirt and cream-colored slacks and suede shoes with thick soles and heels. His sleeves were folded neatly on his upper arms so that his biceps bulged against the fabric with the tautness of muskmelons. He gave no indication of noticing my entry into the club, but I knew that he saw me, in the same way you know when a predator's eyes brush across your skin, like the touch of a soiled hand.

I ordered a glass of club soda and ice with a lemon twist at the bar and watched him in the mirror. He leaned over the table and busted an eight-ball rack all over the felt. A solitary ball dropped into a corner pocket, but he didn't move toward his next shot. Instead, he set his cue butt-down on the floor and casually chalked his cue again, stroking the talc across the rounded surface, taking his time, ignoring the other shooter, who waited by the wall rack, obviously impatient for the game to go forward.

"Tell you what," Raguza said. "Three bucks on each ball in the string. Three to you for each one I leave."

The other shooter, a heavy man who looked like a Mexican laborer, nodded without speaking.

Raguza bent over the table and sank one ball after another with the geometrical precision of an artist, banking shots, making combinations, using reverse English, crawling the cue ball along the rail until it whispered against the target ball and dropped it with a deep thud into a leather pocket.

Then he scratched, with three balls still on the felt, the signature of a hustler who never allows the sucker to feel he's been taken. But when Raguza went back to his table and joined a high-yellow woman who wore a knit tank top over a bulging bra, I could see the look of triumph in his eyes, the curl at the corner of his mouth.

The back door opened and I felt the building decompress, the walls creaking slightly, as Clete came in from the storm and walked through the shadows, past a latticework partition into the men's room.

Clete had accused me of planning to take Lefty Raguza off the board. The truth was I had no plan. Or perhaps more honestly I had no conscious one. But I knew that Raguza belonged to that group of human beings whose pathology is always predictable. By reason of either genetic defect, environmental conditioning, or a deliberate choice to join themselves at the hip with the forces of darkness, they incorporate into their lives a form of moral insanity that is neither curable nor subject to analysis. They enjoy inflicting pain, and view charity and forgiveness as signals of both weakness and opportunity. The only form of remediation they understand is force. The victim who believes otherwise condemns himself to the death of a thousand cuts.

So, if your profession requires that you remain within the parameters of the law, how do you deal with the Lefty Raguzas of the world?

The answer is you don't. You turn their own energies against them. You treat their personal histories with contempt. You yawn at their stories of neglect and deprivation and beatings by alcoholic fathers and promiscuous mothers. Worse, you laugh at them in front of other people. The effect can be like a bolt of lightning bouncing around inside a steel box.

The bartender put a bowl of peanuts in front of me. His black hair looked like oily wire combed across his pate. "You a cop?" he said.

"I look like a cop?"

"Yeah," he replied.

"You never can tell," I said.

"We got free gumbo tonight. It'll be done in a minute." Behind him, a stainless-steel cauldron was starting to bubble on a ring of butane flame.

I looked in the mirror at the reflection of Lefty Raguza. But now he had more company than the mulatto woman in the knit top. A man with washed-out blue eyes that did not fit his negroid face and ropelike black hair plaited down tightly on his scalp sat next to him. Sitting across from them was a man whose size and proportions took me all the way back to a specific moment in Opa-Locka, Florida, when Dallas Klein had burst out the back of the bar, trying to flee the consequences of his gambling addiction, and had collided into a man who seemed as big as the sky.

What was the name? Nestor? Ernest? No, Ernesto. His neck rose into his gigantic head with no taper, as though his neck and jowls were one tubular column of meat and bone. The width and curvature of his upper back made me think of a whale breaking the surface of a wave.

I looked toward the men's room. Clete was still inside.

"What are they drinking over there by the pool table?" I said.

"Beer," the bartender replied.

I placed a twenty-dollar bill on the bar. "Send them a pitcher on me."

"Something I should know about here?" he asked.

"Nothing I can think of," I replied.

A few moments later I watched in the mirror as the bartender set the pitcher in the midst of Lefty Raguza's group. I saw Raguza glance in my direction, then tell the bartender to take the pitcher away. Clete was still not out of the restroom. But showtime was showtime, I told myself. I picked up my club soda and walked past the pool table until I was standing behind Raguza's chair.

"You don't like draft beer?" I said.

The tin-shaded light over the pool table threw my shadow across Raguza's hands and wrists. He waited a long time before he spoke. "This is a private party here," he said.

"Does this lady know your history, Lefty?" I said.

"You need to beat feet, Jack. This is not your jurisdiction." His hands were folded, his thumbs motionless. He didn't turn his head when he spoke.

I scraped a chair up behind him and sat down, so that I was looking over his shoulder, like a kibitzer at a card game. I stared into the face of the woman next to him. She tried to smile, then her eyes broke and her face went flat.

"Lefty ever tell you about his psychiatric problems?" I said.

"Excuse me?"

"He likes to beat up women with his fists. It happens so fast they rarely know what hit them."

"I'm not sure what we're talking about," she said. She lowered her eyes and placed one hand on the tabletop. Then she took it away and placed it in her lap.

"A prison psychiatrist once described Lefty as an anal-retentive. That means he was strapped on the training pot for long periods of time. I suspect his Jockey underwear is loaded with skid marks." I laughed and clapped Raguza hard on the back, snorting when I inhaled. "How about it, Lefty? You ever download into your Fruit of the Looms?"

I could see the back of his neck darken, like a shadow creeping from his collar to his boxed hairline. "Lefty has a problem with animals, too," I said to the woman. "If you ask him why he's cruel to a gentle and defenseless creature, he'll probably tell you about all the hard breaks he had when he was a kid. The truth is Lefty hurts pets and innocent people because he's a gutless punk and never could cut it on his own, either as a child or an adult. Lefty was probably a good bar of soap in prison, but don't let him ever tell you he was stand-up or a solid con. He had sissy status even before he got to Raiford and was probably giving head in the bridal suite his first day down. Right, Lefty?"

I let out a wheezing laugh and slapped him hard between the shoulder blades again. The muscles in his back were corded as tight as cable. The woman started to get up from her chair.

"Sit down," Lefty said. "This guy's a drunk. He got run out of Miami, he got run out of New Orleans. He makes a lot of noise, then he goes away."

"Wish I could do that, Lefty, I mean just kind of disappear. But you poisoned ole Tripod. It takes a special sort of guy to do something like that."

Even from the side I could see his face scrunch. "I did *what*?" he said.

"That's the name of my daughter's pet raccoon. He almost died because you mixed roach paste with sardines and put them in his pet bowl." I looked across the table. "What would you do if you were in my place, Ernesto?"

Ernesto's eyes were small and brown, deep-set, nonexpressive. His hair was tied in a matador's twist on the nape of his neck. He shrugged his shoulders and smiled in a self-deprecating fashion.

"How about you?" I said to the man whose blue eyes didn't match his face.

He glanced from side to side, as though the answer to my question lay in some other part of the bar. His plaits looked like centipedes on his scalp. He wore a purple silk shirt and a crucifix and a P-38 G.I. can opener on a chain around his neck. "I don't got nothing to do wit' dis, mon," he said.

"Glad to hear that, because Lefty here has been a bad boy. I wonder if Whitey knows that Lefty has been causing a lot of trouble over in Iberia Parish, like pouring acid all over Clete Purcel's car. I thought you were a pro, Lefty, but the more I see your handiwork, the more I get the impression you're just a little jailhouse bitch who can't get it up unless he's whacking on a helpless female. Is that because you're short?"

I saw the thumb on his left hand twitch slightly.

"Those elevator soles on your stomps aren't strong indicators of self-confidence," I said. I patted him softly in the middle of the back and felt his skin constrict from the blow that didn't come.

"You're wrapped too tight," I said. "Relax, I'm not going to hurt you. You're probably one of those guys who—" I started laughing again, my words breaking apart. "Seriously, you're one of those guys who has a legitimate beef with the universe. It's not easy being a little guy or the product of a busted rubber." I hit him again, and laughed harder, coughing on the back of my wrist, my eyes watering. "Did your mother ever pick you up by inserting Q-tips in your ears? That's a sure sign there are problems in the family."

His neck was blood-dark, the skin around his mouth drawn down like a shark's. His hands were set squarely on the tabletop. He coughed deep in his throat and spoke in a clotted whisper, his eyes fastened on the opposite wall.

"You got to speak up, Lefty," I said.

"I did thirty-seven days in isolation, in the dark, a cup of water and one slice of white bread a day. I can take the worst you got and spit it in your face."

"Really?"

"I'm done talking with you. Find yourself an alcoholic titty to suck on. I can direct you to a topless bar full of guys like you," he said.

A man walked over from the bar and scraped up the cue ball from the pool table. He bounced it off two rails and watched it miss a pocket. "Anybody up for a game of rotation?" he asked.

"Yeah, over here," Raguza said, and threw three quarters on the felt.

Ernesto and the man with the Islands accent grinned at him, happy in the knowledge their friend was back in the groove.

I glanced toward the latticework partition in front of the men's room. Clete was watching us from behind it, the shotgun still inside his raincoat, the brim of his hat low on his brow. I shook my head at him.

I should have known Raguza wouldn't rattle. He had stacked too much hard time in too many joints and had probably thrived in the prison population. Also, he may have seen Clete behind the lattice-work and figured he was being set up to get blown out of his socks.

I got up from the chair and went back to the bar to retrieve my hat. Then Lefty Raguza, like every wiseass on the planet, decided he'd have another run at fate.

"He's no problem. Believe me, the guy's a joke," he said to the others at his table.

A joke. Those words were essentially the same ones Dallas Klein heard just before his executioner pulled the trigger on him.

I put on my rain hat and showed no indication I had heard Raguza's remark, then walked around the end of the bar onto the duckboards. "Need to borrow this. I'll settle up with you later," I said to the bartender.

"Whoa," he said.

"No 'whoa' to it, bud," I said.

I used two dish towels to pick up the stainless-steel cauldron from the stove, then I headed straight for Raguza. His friends saw me coming, but unfortunately for him, he didn't. The woman pushed her chair back, knocking it to the floor, holding her purse in front of her. "Where you think you're going?" Raguza said.

I slipped one wadded towel under the cauldron's bottom and poured the entire contents—perhaps two gallons of steaming gumbo—on his head.

It must have hit him like a whoosh of flame from a blast furnace. He screamed and clutched his face and tried to wipe the curtain of stewed tomatoes and okra and shrimp off his skin. He rolled on the floor, clawing at his hair, kicking his feet. I picked up a pitcher of beer from another table and poured it onto his face. "You okay down there?" I said.

Ernesto and the man from the Islands had risen from their chairs and were coming around the table. Clete stepped out from behind the partition, opening his raincoat so they could see his shotgun, which he held against his side, muzzle-down, his wrist protruding through a slit in the coat's pocket. "You guys want to buy into this, that can be arranged," he said.

The room was absolutely silent, the patrons at the bar frozen in time and place, the bartender's hand motionless on the telephone.

Clete raised his left hand palm-up, curling his fingers, signaling for me to walk toward him, his eyes on Ernesto and the man from the Islands.

I wiped a smear of gumbo off my fingers onto one of the dish towels and dropped the towel on top of Raguza, then started walking toward Clete and the back door. My mouth was dry, my heart racing, my face suddenly cold and damp in the breeze from an air-conditioning unit. Then I saw Clete's eyes shift, his expression constrict, and I heard feet running at my back.

Lefty Raguza tackled me around the waist and threw us both into a tangle of chairs and a table laden with beer bottles. His face was bright and shiny, like a painted Indian's, his skin already swelling where it had been scalded. He clenched his right hand deep into my throat and hit me full in the face with the other. Then he was all over me.

He head-butted me, got a thumb in my eye, and tried to grab my genitalia. I could smell the deodorant under his armpits and the bile in his breath and the testosterone in his clothes; see the patina of blond hair on his skin, the mucus at the corner of his eye, a pearl of sweat drip from a nostril. I could see his buttocks clench as he wrapped his legs around me and the sensual pleasure on his mouth when he thought he was connecting with bone and organ.

I got my fingers around the neck of a beer bottle and broke the bottle across his face. But it did no good. When I was almost to my feet, he tackled me again, this time around the knees, locking his arms around my calves as I toppled forward. Then he felt the .25 automatic Velcro-strapped to my ankle.

"Got you," he said, working his hand down to the holster. "Gold BB time, dickwad."

He was on all fours, the .25 auto peeling loose from the holster, his right hand gripped like a machinist's vise on my foot so I couldn't move it. The cool green fire in his eyes was like a lascivious burn on my skin. I cocked my left foot and drove my loafer straight into his mouth.

I saw his lips burst against his teeth and the shock of the blow climb into his eyes. I stomped his mouth again, in the same place, at the same angle, doing even more serious damage. Then I caught him across the nose and saw something go out of his eyes and face that was not replaceable.

But the succubus I had tried to exorcise by marrying a woman of peace still held title to my soul. I saw the room distort and the faces of the people around me turn into Grecian masks, and I heard a sound in my ears like the steel tracks of armored vehicles wending their way across an unforgiving land. I heard people screaming and I did not know if their voices were from my sleep or if my own deeds had transformed me into an object of horror and pity in the eyes of my fellow man.

I ran Lefty Raguza's head into the corner of the pool table and saw a horsetail of blood leap across the felt. I kicked his legs apart, as though I were about to frisk him, then lost my purpose and smashed his face down on the table's rim—once, twice, perhaps even a third time. When he fell to the floor his nose was roaring blood, his eyes filled with a new knowledge about the potential of evil, namely, that others could possess elements of darkness in their breast that were the equal of his own.

"Suffering Mother of Jesus, back off, Dave!" I heard Clete say.

"What?" I said, my own voice wrapped inside a sound like wind blowing in a tunnel.

"Dude's finished. He's bleeding from every hole in his body. You hear me? Back away. He's not worth it. The guy may be hemorrhaging."

I could feel the room come back in focus, see the faces staring at me in the gloom, their mouths downturned, their eyes marked with sadness, as though everyone there had in some way been diminished by the violence they had witnessed. Clete was standing between me and Lefty Raguza now, the shotgun still inside his coat.

"I just need a few more seconds with him," I said. "Can't just walk away and leave loose ends."

"No, we bag it and shag it," he replied, reaching for my arm.

I pulled loose from his grasp and knelt beside Raguza. I reached down in my raincoat pocket, then bent over him, my back obscuring the view of Clete and Raguza's friends, my hands going down almost involuntarily to Raguza's face and the blood that rilled back from the corners of his mouth. When I got to my feet, the ends of my fingers looked like they had been dipped in a freshly opened can of paint.

Clete stuck one arm in mine and pulled me with him, out the door, into the night, into the clean smell of ozone and trees that were dripping with rain. A crowd had formed around Lefty Raguza, and I heard a man in a Cajun accent say, "What's that in his t'roat? Get it out of his t'roat. The guy cain't get no air."

There was a pause, then a second man, also with a Cajun accent, replied, "It's toot'paste. No, it ain't. It's a crunched-up tube of bug poison. Holy shit, the guy done this is a *cop*?"

CHAPTER
19

CLETE DROVE BECAUSE MY HANDS would not stop shaking in the aftermath of what I had done to Lefty Raguza. The wind had knocked an oak limb down on a power line by Four Corners, darkening part of the city, killing all the traffic lights. Clete sped through the black district, then skirted the university, splashed through the bottom of an underpass, and caught the four-lane to New Iberia. He made it as far as the first drive-by liquor store south of town.

"What are you doing?" I said.

"Time for some high-octane liquids. I'm over the hill for this stuff. You want a Dr Pepper?" he said, getting out of the truck.

"Leave the booze alone, Clete."

"You should have seen your face back there. You scare me sometimes, Dave."

His words and their content seemed to have been spoken to me by someone else. I watched him walk inside the liquor store and put a six-carton of beer and a pint of Johnnie Walker on the counter. He bought a length of boudin, and while the clerk warmed it in the microwave, he went to the cooler and brought back a king-size bottle of Dr Pepper. I wanted to walk inside and ask him to repeat what he'd said, as though my challenge to him could take the sting out of his remark. Then I realized that my attention was less on Clete than on his purchase—the ice-cold bottles of Dixie, their gold-and-green labels sweating with moisture, the reddish-amber wink inside the Johnnie Walker. I rubbed my hand on my mouth and stared at the trees changing shape in the wind, a yellow ignition of light splintering through the clouds without sound.

Clete pulled open the driver's door and got inside, wiping the rain out of his eyes with the back of his wrist. He handed me the Dr Pepper and twisted off the cap on the Johnnie Walker. He looked sideways at me before he drank. "This is rude as hell, Dave, but my nervous system is shot," he said.

Then he took a deep hit and chased it with Dixie. The color bloomed in his face and his chest swelled against his shirt. "Wow, that's more like it," he said. "I swear that stuff goes straight into my johnson. Four inches of Scotch or gin and I need to lock my schlong in a vault."

"What was that crack about my face?" I asked.

"I thought you were going to do the guy."

"He deserved what he got. I'd do it all over again."

"You want to lose your badge over a shithead like Raguza? This isn't Iberia Parish. We got no safety net here, Streak."

He drank again from the Scotch bottle and out of the corner of his eye saw me watching him. "Drink your Dr Pepper," he said.

"Tell me that again and see what happens."

He turned on the radio and began changing the stations. "The Cubs got a game on."

I turned the radio off. "Where do you get off lecturing me, Clete?" I said.

He put his booze down and rested his big arms across the top of the steering wheel. "Here's what it is. The problem's not you, it's me. I wasn't kidding about leaving my big-boy in a safe-deposit box. I got myself in a jam with Trish. It's not just sexual. I really dig her. But I think she and her friends are planning a serious score."

He was obviously redirecting the subject, protecting me from my own bad mood and the darkness that still lived inside me. But that was Clete Purcel, a man who would always allow himself to be hurt in order to save his friends from themselves.

"A serious score where?" I asked.

"Maybe a takedown on a casino."

"They pulled off that savings and loan job in Mobile, didn't they?"

"If they did, they got lucky. They're all amateurs. They get up each day and pretend they're country singers or boxers or Hollywood screenwriters. It's like being in a roomful of schizophrenics. Look, I may have a few bad entries in my jacket, but I'm not a criminal, for Chrissakes."

"Get away from them."

"What do I do, just throw Trish over the gunnels because she wants to nail the guy who killed her father?"

"In a word, *yes*." When he didn't answer, I said, "I think they already creeped Bruxal's house."

"How you know that?"

"Joe Dupree at Lafayette P.D. told me. A couple of guys impersonated repairmen from the gas company and got free run of the house for a half hour."

"What for?"

"Who knows? Stop drinking if you're going to drive."

"They were actually inside Bruxal's house?"

"Ask Trish Klein."

"Dave, you have a talent for making people feel miserable. Every woman I meet turns my life into a nightmare. And all you can say is 'Stop drinking if you're going to drive'? Twenty minutes ago you were trying to kill a guy with your bare hands. Why don't you show a little empathy for a change?"

We were back to normal. He spun gravel under the tires and roared onto the highway, fishtailing on the asphalt, bent over the wheel like a sorrowful behemoth.

I HAD LEFT A NOTE for Molly before I had picked up Clete and gone to Monarch Little's house. When I got home the note was still on the kitchen table, with an additional message written in Molly's hand at the bottom: "Got too tired and couldn't wait up. Pecan pie and milk in the icebox. Love, Molly."

I checked the message machine and the caller identification on the telephone. No one had called that evening. I stripped in the bathroom, stuffed my bloody shirt and trousers deep in the clothes hamper, and got in the shower. Molly was still asleep when I lay down beside her. Outside, the rain ticked in the trees and occasionally the flasher lights on emergency vehicles passed on the street. But none of them stopped in front of my house.

Lefty Raguza had obviously not dimed me with the Lafayette P.D. Would he come around again and try to square things on his own? I doubted it. His real problem would be with Whitey Bruxal. Men like Whitey want respectability almost as much as they desire power and obscene amounts of money. Raguza had just managed to drag Whitey's name into a back-of-town barroom brawl resulting from Raguza's cruelty to an animal. I had a feeling Whitey's bedside visit to his employee would not be a sympathetic one.

But I had a problem of my own that would not go away, nor would it let me sleep. After four hours, I gave up any hope of escaping the gargoyle that lived within me. I sat on the side of the bed, my hands in my lap, my head filled with images that no power on earth could relieve me of. The digital clock on the nightstand read 4:13 a.m. "What's wrong, Dave?" I heard Molly say.

"I tried to kill a guy tonight," I replied.

I felt her weight shift on the mattress, her legs and bottom slide loose from the sheets. She walked around the side of the bed and sat beside me. She picked up my hand and looked hard into my face. "Tried to kill which guy?" she said.

"The man who poisoned Tripod. I kicked his face in, then I shoved that tube of roach paste down his throat. I mean down his throat, too. I wanted him to strangle on it."

She looked into space, her hand still covering mine. "How bad did you hurt him?"

"Enough so he'll never poison one of our animals again."

"Dave, when you say you wanted to kill this man, you're describing an emotion, not an intention. There's a big difference. Had you really wanted to kill him, he'd be dead."

I thought about what she had just said. The implications were not necessarily flattering. "I never shot anyone who didn't try to kill me first," I said, now defending a history of violence that went all the way back to Vietnam.

"This man is evil and I wish you hadn't gone after him on your own. But stop judging yourself so harshly. You were protecting a creature who can't protect himself. You don't think God can understand that?"

I'm not a theologian, but I believe absolution can be granted to us in many forms. Perhaps it can come in the ends of a woman's fingers on your skin. Some people call it the redemptive power of love. Anyway, why argue with it when it comes your way?

THE NEXT MORNING was Saturday and Helen was home when I called her. I told her about my behavior of the previous night, every detail of it, including the fact Clete had backed my play with a twelve-gauge pump. When I finished my account, I could hear a whirring sound in the receiver and feel a steel band tightening across my sternum.

"You still there?" I said.

"I don't know what to say."

"Nobody called in a nine-one-one?"

"That's your main concern here?"

"Raguza dealt the play. Considering what he did to Tripod, I think he got off light."

"There's no point talking to you. You hear nothing I say."

"I called to tell you I'll take the heat. If it costs me my job, that's the way it is. I don't want you compromised."

"I'm having a hard time with this show of magnanimity."

"I did what I felt I had to. I'm sorry if I've hurt you or the department," I said. "I know Raguza, Helen. He's the kind of guy you put out of action before he burns your house down."

It was quiet a moment, then I heard a sound like dry bread being crunched and I realized she was eating toast. I thought our conversation was over, that my moment in the confessional box had come and gone. As was often the case in my dealings with the complexity of Helen Soileau, I was wrong.

"One day they're going to kill you, Pops. When that happens, a big part of me is going to die with you," she said.

I went outside and worked in the yard, flinging shovel-loads of compost into the flower beds, my eyes burning with sweat. Then I jogged two miles in the park, but Helen's words stayed with me like an arrow in the chest. Just as I returned home, out of breath, aching for a shower, Betsy Mossbacher pulled a steel-gray Toyota into my drive.

"Hello," I said.

She didn't reply. She got out of her car and looked me flat in the face. Her jeans were belted high on her hips, her cowboy boots powdered with dust.

"What's the trouble?" I said.

"You are."

"You'll have to explain that to me."

"You went over to Lafayette and beat the crap out of Lefty Raguza."

"What about it?" I said.

My cavalier attitude seemed to light a fire in her chest. Her eyes stayed fixed on my face, as though she was deciding how much information she should convey to a fool. "You listen," she said. "We have knowledge about the inner workings of Whitey Bruxal's circle that you don't. You understand the connotations of what I'm saying?"

"You've got him tapped?"

She didn't acknowledge my question. "Bruxal thinks Trish Klein and her merry pranksters are planning to take down one of his operations. He also thinks your fat friend Clete Purcel is involved. So what do you guys do? You remodel Raguza's head and stuff a tube of Super Glue down his throat."

"It was roach paste," I said.

She blinked, I suspected from a level of anger that she could barely contain. "You think this is funny?"

"No, I don't," I replied.

"Good. Because we now have the sense Whitey believes you and Purcel may both be working with Trish Klein. In fact, it wouldn't surprise me if you are."

"Wrong. Look, you know anything about Whitey's house getting creeped?"

"No," she said, surprised.

"I think Trish Klein's friends did it. They convinced Whitey's wife they were from the gas company."

I could see the consternation in her face. It was obvious the Lafayette P.D. was not sharing information with her, perhaps because she was a woman, perhaps because she was a Fed, or perhaps both.

"What were they after?" she asked.

"You got me. But whatever it is, Purcel is not part of it."

"That's not the impression we have. Your friend's anatomy seems turned around. I think his penis and main bowel are located where his brains should be," she said.

"You don't have the right to talk about him like that," I said.

"You still don't get it, do you? I work with a few people who aren't as charitable as I am. They wouldn't be totally unhappy if Whitey decided to have your friend clipped. Of if Whitey decided to put up a kite on an Iberia Parish detective who's known for his hostility toward the Bureau."

"You're a rough bunch."

"You don't know the half of it," she said.

Then I saw a look in her face that every veteran police officer recognizes. It was the look of a cop out of sync with her peers, her supervisors, and the political and bureaucratic obligations that had been dropped on her. There may be room in government service for the altruist and the iconoclast, but I have yet to see one who was not treated as an oddity at best and at worst an object of suspicion and fear.

"I talked with Monarch Little last night," I said. "He admitted he called Tony Lujan and tried to shake him down just before Tony was killed. They were supposed to meet out by the Boom Boom Room, but Monarch claims he decided not to go."

"So?" she said.

"I believe him. I think Monarch is an innocent man."

She bit off a piece of her thumbnail and looked down the street. "Who do you think did it?"

"Right now I'd bet money on Slim Bruxal."

"Could be," she said. "Tell Purcel to keep his wick dry and stay away from casinos. One other thing—"

"I don't know if I can handle it."

"I talked to the sheriff before I came over here. She seems to be very protective toward you. I'd thank my stars I had a boss like that."

I decided not to comment on her ongoing inventory of my personal life. I wrote my cell number on a slip of paper and handed it to her. "Call me with anything you get on Trish Klein. I'll do the same," I said.

"I hope you're telling me the truth."

"I don't want to offend you, but I think you should give some serious thought to the way you talk to other people, Agent Mossbacher."

"No shit?" she replied.

After she stuck my number in her shirt pocket, she backed into my garbage can and mashed it between her bumper and an oak tree. "Oh jeez, I can't believe I did this again," she said, twisting the steering wheel, bouncing over the curb in a shuddering scrape of steel against concrete.

I was convinced they grew them special in Chugwater, Wyoming.

ON SUNDAY, Molly and I went to Mass at the university chapel in Lafayette, then ate deep-fried crawfish at Foti's in St. Martinville and took an airboat ride on Lake Martin. It was a wonderful afternoon. The lake was wide, the water high from the storm, the shoreline bordered with flooded cypress and willow trees whose leaves riffled in the breeze. Strapped into the elevated seats on the airboat, roaring across the lily pads, ear protectors clamped down on our heads, we had an extraordinary view of the Edenic loveliness that at one time characterized all of Louisiana. Each time the airboat tilted into a turn or swerved across a slough that was little more than wet sand, Molly hugged my arm like a teenage girl on a carnival ride.

But I couldn't get my mind off my conversation with Betsy Mossbacher. Obviously she had learned through a phone tap that Whitey Bruxal believed he was about to be taken down by the daughter of a man he had ordered killed. It was probably true he had ice water in his veins; indeed, he had probably been respected for his intelligence and mathematical talents by Meyer Lansky, the financial wizard of the Mob. But I believed that Whitey, like his mentors in Brooklyn and Miami, was driven by avarice, and like any man addicted to the love of money, his greatest and most abiding fear was not the loss of his life or even his soul.

"What are you thinking about?" Molly asked.

"Nothing," I said.

We were walking from the airboat landing to her car. The sun hung just above a line of willow trees on the far side of the lake, and a long, segmented line of black geese wended its way across it. Molly took my hand in hers. "You still thinking about that incident the other night?" she said.

"A little bit."

"You took Communion, didn't you?"

"I was drunk when my friend Dallas Klein died. If I hadn't been drinking, I could have taken a couple of those guys out."

"Let the past go, Dave."

"It doesn't work that way."

"What doesn't?"

"We're the sum total of what we've done and where we've been. I still see Dallas's face in my sleep. It's no accident Whitey Bruxal ended up here," I replied.

I saw a look of sadness come into her eyes that I would have cut off my fingers to remove.

I should have been happy with all the gifts I had. Actually, I was, more than I can describe. But I had figured out a way to pay back Whitey Bruxal for Opa-Locka, Florida, and the slate was about to get wiped clean, one way or another.

CHAPTER
20

THE BRUXAL HOME looked like it had been airlifted from Boca Raton and dropped from a high altitude onto a rolling stretch of white-railed horse country fifteen miles north of Lafayette. It was three stories, built in a staggered fashion of pink stucco, with a tile roof and heavy oak doors and scrolled-iron balconies. In the side yard was a turquoise pool surrounded by banana trees, trellises heavy with trumpet vine, potted palms, and the overhang of giant live oaks. Immaculate automobiles that could not have cost less than seventy thousand dollars were parked in the driveway and the porte cochere, almost as though they had been posed for a photographic display demonstrating the munificence of a free-market system that was available to rich and poor alike.

Beyond the barn a red Morgan, a mare, galloped in a field. I thought of the winged horse emblazoned on the T-shirt worn by Yvonne Darbonne the day she died. I thought of her young life destroyed by rape at the hands of Bellerophon Lujan, and I thought of the boys who had gangbanged her in a fraternity house when she was stoned, and I thought of the innocent people all over the world who suffer because of the greed and selfishness of the few.

These were not good thoughts to entertain as I pulled an unmarked departmental car next to the SUV Slim Bruxal had driven the afternoon he busted up Monarch Little at the McDonald's on East Main in New Iberia.

I had called Whitey earlier, at his office, and had asked to see him.

Most criminals of his background would have hung up or told me to talk to their attorney. But Whitey was an intelligent man and had done the unexpected, inviting me to his home at lunchtime. If I was to have any degree of success with him, I needed to empty my mind of all residual anger about him and his friends, even my conviction that they had murdered Dallas Klein, and concentrate on one objective only, and that was to leave in Whitey's head a tangle of snakes that would eat him alive.

When he opened the door, he stepped out on the porch and looked in the yard, virtually ignoring my presence. "You seen the gardener?"

"No," I said blankly.

"That's all right. Come on in. I got this new gardener. He chopped up the hose in the lawn mower. What are you gonna do? People don't want to work for a living anymore."

I had to hand it to him. Dressed in white slacks and a black short-sleeved shirt with a silver monogram on the pocket, his white hair clipped and neatly combed, he was the image of an athletic, self-confident man in his prime. The fact I had stomped the shit out of his right-hand man seemed inconsequential to him. He hit me on the shoulder and told me to come into the living room with him.

"So what's on your mind?" he said, walking ahead of me.

"I've got a dilemma," I said.

"Yeah?" he replied, sitting down in a chair upholstered in red velvet.

Through the front window I could see the driveway, a big live oak in the yard, and the four-lane highway that led to Opelousas. "The Iberia Parish D.A. is an ambitious guy. He wants to wrap up Tony Lujan's homicide and maybe make a lot of black voters happy at the same time. Get my drift?"

"No, I don't get your drift."

"Monarch Little skates. Your boy takes the bounce. I don't know if Lonnie is going to ask for the needle or not."

"Say that again."

"Lonnie Marceaux wants to be governor or a United States senator. He's not going to get there by convicting a black dirtbag nobody cares about. Lonnie wants to screw you, Mr. Bruxal. By screwing you, he can also bring down Colin Alridge. *That* will buy him the national attention he needs."

"Call me Whitey. Slim didn't kill Tony. Tony was his friend. Where you get off with this?"

"Tony was going to give up Slim on the hit-and-run death of the homeless man. There's another theory about Slim's motivation as well."

"Theories are like skid marks on the bowl. Everybody's got them. I think you're here to squeeze my balls."

I glanced out the window at the highway, then grinned at him. "You're not going to own anything to squeeze, Whitey," I said.

For the first time his brow wrinkled.

"The Feds have you and Bellerophon Lujan on racketeering charges. Lonnie wants a piece of you, too. That's where your son comes in," I said. "Second in line does the time. From Lonnie's perspective, your ass is grass."

"You saying Bello is rolling over on me?"

"I'm saying it's a done deal. Come on, you're a smart man. Bello's a coonass, born and bred in South Louisiana. You're from Brooklyn. People here think New York is a place where homosexuals go to get married and every other woman has an abortion."

"Why you keep looking out the window?"

I ignored his question. "This is the short version. They're about to freeze your assets. As you probably know, a RICO conviction will allow the Feds to seize everything you own. In the meantime, you've got other issues and other enemies to deal with."

"*Issues?* I don't like that word. Everybody is always talking about *issues.*" Then, paradoxically, he said, "What issues? What enemies?"

He saw me looking out the window again, this time at a vintage Cadillac convertible with a fresh pink paint job coming up the driveway from the four-lane. "Who's that guy?" he said.

"He does scut work for us. I told him I'd be here. You mind?"

"What's his name?"

"Clete Purcel."

"That fat guy is Purcel? Yeah, I do mind. His squeeze is this Trish Klein broad. What are you guys working here?"

I got up and opened the side door to the terrace. "Hey, Cletus, over here," I said.

"Hey, you answer my question," Whitey said.

But again I didn't reply. Clete walked through the dappled shade of the live oak, his face affable and handsome behind his yellow-tinted aviator's glasses. I could feel the air-conditioned coolness from the living room rushing past me into the heat and humidity of the afternoon.

"Hey, how's it hangin'?" he said to Whitey as he came through the door, uninvited.

But I had underestimated Whitey. He might have been a creature of his times, his psychological makeup as hard as the concrete he grew up on, but he was nevertheless capable of mustering a level of dignity, even if it was feigned, that men of his background seldom possess.

"It's lunchtime and I was going to ask Mr. Robicheaux to join me," he said. "Because you're his friend, you're welcome, too. But this is still my home, the place where my family lives. Any guest in my house has to respect that."

"You got it, Whitey. But I've had the pleasure of meeting your employee Lefty Raguza. He's not a family-type guy," Clete said.

"What might have happened outside this house has no application inside it, you follow? You want to eat, there's a spread laid out for us in the dining room. You want to act rude, it's time for you to go," Whitey said.

"Here's a story for you," Clete said. "We've got a congressman here who was asked to describe Louisiana on CNN. He goes, 'Half of it is underwater and half of it is under indictment.' Right now, in your case, that means you're anybody's hump. Forget the lunch. Let's talk business."

"What business I got with you?"

"The word is your kid's a closet bone smoker. The Iberia D.A. has got the handle he needs to jam him and you both. Dave didn't tell you?"

The transformation that took place in Whitey's face was like none I had ever seen in another person. The eyes didn't blink or narrow; the color in them did not brighten with anger or haze over with hidden thoughts. The jawbone never pulsed against the cheek. Instead, his expression seemed to take on the emotionless solidity of carved wood, with eyes as dull and cavernous as buckshot. I believe I could have scratched a match alight on his face and he wouldn't have blinked.

"What'd you call my boy?" he asked.

Clete pressed the palm of his hand against his chest. "I didn't call him anything. That's his rep in a couple of drag joints in Lafayette. I thought you and Dave had talked. The D.A. thinks the Lujan kid came on to your son and your son blew up his shit. The point is when piranhas smell blood, they clean the cow to the bone. You want your casino interests let alone? Maybe I can make that happen. I'm getting through to you, here?"

"Yeah, you're both working with this twat Trish Klein," Whitey said.

Clete looked at me. "You heard the man, Streak. I told you it was a waste of time. Hey, Whitey, this isn't Miami. Louisiana is a fresh-air mental asylum. Dave knocked a tooth out of the D.A.'s mouth and he's still got his shield. What does that tell you? You think we're here to shake you down for chump change? While you're in the slams, what do you think Bello Lujan is going to be doing—protecting your assets till you get out? He'll turn your pad into a cathouse and your horses into canned dog food."

We left Whitey standing in his living room. Outside, as we crossed the thick, carpetlike texture of his St. Augustine grass, I heard the red Morgan running in the pasture. Her neck and flanks were dark with sweat, her mouth strung with wisps of saliva. She clattered against a rail and I would have sworn she nickered at me.

Clete got in his Caddy and headed down the driveway. Just as I started my engine, I saw Whitey come out the front door.

"Hey, Robicheaux, wait up," he called.

I rolled down the window. "What?" I said.

"What he said about my boy?"

"Yeah?"

"People are saying that, or your friend was just working my crank?"

"Your kid has problems. Homosexuality is probably the least of them."

"You got a kid?"

"An adopted daughter."

"How would you like it if somebody talked about her like you talk about my boy? How would you like it if my lawyers came after you through your family?"

"We're not like you, Whitey. Dallas Klein's blood is on your soul. On the day you die, I believe his specter will stand by your bedside. Nothing you do from now until then will change that fact. Your son is a monster. I have a feeling you know it, too."

For a moment I saw a look in Whitey's eyes that made me believe there are some people who are truly damned. Then the moment passed and he squinted into the haze and pinched the humidity out of his eyes. "I went to school under the Catholic nuns," he said. "They taught us after we pissed not to shake off more than two times. Know what we did? We all ran down to the john and shook it off three times to see what would happen. Good try, Robicheaux, but you and your friend belong here. Like you say, it's a place for jerk-offs."

Upstairs, Slim Bruxal pushed open a window and leaned outside, his upper torso naked. "Hey, Dad, can somebody give Carmen a ride back to the dorm? I've got a softball game," he said.

My LIFE IS NOT GIVEN to prescient moments. But occasionally I have them, particularly with the advance of age. When they occur, they leave behind a sensation like a cold burn on the heart.

The sky was painted with horsetails, the trees blowing hard along the highway as I followed Clete out of Lafayette. Then he pulled into a truck stop and went inside, not glancing back to see if I was behind him.

When Clete made choices, even minuscule ones, that geographically separated him from his friends, he was usually embarking on an odyssey that invariably brought harm to only one person—himself.

I pushed open the door in the café area and saw him at the end of the counter, his aviator glasses in his pocket, the lines at the corners of his eyes like pieces of white thread, a bottle of beer and a foaming glass and a saltshaker in front of him. I cupped my hand on his shoulder.

"It's twenty minutes after one," I said. "You haven't eaten, either."

"I'm on a diet," he replied.

I sat down on the stool next to him and asked the waitress for coffee. "You did great back there, Cletus."

"Remember when we caught Augie Giacano jackrolling an old lady and threw him down a fire escape? Then we dimed him with Didi Gee so he'd get in trouble with his own people?"

"When *you* threw Augie down the fire escape."

"Whatever. We didn't get pushed around by Brooklyn skells like Whitey Bruxal." He salted his beer and drank from it. He touched at his mouth with a paper napkin, then put the napkin aside, finished the glass in one swallow, and filled it again.

"Eat a hamburger with me," I said.

"Everything is *muy copacetico,* Streakus. No *problemas* here." His eyes drifted to the television anchored on the café wall. "Check out those tropical storms in the Atlantic. The Florida Straits are starting to look like a turnstile."

"I've got to get back to the department."

"See you later."

"I'm not leaving you here alone."

"*What?* I'm supposed to feel like the walking wounded?"

"Maybe."

"You don't get it, Dave. You never did. We're dinosaurs. This isn't the same country we grew up in. The scumbags own it, from top to bottom. Except they're legal now and have college degrees and wear two-thousand-dollar suits. Back in our First District days, we would have fed these motherfuckers into an airplane propeller."

A truck driver down the counter wearing a greasy bill cap looked at us, and the waitress studied the television screen with undue attention, then turned up the volume. A CNN announcer was talking about a hurricane that was strengthening off the Bahamas.

"The Bobbsey Twins from Homicide are forever," I said.

"Keep telling yourself that."

"Snap out of it, Clete."

This time he didn't argue with me. But reticence in Clete Purcel was rarely a sign of acquiescence. Instead, it was the exact opposite. He put on his yellow-tinted shades and looked at the television screen, his face composed.

"You're going to see Trish today?" I said.

"What about it?"

She's too young for you. You're going to get hurt real bad, perhaps irrevocably, I thought.

He stared into my eyes. "Yeah," he said.

"Yeah, what?" I said, trying to smile innocuously.

"Yeah, keep your thoughts to yourself," he replied.

It was one of the moments when the truth serves no purpose other than to keep our wounds green. Was Clete right? Were we at the end of our string, flailing at forces that had societal and governmental sanction, convincing ourselves, like fools popping champagne corks aboard a sinking liner, that our violence could extend our youth forever into the future and that the party would never come to an end?

He felt my eyes on the side of his face. "Why you giving me that weird look?"

"Because you're the best, Clete. Because I love you."

The trucker down the counter was cutting up a steak on his plate. He glanced sideways at us, then at our reflection in the mirror. Clete leaned over so he could see past me.

"What's up, bud?" Clete asked.

"Not a whole lot," the trucker said, returning to his steak. He had created a puddle of ketchup sprinkled with pepper on his plate, and he was dipping each piece of meat in it before he forked it into his mouth.

"That steak looks righteous. You want a beer?" Clete said.

"I got to drive. Another time," the trucker said.

"I'm Clete Purcel. This is Dave Robicheaux."

"I'm Joe Vernon Mack."

"You're looking at the Bobbsey Twins from Homicide, Joe Vernon," Clete said.

"Pleased to meet y'all," the trucker said, chewing contentedly.

Clete picked up both our checks and paid for them at the cash register, then the two of us walked outside into the wind.

I ARRIVED BACK at the department shortly before 3 p.m. A note from Helen on a pink memorandum slip was waiting for me in my mailbox. It said: "See me." When I walked down to her office, her door was ajar and I could see her standing behind her desk, talking on the phone. She waved me inside.

"He's here now," she said into the receiver. "Look, Lonnie, you made some ugly remarks about both him and me. He was defending me and this department as much as himself. You want to make trouble over this, you'll have me to deal with as well. My advice is that you be a man and accept the fact you shot off your mouth and that you got what you deserved."

I could hear Lonnie Marceaux's voice coming out of the receiver like a piece of wire being pulled through a metal hole.

"Stop shouting," Helen said. "He's a good cop and you know it. If you want, I'll contact the *Daily Iberian* and the wire services in Baton Rouge and we can both make a statement about what happened. It's your call."

She held the receiver away from her head and looked at it.

"He hang up?" I said.

"Or shot himself. Except we don't have that kind of luck around here. Somebody at Lafayette P.D. told him you busted up Lefty Raguza. He thinks you're running your own program, one that probably conflicts with his. Lonnie wants it all, Dave."

"All what?"

"He's going to indict Monarch Little for the Lujan homicide and bring racketeering charges against Whitey Bruxal. He's also got Colin Alridge in his bomb sights. Alridge is running for lieutenant governor. Lonnie says he's going to drive a nail through one of his testicles."

"Why don't you use a more severe image?"

"Those are his words, not mine." She placed her hand on the windowsill and gazed out at the cemetery, and I knew she was no longer

interested in talking about Lonnie. "I got a call earlier from the sheriff of Orleans Parish. He says a warrant is being cut for Clete Purcel's
arrest."

"For flooding the casino?"

But my question didn't register. "The Orleans sheriff says there're
rumors Clete is mixed up with the people who did the savings and
loan job in Mobile. This parish isn't going to be a haven for people
who think they don't have to obey the law."

"I'll talk with Clete."

"You tell him I said he gets this shit off our plate or he leaves
town."

"I understand you perfectly. Thanks for standing up for me with
Lonnie," I said.

She looked me dead-on, her expression caught again in that
strange androgynous moment when she seemed to linger between
two identities, her face both beautiful and intimidating, a Helen I didn't
really know. "Don't try to jerk me around, Dave. Fun and games are
over," she said.

I WALKED BACK to my office, unsure of my next move. I was convinced I had gotten nowhere with Whitey Bruxal. Worse, all my
investigative work into the deaths of Crustacean Man, Yvonne Darbonne, and Tony Lujan had produced only circumstantial evidence
and theories. Most depressing of all was the fact that, regardless of
what I did, Lonnie Marceaux was going to use the evidence selec-
tively to advance his own career, even if he had to prosecute Monarch
Little, an innocent man, for the murder of Tony Lujan.

I'd had a run at Bruxal earlier, hoping to sow seeds of suspicion
about his business partner, Bello Lujan. But why quit now? I asked
myself. Some activities are like prayer. After you've been shelled off
the mound, what do you have to lose?

I waited until quitting time to drive to his horse farm outside Loreauville. From the state road I saw him in front of a long white stable,
dressed in strap overalls, working on a faucet that fed a galvanized

water tank. He looked up when he heard my truck thumping across the cattle-guard, his Stilson wrench suddenly motionless.

How do you deal with a man like Bellerophon Lujan? Do you hate him? He certainly deserved the odium attached to his name. He was ignorant, driven, corrupt, racist, superstitious, and violent, his wealth ill-gotten, his libidinous appetites legendary. I believed he had probably raped Yvonne Darbonne. And long before he had destroyed her and her faith in her fellow human beings, he had ruined his son's life with control and verbal abuse that disguised itself as love.

But as much as I despised Bello's deeds, I could not hate the man. As my truck approached the horse tank, I saw him grin slightly at the edge of his mouth, and for just a moment I remembered the kid who had waited in the cold with a shine box at the Southern Pacific depot, hoping to catch a few customers before they checked in to the Frederic Hotel.

"You going to take a swing at me?" I said as I got out of my truck.

"I wouldn't do that," he said, twisting the wrench on a three-inch nut. "I'm putting in a frost-free faucet this year, me. All these storms and droughts and hurricanes we been having? That means we gonna have some bad winters, yeah."

His accent, even his syntax, had changed, the rough edges of New Orleans gone, as though the voice of a simple Cajun boy of years ago were speaking. Except that early innocence was not one Bello would ever be allowed to reclaim, whether he knew it or not. I picked up a paint-skinned wood chair by the stable entrance and carried it back to the tank and sat down. The sun was low and buried inside rain clouds, the pasture dark with shade, the grass channeled by the wind. "You have a restful place here," I said.

"The best," he replied. His eyes took on the glimmerings of vindication and pride. But I believed another element was at work inside Bello during that moment. I suspected he was beginning to understand that the symbols of his triumph over the world would never pass on to his son, and that his victory over privation and rejection by the wellborn had become ashes in his mouth.

"See this?" I said.

"Yeah, one of those pocket voice recorders."

I clicked the recorder on, then off with my thumb. "I had a talk with Whitey Bruxal earlier today. I had this recorder running in my pocket. I was going to take you over the hurdles with it, Bello."

He was grinning and I could see he didn't understand.

"I was going to play back snippets to you and let you have a little glimpse of what your business partner has to say when you're not around," I said. "But you're an intelligent man and I won't treat you as less."

"I ain't sure what that means."

"You can believe this or not. Either the Feds or Lonnie Marceaux are going to hang you by your thumbs. No matter how you cut it, you've got Whitey Bruxal as your fall partner."

"What you mean, fall partner?"

"He's the guy you're going down with. Is Whitey the kind of guy who will take a maximum sentence rather than rat out a friend? I don't know the answer. But I bet you do."

"He was working a deal wit' you?"

"Put it this way. I doubt if Whitey would tell the truth to a corpse. But if I were on a burning plane with him and the plane carried only one parachute, I have a feeling who would end up wearing it."

Bello fitted the Stilson back on the faucet head and began to squeak the nut tighter, as though my words were of little interest to him. But I could see the fatigue in his face, and in his eyes the tangle of thoughts that probably waged war inside his head twenty-four hours a day.

"What would you do?" he asked.

"I don't think you'll ever experience any rest until you own up to your mistakes, Bello."

"Starting wit' what?"

"I think you attacked Yvonne Darbonne. I think her death is eating you alive. No amount of Holy Roller shouting in tongues is going to change that fact or relieve you of your guilt."

"Who tole you I did that?"

"It's written all over you."

The heavy, oblong steel head of the Stilson rested on the rim of the aluminum tank, his hand grasped tightly around the shank. The back of his hand was brown, mottled with liver spots and lined with veins that looked like knotted package twine. I could hear a horse blowing inside the stable.

I supposed it was not a time to say anything. But there are moments when caution and restraint just don't cut it. "Why'd you do it, partner? She was just a kid."

"Maybe there're reasons everybody don't know about. Maybe t'ings just happen," he replied.

"Run that crap on somebody else."

"What do you know? You got everyt'ing. They killed my boy. You know what it's like to have your kid killed?"

"Who's 'they'?"

"The niggers. Monarch Little and all them niggers with black scarfs on their head, selling their dope, pimping their women, corrupting the town."

It was hopeless. I think there are those who are psychologically incapable of honesty and I think Bello was one of them. I got back in the truck and left him to himself. In all candor, I doubt if a worse punishment in the world could have been visited upon him.

BUT I STILL HAD MILES TO GO before I slept. I called Molly on my cell phone and asked if we could have a late dinner.

"You have to work?" she said.

"Clete's in some trouble."

"What kind?"

I searched my mind for an honest answer. "There's no adequate scale. The rules of reason and logic have no application in his life," I said.

"Sound like anybody else you know?" she replied.

"Put my supper in the icebox."

"It already is," she replied.

The owner of the motor court where Clete lived told me Clete and a young woman had gone to a street dance in St. Martinville.

They weren't hard to find. In fact, as I drove up the two-lane through the dusk, through the corridor of live oaks that led out of town and the miles of waving sugarcane on each side of the road, I saw Clete's Caddy parked in front of a supper club left over from the 1940s. It was a happy place, where people ate thick steaks and drank Manhattans and old-fashioneds and sometimes had trysts involving a degree of romance in the palm-shrouded motel set behind the club. Above the entrance way was a pink neon outline of a martini glass with the long-legged reclining figure of a nude woman inside.

The refrigerated air in the dining room was so cold it made me shiver. Each table was covered with white linen and set with a candle burning inside a glass chimney. A man in a summer tux was playing a piano that was so black it had purple lights in it. Clete was at a table by himself, a collins drink in his hand, his face flushed and cheerful, his eyes shiny with alcohol.

"Where's Trish?" I said.

"On the phone."

I sat down without being asked. "Helen says Orleans Parish is cutting a warrant for your arrest."

"So I'll get out of town for a little while. You want a steak?"

"The Orleans sheriff told Helen he knows you're mixed up with bank robbers. What's the matter with you, Clete? You know how many people in South Louisiana want an excuse to blow you away?"

"That's their problem."

I was so angry I could hardly speak.

"There used to be a slop chute in San Diego that had a sign over the door like the one out there. You ever go to San Diego?" he said.

"No. Listen, Clete—"

But he had already launched into one of his alcoholic reveries that served only one function—to distract attention from the subject at hand.

"It was a joint that had a neon sign with a gal inside a pink martini glass. We used to call her the gin-fizz kitty from Texas City. A whole bunch of Marines had fallen in love with this same broad who worked the bars outside Pendleton. They said she could kiss you into next week, not counting what she could do in the sack. Bottom line is she got all these guys to put her name down as beneficiary on their life insurance policies. When CID finally caught up with her, we found out she'd been a whore in Texas City. We also found out a half-dozen guys she screwed ended up in body bags. How about that for passing on the ultimate form of clap? Hey, I was one of them. Get that look off your face."

He drank from his collins glass, then started laughing, like a man watching his own tether line pull loose from the earth.

"I want to take you outside and knock you down," I said.

"It's all rock 'n' roll, Streak. Going up or coming down, we all get to the same barn. What can happen that hasn't already happened in my life?"

"I think you've melted your brain. Don't you realize the implications of the story you just told me?"

"*What,* that Trish is hustling me? Don't make me mad at you, big mon."

But there was more hurt in his face than indignation. In the back of the club I saw Trish Klein replace the receiver on a pay phone, then stare in our direction, her mouth red and soft, her heart-shaped face achingly beautiful in the pastel lighting. I got up from the table and left without saying good-bye.

I PLANNED DURING the next two days to talk to Trish Klein in private about her relationship with one of the best and most self-destructive and vulnerable human beings I had ever known. I got the opportunity in a way I didn't suspect.

CHAPTER
21

ON WEDNESDAY, Joe Dupree at the Lafayette P.D. called me just before noon.

"She's in lockup?" I said.

"I never saw anybody look so good in a jailhouse jumpsuit."

"For shoplifting at the Acadiana Mall?"

"It's a little more complicated than that. She walked out of the store with a four-hundred-dollar handbag she didn't pay for. She caused a big scene when security stopped her. She claimed she was just showing the purse to a friend for the friend's opinion on it. She probably could have gone back inside and settled the issue by putting it on her credit card. She had a gold Amex and two or three platinum cards in her billfold. Instead, she ended up throwing the purse in the store manager's face."

"She's not posting bail?"

"To my knowledge, she hasn't even asked about it." I could hear him chewing gum in the receiver.

"What are you telling me?" I asked.

"I think she likes it here."

After lunch, I drove to Lafayette in a cruiser, checked my firearm in a security area on the first floor of the jail, and waited on the second floor in an interview room while a guard brought Trish Klein down in an elevator.

The guard was a stout, joyless woman who had once been taken hostage at a men's prison and held for three days during an attempted jailbreak. I used to see her at Red's Gym, pumping iron in a roomful of men who radiated testosterone—dour, painted with stink, possessed of memories she didn't share. She unhooked Trish at the door. I rose when Trish entered the room and offered her a chair. The guard gave me a look that was both hostile and suspicious and locked the door behind her.

"Did you ever hear the story about Robert Mitchum getting out of Los Angeles City Prison?" I said.

"No," she said.

"Mitchum spent six months in there on a marijuana bust and figured his career was over. The day he got out, a reporter shouted at him, 'What was it like in there, Bob?' Mitchum said, 'Not bad. Just like Palm Springs, without the riffraff.'"

She showed no reaction to the story. In fact, she wore no expression at all, as though both her surroundings and I were of no interest to her.

"What are you doing in here, kiddo?" I said.

"Kiddo, up your ass, Mr. Robicheaux."

"That's clever, but people with your background and finances don't go out of their way to put themselves in the slams."

"I don't like being called a thief."

"Yeah, I bet it was shocking to learn your photo is in the Griffin Book at casinos from Vegas to Atlantic City."

"Why are you here?"

"Because I think you and your friends are planning a big score on Whitey Bruxal. I think you're setting up your alibi."

She looked out the window at the street. "You don't know what you're talking about," she said.

"You guys are going to get yourselves killed. That's your own choice, but you're taking Clete Purcel down with you."

"He's a grown man. Why don't you stop treating him like a child?"

Down the corridor I could hear someone yelling, a scuffling sound of chains clinking, and a heavy object crashing against a metal surface, perhaps against the door of an elevator. But Trish Klein paid no attention to the distraction.

"Clete's been my friend for over thirty years. That's more time than you've been on earth," I said, regretting the self-righteousness of my words almost as soon as I had spoken them.

"I suspect I should go back upstairs now," she said.

"You don't think Whitey is onto you? This guy was a protégé of Meyer Lansky. Your people impersonated gas company employees and creeped his house. Want to hear a couple of stories about people who tried to burn the Mob?"

She didn't answer, but I told her anyway. One account dealt with a man in Las Vegas whose skull was splintered in a machinist's vise, another who was hung alive by his rectum from a meat hook. I also told her what insiders said was the fate of a middle-class family man in a Queens suburb who accidentally ran over and killed the child of his neighbor, a notorious Mafia don.

"These bastards might look interesting on the movie screen, but they're the scum of the earth," I said.

"I wouldn't have guessed that, Mr. Robicheaux. I always thought the people who murdered my father were closet humanists."

It was obvious that my best efforts with Trish Klein were of no value. It was like telling someone not to gargle with Liquid Drano. I was about to call for the guard and leave Trish and her friends to their own fate, when she lifted her eyes up to mine and for just a moment I understood the tenacity of Clete's commitment to her.

"A week before my father's death, he took me snorkeling off Dania Beach," she said. "We cooked hot dogs on a grill in a grove of palm trees and played with a big blue beach ball. Then two men parked a convertible under the trees and made him walk off with them, down where the water was hitting on the rocks. I remember how sad he looked, how small and humiliated, like he was no longer my father. I couldn't hear what the two men were saying, but they were angry and one man kept punching my father in the chest with his finger. When my father came back to our picnic table, his face was white and his hands were shaking.

"I asked him what was wrong and he said, 'Nothing. Everything is fine. Those guys were just having a bad day.'

"Then he put my snorkel and mask on my head and walked me down to the water and swam backward with me on his chest, until we were at the end of a coral jetty. He said, 'This is where the clown fish live. Anytime you're having a problem, you can tell it to the clown fish. These guys love children. Come on, you'll see.'

"That was the first time I ever held my breath and went all the way under the water. There were clown fish everywhere. They swam right up to my mask and brushed against my shoulders and arms. I never thought about those men again, not until years later when I realized they were probably the ones who murdered my father."

I wanted to be sympathetic. Dallas had been a good man, a brave soldier, and a devoted parent. But he had been corrupted by his addiction and had become a willing party to an armored car and bank heist that cost not only his life but also the life of the teller who had tried to foil the robbery by pushing shut the vault door. Now Trish's single-minded obsession with vengeance might cost Clete Purcel *his* life, or at least a large chunk of it, and that simple fact seemed totally lost on her.

"Why not let Whitey and his pals fall in their own shit? It's a matter of time before either the Feds or the locals take them down," I said.

"You said Bruxal was friends with Meyer Lansky?"

"That's right."

"Did the system get Lansky?"

"He died of cancer."

"When he was an old man. You're a laugh a minute, Mr. Robicheaux."

I banged on the door for the guard to let me out. I was determined to let Trish have the last word, to be humble enough to remember my own mistakes and not contend with the certainty and confidence of youth. But when I looked at the earnestness and ego-centered determination in her face, I saw a moth about to swim into a flame.

"You probably noticed the hack who brought you in here seemed out of joint," I said.

"The hack?"

"The female correctional officer. She was held three days in a male prison riot and passed from hand to hand by guys psychiatrists haven't found names for. She ended up in these guys' hands because she thought she knew what was inside their heads and she could handle whatever came down the pike. Don't ask her what they did to her, because she's never told anyone, at least no one around here."

I saw her fingers twitch on top of the table.

On the way back to Lafayette, I left a message with Betsy Mossbacher's voice mail.

LATER THAT AFTERNOON, she called me on my cell phone. "You visited the Klein woman in jail?" she said.

"Briefly. But I didn't learn a whole lot."

"What'd she tell you?"

"A story about her father and swimming with clown fish."

"Clown fish?"

"I guess they're a symbol of childhood innocence for her. Anyway, I think she deliberately got herself arrested."

"We have the same impression at the Bureau. Some of her griffins have been showing up at three or four casinos where Whitey Bruxal is a part owner. It seems they make a point of standing in front of security cameras and getting themselves escorted off the premises."

I waited for her to go on.

"Did I catch you on the john?" she said.

"No," I lied. "I didn't know you had finished. You think they're planning to take down a casino?"

"I'd say it's a diversion of some kind. But my supervisor says I always overestimate people's intelligence."

"You guys deal with higher-quality perps," I said.

"Actually, he was talking about you and Purcel."

Two uniformed deputies entered the restroom, talking loudly. One of them slammed down the seat in the stall next to me. "Hey, there's no toilet paper on the roller. Get some out of the supply closet, will you?" he called out to his friend.

•   •   •

THAT NIGHT I DREAMED of New Orleans. Not the New Orleans of today but the city where Clete and I had been young patrolmen, in a cruiser, sometimes even walking a beat with nightsticks, at a time when the city in its provincial innocence actually feared Black Panthers and long-haired kids who wore love beads and Roman sandals.

This was before crack cocaine hit New Orleans like a hydrogen bomb in the early eighties and the administration in Washington, D.C., cut federal aid to the city by half. Oddly, prior to the eighties, New Orleans enjoyed a kind of sybaritic tranquillity that involved a contract between the devil and the forces of justice. The Giacano family ran the vice and maintained implicit understandings with NOPD about the operation of the city. The Quarter was the cash cow. Anyone who jackrolled a tourist got his wheels broken. Anyone who jackrolled an old person anywhere or stuck up a bar or café frequented by cops or who molested a child got his wheels broken *and* got thrown from a police car at high speed on the parish line, that is, if he was lucky.

The Giacanos were stone killers and corrupt to the core, but they were pragmatists as well as family men and they realized no society remains functional if it doesn't maintain the appearances of morality.

New Orleans was a Petrarchan sonnet rather than an Elizabethan one, its mind-set more like the medieval world, in the best sense, than the Renaissance. In the spring of 1971 I lived in a cottage by the convent school on Ursulines, and every Sunday morning I would attend Mass at St. Louis Cathedral, then stroll across Jackson Square in the coolness of the shadows while sidewalk artists were setting up their easels along a pike fence that was overhung by palm fronds and oak boughs. At an outdoor table in the Café du Monde, over beignets and coffee with hot milk, I would watch the pinkness of the morning spread across the Quarter, the unicyclists pirouetting in front of the cathedral, jugglers tossing wood balls in the air, street bands who played for tips knocking out "Tin Roof Blues" and "Rampart Street Parade." The balconies along the streets groaned with the weight of potted plants, and bougainvillea hung in huge clumps from the iron grillwork and bloomed as brightly as drops of blood in the sunlight. Corner grocery stores, run by Italian families, still had wood-bladed

fans on the ceilings and sold boudin and po'boy sandwiches to working people. Out front, in the shade of the colonnade, were bins of can-
taloupe, bananas, strawberries, and rattlesnake watermelons. Often,
on the same corner, in the same wonderful smell that was like a breath
of old Europe, a black man sold sno-balls from a pushcart, the ice
hand-shaved off a frosted blue block he kept wrapped in a tarp.

Traditional New Orleans was like a piece of South America that
had been sawed loose from its moorings and blown by trade winds
across the Caribbean, until it affixed itself to the southern rim of the
United States. The streetcars, the palms along the neutral grounds,
the shotgun cottages with ventilated shutters, the Katz and Betz drug-
stores whose neon lighting looked like purple and green smoke in the
mist, the Irish and Italian dialectical influences that produced an
accent mistaken for Brooklyn or the Bronx, the collective eccentricity
that drew Tennessee Williams and William Faulkner and William
Burroughs to its breast, all these things in one way or another were
impaired or changed forever by the arrival of crack cocaine.

Or at least that is the perception of one police officer who was
there when it happened.

But in my dream I didn't see the deleterious effects of the drug
trade on the city I loved. I saw only Clete and me, neither of us very
long out of Vietnam, walking down Canal in patrolmen's blues, past
the old Pearl Restaurant, where the St. Charles streetcar stopped for
passengers under a green-painted iron colonnade, the breeze blowing
off Lake Pontchartrain, the evening sky ribbed with strips of pink
cloud, the air pulsing with music, black men shooting craps in an
alley, kids tap-dancing for change, the kind of moment whose perfec-
tion you vainly hope will never be subject to time and decay.

When I woke in the early dawn, with Molly beside me, I didn't
know where I was. It was misting and gray in the trees, and out on
the bayou I could hear the heavy droning sound of a tug pushing a
barge down toward Morgan City. The ventilated shutters on the front
windows were closed, and the light was slitted and green, the way it
had been in the cottage where I lived on Ursulines.

"You okay, Dave?" Molly asked, curled on her side under the sheet.

"I thought I was in New Orleans," I replied.

She rolled on her back and looked up at me, her hair spread on the pillow like points of fire. She cupped her hand around the back of my neck. "You're not," she said.

"It was a funny dream, like I was saying good-bye to something."

"Come here," she said.

She kissed me on the mouth, then touched me under the sheet.

Later, after I had showered and dressed, Molly made coffee and heated a pan of milk and poured our orange juice while I filled our bowls with Grape-Nuts and sliced bananas. Both Tripod and Snuggs came inside, and I split a can of cat food between the two of them and gave each his own water bowl (Tripod, like all coons, washed his food before he ate it) and spread newspaper on the linoleum to preempt problems with Tripod's incontinence. The mist outside had become as thick and gray in the trees as fog, and I couldn't see the green of the park on the far side of the bayou.

But my problem was not with the weather. I could not get rid of the sense that something bad was about to happen, that an evil medium of some kind, if left unchecked, was about to hurt someone.

All drunks, particularly those who grew up in alcoholic homes, have that same sense of angst and trepidation, one that has no explainable origins. The fear is not necessarily self-centered, either. It's like watching someone point a revolver at his temple while he cocks and dry-fires the mechanism, over and over again, until the cylinder rotates a loaded chamber into firing position.

What was it that bothered me so much? Loss of my youth? Fear of mortality? The systemic destruction of the Cajun world in which I had grown up?

Yes to all those things. But my greatest fear was much more immediate than the abstractions I just mentioned. As every investigative law officer will tell you, the clues that lead to a crime's solution are always there. It's a matter of seeing or touching or hearing or smelling them. Nothing aberrant happens in a vacuum. The causality and connections wait for us just beyond the perimeter of our vision, in the same way a piece of spiderweb can attach itself to your hand when you grip the undersurface of a banister in a deserted house. The perps aren't smart. They just have more time to devote to their work than we do.

"Lost in thought?" Molly said.

"The deaths of Crustacean Man, Yvonne Darbonne, and Tony Lujan are all related. But I don't know if any one of those cases will ever be solved."

"Time's on your side."

"How?"

"Down the line, everybody pays his tab," she said.

"I'm not always so sure about that."

"Yes, you are."

"How you know?" I asked.

"Because you're a believer. Because you can't change what you are, no matter what you say about yourself."

"Is that right?" I said.

"I don't hang around with the B team, troop," she said.

Five minutes later, the phone rang. It was Wally, our dispatcher. "Got a nine-one-one from Bello Lujan's wife. She said the black man who works for her went out to the stable and found Bello on the flo', inside the stall. She said a horse kicked him. We got Acadian Ambulance on the way."

"Why'd you call me?"

"'Cause Miz Lujan sounded like my wife does when she tells me to get a dead rat out from under the house. I don't trust that woman."

"Keep me updated, will you?"

"Why is it every time I call you I seem to say the wrong t'ing? The problem must be me."

Just before I went out the door, the phone rang again. "Here's your update. Acadian Ambulance just called. Ole Bello won't be posing wit' the roses for a while. Helen went to New Orleans, so you want to take over t'ings?" he said.

"Will you get the crackers out of your mouth?"

"If the guy blew his nose, his brains would be in the handkerchief. That's the way the paramedic put it. He says it wasn't done by no horse, eit'er. That clear enough?"

• • •

THE EMERGENCY VEHICLES parked by Bello's stable still had their flashers on, rippling with blue, red, and white light inside the mist. I stooped under the crime scene tape and walked down the concrete pad that separated two rows of twelve-by-twelve stalls. Koko Hebert was already on the job—gloved, furrow-browed, morose, his gelatinous girth like curtains of fat hanging on a deboned elephant. In the gloom of the stable he kept turning his attention from the stall to the sliding back doors, both of which were pushed back on their tracks. Out in the pasture, a sorrel mare was eating in the grass, one walleye looking back at the stable.

Bello Lujan lay on his left side in the stall. The floor of the stall was comprised of dirt and sand, overlaid with a layer of straw. The wound in the back of Bello's skull was deep and tapered and had bled out in a thick pool on the straw. His eyes were open and staring, his face empty of expression, in fact, possessed of a serenity that didn't fit the level of violence that had been done to his person. A bucket of molasses balls was overturned in the corner of the stall. I suspected he never saw his assailant and perhaps, with luck, he had not suffered, either.

"You got a weapon?" I said.

"It's outside, in the weeds. A pick with a sawed-off handle. The black guy who found him says the chain was down on the stall and the sorrel was out," Koko said. "There're some tennis-shoe impressions on the concrete. Watch where you walk."

"How do you read it?" I asked.

"Bello went into the stall with the mare and somebody came up behind him and put it to him long and hard."

"What do you mean, long and hard?"

"That hole in the back of his head isn't the only one in him. He took one in the rib cage and one in the armpit. Take a look at the slats on the left side of the stall. I think Bello bounced off the boards, then tried to get up and caught the last one in the skull." Koko laughed out loud. "Then he got shit on by the horse he was trying to feed. I'm not kidding you. Look at his shirt."

"Why don't you show some respect?" I said.

Koko coughed into his palm, still laughing. "Do you ever get tired of it?"

"Of what?" I said.

"Being the only guy in the department with any humanity. It must be tough to be a full-time water-walker," he said.

"Hey, Dave, come see a minute," Mack Bertrand said from the back entrance. He had arrived shortly before I did and had done only a preliminary survey of the crime scene. A camera hung from his right hand.

"I'll talk to you about that remark later, Koko," I said.

"I can't wait," he said.

I joined Mack outside. "What do you have?" I said.

"Take a look at the murder weapon. What's interesting about it is the tip of the pick has been sharpened down to a fine point, probably on a grinder. When's the last time you sharpened a pick like that?"

"Never."

"So in all probability we've got a premeditated homicide here and the killer came prepared to do maximum damage," he said.

I squatted down and looked at the pick. Mack was right. The point had been honed down to a thinness that would break if it was driven into rock or hardpan. Streaks of blood and pieces of hair coated at least four inches of the steel surface. "You've got a good eye, Mack," I said.

"Walk with me to the back fence."

The rear of the lot was strung with what is called a back-fence, one that is made up of steel spikes and smooth wire and is less attractive than a rail or slat fence but cheaper to construct and more utilitarian. On the other side was an ungrazed pasture, then a line of water oaks and pecan trees that separated the pasture from a sugarcane field. Mack pointed to a channel of dented grass in the pasture.

"My guess is somebody crossed the pasture on foot this morning, maybe somebody who parked his vehicle up there on the turnrow by the sugarcane field," Mack said. "What do you think?"

I nodded without speaking.

"No, I mean who do you think would do this? Just between us."

I rested my arm on a steel fence spike. I hated to even think about the possibilities that Mack's question suggested. "I twisted the screws on Whitey Bruxal. Maybe Whitey thought Bello was about to roll over on him," I said.

"The Mob uses pickaxes?"

"Whitey's smart. He doesn't follow patterns. That's why he's never done time."

"I'm really bothered by this, Dave. Bello came to our church for help. I sent him over to the Holy Rollers. You ever figure out what was driving him?"

"Take your choice. Years ago he tried to lynch a black man. His wife thinks he attacked Yvonne Darbonne. He tried to revise his own life by controlling and destroying his son's. Everything he touched turned to excrement."

"He *raped* the Darbonne girl?"

"I just have the wife's interpretation of events. She's not an easy person to talk with. She says Bello raped Yvonne Darbonne the same day Darbonne shot herself."

"Jesus Christ. Yvonne Darbonne was gangbanged that day."

"That's my point. I don't know if Mrs. Lujan is telling the truth. I don't believe she's totally connected to reality."

"Who is?" Mack said.

It was damp and cool inside the mist, and the pasture on the other side of the fence was emerald green, except for the trail of bruised grass that led from the wire back to the turnrow in the sugarcane. Across the road, Bello's house sat heavy and squat and white inside the mist, his flower gardens blooming, the bayou high and yellow in the background. He had owned everything a man could want. But his war with the world and his imaginary enemies had never ended. Was the serenity I had seen on his face in the horse stall simply the result of his nerve endings collapsing? Or in life had the aggressive leer of the moral imbecile been a form of pathological rictus that hid the frightened child?

"You already saw the tennis-shoe impressions in the stable?" Mack asked.

"Yeah, I need to talk to the black man who found Bello."

"He's up at the main house. Want me to see if I can get any latents off the fence?"

"Sure, go ahead," I said, still unable to process my own thoughts about the life and death of Bello Lujan.

"I heard that crack Koko made. Don't let him get to you, Dave. He's full of rage over his kid getting killed in Iraq and doesn't know who to blame for it."

"I wasn't thinking about Koko. I knew Bello before either one of us learned to speak English. He was a tough kid."

"Yeah?" Mack said, waiting for me to go on.

"He was like most of my generation. The poor bastard believed everything people taught him."

"Taught him what?"

"If he had money, he could forget he shined shoes down at the S.P. station. Bello never could understand that the kid with the shine box was probably the best person he would ever know."

Mack put his empty pipe in his mouth and stared at the channel of broken grass in the pasture. He was trying to be polite, but it was no time for my lament on the problems of my generation and the lost innocence of a French-speaking culture that has become little more than a chimerical emanation of itself, packaged and sold to tourists.

"Dave, either we have a random killing, one done by a maniac who didn't know the vic, or somebody who knew Bello's daily routine and literally tried to eviscerate him. I hope to get you some prints off the pick handle, but—"

"But what?"

"I think the perp spent some time on this. I don't think he threw down the weapon so we could find his prints all over it. I think the guy who did this is methodical and intelligent. Does that bring anyone to mind?"

"Yeah, Whitey Bruxal."

"My thoughts shouldn't stray too far past the lab, but when they kill like this—I mean, when they try to tear out somebody's insides—the motivation is usually sexual or racial. Sometimes both."

"What are you saying?"

"I'm not sure myself. Does Mrs. Lujan strike you as a charitable and forgiving spouse?"

"Thanks for your help, Mack. Give me a call from the lab, will you?"

"My pleasure," he replied. "Hey, Dave, you going to talk to Yvonne Darbonne's father? I mean, to exclude him?"

"Why?"

"No reason. He's a good man. His daughter was the same age as one of mine. I don't know if I could live with that kind of grief. I still have a hard time accepting the kinds of shit kids get into today. Drugs, abortion, hepatitis B, AIDS, herpes. They're just kids, for God's sakes. Before they're twenty, they're screwed up for life."

You're right again, Mack, I thought. But what was the solution? An authoritarian government? I feared how many people would answer in the affirmative.

I drove back onto the state road, then crossed a bridge over a coulee and parked in the turnrow by the sugarcane field where the killer probably entered the pasture on his way to Bello's stable. But the turnrow was churned with tractor, harvester, truck, and cane-wagon tracks, and littered with beer cans, snuff containers, and used rubbers as well, and I doubted that we would recover any helpful forensic evidence from the scene.

I watched the paramedics drive away with Bello's body, then I questioned the black man who had found Bello in the stall. The black man was not wearing tennis shoes and he did not believe any of Bello's other employees wore them, either. In fact, he said Bello insisted his employees wear sturdy work boots in order to prevent injuries and to keep his insurance premiums down. That sounded like classic Bello.

The black man also said he had never seen the pick before.

Then I rang the chimes on the front door of the Lujan home and was let inside by the maid.

I have either visited or investigated homicide scenes for over thirty-five years. Clete Purcel and I cut down a corpse that had been hanging in a warehouse for four months. We dug one dancing with maggots out of a wall. We scraped a twentieth-floor jumper off the steel stairs of a fire escape. We had to use tweezers to pick the remnants of one out of a compacted automobile. Twenty-five years ago I saw the interior of a house after rogue members of NOPD had put a hit on a whole family. Murder is an up-close and personal business, and rarely does a journalistic account do it justice. You want a capital sentence in a homicide prosecution? Make sure the jury gets the opportunity to study some color photographs before they go into deliberation.

But the worst part of any homicide investigation usually involves notification and questioning of family members. They want to know if their loved ones suffered, if they died in a brave or cowardly fashion, if the body was degraded. Often their eyes beg, but not for the truth. They want you to lie. And often that is exactly what you do.

Mrs. Lujan did not fall into the category I just described. In fact, when I was escorted by the maid onto the sunporch, I was stunned by what I saw. Mrs. Lujan was standing up with the aid of a walker, dressed in a pink skirt and white blouse, her face bright with purpose, her hair brushed and tied with a ribbon in back. She extended her hand and smiled wanly.

"How are you, Mr. Robicheaux?" she said.

"I'm sorry to bother you at a time like this. I can come back later if you like," I said.

"Call me Valerie. You're only carrying out the obligations of your office," she said. "Do me a favor, though. Would you open the jalousies and let the mist in? I love the cool smell of the morning. When I was a child in New Orleans, I loved the coolness of the mist blowing in from Lake Pontchartrain. My father often took me to the amusement park by the water's edge. Do you remember the amusement park on the lake?"

Her detachment from Bello's murder might have been written off as the effects of shock or perhaps even a thespian attempt to deal with tragedy in a dignified fashion. But I believed that in the mind of Valerie Lujan all the grief the world could expect of her had already been extracted by the death of her son, and she felt no shame in refusing to mourn a husband whose sexual appetites had taken him far from his wife's bed.

"Did Bello give you any indication that Whitey Bruxal might have wanted him dead?" I said.

"Why would Mr. Bruxal want to harm Bello? Tony was friends with Slim, but Bello didn't associate with Mr. Bruxal."

"They were business partners."

"They may have invested in the same enterprises, but they were hardly partners." She eased herself down on the couch and sighed pleasantly. "My, it feels good to stand up. I'm volunteering at the university to teach a noncredit drama course. I haven't done anything so uplifting in years."

"I see."

"You don't think well of me, do you?"

I dropped my eyes. "I think you've carried a heavy load much of your life, ma'am."

"I spoke by telephone this morning with my spiritual adviser, Reverend Alridge. His insight has helped me enormously. My husband was a racist, pure and simple. He sexually exploited Negro women and consequently inflamed their men. That may have contributed to Monarch Little's murdering my son. Now it may have cost Bello his life as well."

"You're saying Monarch Little killed your husband?"

"If I understand correctly, Bello was killed with a maddox or a pick of some kind. You're a realist and I don't think given to political correctness, Mr. Robicheaux. Who else except a depraved Negro criminal would kill like that?"

I looked away from the glare in her eyes. In my mind's eye I saw Monarch Little in his baggy pants and weight lifter's shirt, with an oversize ball cap askew on his head. I also saw the two-hundred-dollar tennis shoes, with gas cushions in the soles, that he wore as part of his cartoon-character persona.

Wrong fashion choice, Monarch.

"Come visit me again, Mr. Robicheaux. Somehow something good will come out of all of this. I have faith for the first time in years. I hope you find it, too," Mrs. Lujan said.

Her unevenly recessed eyes were liquid with the warmth of her own sentiment. I had the feeling Mrs. Lujan had just taken up serious residence in the kingdom of the self-deluded and would be a long time in freeing herself from it.

I DROVE TO the rural slum on the bayou, just outside the city limits, where Monarch lived. A junker car was parked in the drive, but no one answered the door. His neighbor, an elderly black woman picking up trash from a drainage ditch, told me Monarch was in town.

"He's working?" I said.

"His mother died. I ain't sure what he's doin'."

"Died? I thought his mother was coming home from the hospital."

"She had a heart attack two days ago. Monarch gone off wit' his friends. They t'rowed all their beer cans in my li'l yard. Tell Monarch he ought to be ashamed of hisself, his mother not yet in the ground."

"Ashamed why?"

She picked up a crushed beer can, threw it hard in her gunnysack, and didn't reply.

I drove back to New Iberia and crossed the Teche on the drawbridge at Burke Street. The water was high on the green slope of the banks, the surface dimpled with rain, and black people were fishing with cane poles and cut bait from under the bridge. Then I turned down Railroad Avenue into New Iberia's old brothel district, the one place in our town's history where indeed the past had never become the past.

CHAPTER
22

Just as the street-corner crack whores had supplanted their five-dollar antecedents in the cribs that had lined Railroad Avenue, Monarch Little, in his way, had kept the traditions of the red-light district alive by returning to the neighborhood as victim if not as purveyor.

It was still raining lightly when I pulled my truck under the overhang of the oak tree where Monarch used to deal dope. The weight set he had used to add inches to his arms and shoulders still sat on the hard-packed dirt apron under the tree, rusting, beaded with moisture. A kid who was nicknamed "Rag Nose" because he had burned out the inside of his head sniffing airplane glue was sitting on the backrest of a bench a few feet away, looking innocuously up and down the street, as though I were not there.

He was well over six feet tall, with a head that looked like an elongated coconut. His feet were sockless and stuffed in unlaced high-top tennis shoes.

"Seen Monarch around?" I said.

"No, suh, ain't seen him." He tapped his feet up and down on the bench, flexing a toothpick in his mouth, furrowing and unfurrowing his brow as though hundreds of thoughts were flying through his mind.

"Still going to your meetings?" I said.

"Yes, suh. All the time. I'm taking off for one in a few minutes." He looked at his wrist, then realized he wasn't wearing a watch.

"I need to find Monarch," I said.

He scratched his head. "Yeah, Monarch be out at his house maybe, or working, or driving round wit' his friends."

"Your real name is Walter, isn't it?"

"Sometimes it is," he replied, and picked at a scab on the back of one hand.

"I don't work Vice, Walter. I'm not here to hurt Monarch. I'd like to see him stay out of trouble. But I can't do that if his friends lie to me."

The soles of Walter's tennis shoes tapped on the bench again. He looked up into the tree, then at the mist blowing across the roofs of the houses, then at the wet glaze on the little white grocery store that tried to survive in a neighborhood long ago given over to dealers and whores and kids like Walter who had permanently fried their grits. I saw Walter teeter on the edges of honesty and trust, then the moment faded and he looked down at his shoes. "Ain't seen him," he said.

But events were not on Walter's side. A black woman whose street name was Sno'ball pulled a child's wagon from around the far side of the grocery store. The wagon was loaded with twenty-pound sacks of crushed ice.

"See you, Mr. Dave," Walter said, and was gone like a shot.

Sno'ball, so named because she was fat, coal-black, and wore white dresses, towed the wagon down the street toward a tan stucco house whose yard was strewn with garbage. The front porch of the house was wide and breezy and offered shade during the hottest hours of the day, but it was also cluttered with broken wood furniture, a rain-soaked couch, and a mattress that had been blackened by fire.

I caught up with Sno'ball. "Early for a beer party," I said.

"Refrigerator is burnt out. Bunch of steaks in there gonna spoil," she said.

"Going to invite me to your cookout?" I said.

She smiled and continued pulling the wagon up the sidewalk, tugging it across the slabs that were pitched and broken by oak roots that grew from a tree in the yard of the stucco house. Sno'ball's smile and good disposition did not go with the type of work she did. She was a tar mule for Herman Stanga, a black piece of shit who should have been hosed off the bowl long ago. Why she worked for Herman was anyone's guess.

"I need to give Monarch Little some information, 'Ball," I said.

"I'll tell him. I mean, if I see him."

"Want me to help you carry the ice inside?"

"I got it."

"I don't mind," I said. I hefted up two bags, wet and cold under each arm, and started up the walk toward the porch.

"Mr. Dave, we got it under control here," she said.

I ignored her and walked up the stone steps, crossed the porch, and entered the house. Even though the back and front doors and the windows were open, the smell was overwhelming. I thought of offal, burned food, unwashed hair, feces, black water backed up in a toilet. Broken crack vials were ground into the wood floor; the plaster walls were spray-painted with gang signs and representations of genitalia; a mattress with blood in the center lay on the living room floor. I saw a half-dozen people go out the back door, their faces averted so I would not recognize them.

"Where is he, 'Ball?" I said.

"In the bat'room. He wasn't ready for it. He didn't have no tolerance."

The bathroom door was ajar. I eased it open and saw Monarch in the tub, shirtless, his eyes closed, pillows stuffed around him so he would not slip below the waterline and the melting ice that covered his chest. I could see the hype marks inside his right arm.

"Brown skag?" I said.

"Yes, suh."

"Who shot him up?"

"Himself. Monarch still a king. Don't matter what people do to him. He was born a king."

I opened my cell phone and called for an ambulance. While I was talking I heard Sno'ball pour a sack of ice into the tub.

"Did Herman give him the dope?" I said.

She pursed her lips and made a twisting motion in front of them, as though she were locking them with a key. "Bust me if you want. But I stayed wit' him. You want to talk to Herman, Herman ain't here. Herman ain't never here. Y'all don't like this house, Mr. Dave, burn it down. But don't pretend y'all don't know what goes on here."

"What time did Monarch get here?"

"Eight-t'irty."

"You're sure. It wasn't earlier, it wasn't later?"

"I just tole you."

Ten minutes later Acadian Ambulance pulled Monarch out of the tub and loaded him onto a gurney. I walked with them to the back of the ambulance. Monarch's eyelids suddenly clicked open, just like a doll's. "What's happening, Mr. Dee?" he said.

"Your soul just took an exploratory ride over the abyss," I replied.

"Say again?"

"If you die, I'm going to kick your butt," I said.

"You're an unforgiving man," he said.

I pulled one of his tennis shoes off his foot.

"What you doing?" he said.

I watched them drive away with him. Monarch's tennis shoe felt sodden and cold and big in my hand. It was a size twelve, larger, I was sure, than the imprints stenciled on the concrete pad in Bello Lujan's stable. "Tell me again, Sno'ball. What time did Monarch get here?" I said.

"It was eight-t'irty. Some guys dropped him off on the corner. They'd been drinking. I know the time, 'cause I looked at my watch and wondered why Monarch was drinking so early in the morning. He come walking down the street and I axed him that. He said his mama died and would I tie him off."

"You shot him up?"

"No, Monarch is my friend. And I ain't gonna say no mo' 'bout it."

So the combination shooting gallery and crack house would not be an alibi for Monarch Little. But for all practical purposes, the size of his huge pancakelike feet and his obvious grief over his mother's death had eliminated him as a viable suspect in the homicide of Bellerophon Lujan.

"Am I going down on this, Mr. Dave?" Sno'ball asked.

"Don't let me catch you near this house again."

"Herman ain't big on the word 'no.'"

"Tell Herman that of this day he has a bull's-eye tattooed on his forehead."

She laughed to herself, looking down the street at the grocery store and a skinny kid trying to pick up Monarch's weight set. The sun was just breaking out of the mist, shining through the tree over the kid's head.

"You eat lunch with cops?" I asked.

She fixed her hair with one hand. "If they paying," she said.

We drove to Bon Creole, way out on St. Peter's Street, and had po'boy sandwiches, then I drove her back into New Iberia's inner city and left her on a street corner used by both pimps and dealers. It was a strange place to deliver a young woman who I believed to be a basically decent and loyal human being. But it was the world to which she belonged, and for those who lived in its maw, its abnormality was simply a matter of perception.

I ARRIVED AT the department shortly after noon. Helen had just returned from New Orleans, where she had been attending a meeting of Louisiana law enforcement administrators on civil preparedness. She caught me in the hallway and walked with me to my office. "What did you get on Bello's homicide?" she asked when we were inside.

She had not yet had a chance to talk with Koko Hebert or Mack Bertrand. I told her everything I knew about the initial investigation at the crime scene, then told her about Monarch Little overdosing.

"You're excluding him?" she said.

"At least for the time being. He may have had a window of opportunity, but there's no evidence to put him at the crime scene."

"But Valerie Lujan thinks Monarch did it?"

"If there weren't people of color around for her to blame her problems on, she'd probably kill herself."

"You've got somebody in mind for this, Dave. I can see it in your face."

"I stoked Whitey Bruxal up. I told him Bello was going to roll over on him. The possibility that Whitey took him out doesn't make me feel very good."

"Before you climb on a cross, you might consider this. It was a premeditated act. The killer hated Bello and wanted him to suffer. The killer also knew Bello's routine. Maybe the perp nursed a grudge for years. Bello had that kind of influence on people. Maybe Bruxal didn't have anything to do with it."

The phone on my desk rang. It was Mack Bertrand, calling from the crime lab.

"We have prints from several areas on the pick, some good, some bad," he said. "Most of them were probably left there by the same individual. Regardless, we got no hits with AFIS."

"Not even possibilities?"

"Nothing."

I had felt my hopes rise, then fade. "So maybe our suspect is a local with no record," I said.

"Could be. Bello was a sexual predator."

"You think this is a revenge killing, pure and simple?"

"I'm at a loss on this whole investigation, Dave, I mean, into the Lujan boy's death and Crustacean Man and the suicide of the Darbonne girl. I've come around to your way of thinking. It's all part of one piece, but I don't see the key."

"Helen's in my office now. I'll bring her up to date and get back to you later," I said.

"Something bothers me about the prints on the pick," Mack said. "The steel head looks like it's been partially wiped off. The same with the bottom of the handle. But the prints on the middle of the handle are defined and unsmudged. You following me?"

"I'm not sure."

"If someone wanted to wipe fingerprints off a murder weapon, in this case a pick, wouldn't he want to wipe off the entire weapon—both the handle and the head? I think an individual wearing gloves sharpened the pick and later used it to kill Bello. When he swung the pick, he smudged the prints on the bottom of the handle. That's just speculation, of course. My wife says I spend too much time in my head with this stuff."

No, you don't, Mack, I thought.

Helen had been sitting on the corner of my desk, on one haunch,

as she always did when she was in my office. After I hung up, I told
her what Mack had said. I could see the frustration grow in her face.
"Lonnie Marceaux is going to have a field day with this," she said.

"What does this have to do with Lonnie?"

"He's hired an ad firm in Baton Rouge to build him up as a cru-
sading prosecutor surrounded by drunken and corrupt flatfeet. I
think he also wants to hand me my ass."

"Maybe I should have a talk with him."

She pointed a finger at me. "That's the last thing you're going to
do. You copy that, bwana?"

"Yes, ma'am."

"Because if bwana not copy, bwana gonna have the worst experience in his life."

Don't contend, don't argue, I heard a voice say inside me. "How
did the civil preparedness meeting go?" I asked.

She had not expected my response. She tilted her head sideways,
almost looking at me in a new way, her eyes taking on a strange
lavender cast that was both sensual and curious, as though I were of
romantic interest to her. I felt my cheeks color.

"We toured the levees. A one-hundred-sixty-mile-an-hour storm
will turn New Orleans into a bowlful of oil and black sand," she said.
She squeezed my shoulder and looked me in the face. "No matter
how this plays out, Streak, I don't want you beating up on yourself
anymore. Even though I yell at you sometimes, you're one of the best
people I've ever known."

I SPENT THE NEXT HALF HOUR cleaning out paperwork from my
intake basket, putting off an inevitable stage in the investigation that I
was not looking forward to. Finally I picked up the phone and called
Cesaire Darbonne at his home. How do you tell a father whose
daughter has died of a gunshot wound in his driveway that he is a
possible suspect in a homicide? As Mack Bertrand said, how much
grief does one man need?

"This is Dave Robicheaux, Mr. Darbonne," I said. "I'd like to
return your daughter's diary if you're going to be home this afternoon."

"I got to go to the grocery store, but if I'm not home, I'll leave the door unlocked."

"I'd rather give it to you in person."

"Yes, suh, 'bout an hour from now okay?"

"I'll see you then. Thanks for your goodwill, Mr. Darbonne," I said.

I eased the receiver back into the cradle, a terrible sense of discomfort seizing my chest. Oftentimes in an investigation involving a violent crime, when the degree of injury and the desire for revenge can last a lifetime, what people do not say is more important than what they do say. Rape victims want to see the perpetrator's nails ripped out. Relatives of homicide victims, regardless of their religious principles, struggle a lifetime with their anger and desire for revenge, even after the perpetrator is dead, almost as though his specter has taken up residence in their homes.

Cesaire Darbonne had not inquired about any new details we may have discovered regarding his daughter's death. Even though the fatal shooting of Yvonne Darbonne had gone down as a suicide, wouldn't the father have asked if I had learned who drove her home on that terrible day, who had given her the gun, who had filled her young body with drugs and booze? I tried to think of an explanation for his lack of curiosity. I didn't want to think the thoughts I was thinking.

I called Mack at the lab. "How well do you know Cesaire Darbonne?" I said.

"He's a distant cousin of my wife. Why?"

"I just talked with him. He showed no apparent interest in any details we might have discovered about his daughter's death."

"He's a simple man, Dave. For a guy like Cesaire, the government is an abstraction. He lost his livelihood as a sugar farmer because of decisions somebody made in Washington. He said if he hadn't been looking for work the day his daughter died, he would have been home to take care of her. I suspect he feels like a windstorm blew through his life and flattened everything around him."

"Have you ever known him to be violent or vengeful?"

"He used to run a bar. About fifteen years ago, a couple of black guys tried to rob him. I think Cesaire fired a gun in the air and chased them off. I don't know if you'd call that violence or not."

"Thanks, Mack."

After I hung up I removed Yvonne Darbonne's diary from my desk drawer and read again through the entries that alluded to her love affair with the unnamed young man who had "cheeks red as apples." One passage in particular seemed to speak worlds about both the nature of their relationship and the poetic soul of the Cajun girl who waited tables at Victor's and dreamed of studying journalism at the university in Lafayette. She had written of a female seducer and an unwilling boy finally submitting on a bed of "blue-veined violets." Then there were two quoted lines that suggested benign domination but domination nonetheless:

> *Hot, faint, and weary with her hard embracing,*
> *Like a wild bird being tamed with too much handling.*

I had read them before, but I couldn't remember where. I punched in a Google search on the department's computer and came up with Shakespeare's narrative poem *Venus and Adonis*.

What did it all mean? Probably nothing of an evidentiary nature, but it did lend further credibility to the fact that Tony Lujan had homoerotic tendencies and they accounted in part for his dependent relationship with Slim Bruxal.

I placed the diary in a brown mailing envelope and signed out a cruiser.

It had started to rain again when I drove up the Teche on the broken two-lane back road that led past the sugar mill. The mill was as big as a mountain against the sky, gray and strung with wisps of smoke. Down below, across the road, the community of dull green frame houses by the bayou glistened in the rain, their dirt yards as shiny and hard-looking as old bone. I parked in Cesaire Darbonne's driveway and tapped on his front door. Through the screen I could see him drinking coffee in his kitchen, a radio playing on a shelf, his eyes staring out the back window at the rain falling on the bayou.

He walked to the front door, his eyes showing neither interest nor apprehension at my presence on his small gallery. When he unlatched the screen, I saw the chain of heart-shaped scars wrapped across the back of his left hand and around his forearm. "Would you like to have some coffee wit' me, Mr. Robicheaux?" he asked.

"I'd appreciate that," I replied.

He walked ahead of me into the kitchen. The interior of his home was spotless, the furniture free of dust, his dishes in a plastic rack by the sink, the kitchen linoleum drying from a recent mopping.

"I used to fix coffee and cinnamon toast every afternoon at t'ree when Yvonne was going to school," he said. "I don't fix cinnamon toast no more, but I still drink coffee every day at t'ree o'clock. I drip it one tablespoon at a time, just like my daddy done."

I sat at his kitchen table and placed Yvonne's diary, still inside the brown envelope, on top of the table while he prepared coffee and hot milk for me at the drainboard. I could feel sweat start to break on my forehead. I did not want to hurt this man.

He walked toward me, the spoon jiggling slightly in the saucer, his eyes concentrated on not spilling the coffee.

"I need to ask you where you were early this morning," I said.

His eyes lifted into mine with an acuity and sense of recognition I never want to see in a man's face again. "You t'ink I'm the one done that to Bello Lujan?" he said.

"You know about his death?"

"It was on the radio." He set the coffee in front of me, his eyes riveted on mine.

"We have to exclude people, sir. It's part of our procedure. Our questions shouldn't be interpreted as accusations," I said, using the first-person plural in a way that made me wonder about my own principles.

"I went to the Winn-Dixie at sunup. I got gas in my truck down by the drawbridge. I had a flat out yonder in the road and changed my tire right by the mill gate."

He sat down across from me, his pale turquoise eyes never leaving mine. Not one strand of his silver hair was out of place; his skin had hardly a wrinkle or imperfection in it, except for the scars on his left forearm and the back of his hand. But the level of indignation in his eyes was like the edge of another personality asserting itself, one that was not given to latitude in its dealings with others.

I took his daughter's diary out of the envelope and set it in front of him. "Violent and evil men took my wife Annie from me, Mr. Darbonne. The same kind of cruel men murdered my mother. But as bad as my losses have been, I think the greatest suffering any human being can experience is the loss of a child. But I have a job to do, and in this case it's to exclude you as a suspect in the homicide of Bello Lujan."

I removed a ballpoint pen from my shirt pocket and set it on top of the brown envelope and pushed them toward him. "Now, I need you to write down the names of the people who saw you this morning and the approximate times their sighting of you or their conversation with you took place. If you don't know a person's name, just describe what he or she does at the location the person saw you."

He pushed the envelope and pen back toward me. "Why I want to hurt Bello Lujan, me?" he said.

If there was to be a moment of truth in this investigation, I thought, it was now. "There's a possibility Bello attacked your daughter on the day of her death," I said.

He canted his head to one side and tilted up his chin, as though a cold draft had touched his skin. His mouth parted and the color in his eyes seemed to darken. He placed both his hands on the tabletop. "Bello Lujan raped Yvonne?" he said.

"It's a strong possibility."

"And that's why she took them drugs?"

"Yes, sir, I think that may well have been the case."

He stared into space, one hand resting on top of Yvonne's diary. "Why ain't nobody tole me this?"

"What Bello did or didn't do the day of Yvonne's death is still a matter of speculation, Mr. Darbonne."

"If I'd knowed this—"

I waited for him to finish his statement, but he didn't. "You would have killed him?" I said.

He didn't reply. He took back the pen and brown envelope and began to write, listing the places where he had been that morning and the time period he was there and the people who had seen him.

"Do you own a pick?" I said.

"I got one out in the shed. I brought it from the farm I used to own."

"Let's take a look at it," I said.

We went outside, in the rain, with pieces of newspaper over our heads, and walked down the slope of his yard to an old army surplus radio hut where he kept his tools. He unlocked the door and clicked on a light. Like his home, everything was squared away, his nails in capped jars on his workbench, his tools oiled and sharpened and hung in rows on the walls, his paint cans and petrochemical containers arrayed neatly on a polyethylene tarp so they wouldn't form rings on the floor.

"My pick ain't here," he said.

"I see. Could it be somewhere else?"

"No, suh. I hang it between them two nails. It's been hanging there since last spring, when Yvonne and me put in a vegetable garden."

"Does anyone else have a key to the shed?"

"No, suh."

"Would you mind coming down to the department and being fingerprinted?"

It was dry and bright inside the shed, and the rain was slanting outside the door and clicking on the roof. The inside of the shed had a pleasant, warm odor to it, like leaves and field mice and oats in heavy burlap bags. "Sir?" I said.

"I don't mind," he said. He wiped the rainwater out of his eyes with his left hand.

"If you don't mind my asking, how did you get those scars on your arm?"

"Duck-hunting accident 'bout twenty years ago. Just like all this, a big dumb accident. One t'ing turn into another and you cain't turn none of it around. All she wanted to do was go to colletch. Everyt'ing gone to hell just because she wanted to go to colletch. She met that Lujan boy and t'ought she was gonna be his sweetheart. How come she didn't tell me none of this? I wish I wasn't never born."

CHAPTER
23

WHITEY BRUXAL'S CAPACITY for deceit and cunning was not to be underestimated. On Friday morning his attorney, a dapper grimebag by the name of Milton Vidrine, called Helen Soileau at the department. Milton had put himself through law school as a bug exterminator, then had made a good living chasing ambulances in Baton Rouge. In fact, he became known as "Twilight Zone" Vidrine because he was an expert at showing up in emergency wards and intensive-care units and convincing half-comatose accident victims to sign settlement agreements and liability waivers that often left the accident victims destitute. Vidrine said he wanted to talk to Helen and me simultaneously. Coincidentally, I was sitting in her office when the call came in. She clicked on the speakerphone but did not tell him that I was there.

"What's this about?" she said.

"Mr. Bruxal wants you to have a clear understanding about a situation that is not of his making and over which he has no control," Vidrine replied.

"What might that be?" Helen said.

"I'd like Detective Robicheaux to be present."

"I'm the administrative authority in this department. Do you want to tell me what this is about or do you want to put it in a letter?" she said.

He paused a moment. "Detective Robicheaux has a reputation as a hothead and a violent man. His alcoholic history is no secret in

291

Lafayette. But Mr. Bruxal wants to make sure Detective Robicheaux is not harmed in any way. This call is more a matter of conscience than legality."

Helen was standing against the glare of the window, her face wrapped in shadow, but I could see her laughing silently at the absurdity of a man like Milton Vidrine referring to matters of conscience.

"I'm right here, Mr. Vidrine. Thanks for the character assessment and for getting in touch," I said, leaning forward in my chair.

Milton Vidrine might have been disarmed for two seconds at the revelation that I had been listening to his remarks, but no more than two seconds. "Mr. Bruxal has fired his employee Thomas Leo Raguza and wants to inform all parties concerned that he takes no responsibility for this man's actions," he said.

"I'm not sure how I should interpret that," I said.

"You gave Mr. Raguza a severe beating, Detective Robicheaux. Mr. Bruxal has no knowledge about your previous relationship with Mr. Raguza or why or how he provoked you. But Mr. Bruxal does not want to employ anyone who bears hostility toward any member of local law enforcement. He's also concerned that Mr. Raguza could be a threat."

"Say that last part again," Helen said.

"My client believes Mr. Raguza is unstable and should be considered potentially dangerous."

"Bruxal just recently made this discovery?" I said.

"I'm passing on the information as it was presented to me," he replied.

"Here's some more information for you. Lefty Raguza and your client were involved in the murder of a friend of mine. His name was—"

Before I could continue, Helen propped her arms on her desk and leaned down to the speakerphone. She placed her thumb on the phone's "memo" button. "As of this moment this phone conversation is being recorded. Your statement about the danger posed to a member of the Iberia Parish Sheriff's Department by Thomas Raguza is duly noted. I'm also at this juncture informing you that I consider this information a disguised conveyance of a threat against a member of my department."

"That's ridiculous," he said.

"Every white-collar guy we slam the cell door on uses those same words," she said.

"I'm going to have a talk with the district attorney, Mr. Marceaux."

"Good, you two deserve each other. Now, you keep your goddamn distance from my office," she said.

Helen pushed down on the disconnect and shut off the speakerphone. She realized I was smiling and gave me a look. I dropped my eyes and examined the tops of my fingers. "I'm sick of this bunch wiping their feet on us. Was it you or Purcel who said most of the world's ills could be corrected with a three-day open season on people?"

"It was Ernest Hemingway."

"I've got to read more of him." She sat down behind her desk and brushed at a spot above her eyebrow with one knuckle, the anger subsiding in her face. "What do you think they're up to?"

"Disassociating themselves from Raguza and at the same time pointing him in my direction."

She seemed to think about what I had said, her eyes wandering around the room. But that wasn't it. "We're anybody's punch," she said.

"Pardon?"

"Every corrupt enterprise in the country ends up here. They fuck us with a Roto-Rooter and make us like them for it."

"Who's 'they'?"

"Anybody with a checkbook." Then she blew out her breath. "What's the status on Cesaire Darbonne?"

"He's getting printed as we speak."

YOU HAVE TO BELIEVE IN SOMETHING. Everyone does. Even atheists believe in their unbelief. If they didn't, they'd go mad. The misanthrope believes in his hatred of his fellow man. The gambler believes he's omniscient and that his knowledge of the future is proof he is loved by God. The middle-income person who spends enormous amounts of time window-shopping and sorting through used clothing at garage sales is indicating that our goods will never be ashes blowing across the grave. I suspect the drunkard believes his own self-destruction is the penance required for his acceptability in the eyes of his Creator. The adherents of Saint Francis see divinity in the faces of the poor and oppressed but take no notice of the Byzantine fire surrounding themselves. The commonality of all the aforementioned lies in the frailty of their moral vision. It is also what makes them human.

Most cops and newspeople, usually at midpoint in their careers, come to a terrible realization about themselves, namely, that they are in danger of becoming like the jaundiced and embittered individuals they had always pitied as aberrations or anachronisms in their profession. But when people lie to you on a daily basis, when you watch zoning boards sell out whole neighborhoods to porn vendors and massage parlor owners, when you see the most expensive attorneys in the country labor on behalf of murderers and drug lords, when you investigate instances of child abuse so grievous your entire belief system is called into question, you have to reexamine your own life and perspective in ways we normally reserve for saints.

At that moment you either reaffirm your belief in justice and protection of the innocent or you do not. But unlike the metaphysician, you do not arrive at your faith through the use of syllogism or abstraction. You often rediscover your faith by taking up the cause of one individual, one innocent person who you believe deserves justice and the full protection of the law. If you can accomplish this, the rest of it doesn't seem to matter so much.

I wanted to believe in Cesaire Darbonne. Like many cane farmers in South Louisiana, he had been driven under by a trade agreement allowing the importation of massive amounts of cheap sugar into the United States. The French-speaking provincial world he had grown up in, one of serpentine bayous and endless fields of green cane bending in a Gulf breeze, was becoming urbanized and overlaid with subdivisions and strip malls. But the greatest tragedy in his life was one he could have never foreseen.

His daughter, like mine, seemed to have possessed all the innocence and love and goodness that every father wishes for in his child. No one, and I mean absolutely no one, can understand the level of pain and loss and rage a father experiences when he wakes each day with the knowledge that his daughter has been raped or murdered. The images of her fate haunt him throughout his waking hours and into his sleep, and the thoughts he has about her tormentors are of a kind he never shares with anyone, lest he be considered perverse and pathological himself.

At 2:15 p.m. Mack Bertrand rang my extension. "It's a match," he said.

"Don't tell me that," I said.

"Cesaire's prints are all over it. What else you want me to say? Didn't you say his pick was missing from his toolshed? It's obviously his."

"The guy doesn't need this," I said. "Look, Mack, the motive isn't there. I'm convinced he didn't know Bello raped his daughter."

"How can you be sure?"

"He was stunned when I told him."

"Maybe that's just the impression you had. You're a sympathetic soul, Dave. Valerie Lujan hated her husband. She wouldn't have been above passing on the information to Cesaire."

"No, Mr. Darbonne looked like he'd been poleaxed. Maybe he killed Bello, but it wasn't because he knew Bello attacked his daughter."

"Good luck with it."

"With what?" I asked.

"This case. It's like trying to get cobweb out of your hair, isn't it?" he said.

I BROUGHT HELEN up to the minute, then spent the rest of the afternoon trying to verify Cesaire Darbonne's alibi. A clerk remembered seeing him at the Winn-Dixie and so did the clerk at the gas station by the drawbridge. But the preponderance of his alibi rested on his claim that he had changed a flat by the sugar mill entrance, and

unfortunately none of the security people at the mill could recall seeing him. Cesaire had another problem as well. Bello Lujan's horse
farm was less than fifteen minutes' drive from Cesaire's house.
Cesaire could have visited the Winn-Dixie, bought gas, changed a flat
tire, and still had time and opportunity to murder Bello.

I returned to the office just before 5 p.m.

"You want to get a warrant?" Helen said.

"Not yet," I replied.

"I think Cesaire is looking more and more like our boy," she said.

"It's too pat. The murder weapon was left a few feet from the
body with Darbonne's fingerprints all over it. But Mack Bertrand
believes the last guy who handled the pick was wearing gloves. Why
would Darbonne wear gloves, then drop his own pick at the crime
scene with his fingerprints on it?"

"We're back to Whitey Bruxal?"

"Maybe."

"But Bruxal couldn't hang a frame on Cesaire Darbonne unless he
knew Darbonne had motivation, in other words knowledge that his
daughter was attacked by Bello. Which doesn't seem to be the case. I
think Bruxal is out of the picture. What bwana say now?"

She had me.

JUST AS I WAS ABOUT TO LEAVE the department for the day, I got
a call from Koko Hebert.

"I've got scrapings from under Bello's fingernails," he said. "He
either had a real good piece of ass before he died or he fought with his
attacker."

"Koko, if you still feel a need to prove you're offensive and obnoxious, I want to set your mind at ease. You don't have to carry that
burden anymore. You've assured everybody in the department you're
the real article."

"Fuck you," he said. "Pending lab analysis, I'd say the skin tissue
came from a person of color. Normally we can't tell race by looking
at tissue scrapings, because it dries out quickly and becomes visually

indistinguishable from the victim's. But Bello got a roll of it under two of his fingernails and they look like they came off a black person. Gender is another matter. We've got to go to a lab in Florida for that. Because Bello probably porked half the black girls in this parish, I'm not sure if my tissue scrapings will be relevant. Sort that out, Robicheaux, then give me a call if you need more explanation."

You didn't trade shots with Koko Hebert unless you were willing to take a heavy load of shrapnel.

I WENT HOME and had a light supper with Molly, then drove up the bayou in the sunset to Loreauville and Bello Lujan's stable. The fields were green and sweet-smelling, the clumps of oaks along the road pulsing with birds. The crime scene tape flickered and bounced in the wind. I walked behind the stable and looked at the spot where Mack had found the murder weapon, then studied the breadth of the field where the killer had run toward the steel back fence. What had I missed? Not just here, but in all the interviews involving Yvonne Darbonne and Monarch Little and Slim Bruxal and Crustacean Man and Tony and Bello Lujan. The key glimmered on the edge of my vision, like a shard of memory you take with you from a dream. It lay in an insignificant remark, an oblique reference that I had passed over, a piece of physical evidence that was like a grain of sand on a beach. But what?

On the other side of the steel fence, two little boys and a girl, all of them black, were flying a kite emblazoned with the American flag. The girl, who was not over eight or nine, was holding the kite string. They had made a fort of propped-up plywood inside a stand of persimmon trees and inside the walls had spread a blanket on the ground. A box of snack crackers, a plastic pitcher of what looked like Kool-Aid, three candy bars, and a can of tuna had been dumped out of a grocery bag onto the blanket.

"You guys doin' all right?" I said.

"We're camping out, least till dark," one of the boys said.

"Y'all weren't out here early this morning, were you?"

"No, suh," the same boy said.

"That's a fine fort you've got there," I said.

"Yes, suh," the same boy said.

His eyes left my face and looked up at the kite popping against the sky. The other boy seemed to concentrate unduly on the kite as well. The girl had wrapped the string around her wrist and was making a game of pulling on the string and releasing it, so that the kite rose, then sagged and rose again in the sunset. She wore elastic-waisted jeans and pink tennis shoes and a white blouse with tiny flowers printed on it. She had big brown eyes and pigtails and a round face and skin that was as dark and shiny as chocolate. Her expression was a study in innocence.

"You guys didn't go inside that yellow tape on the stable, did you?" I said.

No one answered.

"What's your name?" I asked the girl.

"Chereen," she said. "What's yours?"

"Dave Robicheaux. I'm a police officer. Did y'all see anybody run across this field early this morning?"

"We wasn't out here," she replied.

"But later maybe you guys went over to see what was going on?"

They looked at one another, then at the birds freckling the sky.

"Y'all sure you don't want to tell me something?" I said.

"Want some crackers and Kool-Aid?" the girl said.

"Thanks just the same. Don't you guys go on the other side of that yellow tape, okay?"

"No, suh, we ain't. Gonna stay right here, outside the fence."

I waved good-bye to them and walked away. When I glanced back over my shoulder, one of the boys was working open the can of tuna while the other boy filled three plastic glasses with Kool-Aid.

I DROVE BACK into New Iberia and visited Monarch Little at Iberia General. He was sitting up in bed, watching a Chicago White Sox game on the television mounted high up on the wall, the sheet drawn up over his sloping girth. I sat down on the side of his bed and picked up each of his hands and examined his skin from his wrists to his upper arms.

"What you doin'?" he said.

"Lean forward," I said.

"What for?"

"So you don't end up charged with murder. For once in your life, try cooperating with someone who's on your side."

He sat motionless while I looked closely at his face and hair and throat and the back of his neck.

"Take off your shirt," I said.

"Mr. Dee—"

"Just do it."

He pulled off his pajama top, held his massive arms straight out, and let me examine his chest and back.

"That's it," I said.

"That's what?"

"You didn't kill Bello Lujan."

"That's a big breakt'rew for you? I ain't never killed nobody."

"Why'd you put all that skag in your arm, Monarch?"

"Felt like it."

"You almost caught the bus, partner."

"Maybe I'd be better off."

"What about all those soldiers in Iraq? What kind of day do you think they're having?"

"I tried to join the army. They didn't want me."

My question to him had been a cheap shot and I deserved his reply. I sat in a chair next to his bed for a long time and didn't say anything. He tried to concentrate on the televised baseball game, but it was obvious he was becoming more and more uncomfortable with both my presence and silence.

"You got some wiring loose in you, Mr. Dee," he said.

"I want you to call me as soon as you get out of here," I said.

"What for?"

"My wife wants you to come over for dinner."

There was a broken smile at the corner of his mouth. "Who you kidd—" he began.

"Don't mock her invitation. She used to be a Catholic nun. She'll rip your arms off and beat you to death with them," I said.

He made a show of crushing the pillow down on his own face, but I could hear him laughing under it.

THAT NIGHT the weatherman on the late news talked about another storm building in the Caribbean, one that was expected to reach hurricane velocity as it approached Cuba. I fell asleep on the couch while dry lightning flickered in the trees and leaves gusted in the street. I dreamed about baseball and summer evenings in City Park back in the 1950s, when we played pepper games in front of the old wood and chicken-wire backstop that was overhung by oak trees dripping with Spanish moss. In the dream the air smelled of boiled crabs and barbecue grease flaring on hot charcoal, and I could hear a Cajun band playing "Jolie Blon" down by the old brick firehouse. The dream seemed to reflect an innocent time in our history, an idyllic vision I have never been able to disengage from. But in reality there were many elements of the 1950s that were not so innocent, and Monarch Little was there, in the dream, to tell me that. Or at least that was what I thought.

He was standing at home plate with a bat propped on his shoulder, in an era when people of color were not allowed in the park, whacking grounders to the three black children I had seen flying a kite by Bello Lujan's back fence. Except in the dream the children were uninterested in Monarch and his baseball bat, and were sitting on the close-cropped grass just beyond the infield, eating a picnic lunch. One of the children was opening a can of tuna.

I woke from the dream like a man breaking through a pane of glass.

THE NEXT MORNING was Saturday. I got up at seven and dressed in the kitchen so I wouldn't wake Molly. I fed Snuggs and Tripod on the back steps, left Molly a note on the chalkboard we used for messages, took a half-carton of orange juice out of the icebox for myself, and drove down St. Peter Street to Iberia General. Monarch was just checking out of the hospital as I came through the reception area.

"I need to talk with you," I said.

"I got a cab coming," he said.

"After we talk, I'll take you wherever you want to go. My truck's outside."

"I ain't eat yet," he said.

"That makes two of us," I said.

We headed toward the McDonald's on East Main. The clothes Monarch had been wearing when the paramedics pulled him out of the ice water at the crack house had been washed and dried at the hospital and, riding in the truck, with the windows down and the trees and shadows sliding by us, he looked cool and comfortable, strangely at peace with himself. I pulled into the line of vehicles at the take-out window.

"You lay down your sword and shield?" I said.

"What you mean, 'sword and shield'?"

"You're not 'gonna study the war no more.' Those are lyrics from a hymn. The singer is telling the listener he's resigned from the fray, that he's made his separate peace."

"What the FBI do to me, what y'all do to me, it don't matter one way or the other. I just ain't gonna fight wit' it no more. I'm t'rew wit' dope, t'rew wit' gangs, t'rew wit' the life. If I stack time, that's the way it be."

"That's what I was talking about."

"Then why you got to say everyt'ing in code?" he said.

The electronic order box came on and I ordered eggs, sausage, biscuits, and coffee and milk for both of us. "T'row a couple of fried pies in there," Monarch said.

"Two fried pies," I said to the box.

I got our order at the second window in the line, then parked under the big oak tree by the front. I couldn't believe how much food Monarch could stuff into his mouth at one time.

"What you want to know?" he asked, pieces of scrambled egg falling off his chin.

"When I questioned you about Tony Lujan's death, you said you were supposed to meet him out by the Boom Boom Room, but you changed your mind."

"Right."

"Why?"

"I was gonna jack him for money. It was a bad idea. So I didn't go. He ended up shotgunned to deat', but I didn't have nothing to do wit' it."

"Yeah, I know all that. But why was it a bad idea?"

"I just tole you. I was gonna jack him—"

"No, that's not the explanation you gave me originally. You were afraid something was going to happen."

"Yeah, I said what if Tony called up Slim Bruxal and Slim and them other colletch boys showed up wit' ball bats."

"Why baseball bats?"

"'Cause they done it before. I checked them out. They had a beef behind a nightclub in Lake Charles wit' a couple of soldiers from Fort Polk. They got ball bats out of their car and busted up a soldier and smashed all the windows out of his car."

"Slim and Tony did this?"

"And about ten more like them."

"Why didn't you tell me all this earlier?" I said.

"'Cause you ain't axed me," he replied, biting into a fried pie.

I drove Monarch to his house up on Loreauville Road, then went to the department and in the Saturday-morning quietness of my office pulled out all my files and notes and photographs dealing with the unsolved vehicular homicide of Crustacean Man.

Just before noon I called Koko Hebert at his home. Strangely enough, he acted halfway normal, making me wonder if much of his public persona wasn't manufactured.

"Do I think the fatal wound is consistent with a blow from a base-ball bat?" he said.

"Yeah," I said.

"It could be."

"Come on, Koko. I need a warrant. Give me something I can use."

"The bone was crushed, the damage massive. All kinds of shit can happen in a high-speed hit-and-run we can't reconstruct. It's like somebody getting caught inside a concrete mixer."

"I'll bring you the photos. The wound is concave and lateral in nature, the indentation uniform along the edges."

"Stop telling me what I already know. Yeah, a baseball bat could have done it. I'll come down and make an addendum to the file if you need it."

"Thanks, partner."

"Who's the warrant on?"

"Some kids who would like to pour the rest of us into soap molds," I said.

I DOUBTED IF I'd be able to get the warrant until Monday morning, but there were other things to be done that weekend, other elements in the dream that had caused me to sit up as though a piece of crystal had shattered in my sleep.

I drove to Loreauville and crossed a drawbridge and passed a shipyard where steel boats that service offshore oil rigs are manufactured. I drove down an undulating two-lane road through water oaks and palmettos and asked an older black man clipping a tangle of bougainvillea from the trellised entrance to his yard if he knew a little girl by the name of Chereen. The house behind him was made of brick and well maintained. A speedboat mounted on a trailer was parked in his porte cochere.

"That's my granddaughter's name. Why you want to know?" he said.

I opened my badge holder and hung it out the window. "My name is Dave Robicheaux. I'm with the Iberia Sheriff's Department. I thought she might have some information that could be helpful to us," I said.

The black man wore old slacks and tennis shoes, but his shirt was pressed, his back erect. The distrust in his eyes was unmistakable. "She's nine years old. What information she gonna have?"

"It concerns evidence she and two other children may have found at a crime scene," I said.

"You talking about the Lujan farm?"

"I need to talk to your granddaughter, sir."

"Maybe I need to call my lawyer, too."

I pulled my truck in his driveway and cut the engine. I opened the door and stepped out on the grass. "She and her friends were playing in a plywood fort by Bello Lujan's back fence. Mr. Lujan was murdered. Where's your granddaughter?"

"She don't know nothing about no murder."

I could feel my patience draining and my old nemesis, anger, blooming like an infection in my chest. Like most southern white people, I did not like paying the price for what my antecedents may have done.

"The man who killed Bello Lujan is still out there. You want him prowling around your neighborhood? You want him looking for your granddaughter, sir?" I said.

He spiked his clippers into the lawn and blotted his neck with a folded handkerchief. "Come wit' me. They in the backyard," he said.

I followed him around the side of the house. The three children I had seen flying a kite behind Bello's property were playing croquet in the shade of oak trees. "You guys remember me?" I said.

They looked at one another, then at Chereen's grandfather. "Tell him what he want to know," he said.

I squatted down so I was eye level with the children. "When y'all were having your picnic at your fort, you opened a can of tuna fish, didn't you?" I said.

All three of them nodded, but their eyes didn't meet mine. I pointed to the little boy who had opened the can. "What's your name?" I asked.

"Freddy."

"What did you use to open the can, Freddy?"

"Can opener," he replied.

"Was it an unusual can opener?" I said, smiling at him now.

"A little bit, maybe," he said.

"Where'd you get it?" I said.

"I found it," Chereen said, before her friend could answer. "In the field behind the horse barn."

"Do you still have it?"

"It's at the fort. Wit' the crucifix and the broke chain it was on," she said.

"A crucifix and a chain? Those things and the can opener were all together?" I said.

"Yes, suh, lying in the weeds. Not far from the fence," Freddy said.

"I'm glad you guys found and saved those things for me. But you should have told me this yesterday. A man was killed and his killer is still out there, maybe preparing to hurt someone else. When I asked y'all if you had been inside the tape, you told me you hadn't. So I had to figure all this out on my own. By keeping silent about the things you had found, you were telling me a lie. Indirectly, you were helping a very bad man get away with a terrible crime."

"They got the point," the grandfather said.

When I stood up, I could hear my knees pop. "How old are you, sir?" I asked.

"Sixty-one," he replied.

I wanted to ask him how much value he set on pride. Was it worth the innocent lives of others in danger? I wanted to ask him if he thought he could negotiate with the kind of evil that dwells in a man who could tear a fellow human being apart with a steel pick. I wanted to tell him I was not the source of his discontent and enmity and that as a child of poor and illiterate Cajuns I shared his background and had done nothing to warrant his irritability.

I had all these vituperative thoughts, but I expressed none of them. Instead, I shook his hand without his having offered it. He stared at me blankly.

"Will you accompany me and the children to their fort, sir?" I said.

He brushed some garden cuttings off his shirt with the backs of his fingers. "Yeah, I could use a break. I'll get some Popsicles out of the icebox to take along. Appreciate the job you doing even though I don't probably show it," he said.

• • •

AFTER I DROVE WITH THE CHILDREN and their grandfather to the plywood fort, I returned to the office and logged the neck chain, crucifix, and the small P-38 army-issue can opener into an evidence locker. Then I called Helen Soileau at home.

"Bello Lujan's killer is a guy from the Islands. He's a friend of Lefty Raguza," I said.

"How do you know?" she said.

"Some kids playing on Bello Lujan's property found a chain and crucifix and G.I. can opener by Bello's back fence. I saw this guy wearing this stuff the night I had a run-in with Lefty at that zebra club in Lafayette."

"You're sure?" she asked.

"There's no question about it. I figure Bello broke the chain from the guy's neck and it fell down inside his shirt. It didn't fall onto the ground until he was almost to the fence."

"That doesn't put the guy at the murder scene. Whitey Bruxal was Bello's business partner. It's not improbable his hired help hung around Bello's stable. But if we can put the neck chain and whatever with the scrapings from under Bello's nails, we might have something. Find out where the gumball is and bring him in."

I called Betsy Mossbacher on her cell phone. She picked up on the second ring.

"I need to find the guy from the Islands who works for Whitey Bruxal. His hair looks like a braided mop somebody dipped in a grease bucket. Know who I'm talking about?" I said.

"He's an illegal by the name of Juan Bolachi. He's got the smarts of a used Q-tip. What do you want him for?"

"He may have been involved in the murder of Bello Lujan."

"Our surveillance indicates he already blew town. Good luck finding him. He mucks out stables anywhere between Hialeah and Belmont Park and a couple of quarter-horse tracks in the Southwest. You're sure this is the guy?"

I called Helen again at her house, even though it was Saturday and I knew my obsessiveness was beginning to test her patience. "The guy from the Islands already split. I've got an address for him in

Lafayette. Maybe we can match DNA from some items in his residence with the scrapings from—"

"Ease up, bwana. It's starting to get away from you."

"I'll work on it this weekend. On my own time."

"The evidence you've found is one nail in the coffin. But we're going to need six more like it. Now cool your jets, Streak."

In terms of the evidentiary aspects of the case, she was right and it was pointless to argue with her. But Helen believed in the viability of the legal process much more than I did. If the building that you wish to see demolished already has a crack in it, why wait on time and decay to finish the job? I tried another tack before she could hang up.

"I think I know how Crustacean Man died," I said. "Monday morning I want to get a search warrant on the Lujan and Bruxal homes and Slim Bruxal's fraternity house."

I heard her sigh. "What do you have?"

"Monarch Little says Slim and Tony and their friends used baseball bats in a beef with some soldiers behind a nightclub. I think they used one on Crustacean Man as well. Koko will back us up on the warrant."

"Why would college kids deliberately murder a derelict?"

"Why did they gangbang Yvonne Darbonne when she was stoned and drunk and already traumatized by rape? Because they're sociopaths. Because their parents should have used better rubbers," I replied.

"Get the warrants," she said.

CHAPTER
24

We had the warrants by 11 a.m. Monday. We coordinated with both the Lafayette P.D. and the Lafayette Parish Sheriff's Department and arranged to serve all three search warrants simultaneously to ensure that no one at any of the three locations notified the other targets we were on our way.

At exactly 2:45 p.m. Helen and two plainclothes descended on the Lujan home, Lafayette Parish detectives searched the Bruxal home, and Joe Dupree at the Lafayette P.D. accompanied me and Top, our retired NCO, to Slim Bruxal's fraternity house.

Summer school was out of session and the white three-story Victorian home that had been the second-to-last stop in the short life of Yvonne Darbonne was almost empty. The air-conditioning units in the windows were turned off, either to save electricity or perhaps because they were broken, and the entire building seemed to radiate heat and the smell of moldy clothes and spoiled food someone had forgotten to empty from a garbage container. In fact, without the forced humor and irreverent shouting that passed for camaraderie among the usual residents, the house was a dismal and depressing environment, as though the floors and water-stained wallpaper and dark corridors contained no memories worth remembering and had served no purpose higher than a utilitarian one.

A thick-bodied, crew-cut kid with green and red tattoos on both arms was reading a magazine on the back porch. He told us he couldn't remember seeing any baseball bats on the premises.

"What's your name?" I asked.

"Sonny Williamson."

"You have a speed bag in the backyard, Sonny. You must have other sporting equipment here. Where would it be?" I said.

He lowered his magazine and studied the back hedge. "I got no idea," he said.

"Get up," Joe said.

"What?" the kid said. His close-cropped hair was oily and bright on the tips, his upper arms sunburned.

"You deaf as well as impolite?" Joe said.

"No," the kid said, slowly rising to his feet.

"You're going to give us the tour. If I think you're concealing evidence in a homicide investigation, I'm going to turn your life into a toilet," Joe said.

"What's your problem, man?" the kid said.

"You are. I don't like your tats. If you ask me, they really suck. Where'd you get them?" Joe said.

"In Houston."

"You should get your money back. These guys using you for queer-bait?" Joe said.

"*Queer-bait?* What's going—"

"Shut your mouth. Where are the baseball bats?" Joe said.

"There's some shit out in the garage. You want to look through it, be my fucking guest," the kid said.

"Thanks for your help. Now, sit down and don't move until I tell you," Joe said.

Just then Joe's cell phone vibrated on his hip. He glanced at the incoming number on the digital display and took the call while Top and I went into the garage. The heat was stifling, the tin roof ventilated by rust against a white sun, nests of mud daubers caked on the rafters.

"There it is," Top said, pointing to a canvas duffel bag stuffed with baseball bats.

"Take them out to the car, will you, Top? I want to have a talk with the kid on the porch," I said.

"You believe he's really a college student?" he asked.

"Sure, why not?"

"I joined the Crotch because I didn't think a university would accept a guy like me," he said, hefting the duffel by its strap onto his shoulder. "I ended up at Khe Sanh. I think I screwed myself."

"It could have been worse."

"How?"

"You could be an alumnus of a fraternity like this one," I said.

His eyes crinkled at the corners, the collection of aluminum and wood bats rattling against his back.

I walked back into the yard. The sun had gone behind a cloud and the wind was blowing in the trees. The kid reading the magazine glanced up at me. His eyes had the tint and complexity of clear blue water, devoid of thought or moral sentiment.

"Show me around the inside, will you, Sonny?" I said.

He tossed his magazine aside and walked ahead of me. But before I entered the house, Joe Dupree stopped me. He had just put away his cell phone and seemed to be puzzling through the conversation he'd just had. He gestured for me to follow him back into the yard, out of earshot of Sonny Williamson. "That was a friend of mine at the courthouse. Trish Klein just pleaded no contest on the shoplifting charge, paid a fine, and went back on the street," he said.

"Have you gotten any reports of crimes committed against Bruxal or his interests?" I said.

"None," he said.

"Maybe she wasn't using the jail as an alibi after all."

"I'm still convinced her people were the ones who creeped Bruxal's house," he said.

"You hear anything from the Feds?" I asked.

"A couple of calls from this Mossbacher woman. She seems on the square, but she doesn't know any more than we do."

"You got anybody tailing Trish Klein?"

"With our budget for overtime? We don't have the manpower to patrol our own parking lot," he replied. "You about to wrap it up here?"

"Just about," I said.

I can't tell you exactly why I wanted to go inside the fraternity house with the kid named Sonny Williamson. Maybe, like most people, I wanted to believe in the Orwellian admonition that human beings are always better than we think they are. Ask a street cop how often he has glanced in his rearview mirror at a handcuffed suspect whose clothes are stippled with his victim's blood, hoping to catch a glimmer of humanity that will dispel his growing sense that not all of us descend from the same tree.

"You have an interesting name," I said in the kitchen.

"Why's that?"

"Sonny Boy Williamson was a famous bluesman from Jackson, Tennessee, same town that produced Carl Perkins," I said.

He seemed to think about the implications of my statement. "Never heard of either one of them. What do you want to see?" he said.

"The bedrooms."

"They're all upstairs."

"Good," I said.

It was obvious he didn't like embarking on a mission whose purpose was hidden from him. He stopped on the second landing and gestured vaguely down the hallway. "About a half-dozen guys sleep here, but they're gone for the summer," he said.

I looked down from the banister at the living room area below and the thread-worn carpet and scarred furniture. "Your parties usually take place down there?" I said.

"Right, when we have parties."

"Remember a party about the time of spring break?"

"Not particularly."

"Think hard."

"I don't remember," he said, shaking his head.

"Don't you guys sometimes call that 'booze and cooze night'?"

"No, man, we don't."

I rested one hand on his shoulder, as a blind man might if he wanted someone to cross a dangerous street with him. "Show me the bedrooms, Sonny. I've got a lot of faith in you. I can tell you're a guy who wants to do the right thing."

The afternoon heat was trapped against the ceiling, the air motionless, gray with motes of dust. A drop of sweat ran in a clear line down the side of Sonny's face. "See for yourself. It's just empty rooms," he said, flexing his back.

"But you know the one I'm interested in. She was stoned when she got here, then she loaded up again and probably couldn't walk too well. So one guy probably offered to help her, you know, show her to the bathroom or give her a place to lie down. It would have been just one guy, right? She wouldn't have gone upstairs with two or three. That would have caused all kinds of alarm bells to go off in her head, and besides, it would look bad. Who was the guy, Sonny? I don't think it was Tony Lujan and I know she didn't like or trust Slim Bruxal. Who's the guy who walked Yvonne Darbonne upstairs?"

He had stepped back from me, causing my hand to drop from his shoulder. His neck was slick with sweat, his breathing audible in the silence. "I wasn't there," he said.

"How can you say you weren't there if you don't even remember the party? You mean you don't attend fraternity parties?"

He stared at me dumbly, unable to reason through the question. I pushed open a bedroom door that was already ajar. The closet was empty, the drawers pulled loose from the dresser, the bed little more than a stained mattress askew on a set of springs.

"Is this y'all's fuck pad?" I said.

"You're all wrong on this."

"Right. Were you one of them, Sonny?"

"One of who?"

"She'd already been raped earlier in the day. She was drunk and stoned and unable to protect herself. Did your buds say she was a good lay? Did you have a go at her yourself?"

"I ain't saying anything else."

"You don't have to, Sonny. People stack time in different ways. I think you've got a life sentence tattooed right across your forehead."

I left him in the hallway and walked down the stairs and out into the yard, into wind and the shadows of trees moving on the grass and flowers blooming in a garden across the street and automobiles passing in columns of sunlight that shone through the canopy of oaks overhead. I walked into the ebb and flow of a world separate from the systematic ruin of a young woman's life.

As I was getting into the cruiser, Sonny Williamson came out on the gallery, his arms pumped. "What do you mean, life sentence?" he shouted. "What's your problem, man?"

No BASEBALL BATS were found in the search at the Bruxal or Lujan homes, and the search team had already left the Bruxal property when Top and I arrived. But it was obvious a calamity of some sort had struck the Bruxal family. An upstairs window was broken; an earthen pot lay shattered on a terrace, the root system of the plant cooking in the sun. All the doors were wide open, the air-conditioning gushing out into the heat. The waxed black Humvee had been backed into a stucco pillar by the carriage house and left there, glass and electrical connections leaking from the crushed taillight socket.

Top parked the cruiser in the drive and he and I rang the bell on the porch and heard it chime deep in the house. But no one came to the door, which yawed open on a living room littered with huge amounts of paper that looked torn from binders. We went around to the back of the house and saw Slim Bruxal under a shed attached to the side of a barn, grooming the red Morgan I had seen running in the pasture on my previous visit.

Slim did not look well. One eye was swollen and bloodshot. A fresh abrasion flamed high on his other cheek. His T-shirt was sweaty and dirt-streaked and stretched out of shape at the neck.

"Who messed up your face?" I said.

"My father did. After he went nuts and chased my mother out of the house."

"When?"

"Ten minutes ago," he said. "His goddamn money got transferred out of the Islands into a bunch of domestic accounts. He blamed it on her and me. He says somebody got ahold of all his bank account numbers."

"Really?" I said, my expression blank.

"Yeah, *really*."

Slim's face reminded me of a hurt child's, and I had a feeling the injury his father had visited upon him would not go away for a very long time. I asked Top to go to the cruiser and radio Helen we'd be late getting back to the department.

I stepped under the shed and rested my arm across the mare's croup. I felt her skin wrinkle, heard her tail swish and one hoof thump into the compacted dirt under her.

"I think you're an intelligent man, Slim, and I won't try to jerk you around. But one way or another, your kite is about to crash and burn. So is your old man's. We won't get you and your father on everything y'all have done, but we'll get you on part of it and that'll be enough.

"You killed the homeless man with a baseball bat. It wasn't planned, but that's what happened. You and Tony were cruising down the back road, maybe drinking a little brew, blowing a little weed, and you saw this wino walking along the edge of the ditch. Then you thought it'd really be funny to load this guy in your car and maybe take him to a party, push him inside the door and leave him there, rolling around on the rug, wrapped in grunge and puke, people tripping over him, wow, what a gas, huh?"

All movement had drained out of Slim's body. He stood frozen in the shade, breathing through his mouth, and I knew I had described at least part of what had actually happened on the back road.

He dipped a big round pale yellow sponge into a water bucket and ran it along the horse's neck, his eyes darkening with thought, his mouth downturned at the corners, the water sliding off the horse's withers onto Slim's shoes.

"Except the guy didn't like what you guys had planned for him, and he got out of the car and started running," I continued. "Tony was driving and tried to cut him off, but, guess what, he hit the guy with the right fender and broke the guy's hip. If you guys had just done a hit-and-run on a drunk, you could have bagged ass, left him on the road, and nobody would have ever been the wiser. In fact, you could have even done a nine-one-one call on him and saved his life. But he had seen your faces and he could identify the Buick as well, and that meant only one thing—it was time for this poor bastard to go to that big wineshop in the sky.

"So you got out of the Buick with a baseball bat and parked the guy's head in the fourth dimension. Tell me I'm wrong."

He looked me in the face, without really seeing me, thinking about the words, if any, he was about to say.

"Good try, but I don't think you got jack shit to go on," he said.

And I knew at that moment the baseball bats we had found in the fraternity garage probably did not contain the one that had delivered the fatal blow to Crustacean Man. Slim had slipped the punch again. All he needed to do now was to keep sponging down his horse and not say anything. But the anger at his father, and by extension at me, still lingered in his face, and I had another run at him.

"You've got somebody else's death on your conscience, too, even though you may never be held legally accountable for it. But one way or another, I'm going to make your life miserable until you own up for what you little sonsofbitches did to Yvonne Darbonne."

His hand tightened on the sponge, squeezing a curtain of water down the horse's withers. Then he threw the sponge into the bucket, hard, splattering his jeans.

"You just don't get it, do you?" he said. "I was the only guy looking out for her. She got stoned out of her mind at the house and puked in the toilet on the second floor. Then some guys took her in a room and she got it on with all three of them. That kind of shit doesn't go on when I'm in the house. We've got a little sister sorority we look out for, and we don't need a reputation for gangbanging freshman coeds. *I* broke it up and *I* took her home. Where was Tony? Glad you asked. Passed out under a picnic table in the backyard with potato salad in his hair."

"You drove Yvonne Darbonne back to New Iberia? To her house?" I said.

"You got it," he said. "I was going to take her inside her house, but she got a gun out of the glove box and started waving it around. It was a twenty-two Tony and me target-practiced with. I tried to take it away from her, but she turned it into her face and pulled the trigger. That's what happened, man. You want to put me in prison for that, go ahead. But get this straight. I helped her when she didn't have any other friends, including Tony, who in case you didn't know it was a closet homo."

"If you were an innocent man, why'd you run?"

"Because I'm Whitey Bruxal's son. Because I don't like being a backseat hump for every cop in South Louisiana."

His cheeks were pooled with color in the warm gloom of the shed, and for just a moment he reminded me of his dead friend Tony. I could hear the wind coursing in the pasture, feel the mare shift her weight under my hand.

"You killed Tony, though, didn't you? You knew sooner or later he was going to dime you with the D.A. Maybe he came on to you and you got disgusted with his weakness and cloying dependence and decided to do both of you a favor and blow out his wick."

"You got part of it right. He started crying and tried to grab my package. I told him he turned my stomach and he could deal with Monarch Little on his own. If I'd stayed with him, maybe he'd still be alive," he said. "Believe it or not, that doesn't let me sleep too good sometimes."

What do you believe when you have conversations with people for whom the presence of evil is a given and simply a matter of degree in their daily lives? Do you just walk away from their words or let them invade your own frame of reference? How do you play chess with the devil?

You don't.

"I advise you to come into the department with your lawyer and make a formal statement about the circumstances surrounding Yvonne Darbonne's death," I said. "With luck and a little juice, you'll probably skate."

"Yeah, right," he said, clipping a rope onto the horse's hackamore. "I'm the least of your worries, Mr. Robicheaux. You got no idea what my father and Lefty Raguza are capable of. My father beat up his wife and son because he lost his money. Think what he might do to somebody else's family."

"Say that last part again?"

He walked the mare into the barn, his T-shirt gray and glued with moisture against his back. I grabbed him by the arm and turned him around. "Did you hear me?" I said.

He pulled up his T-shirt, exposing a burn scar on his stomach. It was V-shaped, welted, the color of a tire patch.

"I was five years old," he said. "He said he dropped the iron, that it was an accident. He told me he was sorry. I think he meant it. That's just the way he's wired. Now give me some peace."

BETSY MOSSBACHER called me at the office five minutes after I walked in. "Do you know where the Klein woman is?" she said.

"Out of jail," I said.

"I know that. She slipped the surveillance on her."

"Is this related to Whitey Bruxal's problems over a money transfer from the Islands?"

"You better believe it. Somebody rolled thirteen million dollars out of his accounts in the Caymans into a half-dozen banks in Jersey and Florida, all of them in the name of Whitey Bruxal or businesses he owns. In the meantime, an anonymous caller had already alerted the IRS the money was on its way. All that thirteen million is undeclared income."

"Trish's friends impersonated gas company employees and retrieved Whitey's account numbers from his computer," I said, more to myself than to her.

"That's my guess. All they needed were the nine-digit numbers to do the transfers. It gets better, though. While Trish Klein and her friends were sending signals that they were about to pull a big score on Whitey's businesses, he was funneling his cash flow into the Caymans. During the last two weeks he parked another two million over there. This is the slickest sting I ever saw. They've ruined the guy and they used the government to do it."

She laughed into the receiver.

"Can I get a job with you guys?" I asked.

"In your dreams," she said.

BUT THE HUMOROUS MOMENT with Betsy Mossbacher soon gave way to the realities of my own departmental situation and the political ambitions of Lonnie Marceaux. Just before quitting time, he called Helen's office and said he wanted to see both of us at 8 a.m. the next day. He refused to discuss the content of the meeting so we would be kept wondering or perhaps, even better, apprehensive and anxiety-ridden until the next morning. When Helen pressed him, he replied, "Get a good night's sleep. We'll all have a better perspective tomorrow."

He was in fine spirits when we showed up, tilting back in his chair, his fingers crisscrossed in a pyramid, his carefully clipped hair gleaming with brilliantine. "How is everyone this morning?" He beamed.

"What's up, Lonnie?" Helen said.

"It's time to move forward, much more aggressively than we have been," he said as soon as we were seated.

"Move forward with what?" Helen said.

"An arrest in the homicide of Bello Lujan," he said.

"Arrest whom?" I said.

He rested his chin on the backs of his fingers, staring good-naturedly out the window. "*Dave,*" he said patiently.

"I'm listening," I said.

"We've got the murder weapon with fingerprints all over it. We've got the motive. We've got a suspect with no alibi. But I can tell you also what we haven't got," he said.

"I'll bite," I said.

I could see a tic inside his feigned air of tolerance and goodwill. "What we don't have is somebody under arrest," he said. He rocked his chair back and forth, the spring going *scrinch, scrinch, scrinch.* "Why don't we have somebody under arrest? I think you're a member of that wandering group of penitents, the incurably liberal-hearted, Dave. Because you believe Cesaire Darbonne is a simple man of the earth, one who has already suffered a terrible tragedy, it would be a collective sin of enormous magnitude if we arrested him for killing the man who raped his daughter. Maybe I'm unfair to you, but I believe you're a sucker for any tale that involves social victimhood."

"I don't believe Cesaire knew Bello raped his daughter."

"*You* don't believe? The last time I checked, the grand jury decides those kinds of things."

"How would Bello have known?" I said.

"Somebody told him?" he replied.

"We found a neck chain and crucifix and G.I. can opener near the crime scene that belongs to one of Whitey Bruxal's gumballs, a guy from Jamaica by the name of Juan Bolachi," I said.

"Yeah, I know all about that and it doesn't mean dick," Lonnie said before I could continue.

"We've got scrapings from under Bello's fingernails," I said. "It's just a matter of—"

"A matter of getting this guy Bolachi in custody is what you're trying to say, right? Unfortunately, he's not in custody and all you've got is speculation," Lonnie said. "Everyone has skin tissue under their nails. It doesn't mean the skin tissue came from a killer, for God's sakes."

My hands were beginning to tremble with anger. I pressed them flat against my knees, below the level of his desktop, so Lonnie couldn't see them. "Cesaire Darbonne is an innocent man," I said, all of my arguments spent, my grandiose declaration itself an admission of defeat.

Lonnie touched at a speck of saliva on the corner of his lip and looked at it. "The warrant will be ready at one p.m. today," he said. "Helen, I want Dave to serve it. It's his case. He should see it through to its conclusion."

He pulled on an earlobe and studied the far wall.

Then I realized Lonnie had found his means for revenge. He didn't care whether Cesaire Darbonne was guilty or not. The case was prosecutable and for Lonnie that was all that mattered. His butt was covered and I had to place under arrest a man whose personal tragedy weighed heavily upon me. I didn't like Lonnie, but I thought he had a bottom beyond which he didn't go. His ambition, his manipulation of uneducated people, his pandering to fear and the lowest common denominator in the electorate were all sickening characteristics in themselves but not without precedent in either national or state politics. Now I realized what bothered me most about Lonnie. He didn't care about either the place or the people whom he professed to love and was capable of mocking them while he simultaneously did them injury.

"One day this is going to be over, partner, and we'll all have different roles," I said, getting up from my chair.

"Want to interpret that for me?" he said, slouched back in his chair, still smiling.

"No, I don't," I replied.

"I didn't think so," he said.

"Dave, would you wait for me out in the hallway?" Helen said.

I walked down to the watercooler and had a drink. Through the window I could see the Sunset Limited running down the tracks, hours off schedule, passengers eating breakfast in the dining car. At one time we literally set our watches by the Sunset Limited. It ran every day, from Los Angeles to Miami and back again, and somehow assured us that we were part of something much larger than our-selves—a country of southwestern vistas and cities glimmering at sun-set on the edge of vast oceans, where the waves broke against the skin like a secular baptism. It was the stuff of mythos, but it was real because we believed it was real.

The last car on the train clicked down the tracks and disappeared beyond a row of shacks.

The door to Lonnie's office was half open and I saw him rise to his feet, placing a pen and his glasses in his shirt pocket, indicating he had to be somewhere else and that it was obviously time for Helen to go. The hush inside the office was of a kind that comes before a clap of thunder or a violent act you never anticipate.

"We're professional people, Helen. We need to drop this and con-centrate on the job and not the personal problems of one individual," Lonnie said.

"Not just yet," she replied. "I want you to have a clear under-standing about my position on a couple of matters. Number one, I couldn't care less about your opinion of me. I think you're a fraud and a bully, and like most bullies, you're probably a coward. Number two, you couldn't shine Dave Robicheaux's shoes. If you ever try to demean him again, or use the power of your office to hurt him in any fashion, I'm going to personally rip your ass out of its socket and stuff it down your throat."

You could have worse friends than Helen Soileau.

CHAPTER
25

I PLACED CESAIRE under arrest after lunch. I cuffed his wrists in front of him rather than behind him and allowed him to drape a windbreaker over his hands before I put him in the back of the cruiser. But there was no disguising his level of humiliation and shame. If I ever saw a broken man, it was Cesaire Darbonne.

After he was booked for capital murder, I walked with him to a holding cell and asked the guard to lock me inside with him and to give me a few minutes.

"This is a part of the job I don't like, Mr. Darbonne," I said. "I don't believe you killed Bello Lujan. But even if you did, I and others like me would understand why you did it, even if we considered it wrong."

"It ain't your fault, no."

"Look me in the face, sir."

He stared at me from the iron bench on which he was seated, perhaps unsure whether my request had contained a veiled insult.

"Tell me again you didn't know Bello Lujan assaulted your daughter," I said.

"A man who got to repeat himself don't respect his own word," he said.

He looked at the tops of his shoes.

"I suspect your bail could be as high as a quarter million dollars. Do you have any kind of collateral you can offer the court?" I said.

"No, suh, I t'ink I'm gonna be here awhile."

His intuitions were probably more accurate than he knew. He was in the maw of the system, and anyone who has been caught in it, the guilty or innocent or hapless alike, will be the first to tell you that justice is indeed blind. "I hope it comes out all right for you, sir," I said.

"Nothing gonna come out all right. Ain't no way to turn it around now."

"What do you mean it can't be turned around?"

"I lost my farm and bidness when the gov'ment let in all that sugar from Central America. Ain't fair to put all that cheap sugar on the market. Ain't nothing like it used to be. Li'l people ain't got no chance."

His linkage of his own fate to economic factors was probably self-serving, if not self-pitying, and his condemnation of the world for his own misfortune was the stuff of grandiosity. But who can fault a man with no legs for not being able to run?

"I'm going to see what I can do," I said.

"About what?" he said, his eyes lifting to mine.

MOLLY WAS WASHING her car under the porte cochere when I got home. She wore a pair of blue-jean shorts and an old white shirt that was too tight for her shoulders, and her clothes and hair and skin were damp from the garden hose she was spraying on the car's surface while she wiped it down with a rag. Molly's physical firmness, the curvature of her hips, the way her rump flexed against her shorts, the suggestion of sexual power in her thighs and the swell of her breasts, all reminded me of my dead wife Bootsie, and I sometimes wondered if Bootsie's spirit had not slipped inside Molly's skin, as though the two women who had not known each other in life had melded together and formed a third personality after Bootsie's death.

But I didn't care where Molly came from, as long as she remained in my life, and I loved her as much as I did Bootsie, and I loved them both at the same time and never felt a contradiction or a moment of disloyalty about my feelings.

"Come scratch my back, will you?" Molly said. "A mosquito about six inches long got under my shirt."

She propped her arms on the car's roof while I moved my nails back and forth across her shoulder blades. The water from the hose continued to run, spilling back across her fist, trailing down her forearm. She shifted her weight and her rump brushed against my loins.

"I had to put Cesaire Darbonne in jail today," I said. "I suspect he'll be arraigned tomorrow for capital murder."

"Uh-huh," she said, gazing abstractedly through the shadows in the backyard.

"The guy's broke. He'll probably stay in lockdown out at the stockade."

"And?" she said, removing a strand of damp hair from her eye.

"No bondsman will touch him with a dung fork, at least not without collateral."

"You hurt my feelings," she said.

"Pardon?"

She rolled her shoulders to indicate I should continue scratching her back. "I thought you were putting moves on me to get me into the sack," she said.

"I'm not above doing that."

She deliberately hit me with her rump. "You want to go his bond?" she said.

"I'll have to put up the house and lot. They're half yours."

"Not really, but whatever you want to do is fine with me," she said.

She turned around, stood on my shoes, and hugged me.

"What's that for?" I said.

"I won't tell you," she said, then continued washing her car.

AFTER SUPPER, I drove to Clete's cottage at the motor court. He had closed all the blinds and was sitting barefoot on his bed, dressed in a pair of elastic-waisted khakis and a strap undershirt, reaming out the barrel of a .38 revolver with a bore brush. His television set was tuned to The Weather Channel, the sound turned off. A shaded lamp burned on the nightstand, and under its glow were a can of oil, his sap, a throw-down .22 piece of junk with tape on the wood grips, a six-inch stiletto, and a nine-millimeter Beretta that carried a fourteen-round magazine. I took a can of Dr Pepper out of his icebox and sat down in a straight-back wood chair across from him.

"Expecting the Union Army to come up the Teche?" I said.

"A bud inside NOPD called me and said I'm about to get picked up for destroying the casino. I rented a camp out in the Atchafalaya Basin. Time to do a survey on the goggle-eye perch population," he replied.

Then I made a mistake. I told him about all the recent events involving the deaths of Yvonne Darbonne, Crustacean Man, and Tony and Bello Lujan. I told him about the scam Trish Klein and her crew had pulled on Whitey Bruxal. I also told him about Slim Bruxal's implication that his father and Lefty Raguza might decide to take their pound of flesh.

Clete wiped the oil off the blue-black surfaces of his .38, then flipped the cylinder from the frame and began inserting cartridges one by one into the chambers, his blond eyelashes lowered so I could not read his eyes.

"I can hear your wheels turning, Clete. Forget about it," I said.

"I'm glad I've finally heard the voice of God. You can actually go into people's heads now and explain their own thoughts to them."

"Don't be a smart-ass. I'm trying to—"

He cut me off before I could continue. "We used to do business one way with these assholes—under a black flag. Why do you think Whitey Bruxal is here? It's because he gets a free pass. In the old days, at least he would have been under the control of the Giacanos. Now he can kick the shit out of cerebral palsy victims and be on the Society page."

"You don't think NOPD can find you in a fishing camp? Use your brain," I said.

He spun the cylinder on the .38, the butt end of the loaded cartridges glinting in the light. His green eyes were bright and happy, free of alcoholic influence or fatigue, and I realized when he didn't reply that I hadn't listened carefully to what he had said and I had once again misread the complexities of an antithetically mixed man.

"You were already planning to take out Whitey Bruxal, weren't you?" I said.

"Not exactly. But if these guys make a move on us, we hunt them down and pitch the rule book. What's to lose? We're dinosaurs anyway. The only guys who haven't figured that out are us. Pop me a beer, will you?"

He laid a clear line of oil along the side of the Beretta, then wiped all of its surfaces clean with a rag. He pulled back the slide on an empty magazine and ran the bore brush up and down the inside of the barrel, smiling at me while he did it. In the muted glow of the lamplight he looked like a young man again, one who still believed the world was a magical place full of adventure and goodness and intriguing encounters up every street. In moments like these I sometimes wondered if Clete had ever intended to age and grow old and change from the irresponsible man of his youth, if indeed he had not always courted death as a means of tearing off the hands on his own clock.

"Why you looking at me like that?" he asked.

"No reason."

"You worry about all the wrong things, Streak. In this case, about me and Trish. All that stuff you told me about the Lujan murders and Crustacean Man and the Darbonne girl? There's something missing. This character in the D.A.'s office, what's his name?"

"Lonnie Marceaux."

"This Marceaux guy is the one to worry about. It's these white-collar cocksuckers who'd crank up the gas ovens if they had the chance. You're really going bail for Yvonne Darbonne's old man?"

"I put him in jail. He's an innocent man. What should I do?" I replied.

"How many guys have you known inside who were actually innocent?"

"Some," I said.

"But almost all of them were guilty of other crimes, usually worse ones. Right or wrong, noble mon?"

I poured my Dr Pepper into the sink and dropped the empty can into the trash basket. "See you later," I said, trying to suppress the anger in my voice.

"Put it in neutral a minute and check those satellite pictures on the tube," he said, nodding at the television screen. "The state of Florida must feel like a bowling pin. You were on the water when Audrey hit back in 'fifty-eight?"

"It was 'fifty-seven."

"Think we'll ever have one that bad again?"

"Don't change the subject, Clete. Take Trish and go somewhere a long way from New Iberia. You keep hurting yourself in ways your worst enemies couldn't think up."

He reached under the bed and removed a pint of brandy. He unscrewed the cap and lifted the bottle at me. "Here's to chaos and mayhem and blowing the bad guys out of their socks," he said. He drank the brandy down like soda water, one eye cocked at me over the upended bottle.

I WENT TO AN A.A. meeting in the Episcopalian cottage across the street from old New Iberia High School. When I came out, the sky had turned yellow and purple and was full of dust blowing out of the cane fields. The oak trees in front of the school throbbed with birds, and when the wind changed, the air smelled like a lake that has gone dry. It was an evening when the colors of the sky and the earth and the trees seemed out of accordance with one another. The end of summer in South Louisiana is usually like sliding over the crest of a torpid season of heat and humidity into autumnal days that ring with the sounds of marching bands and smell of burning leaves and the damp, fecund odor of the bayous. But this year was different.

The skies were red at morning, and at night churning with clouds that looked like curds of smoke from giant oil fires. Afternoon showers turned into violent storms, with trees of lightning bursting across the entirety of the sky. I have never given credence to apocalyptical theology or prophecies, but this year I felt a sense of foreboding that I couldn't shake. It wasn't based on an intuitive knowledge about the future, either. I had seen the show before.

It is hard for someone who has not experienced a hurricane to understand the terror of being inside one. Perhaps the fear has its roots in the unconscious. Psychiatrists say the most terrifying moment in our lives occurs when we are delivered out of the birth canal from the safety of the womb—unable to breathe, shuddering against the light, knowing we will die unless we receive the slap of life. Supposedly that moment is sealed forever in a corner of the mind we wish never to reenter. Then one day the world of predictability, the earth itself, caves under our feet.

That moment came for me on a seismograph drill barge anchored by deep-water steel pilings in a bay west of Morgan City in the summer of 1957. On board were 160 pounds of canned dynamite and boxes of canned primers and spools of cap wire that were tipped with a vial of nitroglycerin gel that could be detonated with either an electrical spark or a hard knock against a steel surface.

No one anticipated the ferocity of Hurricane Audrey or the tidal wave it would push ahead of it. Our company chose to ride it out. That experience was one that will remain with me the rest of my life.

The tide dropped at sunset, and for miles there was hardly a ripple of wind on the water. The sky was lidded with clouds that were the color of scorched pewter, but the horizon was still blue, glowing with an iridescence that seemed trapped behind the earth's rim. We went to bed on the quarterboat with a sense of peace about the storm, convinced it was passing far to the west, perhaps over in Texas, and that our fears had been unfounded.

At dawn, the miles of flooded cypress and gum trees surrounding us were thick with birds of every description, as though none of them could find a proper tree upon which to rest. At 9 a.m. my half brother Jimmie and I were building explosive charges for the driller, screwing six cans of dynamite end to end, then screwing on a primer that would attach to a second string of six cans, doing this three times until we had a charge of eighteen cans that we would slide down the drill pipe with the cap wire whipping off the spool behind it.

Without any transition, the sky erupted with lightning, the barometer dropped so fast our ears popped, a line of whitecaps shot from the mouth of the bay into the swamp, like skin wrinkling, and the miles of flooded trees surrounding us bent simultaneously toward the water.

I turned away from the drill and the wind struck my face as hard as a fist. The tarp that was used to shade the drill deck, one that was made of heavy canvas and inset with metal rods and brass eyelets, ripped loose from the pilothouse and disappeared in the wind like a discarded Kleenex. What happened next was an event of such magnitude and intensity that neither Jimmie nor I nor anyone else on board would ever quite understand it or the natural causes that created it. Some thought it was a waterspout. Some believed a secondary system, one with its own eye, had passed over us. But whatever it was, it carried its own set of rules and they had nothing to do with the laws of physics, at least not as I understand them.

There was no sound at all. The wind stopped, the water around the drill barge flattened, then seemed to drop away from the steel pilings, as though all the water were being sucked out of the bay. The gum and cypress trees and willows along the shore straightened in the stillness, their leaves green and bright with sunshine, then the world came apart.

All the glass exploded from the windows in the pilothouse. The instrument shack, made of aluminum and bolted down on the stern, was shredded into confetti. The crew chief was shouting at everyone on the deck, pointing toward the hatch that led down to the engine room, but his words were lost in the roar of the wind. A curtain of rain slapped across the barge, then we were inside a vortex that looked exactly like millions of crystallized grass cuttings, except it was filled with objects and creatures that should not have been there. Fish of every kind and size, snakes, raccoons, blue herons, turkey buzzards, a pirogue, uprooted trees, possums and wood rabbits, a twisted tin roof, dozens of crab traps and conical fishnets packed with enormous carp, hundreds of frogs, clusters of tar paper and weathered boards—all these things were spinning around our barge, sometimes thudding against the handrails and ladders and bulkheads.

I got to my feet just as an avalanche of water and mud surged across the decks. It stank of oil sludge, seaweed encrusted with dead shellfish, sewage, and human feces. The driller, who had been huddled under a pipe rack, vomited in his lap.

Then the sky turned black with rain, and in the west we saw lightning striking the shoreline and in the wetlands and in fishing communities where our relatives lived and in small cities like Lafayette and Lake Charles, and we were glad that it was them and not us who were about to receive the brunt of the storm, even the tidal wave that would curl over Cameron and crush the entire town, drowning over five hundred people.

I USED WEE WILLIE BIMSTINE and Nig Rosewater's agency in New Orleans to go bail for Cesaire Darbonne. Willie and Nig kept my name out of the court record, but Cesaire was released from jail on Wednesday morning and was at my house ten minutes after I arrived home for lunch with Molly.

He removed his straw hat before he knocked on the door. I invited him in but he shook his head. "I just come to t'ank you," he said.

"It's not a big deal, Mr. Darbonne," I replied.

"Ain't many people would do somet'ing like that."

"More than you think."

He looked out at the traffic on the street, his expression neutral, his turquoise eyes empty of any thoughts that I could see. He fitted on his hat, his skin darkening in the shadow it made on his face. In absentminded fashion, he scratched the chain of scars on his right forearm. "You ever want to go duck hunting, I got a camp and a blind. I know where the sac-a-lait is at on Whiskey Bay, too," he said.

"I appreciate it, sir, but you don't owe me anything," I said.

He turned his eyes on me. They were almost luminous, full of portent, and for just a moment I was sure he was about to tell me something of enormous importance. But if that was his intention, he changed his mind and got in his truck without saying anything further and drove away.

"Who was that?" Molly said behind me.

"Mr. Darbonne. He wanted to thank us for getting him out of the can."

"Your food is getting cold."

"I'll be there in a second," I said, still looking down the street, where

Cesaire's truck was stopped at the traffic light in front of an 1831 ante-bellum home called the Shadows.

"What's bothering you, Dave?" Molly said.

"I've never had a more perplexing case. It's like trying to hold water in your fingers. The real problem is most of the people I keep looking at would probably have led normal lives if they hadn't met one another."

"Start over again."

"I have. None of it goes anywhere."

She kneaded the back of my neck, then ran her fingers up into my hair, her nails raking my scalp. "I'll always be proud of you," she said.

"What for?"

"Because you're incapable of being anyone other than yourself."

I closed the door and turned around. I wanted to hold her, to pull her against me, to whisper words to her that are embarrassing when they are spoken in a conventional situation. But she had already gone back into the kitchen.

AFTER LUNCH, I returned to the office and once again got out all my notes on Yvonne Darbonne's death. Except this time I had something else to go on: Slim Bruxal's firsthand account of how Yvonne had died. At 2 p.m. Helen came into my office. "Where's Clete Purcel?" she asked.

"I'm not sure," I replied.

"NOPD just tried to serve a warrant at his cottage. It's empty. The owner says Clete left late last night with a young blond woman. You have no idea where he is?"

"Nothing specific," I replied, squinting thoughtfully at the far wall.

She closed the door behind her so no one could hear her next words. "Don't let them get their hands on him, Dave. They're not talking about six months in Central Lockup. It's Angola on this one. The insurance companies are tired of Clete destroying half of New Orleans."

"Glad to know the city is looking out for the right interests," I said.

She looked at the crime scene photos and case files spread on my desk. "Where are you doing?" she said.

"I think maybe I found the key in the murder of Tony Lujan."

I DIDN'T TRY to explain it to her. Instead, I went looking for Monarch Little. His next-door neighbor told me Monarch was doing body-and-fender work for a man who ran a repair shop in St. Martinville.

"You know the repairman's name?" I asked.

The neighbor was the same woman who had shown great irritation at Monarch for getting drunk with his friends and throwing beer cans in her yard after his mother died.

"Monarch done straightened up. Why don't y'all leave him alone?" she said.

"I'm not here to hurt him, ma'am."

Her eyes wandered over my face. "He's working for that albino man on the bayou, the one always grinning when he ain't got nothing to grin about," she said.

A half hour later I parked by the side of the sagging, rust-streaked trailer of Prospect Desmoreau, the same albino man who had repaired the Buick that had run down Crustacean Man. Monarch Little was under the pole shed, pulling the door off a Honda that had evidently been broadsided.

"You're looking good, Mon," I said.

"My name is Monarch," he said.

"I need your help."

"That's why you're here? I'm shocked."

"Lose the comic book dialogue. I'm looking for a black guy who rides a bicycle and salvages bottles and beer cans from the roadside. A black guy who might have seen what happened when Yvonne Darbonne died."

"The girl who shot herself by the sugar mill?"

I nodded.

The sun was in the west, burning like a bronze flame on the bayou's surface. Monarch was sweating heavily in the shade, his neck beaded with dirt rings.

"Is this guy on the bike gonna be jammed up over this?" he asked.

"No, I just want to know what he saw. I'm just excluding a possibility, that's all."

"There's two or t'ree street people do that. But they're white. They stay at a shelter."

"Quit waltzing me around, Monarch."

"There's this one black guy, he's retarded and got a li'l head. I mean a real li'l-bitty one. You see him digging trash out of Dumpsters or stopping his bike by rain ditches wit' cars flying right past him. Know who I mean?"

"No," I replied.

Monarch lifted up his shirt and smelled himself, then wiped the sweat off his upper lip onto the shirt. "He's retarded and scared of people he don't know. I better go wit' you," he said.

I started to thank him, then thought better of it. Monarch was not given to sentiment. He was also aware that, rightly or wrongly, I would probably never forget the fact he had been a dope dealer. We walked up the grassy slope toward my truck, his shadow merging with mine on the ground. I saw him smile.

"What's funny?" I said.

"Ever see that old movie about this hunchback guy swinging on the catee'dral bells?" he asked.

"*The Hunchback of Notre Dame?*"

"Yeah, that's it. The two of us together look like the guy swinging on the bells. See?" he said, pointing at our shadows. "Everybody t'ought the hunchback was a monster, but he had music inside his head nobody else could hear."

"You never cease to surprise me, Monarch."

If my remark held any significance for him, he didn't show it.

We drove a few miles back down the bayou to a cluster of shacks behind a parking area for harvesting machines and cane wagons. I had not told Monarch the real reason for my interest in the black man Cesaire Darbonne's neighbor had told us was collecting discarded bottles and cans from the roadside the day Yvonne died. I believed Slim Bruxal had told me the truth when he said Yvonne had deliberately turned the .22 Magnum into her face and had shot herself, and I needed no confirmation of that fact from a witness. But there was a detail in Slim's story that I had overlooked. He claimed, and I had no reason to doubt him, that Tony Lujan had passed out in the backyard of the fraternity house and was incapable of driving Yvonne home. I had assumed Slim had driven her back to New Iberia in his SUV, but Slim had said Yvonne had taken the .22 out of the glove box. Her diary indicated she didn't like Slim and had probably avoided him. If she had been riding in Slim's vehicle, how would she have known a revolver was in the glove box?

The bottle-and-can collector was named Ripton Armentor. As Monarch had said, he looked like he had been assembled from a box of discarded spare parts. His shoulders were square, his chest flat as an ironing board, and his torso too long for his legs, so that his trousers looked like they had been taken off a midget. Worse yet, his head was not much larger than a shot put. And as though he were deliberately trying to compete with the physical incongruities fate had imposed upon him, he wore a neatly pressed blue denim shirt with a necktie that extended all the way to his belt, giving him the appearance of an inverted exclamation mark.

He sat on the top step of his gallery and listened to Monarch explain who I was and what I wanted, the cane fields around his house swirling with wind. It was obvious he was retarded or autistic, but paradoxically his expression was electric, one of fascination with the intrigue and sense of adventure that had been brought to his front door.

"You remember that day, Ripton, when the girl died?" I said.

"I ain't seen her die," he said, eager to be correct and to please, his words rushed yet syntactical.

"But you know she died that day you were collecting bottles and cans by the mill?" I said.

"Yes, suh. Heard all about it. Seen it on the TV, too. That's why I come back the next day."

"I'm not quite with you, Ripton," I said.

"I gone back by the mill. See, I was way down the street when I heard it. I t'ought maybe it was my bicycle tire. When it pop, it make a sound just like that. In the wind and all, I t'ought it was my tire going *pop*."

"You heard the shot?" I said.

"Yes, suh. I heard it. Then I seen a car go roaring by. So I went and knocked on Mr. Cesaire's do' and tole him what I seen."

"You talked to Cesaire Darbonne?" I said.

"Yes, suh, that's what I'm saying. I went back and tole Mr. Cesaire about it. A silver car went streaking on by. Gone by like a rocket, *whoosh*."

"What kind of car was it?" I said.

"A silver one, just like I said."

"Why didn't you tell the police about this?" I asked.

"Mr. Cesaire said I ain't had to. Since I'd already give him the numbers, he was gonna take care of it. Didn't need to talk to no police."

A flock of crows rose from the cane field and patterned against the sky. "What numbers, podna?"

"The first t'ree numbers on the license plate. Wrote 'em in down in my li'l book. I keep a li'l book on everyt'ing I pick up from the road 'case the taxman call me in. I still got them numbers inside. You want 'em?"

I could hear clothes popping on a wash line, or perhaps the sound was in my own ears.

CHAPTER
26

I WENT EARLY to the office the next morning and ran the registration on Tony Lujan's silver Lexus and looked once again at all my notes concerning Cesaire Darbonne's background. But what stuck in my mind about Cesaire was not written down in a notebook. Instead, it was his absorption as a duck hunter and the fact he had told me the scars on his left hand and arm had come about from a hunting accident. I called Mack Bertrand at the crime lab.

"I'm doing a little background work on Cesaire Darbonne. Did you tell me he's a distant cousin of your wife?" I said.

"That's right," he replied.

"He was in a duck-hunting accident?"

"Yeah, as I remember. He poked his shotgun barrel into the mud and almost blew his arm off."

"What did he do with the gun?"

"Pardon?"

"After the barrel exploded, what did he do with it?" I asked.

"How should I know?"

"You told me a couple of guys tried to rob his bar and he ran them off by firing a gun in the air."

"Yeah, about fifteen years back. Why you pumping me, Dave?"

"You know why."

"Hasn't the guy had enough grief?"

"That fact won't change what happened. What did Cesaire do with the shotgun after it exploded?"

"Ask him. I'm signing off on this."

"Sorry to see you take that attitude, Mack."

"The guy is already down for one murder and you want to put Tony Lujan's on him, too?" He hung up.

I searched the department computer but found nothing on an attempted robbery at the bar run by Cesaire Darbonne. I spent the next two hours searching through our paper files with the same result. Then I called a retired plainclothes by the name of Paul LeBlanc who h. .i worked for the department forty years before deafness and diabetes forced him to hang it up. Now he lived in an assisted-care facility by Iberia General and at first did not recognize my name.

"Dave Robicheaux," I said. "I was with NOPD before I went to work for Iberia Parish. I used to own a bait shop and boat-rental business south of town."

"The one wit' drinking problems?" he said.

"I'm your man."

"How you doin'?" he said.

"You remember an attempted robbery at a bar owned by Cesaire Darbonne? It was a ramshackle hole-in-the-wall joint up the bayou. We're talking about maybe fifteen years back."

"No," he said.

"You have no memory of it?"

"That wasn't what I said. It wasn't fifteen years back. It was seventeen. The spring of 1988."

"What happened?"

"Wasn't much to it. A couple of colored men tried to pry the back window while Cesaire was mopping up. He come out the back do' and chased them out in a cane field. Fired a shell in the air. I think they were after booze instead of money. I don't think I even wrote it up."

"You didn't write it up?"

"No, I don't think I did."

"What kind of weapon did Cesaire fire in the air, Mr. Paul?"

"Cain't hear you. The earpiece on this phone ain't no good."

"You said he fired a shell, Mr. Paul. Did Cesaire fire a shotgun over these fellows' heads?"

"Maybe it was."

"Was it a cut-down twelve-gauge?"

The phone was silent. "Sir?" I said.

"I'm in my years now. My memory ain't that good."

"We're not talking about an illegal gun charge, Mr. Paul. This is a homicide investigation. Was Cesaire in possession of a sawed-off shotgun?"

"Yes, suh, he was."

"Thank you." I started to lower the receiver into the cradle.

"Mr. Robicheaux?"

"Yes, sir?"

"I been knowing Cesaire Darbonne fifty years. He's a good man."

He *was* a good man, I said to myself.

After I hung up, I went into Helen's office. "I think I got taken over the hurdles. I think Cesaire Darbonne murdered Tony Lujan," I said.

She sat back in her chair, widening her eyes.

"I found a witness to the Yvonne Darbonne homicide. A retarded black man by the name of Ripton Armentor saw a silver car speeding away after he heard a gunshot. He wrote down three numbers from the license tag. He gave them to Cesaire Darbonne the next day."

She closed then opened her eyes. "Oh, boy," she said, more to herself than to me.

"I did some more research into Cesaire's history, too. Seventeen years back, a plainclothes investigated an attempted break-in at Cesaire's bar. Cesaire was in possession of a cut-down twelve-gauge that he probably salvaged from a shotgun that exploded on him after he got some mud in the barrel."

"Cesaire followed Tony the night Tony was supposed to meet Monarch?"

"That's my guess. He blew Tony apart, then planted the weapon in Monarch's car."

"Why Monarch's?"

"Because everyone knows Monarch was selling dope to white teenagers. The autopsy showed Yvonne was full of drugs when she died. Cesaire probably blamed Monarch for her death as much as he did Tony."

"We're going to look like idiots going back to the grand jury on this guy for another homicide. It's like we don't have anyone else in the parish to charge for unsolved crimes," she said.

"Want me to talk to Lonnie?"

"Screw Lonnie. We need to clean up our own mess." She studied a legal pad on her desk, her fingers on her brow. "I just got off the phone with the FBI in New Orleans. They pulled a cell phone transmission out of the air on Lefty Raguza. They think he's in Iberia or St. Martin Parish."

"Lefty wants payback for the beating he took?"

"No, the Feds think he and Whitey Bruxal are going to try to get Whitey's money back by peeling the skin off Trish Klein's pretty ass."

She saw the look on my face. "That's the language this FBI jerk used. Don't blame me," she said. "Where's Clete Purcel, Dave? Don't lie to me, either."

I didn't have to lie. I didn't know. Not exactly, anyway.

THAT NIGHT, Molly and I went to a movie and had dinner in Lafayette. The summer light was still high in the sky when we drove back home, and I could see fishermen in boats out on Spanish Lake, the cypress snags shadowing on the water against the late sun.

"You worried about Clete?" she asked.

"A little. If NOPD gets their hands on him, they're going to put him away."

"He's always come through before, hasn't he?"

"Except that's not what he wants. He's been committing suicide in increments his whole life. He tries to keep the gargoyles away with booze and aspirin and wonders why he always has a Mixmaster roaring in his head."

I could feel her eyes on me. Then I felt her put away whatever it was she had planned to say.

"Buy me some ice cream?" she asked.

"You bet," I replied.

The next morning was Friday. I called Nig Rosewater and Wee Willie Bimstine and Clete's offices in both New Iberia and New

Orleans and was told that Clete was out of town and that his where-abouts were unknown. The only semblance of cooperation came from Alice Werenhaus, the part-time secretary and former nun at the office on St. Ann in the Quarter.

"He's fine, Mr. Robicheaux. He doesn't want you to worry," he said.

"Then why does he keep his cell turned off?"

"May I be frank?"

"Please."

"He doesn't want you compromised. Now stop picking on him."

"I think his life may be in danger, Miss Alice."

She was quiet a long time. "Mr. Purcel will always be Mr. Purcel. He won't change for either of us. I'll do what I can. You have my word."

So much for that.

My other ongoing problem was Cesaire Darbonne. I had gone bond for a man who was probably innocent of the murder he was accused of committing and guilty of a homicide for which he wasn't charged. The greater irony was that the boy Cesaire had probably murdered was not responsible for his daughter's death and the man he had *not* killed was.

After lunch I went to Lonnie Marceaux's office and told him everything I had learned about Cesaire Darbonne's probable guilt in the murder on Tony Lujan.

"Nobody can screw up a case this bad. Are you drinking again?" he said.

"Glad to see you're handling this in the right spirit, Lonnie. No, I'm not drinking. But since you went full tilt on insisting we indict an innocent ian for Bello Lujan's death, I thought I should drop by and give you a heads-up."

"Me a heads-up?"

"Yeah, because the shitprints lead right back into your office."

"I think you have your facts wrong. Of course, that's no surprise. Scapegoating others is a symptom of the disease, isn't it?"

"Say again?"

"It's what alcoholics do. Scapegoating other people, right? It's always somebody else's fault. My office acted on the information you provided, Dave. You want to contest the factual record, have at it. I think you're long overdue for an I.A. review."

I glanced out the window at the storm clouds building in the south and the tops of trees bending in the wind. "At my age I don't have a lot to lose. There's a great sense of freedom in that, Lonnie," I said.

"Care to explain that?"

"You'll figure it out."

I believed Whitey Bruxal had set up Cesaire Darbonne for the murder of Bellerophon Lujan. But my speculation, and that's all it was, posed a problem I had not yet resolved: If Whitey had indeed framed Cesaire, how did Whitey know that Bello had probably raped Cesaire's daughter, giving Cesaire motivation to take his life?

I went to see Valerie Lujan for an answer. She was obviously preparing to go somewhere when I pushed the bell and the maid opened the front door.

"I won't take much of your time," I said.

She was in her wheelchair, wearing a yellow dress that matched her hair, a lavender corsage pinned on her shoulder. A picnic basket containing a pink cake and two bottles of champagne and two glasses rested on the tabletop behind her. "Let him in," she said to the maid.

I sat down in a deep white chair, leaning forward, my back stiff, so as not to look relaxed or accommodating. "Cesaire Darbonne didn't kill your husband, Mrs. Lujan," I said.

"Just a moment," she said, and turned to the maid. "Finish up in the kitchen and tell Luther to bring around the car." Then she addressed me again. "To be honest, I really don't care who killed my husband."

"But we do. Whitey Bruxal thought Bello was going to roll over on him and he used a stable mucker by the name of Juan Bolachi to take him out."

"Then you must arrest him."

"Except there's another problem. Whitey decided to frame Cesaire Darbonne for the homicide, but that means Whitey knew we'd eventually discover that Bello raped Yvonne Darbonne and that her father would be a perfect suspect when a pickax stolen from Cesaire's toolshed was used to tear Bello apart."

She looked at a tiny gold watch on her wrist. The color of her skin and the veins in her arms made me think of milk and pieces of green string. "I'd like to be of assistance, but I'm on my way to the cemetery," she said. "It's Tony's birthday. He always loved strawberry cake with pink icing."

"Who told Whitey that Bello probably raped Yvonne?" I asked.

"I certainly didn't, and I resent your suggesting I did."

"That wasn't my intention. But there *is* one man you do confide in. He's your friend and spiritual counselor, someone who claims to be a man of God, someone you trust, a man you believe would never betray you."

Her eyes fixed on my face with an intensity that seemed far greater than her failing powers were capable of generating. I knew I had hit home.

"You're saying Colin Alridge passed on information about my husband to Whitey Bruxal?" she said.

"You bet I am. No matter what he tells you, Alridge's vested interest is with the gambling industry and the lobbyists who support it. He sold both you and Bello down the drain."

At this stage in her life, she probably believed nothing else could be taken from her. But I had just proved her wrong. She looked out the front window at the turbulence in the sky and the oak leaves flying from the trees in the yard.

"My car is waiting outside, Mr. Robicheaux. I'll be at Tony's graveside the rest of the afternoon," she said. "I hope you'll be gracious and decent enough not to disturb me there. I believe the dead can hear the voices of the living, although we cannot hear theirs. I'll ask my son to forgive you for not finding his killer and for concentrating your efforts instead on tormenting his mother."

I stood up to go, but I didn't want to leave her with the impression that I accepted her victimhood. She wore her infirmity and her personal loss as a shield against the system, and chances were she would take on the permanent role of martyr and saint and be venerated as an icon of bereavement and moral courage until the day of her death. But I believed Valerie Lujan's contract with the devil had been signed many years ago, and she knew that every dollar in her possession had come into Bello's hands through the deprivation of others.

I started to say these things and perhaps other things even more injurious to her. But what was the point? Saints are made of plaster and they neither bleed nor hear. So I simply said, "I was drunk for many years, Mrs. Lujan. But I finally learned everybody has to pay his tab. Good luck to you. The Garden of Gethsemane is a tough gig."

BUT RHETORIC IS rhetoric and a poor substitute for putting away people who belong in jail. That afternoon, as I drove home, I realized that all my investigative efforts since the spring would result in few if any meaningful convictions. Without a confession, I doubted if Cesaire Darbonne would ever do time for the murder of Tony Lujan. The same with Slim Bruxal. I believed he had killed Crustacean Man with a baseball bat, but the case had already grown cold and there was no forensic connection between Slim and the hapless man who had been struck by the Lujan family's Buick. Worse, Whitey Bruxal and Lefty Raguza would never be punished for the executionlike slaying of my friend Dallas Klein, a murder I had been too drunk to prevent.

I helped Molly prepare supper, then I fed Snuggs and Tripod on the back steps. It was shady and cool under the trees, and the wind blowing from the bayou stiffened their fur while they ate. I pulled Snuggs's tail playfully and bounced him gingerly on his back paws. "How you doin', soldier?" I said.

He glanced back at me, his head notched with pink scars, then returned to his food.

"How about you, Tripod? You doin' okay, old-timer?" I said.

Tripod smacked his chops and had no comment.

I wished life consisted of just taking care of animals, the earth, and one's family and friends. In fact, that's what it should be. But it's not, and the explanation for that fact is not one I have ever been able to provide.

"Ready to eat?" Molly said through the screen window.

"Sure," I said, and went back inside.

It was 6:10 p.m. and Molly was in the bathroom when the phone on the kitchen counter rang. Outside, the light in the trees was the color of honey, the tidal current in the bayou flowing inland, the surface networked with serpentine lines of dead leaves.

"That you, Mr. Robicheaux?" the voice said.

"Cesaire?" I said.

"This connection ain't good. I'm at a pay phone not far from Whiskey Bay. I seen your friend wit' a blond woman. He was driving a pink Cadillac convertible wit' a white top."

"Right, that's Clete Purcel. You saw him?"

"Yes, suh. But that ain't why I called. A couple of gangsters followed him and the woman out of a parking lot in front of a bar. One of them was the father of Tony Lujan's friend."

"Whitey Bruxal?"

"I ain't sure of his name. I just know his face. He called the man wit' him 'Lefty.' This guy Lefty's face looked like a busted-up flowerpot. I t'ought I ought to tell you about your friend."

"Why are you at Whiskey Bay, Mr. Darbonne?"

"I got a camp here. Is your friend gonna be okay?"

CHAPTER
27

AFTER I CLOSED the bedroom door, I removed my cut-down twelve-gauge pump from the closet, sat on the side of the bed, and pushed five shells loaded with double-aught buckshot into the magazine. I strung my handcuffs through the back of my belt, clipped on my holster and 1911-model United States Army .45, Velcro-strapped my .25 automatic on my ankle, and picked up the receiver from the telephone on the dresser. I paused for a moment, thinking of Clete and the alternatives his situation offered, then replaced the receiver in the cradle without punching in a number. I heard the doorknob twist behind me.

"What are you doing?" Molly asked.

"That was Cesaire Darbonne. I think Whitey Bruxal and Lefty Raguza have followed Clete and Trish Klein to a camp in the Basin."

"Call the department."

"Clete's wanted by NOPD. He'll be locked up."

"That's Clete's problem."

"It may be a false alarm," I said, starting toward the door.

"You simply accept the word of Cesaire Darbonne? A man you believe mutilated the body of a college student with a shotgun?"

"I've got my cell. I'll call you."

"I'm going with you."

"Not on this one."

"Don't do this, Dave."

"If you don't hear from me in two hours, call nine-one-one."

Perhaps my attitude was willful and even cruel, but I had a terrible sense that maybe this time Clete's luck had finally run out. That thought caused a sensation in my throat that was like swallowing glass.

IT TOOK ME almost an hour to reach the levee area where Cesaire had called from. He was waiting in his truck in front of a bar that had been knocked together from unpainted plywood and covered with a tin roof that had been peeled off a barn. On the other side of the levee was a wide bay flanged by flooded woods. To the north I could see car lights crossing the elevated highway that traversed the massive network of bayous, rivers, oxbows, lakes, and cypress swamps that comprised the Atchafalaya Basin. The sky was piled with clouds that had turned purple and gold in the sun, the miles of flooded trees bending steadily in the wind. As I got out of my truck, a smell like burning garbage struck my face.

"Can you show me where they went?" I asked.

"Down the levee and back in them woods," he said, pointing. "There's high ground back in them gum trees and palmettos. It don't never go underwater unless it storms real bad."

I didn't shake hands with him, which is considered a personal affront in South Louisiana. But as Molly had suggested, it would have been foolish to dismiss the darker side of this man's nature. When people seek vengeance, they dig up every biblical platitude imaginable to rationalize their behavior, but their motivations are invariably selfish. More important, they have no regard for the damage and pain they often cause the innocent.

"Why you doing this, Mr. Darbonne?"

"You went my bond. You treated me decent. You cared about my li'l girl."

"I did those things because I thought you had been unjustly accused. You didn't kill Bello Lujan, did you?"

"No, suh."

"But you murdered his son."

His turquoise eyes were empty, unblinking, his face devoid of any emotion I could detect. "I ain't never tole you ot'erwise," he said.

"Then you planted the weapon in Monarch's car and set fire to it," I said.

"He ain't selling dope no more."

"I wish you had trusted me, Mr. Darbonne."

"To do what? Still ain't nobody in jail for what they done to my li'l girl."

How do you explain to a man whose daughter has killed herself that there is no "they," that the pitiful, guilt-driven man who raped her was a victim himself, that the fraternity boys who gangbanged her couldn't think their way out of a wet paper bag, that Slim Bruxal, who had the feral instincts of a vicious street punk, had acted with a degree of conscience and tried to return her safely home? How do you deal with the moral authority of ignorance?

"You're not setting me up, are you, partner?" I said.

"What you talking about, you?"

"Get in," I said.

We drove down the levee, the wind buffeting the truck. Out in the swamp I could see black smoke rising out of the trees from trash or stump fires, then flattening above the canopy.

"Turn down the grade," Cesaire said, pointing at a steep set of vehicle tracks that led down the side of the levee into stands of gum and persimmon trees.

As we dipped down the smooth green incline of the levee, I could see the sunset through the canopy, the leaves of the cypress ruffling in silhouette. But the poetic moment was lost as soon as we entered the shade. Inside the heated enclosure of the woods, an ugly stench hung in the air, one that called to mind a dead bird caught in a flaming chimney.

I drove at least two hundred yards on top of dried-out humus and layers of leaves that had turned gray with damp rot. The trees were strung with air vines, the ground dotted with palmettos. In the distance I could see ponds of water, like greasy oil slicks among the tree trunks, and a spacious cabin elevated on cinder blocks, wind chimes and birdhouses hanging from the eaves of the peaked tin roof.

But the cabin was not the focus of my attention. Off to the left was the scorched hulk of a Cadillac convertible, strings of smoke rising from what had once been a flamingo-pink paint job. The hatch had been popped, perhaps by the heat of the gas tank burning, and the top had collapsed in a soft gray patina of ash on the seats. There was no sound of life around either the Caddy or the cabin. I stopped the truck and cut the ignition.

"I want you to stay here, Mr. Darbonne. I'm going to take a look at my friend's car, then I'm going inside the cabin. If everything goes all right, I'll be back in a few minutes. But I want you to stay right where you are."

"What's the deal wit' this Bruxal guy? How come he's after your friend and his woman?"

"It's complicated, but the short version is Whitey Bruxal ordered Bello Lujan killed and then put it on you. He did to you, Mr. Darbonne, what you did to Monarch Little."

Cesaire stared at me in the deepening shadows. A mosquito lit on his neck, sucking his blood, but he gave it no notice. "That's the man took the pickax out of my toolshed?"

"When we're finished here, I'm going to help you in whatever way I can. If I don't return in ten minutes, walk back to the bar and call nine-one-one."

I opened the door quietly, slipped my cut-down pump from the gun rack behind the seat, and got out of the truck. I walked toward the Cadillac, my heart pounding.

The heat from the fire had curled all the leaves in a water oak that towered above the Caddy's shell. The tires had exploded and the air stank of burnt rubber and the leather in the seats and the wiring and hoses that had melted in the engine. But one odor in particular overpowered all the others. It was one that lived in my sleep, and the image and sound that went with it—a burst of flame from a nozzle, an incongruous mewing sound, like that of a newborn kitten—were etched forever in my unconscious, and no amount of booze or hospital dope will ever remove them.

I walked through a dry coulee full of leaves and came up on the driver's side of the Caddy. The door hung ajar and the window was rolled down. The convertible top had settled like an ashy veil on the shape of a man who sat slumped forward on the steering wheel.

The figure was that of a big man, or at least he had been a big man until the fire had seared and buckled his flesh and boiled his blood and deformed his features. I touched the door handle, then pulled my hand away from the heat that was still trapped inside the metal. I removed a handkerchief from my pocket and clasped the handle with it and pulled the door completely open.

The veil of ash on the man's head fell away and powdered in his lap. His mouth was locked open, his eyes cavernous and poached, his ears little more than red-black stubs. I backed away and fell to one knee, the butt of my shotgun propped up in the leaves. I tried to suppress the sob in my chest, but to no avail. I cried, as a child would, my back heaving, my hand clenched over my eyes. A Beretta lay on the floor, by the foot pedals, the pistol grips blown off by the rounds that had exploded in the magazine. It was the same model, with a fourteen-round magazine, that Clete had carried.

I backed away into the coulee and looked again at the cabin. The sun had dipped over the horizon, and someone in the cabin had either lit a lantern or turned on a battery-powered light. I circled far to one side of the cabin, so I could see the back as well as the front entrance. Farther down the slope was a canal and a boathouse and a shed inside of which at least two vehicles were parked.

I knelt behind a tree and studied the cabin. My cell phone was in my pocket and I could have called for help. But I knew I wouldn't, and I also knew I was not even going to think about the things I was about to do. I would just do them and add up the score when it was all over. My ears were filled with a sound like a train entering a tunnel, a taste like copper pennies in my mouth. My hands were damp and tight on the stock and pump of the twelve-gauge, my breath almost rasping with anticipation. In my mind's eye, I already saw the pink mist I was going to create out of the faces inside the cabin.

I moved quickly up the coulee until I was in a place that was overhung with cypress boughs and black with shadow, swimming with clouds of mosquitoes and gnats. The back entrance was actually a ramp that led to a screened porch that was stacked with collapsible-wire crab traps. I saw a silhouette against a back window, then the silhouette disappeared and the glass was filled with an unobstructed yellow radiance again.

This one is under a black flag, Cletus. This one is for you, I thought.

I entered that adrenaline-fed dead zone of bloodlust that requires no pretense of moral justification for its inhabitants. I pushed off the safety behind the shotgun's trigger guard with my index finger and sprinted across the backyard, bent low, my neck running with sweat, the wind suddenly cold on my face. Then I pounded up the ramp, ripped open the screen, and crashed over a tangle of fishing tackle and cartons of preserve jars into the cabin's interior, the sound of my shoes like hammers on the floor, the shotgun's stock against my shoulder.

At first I couldn't assimilate the scene and situation I had burst into. Trish Klein lay in a corner, hog-tied wrists-to-ankles, her mouth wrapped round and round with silver duct tape. Clete Purcel was not only alive, he had been propped up in a heavy oak chair, his forearms and calves cinched to the wood with plastic ligatures. His eyes were swollen into puffed slits, his face streaked with blood, his bare chest and shoulders and arms burned by cigarettes. A coarse piece of hemp rope hung down from his throat.

Lefty Raguza had stripped to the waist and slipped on a pair of leather gloves before going to work on Clete's face. Had he not been wearing gloves, perhaps he might have been more successful in pulling a .38 revolver from a shoulder holster hanging on the back of a chair. When I squeezed the trigger on the twelve-gauge, the load of double-aught bucks caught him across the collarbone and in the throat and exited into wallpaper that was printed with garden scenes of children watering flowers from sprinkler cans.

Lefty fell heavily against the wall, as though stunned that an event he had always associated with other people was now happening to him. In fact, the cool green fire in his eyes never died. As he slid toward the floor, he looked straight ahead, never blinking, his gaze steady, his mouth pursed like a fish's when it feeds at the surface of a lake. One hand came to rest on his genitalia, then he made a puffing sound and died.

I heard Trish Klein trying to talk behind the tape over her mouth, then Clete raised his head and spit and whispered something I couldn't understand. I ejected the spent shell from the chamber and heard it hit the floor.

"What is it?" I said, my ears still ringing from the roar of the shotgun inside the room.

Clete nodded at a door to a side room.

Too late.

Whitey Bruxal came out shooting. He was holding a chrome-plated .25-caliber automatic straight out in front of him, squeezing off rounds as fast as he could pull his finger, his face averted from the shotgun blast he knew he would probably have to eat. One round lasered across my scalp, then a second one caught me on the rotator cuff, just as though someone had punched the bone with a hammer and cold chisel.

I spun away from him, my left arm held out defensively in front of me, and swung the shotgun haphazardly in his direction. When I fired, the shotgun jerked upward in my hand and I saw Whitey tilt forward, as though he had been struck by a violent attack of nausea. He laced both arms across his stomach, his mouth open, and sat down heavily in a chair. His forehead was pinpointed with sweat and the level of pain and terror in his eyes made me look away from his face.

I lay the shotgun across the tabletop and pressed a towel between Whitey's forearms and the exposed entrails he was trying to hold inside his stomach cavity.

"Hang on," I said. "I'm calling for the paramedics."

"You read it all wrong, Dave. In the bedroom," I heard Clete say hoarsely behind me.

But at that point I trusted none of my own faculties. My shoulder ached miserably and my ears were popping as though I were aboard an airplane that had suddenly lost altitude. Who was the man in the burned Caddy? How did the car burn? I sank into a chair and reached for my cell phone.

Then a shadow cast by a light inside the bedroom fell across my hand. I turned my head and stared into the face of Valerie Lujan.

"I'm sorry it's come to this, Mr. Robicheaux. I wish you had left us alone," she said.

She was standing in the doorway now, supported by an aluminum brace whose socket fitted around her left forearm. In her other hand she held a small pistol. Her flesh tone was pink, her eyes clear, as though she had been suffused with new life from an iniquitous enterprise.

I looked at the shotgun, the blue-black of the steel, the damp imprints of my hands still on the stock, the safety still pushed to the off position. But I had not ejected the spent shell after I had shot Whitey. Even if I could pick up the gun, I would never have time to jack another round into the chamber before Valerie Lujan shot me at point-blank range.

"How many mistakes can one man make?" I said.

"Did you think an ignoramus like my husband amassed a fortune by running cockfights and handling oil leases that usually resulted in dry holes? He could hardly write his name. Half the money Miss Klein stole from Mr. Bruxal belongs to me."

I was losing more blood than I had thought and the room was spinning around me. Whitey was bent forward across from me, the tops of his forearms glistening with blue and red lights.

"Let me call nine-one-one. It will save this man's life. You still have a chance to be a friend of the court, Mrs. Lujan," I said.

But the resolution in her eyes was of a kind I knew my words would have no effect on. She stepped farther into the room, her metal brace clinking with her weight. I saw Clete strain against the plastic ligatures that held him in the chair.

"I'm sorry, Mr. Robicheaux. But way leads on to way," she said.

"You ran over the homeless man, not Tony," I said.

"How did you know?"

"Tony wouldn't have gone to prison for his father or even Slim. But he would have for his mother."

"You need to understand something, sir. A vagrant came out of the darkness and struck the side of my car. When we tried to help him, he bragged on the amount of money he was going to make. Then he laughed at Slim Bruxal. *That* was a mistake. You keep your mouth off my relationship with my son, Mr. Robicheaux. In fact, you tell your tale to the devil."

She raised the pistol and aimed it at my face. I could feel my mind racing, searching for words that would turn the situation around, that would impose humanity on a person whose small wasted hand and crippled mind had the power to shut down my life with the casualness of a fool arbitrarily slamming a door.

"Mrs. Lujan, you're not a killer," I said.

"We all are," she said.

I saw her index finger and hand tighten on the pistol's trigger and tiny pearl grips. Then there was a solitary *pop,* like a Chinese firecracker, behind me and the petals of a red flower spilled from the middle of Valerie Lujan's forehead. For less than a second there was a look in her eyes I will never forget, as though she realized that once again an unfair hand had cheated her out of the life that should have been hers. Then all the neurological motors and complexities that defined who and what she was drained out of her face, just like the features of a wax figure softening in front of a flame. The pistol she had been holding struck the floor with more sound than the weight of her body.

Cesaire Darbonne stood in the back doorway, Clete Purcel's throwdown .22 hanging from his hand, the woods behind him thrashing with wind. He stared at the gun, then set it on the kitchen counter and looked at it again. I could hear him breathing in the silence.

"It was lying out there in the weeds, wit' a knife and a blackjack," he said. "I heard the gunfire. I didn't know what else to do. Did I do the right t'ing?"

I didn't reply. Valerie Lujan had said we're all killers. Was she correct? Does our simian ancestry feed daily at the heart? Perhaps better people than I can answer that question. I cut loose Trish Klein and Clete Purcel and silently asked my old friend Dallas to forgive me for failing him years ago on that flyblown, burning day in Opa-Locka, Florida, when I learned that charnel houses can wait for us on the other side of morning. Then I called both the FBI and the St. Martin Parish Sheriff's Department and asked them to send everything they had.

EPILOGUE

Nopd eased up on Clete while he recuperated at Our Lady of Lourdes in Lafayette, although none of us had any doubt that this time Clete was not going to skate. He tried to dismiss his impending legal troubles as well as the events that had taken place at the camp out by Whiskey Bay. Through his window he had a lovely view of the older part of Lafayette, the houses couched deep inside a canopy of live oaks, slash pine, pecan, and hackberry trees. He joked and pretended he had never lost control of the situation on the levee, that bad judgment and mortality still held no sway in his life.

"I'm telling you, I was never scared. Bruxal and his hired lamebrains just weren't the first team," he said. "Soon as they locked me in the trunk, I knew they'd blown it."

He had installed a release latch inside the hatch. When Whitey Bruxal and Lefty Raguza and the man named Ernesto had run Clete's vehicle off the road, they put Trish in the SUV and took Clete's Beretta from him, tossing his stiletto and throw-down into the weeds. Then they stuffed Clete into the Caddy's trunk. Clete's flare pistol, the one he carried with him when he was out on the salt, was behind the spare tire. When Ernesto stopped the Caddy, Clete popped the hatch and fired the flare pistol straight into Ernesto's face.

Unfortunately for Ernesto, Trish and Clete had just gone up the levee to fill a ten-gallon gas can to power the generator at his rented camp. Worse yet, the can had evidently fallen on its side and soaked the carpet on the passenger's side of the car. The explosion of flame from the windows wrapped all the way across the roof.

But Clete's dismissal of his experience at Whiskey Bay was not convincing. When no one was watching, I could see the haunted look in his eyes, not unlike the thousand-yard stare that soldiers bring back from places no one should ever have to revisit.

"Get that expression off your face," he said to me one evening, just after Trish had left.

"I think you should leave the United States, Cletus. Check out the Islands, maybe stay gone a year or so," I said.

"This is our country, Dave. We fought for it. We're not going to give it over to these sonsofbitches," he said. "Get us a couple of Dr Peppers out of the machine, will you? The Bobbsey Twins from Homicide stomp ass and take names and are here to stay, big mon."

That was Clete Purcel, thousand-yard stare or not.

My feelings about the people who died at the camp by Whiskey Bay are simple: I think each of them got what he or she deserved and I'm glad they're dead.

Cesaire Darbonne pled guilty to the premeditated murder of Tony Lujan and was sentenced to life imprisonment at Angola. His lawyer told me later that Cesaire refused to allow him to enter an insanity plea or to ask for leniency from the court. I visit him regularly and believe he is one of those rare individuals who discovers a form of dignity inside jail that would have been denied him outside. I hope one day that his sentence is commuted.

Slim Bruxal? He not only got a free pass, since there was no substantive evidence against him in the death of Crustacean Man, he also got a job as a card dealer at a casino in Las Vegas. But I think Slim has his own appointment in Samarra waiting for him, at which time he'll get to see Crustacean Man again.

But actually within days after Clete's hospitalization, our concerns about his future and all the events that had ensued since the death of Yvonne Darbonne seemed to telescope into the distant past. Hurricane Katrina, the nightmare that New Orleans had feared for years, struck the city with an intensity that was greater than the destructive force of the nuclear weapons visited upon the cities of Hiroshima and Nagasaki in 1945.

The levees broke and the great bowl that surrounds New Orleans filled with water, untreated sewage, and petrochemical sludge. On rooftops and in windowless attics, the residents of the Lower Ninth Ward in Orleans Parish drowned by the hundreds if not thousands. If you have ever heard tapes of those who called on cell phones from those attics and rooftops, you will never forget the desperation in their voices as the water rose around their heads.

If there are saints who walk among us, many of them wear the uniform of the United States Coast Guard. They flew without rest or sleep day after day, suspended from cables, holding the infirm and the elderly and the helpless against their chests, with no regard for their own safety, with a level of courage that others might equal but never surpass.

As of this writing, January 29, 2006, the death toll is over 1,000 souls, and 3,400 are still officially listed as missing.

The irony is that the National Hurricane Center had forecast that New Orleans would be hit head-on by a category five storm. That didn't happen. In the last hours before landfall, the storm shifted direction to the northeast and its full brunt struck Gulfport, Mississippi, rather than New Orleans. Had the forecasters' prediction proved correct, the levees surrounding New Orleans would have been turned into little more than strings of silt and the loss of human life would have been incalculable.

Weeks later, Hurricane Rita churned ashore at Cameron, Louisiana, just south of Lake Charles, the exact same place Audrey made landfall in 1957 when my half brother and I worked on a seismograph barge west of Morgan City. It is no exaggeration to say the southern rim of Louisiana is gone. Fishing villages, towns, hundreds of square miles of sugarcane and rice fields look like surreal footage from a film depicting an apocalyptic event.

But as Clete suggested, you don't surrender the country of your birth to either the forces of greed or natural calamity. The songs in our hearts don't die. The spring will come aborning again, whether we're here for it or not. Clete Purcel always understood that and as a consequence was never defeated by his adversaries.

Southern Iberia Parish was under twelve feet of water after Hurricane Rita. East Main, where we live, was virtually untouched. The flowers along the street are blooming, our lawns green, the days balmy, the bayou hammered with a brassy light through the trees. Why is one person spared and another not? Why do the Yvonne Darbonnes of the world suffer? If age brings either wisdom or answers to ancient questions, it has made an exception for me.

But I don't dwell on the great mysteries anymore. Alafair will be home for Christmas, and Molly and I greet each day as lovers just discovering one another. I live in a place where Confederate soldiers in ragged uniforms hover on the edge of one's vision, beckoning from the mist, calling us back into the past, reminding us that the mythos of winged horses and Grecian warriors was fashioned in our collective souls, that our story is one of ancient gods and peoples, inseparable from our own.

I think it's not bad to be a player against a backdrop like that.

Mentored
   by a millionare

Steve K. Scott